Lincolnshire
COUNTY COUNCIL
D1139612

Flynn has lived for many years in ...
...mpulsive writer, she started with short stories
...es and many of her early stories were broadcast on
...o Merseyside. She decided to write her Liverpool series
...r hearing the reminiscences of family members about
... in the city in the early years of the twentieth century. For
...ny years she has had to cope with ME, but has continued
... write. She also writes as Judith Saxton.

05253448

Katie Flynn

writing as
JUDITH
SAXTON

Chasing Rainbows

arrow books

Published by Arrow Books, 2014

6 8 10 9 7

Copyright © Judith Saxton 1988

Judith Saxton has asserted her right under the Copyright, Designs and
Patents Act, 1988, to be identified as the author of this work.

First published in Great Britain in 1988 by Michael Joseph Ltd

Arrow Books
The Random House Group Limited
20 Vauxhall Bridge Road, London, SW1V 2SA

A Penguin Random House Company

Penguin
Random House
UK

www.randomhousebooks.co.uk

Addresses for companies within The Random House Group Limited can
be found at: www.randomhouse.co.uk/offices.htm

The Random House Group Limited Reg. No. 954009

A CIP catalogue record for this book
is available from the British Library

ISBN 9780099598695

Printed and bound in Great Britain by Clays Ltd, St Ives plc

Penguin Random House is committed to a sustainable future for
our business, our readers and our planet. This book is made from
Forest Stewardship Council® certified paper.

For Alan Hunter,
who invented Lionel and the grandsons and
made me a present of them.

CHAPTER
1

No one would ever guess it was June, Clare thought, gazing out through the plate glass frontage of the caff at the dreary cloud-reflecting tarmac of the car-park, deserted under the steady fall of mild, grey rain. The caff was deserted too, with rows of empty tables and chairs and only herself, Mavis and Deirdre behind the counter to show that it was not closed. The lunch-time rush had been minimal and the trickle of soaked and grumbling shoppers, making their way back to their cars, had not yet begun. Clare and Deirdre had washed up, cleared away and made tea-time preparations. Mavis had wiped the tabletops and chair seats and brushed the floor, her sharp face pulled into a grimace of distaste as her broom collected congealed chips, pastry segments and mud in almost equal proportions.

Now, with nothing left to do, the three of them were lined up behind the counter staring unseeingly at the rain like beauty queens facing a panel of indifferent judges. Only the beauty is missing, Clare thought ruefully, eyeing their reflections in the window pane. Mavis used make-up like a chef uses icing, Deirdre was suffering from one of her recurrent acne attacks and Clare's own face, unremarkable at the best of times, was pale and tired-looking, needing a touch of lipstick and a smear of eye-shadow to compete with Mavis's vivid colouring.

Outside, the city seemed to slumber beneath the rain. From here you could see – just – Norwich Castle up on its mound, and if you went to the door and peered to the right you could also see what used to be the Cornhall and was now the Anglia TV studios. Once, long ago, the car-park had been a cattle market and perhaps because of the number of cattle trucks which parked here it had a country air still, as though you were likelier to meet a calf crossing the road than a Porsche. On the other hand, Clare reflected, it might be the trees. A great big one grew right opposite them, dripping on her Mini, parked beneath its sheltering boughs. Clare winked at the car, then felt a fool and hastily bent down and got a cloth from the bowl beneath the counter. She began to mop the formica, putting heaps of energy into the small task, and Deirdre, fired by her example, dug a listless hand into the wicker basket of teaspoons and began desultorily polishing them on the pink and white gingham skirt of her overall.

'I don't think that'll ever stop raining,' she remarked in a lugubrious tone. 'Have you heard the forecast, Clare?'

Clare was about to say she had not and to suggest that Deirdre had better fetch a cloth rather than use her overall when the door burst open; they were about to have some customers.

Half a dozen large, leather-clad lads erupted through the doorway and congregated in the aisle. They would now go through the rigmarole of choosing a table, though every one seated six and was identical to all the others. It was a matter of some amusement to Clare and her fellow-workers that people did this and, turning to smile at Mavis and Deirdre, Clare was struck by their expressions, unguardedly showing so plainly their attitudes to the sudden invasion.

Mavis saw them as trouble; six chances of being insulted or attacked and the certainty of a floor to clean again and fingerprints all over her tables and chairs. Mavis thought of the cafe as her own despite Mrs Parnell's obviously better claim to such feelings. It had amused Clare when she first started work here that the two women could both refer to 'my tables, my cooker', yet never find it objectionable in the other. But now, looking at Mavis, Clare realised that had the older woman possessed hackles they would have been erected like umbrellas in a rainstorm. Even if the young men did not desecrate her, they would certainly desecrate her tables and chairs!

Deirdre, on the other hand, saw them as a challenge; fun, spiced with danger. Six chances of being dated, propositioned, ultimately seduced. Her face glowed at the prospect. At sixteen one could enjoy such fantasies, Clare realised. Deirdre was probably even now rehearsing what she would tell her friends. *The tall feller, he fancied me, I could tell when he gave me this look . . .*

I wonder what expression crossed my face as they burst in, Clare thought, as the young men settled down at a table and began to study the menu. To me, they're just six cups of tea and half a dozen ham rolls, but then I'm only interested in keeping sales up so that Mrs Parnell thinks I'm worth my salary. A closer look at the customers convinced her though that of the three, she was probably the one closest to the mark. The lads were young and hungry with the swagger natural to men who had just dismounted from huge motor bikes and sauntered into the OK Corral for a double whisky on the rocks. Of course they were probably only riding mopeds and since the caff was not licensed it would be tea and not whisky, but the pretend game was not a female prerogative. Those leather-jacketed lads would imagine themselves motor bike kings, a danger to themselves and others, even if they only had push-bikes hidden away behind the big lorries opposite.

She watched them as they passed the menu round, scratched various parts of their anatomies and laughed gruffly. No, neither vicious or sex-starved, but pretty hungry. Presently one of them stood up, turned towards the counter. He was stocky and fair, the marks of his crash-helmet still clear on the pink, dampish skin of brow and cheek. He strode over to the counter, his eyes still on the menu in his hand, mouth opening, words rehearsing themselves silently on his lips.

Deirdre moved forward into her customer-service position. She lowered her head, pushed out her chest and looked up at the lad through spiky, mascara-ed lashes.

'Yes?'

3

'Can I help you?'

Deirdre and Clare had spoken in unison but the lad turned to Clare without hesitation. It's the mother in me, Clare thought, not without satisfaction.

'Er . . . beans on toast twice, eggs on toast twice, sausage and chips and . . . hmm . . .' He turned to survey his companions. '. . . What was yours, Bender?'

'Spaghetti on toast with sausage, egg and chips on the side,' the boy who had been addressed said. Clare saw that Bender was a chubby youth who could ill afford to stock up with yet more carbohydrates. But it was ever thus; everyone always wanted what they shouldn't have.

'Yes, that's right. And six teas please, Miss.'

The boy's hand hovered at his pocket but Clare turned dismissively towards the kitchen to show him that he would pay for the food after eating and not before.

'Right, I've got that. Shall we bring the teas whilst the food is cooking?'

The boy's affirmative followed Clare into the kitchen where Mavis was already busy tipping blanched chips into the fryer, heating the pan and slotting bread into the toaster. She was not a cook, as she was fond of telling anyone who asked, she was just the cleaner and the washer-upper, but she was invaluable as a kitchen worker.

Clare repeated the order though she knew that Mavis would have had it by heart from the moment the boy had said the final word, then reached up and took the mugs off their hooks and put them onto a tray.

'I'll do the teas and butter the toast when it's cooked. Shall we stick the beans and sausages into the microwave?'

'Nah, we'll do it the slow way for once,' Mavis said, belying her own words as she snatched ingredients from the fridge and tossed them into various utensils.

Clare, her hands busy with the familiar routine of tea-making, allowed her thoughts to wander. She had been rather doubtful when Dr Maddocks had first advised her to get herself a job but he had been right. She really loved the caff and her job here and knew she was good at it, yet it had been touch and go, really, whether she worked or not. She thought back, to that first interview in the surgery, when she had unburdened herself to Dr Maddocks, confessing to her depression and miserable uncertainty because she had to tell someone and refused to burden Clive more than she had burdened him already.

'You're depressed? Think you're useless? Call yourself a failure? My dear girl, is it any wonder you feel like that, shut away in your house for fifty weeks of the year with only Sally and that damned dog of yours! Look, you can't be much above thirty . . . oh, is it thirty-three? Time does fly, I can remember you when . . . but never mind that. Why don't you go with Clive when he leaves next time? You've nothing to keep you here, you've no job, no aged relatives depending on you.'

His tone implied that she really should have managed to acquire one or the other, but Clare was too surprised to take him up on it.

'To Saud? Oh, but I don't think they're allowed to take wives, let alone children. Anyway, Sally would hate it; she'd never leave Pegasus and she'd miss her friends . . . even the dog . . .'

Dr Maddocks snorted. 'Pegasus! Ridiculous name for a perfectly ordinary pony. Fond of him is she?'

'Oh yes, she adores him. Clive and I come a poor second to Pegs. Once the summer holiday starts she'll be with him eight or ten hours a day, sometimes longer. I hardly see her.'

Dr Maddocks snorted again. 'And you're left alone, of course. Well, Clare, if you won't go to Saud with Clive then I think you ought to consider getting yourself a job. Do voluntary work if Clive doesn't like the thought of you earning money, but if I were you I'd go for a properly paid position somewhere. It would take you out of the house and give you something to think of besides your imaginary failings, and something to talk about too. Surely your mother would give an eye to Sally? She's a big girl now, mind, but I know what you are!'

Mrs Flower was fifty-three and chief buyer of the ladies department in a large store. She was not fond of children and,

5

beyond buying Sally unsuitable clothing at birthdays and Christmas, took almost no notice of her only grandchild.

'No, Mother wouldn't, she's still in full-time work, you know. But Gran could, at a pinch.'

Gran was seventy-five and loved Sally with a dry, humorous affection which was as natural and uncloying as spring sunshine and as good to bask in. It offset Clive's overindulgence and Clare's tendency, which she recognised and deprecated but could not always prevent, of smothering Sally. Between the three of us though, Clare thought rather defiantly, looking at the doctor's raised brows, we've done well by Sally. We've given her lots of love, all different perhaps, but all good. When she thought about it, her own childhood and Sally's had been similar in a surface sort of way. Her father had died when she was not even two years old and Anne Flower had got herself employment and dumped Clare on her own mother as soon as she could. In her turn, Clare had found herself grass-widowed for ten months of every year, and had certainly taken advantage of Gran's willingness to help with a second generation, but there the similarity had ended. She and Clive adored Sally and wanted nothing better than her company. Mrs Flower had been impatient with Clare, wanting nothing more than to see her elsewhere, quietly reading in her room or visiting friends, provided they were not the sort of friends who expected reciprocal visits.

That's why I did the things I did, Clare told herself now, pouring tea into earthenware mugs. I knew Mother didn't really love me, I knew I was rejected in all the things that matter, even though she kept up a pretence of being my Mum. So I kicked over the traces a tiny bit . . . and there was Gran, loving me, guiding me . . .

'Is the tea ready, Clare?' Deirdre's flushed face appeared round the edge of the kitchen door. 'Shall I take it out for you?'

'It's all right, Dee, I'll bring it.' Deirdre's face fell, and Clare put the mugs neatly in two rows on the tray and sailed out into the caff with them. She put them down one by one on the table, earning smiles and mutters, then returned to the kitchen to slice, butter, serve, warm through and do all the other things necessary for the rapid serving of their customers.

Working once more, Clare remembered Clive's behaviour when she had first mentioned the idea of a job. She had broached the subject three days after Clive's return from Saud and had chosen breakfast-time since Sally had already left for school and Clive and she were alone together in the house. They were sitting opposite one another at the kitchen table, Clive with the *Telegraph*, she with tea and toast.

'Clive . . . Dr Maddocks suggested I try to get a job.'

After a moment Clive lowered his paper a trifle and looked at her over the top. At the same time he wriggled his glasses lower down on his nose and peered at her above them. She had always disliked this Dickensian habit and found she disliked it more than ever because of the condemnation she thought she read in his eyes.

'A job? Why should you want a job? I give you enough money, don't I?'

'Yes, of course you do.' He was generous, always had been. 'But that isn't why the doctor suggested it. He said I don't have enough to keep me busy and being at a loose end is what makes me so depressed and unsure of myself.'

Clive would have liked to go back to his paper; she could tell that he was keeping his eyes from the sports page only by a great effort of will. Perhaps that was why he sounded so impatient when he replied.

'Depressed? I haven't noticed.'

'No, Clive, you don't understand.' She despised herself for the ingratiating note which was creeping into her voice but there was nothing she could do about it. Clive was ten years older than she and had been infinitely generous, she felt, when he had stooped from his superior years and asked her to marry him. She could not now consider herself his equal, even after fifteen years of connubial bliss. Now, she tried to force some resolution into her voice, without notable success. 'When you're home I'm happy, of course I am, and busy as well. It's when you're in Saud that I get so low. I don't really know why it should be, but . . .'

7

Clive had thought she was being selfish or if not selfish, at least thoughtless. He reminded her of those occasions in the past when he had come home unexpectedly and stayed a week or even longer. Clare had not liked to point out that he had not done this since Sally had started school some ten years earlier because this sounded like whining and she tried hard not to whine, but nevertheless it was true. For the past ten years, because Clive liked a settled, ordered existence and plenty of time to unwind, he took his leave in one big chunk in the summer, saving a few days so that he could rush home at Christmas to share in the orgy of present-giving and eating which is the British way of celebrating the holiday.

Now, having dealt masterfully with her selfishness in not respecting his right to find her waiting whenever he chose to return, Clive abandoned his newspaper, walked round the table to stand behind her, and kissed the nape of her neck, then tenderly squeezed her shoulders.

'Come on, Clare, things are really hard on you when I'm away, you have all the responsibilities and everything on your shoulders, don't you remember what the doctor said about your miscarriages? He said too much depended on you and you probably wouldn't carry a child full-term whilst I worked abroad. You can't have it both ways, you know.'

He sounded perfectly good-natured, even teasing, and Clare knew she should have explained that being alone so much at first, with a young baby, a rambling house and a huge garden, was indeed too much. Hers had been the responsibility, hers the anguish when things went wrong. Her home and her child had absorbed her twenty-four hours out of the twenty-four and then, suddenly, it was no longer so. She ran the house effortlessly, the garden was mature and only needed to be kept tidy, and her child had grown up and away from her, as children will. Yet she did not feel she could say these things to Clive; he had made her feel that suggesting a job was frivolous, done to annoy him. So she let the subject drop, only repeating from time to time, with what must have seemed like mindless obstinacy, that she really would like to work.

Clive's six-week stay always flew by; so much to do, so

many people to see. He usually took his leave at the height of summer so that he saw more of Sally, but for some reason he had chosen to come back in April this year. It was not until he was packed and ready to depart that he had told Clare why. You get wistful for green in the Kingdom, he had said. He had given in to a longing to see the buds burst and the leaves unfold once more.

It had made Clive seem human and fallible, and Clare loved him more than ever. She forgave him his lapse of understanding over her sudden desire for a job. After all, she had been happy enough for the past fifteen years in the house he had worked so hard to buy, the garden they had created – though most of the work had been hers – and with Sally. She loved Tish, the red setter bitch bought for a surprise gift two Christmases ago, and Pegasus, Sally's adored white pony. She got on well with Mrs Ames who cleaned for her three mornings a week and with Bert Ames who did all the heavy work in the garden. She understood Clive's obvious desire to think of her safe in his home during those long absences abroad, yet she could not entirely smother her resentment. He did not see her fretting the winter away, snowed up sometimes for days on end, unable even to get into the village to buy a loaf. He did not know how long the summer days could seem, when Sally was off on her own with Pegs and the dog whilst she, Clare, weeded the garden, bottled fruit and wished . . . how she wished . . . for company!

So when Clive left Clare had driven to the city and parked the car, meaning to go round the employment agencies and just take a look at what was on offer. She would not get a job, not with Clive against the idea, but looking and perhaps dreaming a little would do no harm. Only, when she got there it was so depressing; there was not a single job on offer for which she was qualified and she had returned to the car feeling even more of a failure than when she had set out. Then she had spotted the caff, and thought a cup of tea would be nice before driving home, and there was the notice in the window . . .
WANTED, PERSON TO COOK AND SUPERVISE IN OWNER'S ABSENCE. SALARY NEGOTIABLE.

She had walked in and there they were standing behind the

counter. Mrs Parnell, Mavis and Deirdre. Mrs Parnell had looked cross, but it was only, Clare discovered later, because no one had answered the advertisement and she could see herself having to put off her long awaited trip to Scotland to visit her married daughter there.

As for applying, it had scarcely been necessary when it came to the point. Clare had said hesitantly, 'There's a card in the window . . .' and Mrs Parnell had whisked her off into the cubbyhole at the back of the kitchen where she did the paperwork, had talked to her, explained that the job was until September but might be for longer, if she did well and if Mrs Parnell decided to retire, or at least take five days out of the seven off.

Almost before she knew it, Clare found she had the job. Mrs Parnell asked her to keep an eye on the flat above the caff, to feed the big ginger cat, Hodge, and the small tortoiseshell, Pocket, and to make sure they were shut in the flat at night, so they could not stray and get kidnapped to be made into fur gloves, a recurring nightmare of hers she confided.

Clare promised to do all these things though she could not help thinking that Pocket would not have cut up well at all; indeed, only miniature mittens would have resulted from any such skulduggery. In fact for the first few weeks at the caff she referred to Pocket as Mitten without realising it so many times that Mavis grew quite cross. Cats, Mavis told her sternly, deserved more consideration. You wouldn't like it if we called you Clara, she added, and Clare, who absolutely loathed the name Clara, mended her ways hastily.

A trial period of a week had passed in a whirl, with Clare so busy and so happy that she had felt years younger, and Mrs Parnell, realising that her trip to see her daughter and the new baby was more than a dream, felt years younger too.

'You're a natural,' she told Clare after a mere five days had gone by. 'You like it, the customers like you, and you'll be good to my girls. Going to stay?'

Clare had said she would stay unhesitatingly. She was tired often, she even lost a little weight, but she loved it. The companionship, being able to cook heaps of food, the customers, the atmosphere, the feeling of being one of a vast army who served the public, all appealed to her enormously. She used her own recipes, tried out new ones, learned Mrs Parnell's favourites, and the thrill when a total stranger complimented her on her walnut and maple cake or asked for a recipe for the peanut crunchies was heady stuff after Sally's omnivorous appetite and Clive's desire to keep his weight down.

Sally loved it too which was odd, perhaps, when you thought how sheltered her life had been, but children are very adaptable. She liked calling for Clare on weekdays and going home in the car instead of on the bus. But most of all, Clare suspected, Sally enjoyed her friendship with Deirdre.

'There you are; that's the last egg.' Mavis slid the spluttering white and orange object onto a plate already laden and pushed it across to Clare. 'Hoff you go!'

Whilst Clare was serving the meal the door opened again and two women came in, with pushchairs and toddlers. They were soaked to the skin and heavily laden with shopping and although strictly speaking prams were not allowed in the caff Clare turned a blind eye; what with the weather and the absence of other customers it would be churlish to object and to see the children go out to puddled pushchairs.

The women sank onto chairs and began to pile their shopping beneath the table whilst Clare, putting down the last plate, turned to help the small boys off with their vast yellow waterproofs and jotted down their order – two teas, two scones and two fizzy drinks with a Kit-Kat to be shared, apparently.

Mavis, standing behind the counter now, clucked dotingly over the children, one of whom suddenly swung a soggy teddy bear at his companion's head, hitting him with sufficient force to make the assaulted child give an outraged squawk. His mother comforted him, trying to wipe rain and tears – and resentment – from his small, puggy face whilst the other mother, apologising profusely, endeavoured to prevent her child from repeating the dose. Mavis smiled, her head tilted to one side, presumably because it was a more doting position than any other.

'Love 'im, you can see he wouldn't 'urt a fly,' she was saying as Clare passed her. 'Look at them curls!' Since the child with the curls was the striker and not the struck Clare concluded that Mavis had been bowled over by beauty, just as bowled over as Deirdre who was informing them even now, in a hissing undertone, that she didn't 'alf fancy the feller with the snake on his tee-shirt.

As Clare turned to use the drinks machine the fair-haired boy was approaching the counter again. He had shed his dark leather jacket and Clare could see for herself the black and gold snake writhing across his chest. The youths had all finished their food, or nearly so, but before she could reach for her order pad to make out the bill, the fair-haired one spoke.

'Any puddings still on? It's late, I know.'

Deirdre, with fluttering lashes, leaned across the counter and spoke with the confidence of one who had helped to cook the puddings. 'That's all on still. What do you fancy? The rhubarb crumble and custard's nice, but so's the apple pie.'

Deirdre had warned Clare, red-faced, that she did not intend to let the words 'spotted dick' cross her lips, no matter what. 'That's vulgar,' she had grumbled. 'Why can't we call it currant pudding?'

At the time Clare had thought she was being rather silly but now she thought about it, she realised the customers never actually asked for it either. They would point to the menu and ask what it was and then say they would try a helping, but they would not come out with the words. Folk, Clare concluded, were almost as queer as the proverb implied; but she would take the menus home and rewrite them tonight. She could take Deirdre's advice and call it currant pudding, or even suet pudding, though there wasn't a crumb of suet in it as she well knew. Still . . .

'Right. We'll have six rhubarbs, then.'

'I'll get them,' Clare murmured as Deirdre made as if to turn into the kitchen. 'You stay here and keep an eye on things.' If Deirdre went through to get the puddings she would be in a hurry to get back, and that might result in rhubarb crumbles arriving before customers less than piping hot. She was already sensitive to public opinion, Clare realised as she handed Deirdre the two glasses of fizzy drink. 'If you take these over for me, I'll make the teas whilst I'm heating the puddings.'

Thanks to the magic of the microwave, the puddings were ready and on a tray about the same time as Mavis finished pouring fresh cups of tea and setting out two buttered scones. Clare whisked through with the tray, dispensed her largesse and went to stand beside Deirdre, who was now eyeing the young men almost hungrily.

Clare, casting a glance, had to admit that in a way she could see why Deirdre was so fascinated. So much shoulder, so many biceps, such an abundance of tanned and hirsute skin! They ate quickly, without talking much, and then they began the sort of movements which meant they were about to leave. Leathers were donned, zips zipped, buttons fastened. Their chairs scraped back and Clare thought smugly that she had been right; they had made no approaches, done no damage. They had simply eaten well, would pay . . . they were sorting out the bill now, with much guffawing and clinking of small change . . . and would go.

The fair-haired boy got up and came over to the counter. Deirdre leaned forward eagerly, eyelashes batting like a gull in a gale, but the boy put the bill and the money carefully – neutrally – down on the counter between the two women and turned away.

'That's right, I think,' he said gruffly. 'Ta very much.'

The youngsters lounged and jostled their way out, donning their helmets, pulling on their great, stiff-fingered gloves, whilst in miniature, at knee-level, the toddlers imitated them, their heads tipped back to stare as the gods of their universe strode out through the doorway, grandly oblivious of the steadily falling rain.

The caff seemed very quiet when the wind of their presence had blown out into the grey afternoon. You could hear a tap dripping in the kitchen and Mavis's glass cloth squeaking as she rubbed officiously at the table so recently occupied. Deirdre stared at the door, her face heavy with discontent; hopes vanished with the bikers, she would have to make do with reality for a bit. Though there was always cooking to be done, so Deirdre, who was here on a Youth Training Scheme, would not be idle. She was being trained and right now, that training had better take the form of being taught to make a chocolate fudge cake. Her cheap labour deserved some reward; perhaps one day her husband would be grateful to the caff, and to Clare, for teaching young Deirdre the difference between plain and self-raising flour and instilling into her frizzy head the importance of elementary hygiene.

The mums and their small sons were absorbed in tea and scones, in fizzy pop and Kitkats and there was no sign of other customers so Mavis might as well keep an eye on things whilst she cleaned down, leaving Clare and Deirdre free to cook.

'Come on, Dee, we'll make some cakes. You've not done a chocolate fudge one before, have you? Well, now's your chance.'

Deirdre sighed deeply but nodded and followed Clare into the kitchen. Once there, in the familiar routine of getting out the scales, greasing the tins, putting ingredients at hand, she relaxed a bit, and broke off a piece of cooking chocolate to nibble when she thought Clare wasn't looking.

'You'll get spots,' Clare said and made Deirdre giggle, though she pointed out that she'd already got them by the score.

'Only I'll grow out of it, I hope,' she added. 'Is Sally coming in soon?'

Clare glanced at her watch. 'I don't know about soon . . . but she'll be here in thirty or forty minutes, I dare say. When we've done the chocolate cake we'll do a couple of very light ones to be filled with fresh cream, they go down well. And some brownies, I think.'

Deirdre's face brightened perceptibly at the mention of brownies, which she loved. She was only a child still for all her attempts at sophistication, Clare told herself, barely a year older than Sally, who was so much a child.

'Gee, brownies! I'll buy some to eat on the bus.'

'Right, I'll make a few extra.' Clare always made everyone pay for what they took though staff, of course, only paid

cost. Deirdre lived out of the city and liked something to
nibble on the way home, though Clare could not help
thinking that brownies were rather anti-social things to
devour on the crowded upper deck.

Deirdre started carefully weighing out for the first cake and
Clare, not to waste time, got out a bowl and made pastry for
her pies. Working steadily, the two of them listened to the
radio turned down low, chatted and gave Mavis a hand when
the odd customer wandered in. The cooking got done most
days like this, though at times Clare almost cursed the
customers, coming in on a quiet afternoon when the three of
them could have polished off twice the work if left to
themselves.

The oven was full and the caff empty by the time forty
minutes had passed. Mavis made them a pot of tea, Clare got
out the shortbread which she made specially for their breaks,
and they took the tray out of the kitchen and into the caff, to
a table at the back, where they could enjoy a sit-down and yet
still get quickly to the oven when the timer went off with its
habitual shrillness.

Clare, sipping her tea with great enjoyment, spotted a
skinny, hunched-up figure dashing across the road and
heading for the door. It burst open, the figure burst in,
dripping, and it was Sally.

'Hi, everyone!' Sally's pale little face lit with pleasure as she
crossed the room towards them. 'Gosh, isn't it wet? I missed
the bus, of course, but I got a lift on the back of Ella's
brother's bike, only I caught my dress in the chain when I got
off.' She displayed a chewed and oily hem for her mother's
moan. 'Don't worry, Mum, we're only in school for another
four or five weeks, then it's jeans and things for ages and ages.
By the time we go back to school it'll be autumn and we'll be
wearing skirts and blouses again, and when next summer
comes round I'll have grown out of this thing.' She flicked her
dress and pulled a face. 'Horrible old rag, it is.'

'Horrible or not, it'll have to do you to the end of term,'
Clare said decidedly. 'I'm damned if I'm buying you a new
dress just for a few weeks.'

'Don't want one.' Sally wrenched off her rain-darkened

15

blazer and threw it in the direction of the nearest chair – it slid straight onto the floor of course – and then went and pressed her nose to the glass display case, wistfully eyeing the cakes on the shelves. 'I'm terribly hungry; we had bones and raw spuds for school dinner and the pudding was incredible . . . sour sick Ella said, only . . .'

Cries of disgust from the other three made her give them a grin, and amend the remark slightly.

'Well, it was rice pudding only it tasted of burn, Mum . . . you wouldn't have given it to Tish, let alone a human schoolgirl. Can I have a bit of cake? Or two?'

Before Clare had a chance to reply Deirdre butted in.

'I say, Sally, did you see them boys on motor bikes as you crossed the road?'

'Boys? No. Where?' Sally turned and surveyed the empty tables as though she expected to see a couple of football teams lined up for inspection. 'It was raining ever so hard; I just put my head down and charged.'

'They were here,' Deirdre said in a dissatisfied tone as though she, too, had expected to find the boys at the table they had left nearly an hour earlier. 'Nice, one of 'em was. You'd have liked him.'

'That she wouldn't,' Mavis declared roundly, frowning at Deirdre. 'Right rough they was, love. Wouldn't have done for you at all. Int that right, Clare?'

'Since none of them had four hooves and a tail you're probably right, Mavis,' Clare agreed peaceably. 'Did you have a good day, darling? Much work?'

'Not bad thanks, Mum. It's all revising for exams now, so it's beautifully quiet in class. Look what I did in English!' She delved around in the bag she had dropped at her mother's feet and produced a fat sketch book. Flipping it open she showed around several pages of horse sketches, competently but not inspiringly drawn. 'Good, eh? Mum, that reminds me, can you get me a plain white tee-shirt? Dee's going to show me how to stencil a horse on it.'

'I never said that, I said I'd show you how to stencil letters,' Deirdre protested.

'If you can do letters, you can do a horse.' Sally crammed

the book back into her bag to the detriment of everything else within and pointed to the cake display. 'Can I have a piece of the cake with nuts on top please? And a glass of milk, if you can spare it.'

'Yes, I'll get the cake out. And you'd better have a sandwich as well since it'll be an hour or so before we can leave. I'll make you one – how do you fancy cheese and tomato?'

'I'll do it,' Deirdre said, jumping to her feet. 'Can I have my break with Sal, Clare? There int much more cooking to do, is there? I'll stay till it's finished; tomorrow being my tech. day and all.'

'Right; thanks, Dee.' Clare made her tea last whilst Deirdre and her daughter got themselves food and then she watched them settle at a window table. The two heads, one dark and smooth, the other peroxided and permed into fashionable frizziness, got closer as they began to talk.

Clare smiled to herself as she and Mavis returned to the kitchen. Those two! So different, yet with so much in common. Dee larded her face with make-up, bleached her hair and then highlighted it, bombarded it with conditioners, special shampoos and spray. Sally washed her hair twice a week and brushed it when she was reminded. Deirdre wore fashionable clothes, straight skirts almost to her ankles or mini skirts which Sally had once very rudely called pussy-pelmets. She had culottes, blousons, spike-heeled shoes. Sally wore school uniform or faded jeans and shabby shirts and jumpers. Deirdre possessed a multitude of bras, uplifts, platforms, wire-supported, strapless. Sally was still waiting to possess something worth putting into a bra. Deirdre wore fishnet stockings and a lacy suspender belt or tights with butterflies and bows all over them. Sally wore white ankle socks. Yet they always found something to discuss, something fascinating or amusing to talk about.

Sparing a glance through the kitchen door at the pair of them, crouched over the table chattering, Clare was glad all over again that she had gone ahead and taken the job. Despite school, she thought that Sally was often lonely. At home of course there was Emma, who lived a stone's throw down the road, but Em was like Sally, young for her age, a country girl mad on horses and with so many brothers and sisters that she could scarcely call her life her own. Sally had no particular friend at school unless you could count Ella, and since Ella appeared regularly in conversation but never in the flesh – or almost never – Clare had concluded that she was one of those mysterious friends who are friends through circumstance and when Sally or she moved away from school the friendship would lapse.

When asked about Ella, Sally had merely replied briefly that she got on 'all right' with Ella because the other girl was not quite such a snob as the rest of her form. Sally's school was fee-paying and girls only, but Clare could not believe it was peopled entirely by snobs. Still, her daughter kept her school life strictly apart from her home life, so she had little opportunity to judge.

Clare wondered, sometimes, whether tongues had been sharpened on Emma because if so, she could understand Sally's strictures. Emma was the middle child of a large family, her father was a farm-worker so they lived in a tied-cottage. She was a quiet little thing, a scholarship girl at another school in the city, and Clare was grateful to her and to her parents for providing Sally with the sort of family life that she would otherwise have lacked. 'Them boys' were all older than Emma, 'the littl'uns' all younger. Clare had never managed to sort the Carter family into its component parts but she believed it to consist roughly of three big boys and three small girls, with Emma, the fourth girl, in the middle.

Mrs Carter was a fat and friendly woman, a bit of a slut, who went charring, when she could get work, picked fruit, did hand-weeding and cooked massive meals for her family whenever she was at home. She mothered Sally and would have mothered Clare as well had Clare allowed it. Instead, Mrs Carter contented herself with bawling friendly greetings whenever they met and sending Sally home, occasionally, with a string bag of early potatoes or a handful of fresh strawberries.

Mr Carter was a common enigma, a small, shrivelled chap with a brick-red face, white forehead and permanent cap and bicycle clips, who seldom spoke when strangers were present and indeed talked remarkably little, Sally reported, when in the bosom of his own family. On the odd occasion when Sally mentioned Mr Carter it was to remark that he ate a lot, liked his beer of an evening and believed a quick backhander did more good than a thousand lectures.

I think I'll get Sally to work as a Saturday girl in the school holidays, Clare decided, getting one cake out of the oven, moving all the others up a shelf, and sliding a tin of raw mixture in at the bottom. Then she can earn herself some money, have more of Deirdre's company, and meet people who aren't either what she terms 'snobs' or villagers she's known all her life. It was odd, really, that she felt Dee was so good for Sally, yet she did. After all, Sally was fifteen; it was high time she gave something other than horses a serious thought and Dee was the very person to concentrate Sally's mind on more frivolous subjects.

Boys, for instance. Why did Sally never think of boys? Of course she did not want the child to think of nothing else, like Dee, but surely a happy medium was possible? And clothes. Even well-fitting jodhpurs would be a change, but Sally's sartorial indifference stretched to riding clothes as well as to ordinary street ones. It was clear that unless something drastic happened Sally was going to spend the rest of her life in jeans.

The thought, she's like me at fifteen, reared its ugly head, only to be hastily and contemptuously dismissed. There was a resemblance in some ways. But by the time I was sixteen I was . . . Oh hell, I don't want her to be like . . . Not that it was my . . . Anyway Sally's quite . . .

Clare's thoughts broke down in confusion as they frequently did when she started thinking about her own childhood. Sally was quiet as Clare had been but in most ways she was different, quite different, Clare reminded herself fiercely. She did not have the strains and stresses of living with Mrs Flower. She had horses and dogs round her. She was encouraged to bring friends home, have some sort of social life. When Sally gets going she won't be trying to prove she's grown-up, she won't be flinging herself at experience in the desperate, stupid way I did, she'll have Clive and me behind her, and Gran of course. She won't be searching for love so desperately that . . .

'Hey, Mum, customers!' Sally's head appeared round the kitchen door, her dimple much in evidence. 'Can I serve them, can I? I'll be ever so quiet and efficient . . . Dee's finishing her cuppa . . . One of 'em's a prefect!'

'Oh, lord, sweetie, but you're in school uniform. I'm sure there's a rule against serving customers in . . .'

''Salright, I'll grab a pinny.' Sally reached up and took Deirdre's spare overall off the hook behind the door. She slid into it and went back to the caff, fastening the buttons. 'Thanks, Mum!'

Clare watched her daughter through the crack in the door as she went smoothly round the end of the counter and approached the couple sitting halfway down the room. The prefect, in school blazer and skirt, was folding a plastic mac over the chair next to her own and the young man opposite, probably also a prefect though plainly at a different place of education, leaned over and took her hand, murmuring something beneath his breath.

Sally arrived, pad and pencil poised. The customers, after some thought, gave their order. Sally came through into the kitchen. She looked rather disappointed.

'She never even looked at me, Mum! Oh well, I suppose that's love for you. They want two coffees and two pieces of date and walnut loaf.'

'You do the loaf and I'll do the coffees,' Clare said automatically. 'You didn't want to be recognised though, did you?'

'Mm, I don't know. Yes I do know, I did want to be recognised! After all, I recognised her! Still, I suppose I'm pretty insignificant to Pamela Forbes.'

Somewhere, in the back of her mind, the name rang a faint bell for Clare. She considered it, then shrugged it aside, dipping milk out of the bain marie and getting matching cups and saucers. But when Sally took the date and walnut loaf out she followed her with the coffee. She put it down on the table, taking the opportunity for a quick stare at the young woman who had not recognised her daughter and again, something stirred, some memory or recollection. But it would not come clearer; declare itself for what it was.

The girl was big and handsome, looking older than her eighteen or nineteen years, with a high colour and dark-auburn hair. The green of her uniform suited her – and didn't she know it, Clare thought crossly, as the girl took the coffee without a word and smiled across at the King's School boy opposite. The boy took his coffee with a murmur of thanks and then, to Clare's surprise he glanced up at Sally, took the place of food from her, and winked. It was so quick and so cleverly done, with his face turned away from the older girl's, that Clare wondered if she had imagined it, until she saw the dimples on her daughter's cheeks and the triumph in the glance Sally shot at her.

Back in the kitchen, she faced Sally, her brows climbing.

'Well, what was all that about?'

'That's Alan Hutchinson, Mum – isn't he nice? Pamela's so full of how important she is she wouldn't even look at me, but Alan's different – he's nice to everyone, even kids like me, and he's captain of rugger, as well!'

'Gosh,' Clare said automatically. 'Umm . . . how old is he?'

'Who, Alan? Oh very old . . . probably eighteen. Emma says he's got laughing eyes. Oh, more customers . . . lots . . . Here, you stay and finish your cakes, Dee and I can manage.'

It was not until long afterwards, when she was in bed that night and on the verge of sleep, that it occurred to Clare to wonder when Emma had clapped eyes on Alan Hutchinson. Emma was at school on the far side of the city, she caught a bus directly to the village, she almost never came into the centre. Not that it mattered. And it did look as though Sally was beginning to take an interest, however slight, in something other than horses.

CHAPTER
2

Clare usually worked late on a Monday, because Tuesday was Deirdre's tech. day so they were short-handed until Sally came in after school. Today was no exception and it was seven o'clock before she and Sally went out to the Mini having tidied up and cleaned down, fed both cats, incarcerated them in the flat's small kitchen with two bowls of milk, two saucers of cat food and two commodious cat litter trays to see them through until Mavis came in next morning.

It was still raining as Clare drove the Mini through the suburbs. Grey rain splashed on grey roads, grey clouds overhung the scene. But, in the unexpected way of English weather, by the time they had left the city behind the sky was paling. Then the clouds parted and frail, late sunshine flooded the land with a chancy, unlikely gold.

'Isn't that a lovely sight?' Clare said approvingly to her passenger, curled up on the back seat resolutely doing her French homework. 'Just when I thought the rain had set in for the week, as well.'

'Mmm,' Sally said, on a musical note. She was not listening. Clare sighed and drove, then remarked on the lushness of the hedgerows and wondered aloud if the wild raspberries up on the common land past Pegasus's stable were ripe yet. Another 'hum' answered her and out of the corner of her eye Clare saw Sally put her cupped hands across her ears; her lips moved silently, chanting verbs, no doubt. Very

22

laudable except, Clare thought crossly, that I happen to want to chat.

The rest of the drive was accomplished in comparative silence; that excluded Clare seeing a rainbow and exclaiming over it, then remarking that the wretched rain was coming on worse than ever after the short break. So when they slowed for the village she was none too pleased when Sally scrambled her books together and broke her long silence.

'There, finished! I say Mum, drop me at Emma's, would you? I'll have a chat with her and she can hear my verbs, then I'll come home later. Supper won't be for about an hour, will it?'

'Yes, in about an hour, I suppose. What about Tish though, love? She'll need to go out, you know, and I can't do that and make a meal. Why don't you come home with me now and then walk Tish down to Emma's so she can have a wee and get some exercise at the same time?'

For some obscure reason Clare found she did not much want to go home alone, but Sally was oblivious to parental feelings, on this occasion at least.

'Well, I could do that but it's awkward when it's raining. There isn't room indoors and I can't tie Tish up in a downpour, can I? Look, if you let her out into the yard for a pee I'll take her for a proper walk later, after supper. How would that be?'

Clare longed to say that Sally must come home first, but it would not have been fair. If Sally had caught the bus straight home after school then she and Emma would have been together for a couple of hours already. With a sigh she put her foot on the brake as the Carters' cottage came into view. It was not really a cottage but a poor, meanly built, semi-detached, brick and tile dwelling with a long front garden heavy with every imaginable vegetable. The house itself looked tight-lipped and forbidding with all its windows and its narrow front door sealed tight against the rain.

'Thanks, Mum.' Sally scrambled out into the rain, leaving her school bag on the back seat but taking her wet blazer. 'See you in an hour, then.'

Clare muttered something non-committal and drove on as

23

Sally splashed up the garden path, not even attempting to avoid the puddles which had formed but cheerfully wading through them. Wretched child, could she not sense, somehow, that her mother did not much want to go home alone, this evening?

Knowing she was being silly did not help, but as Clare swung the car into the drive her heart lifted a little. However, this did not stop her giving the house a sulky, under-brow stare and deliberately scattering gravel in her too-fast turn round to the back. The garage had once been the tack-room of the stable buildings. She drove in, got out, grabbed her own bag and Sally's, slammed the door shut and turned towards the house.

It was long and low, built of rose-red brick under comfortably rustic tiles. When Clive had first bought it they had simply been desperate for something they could afford near Gran, because Clare could not imagine herself not being within walking distance of the woman who had brought her up, but they had soon realised its potential. Over the years they had worked and slaved, pulled down, built up, despaired, rejoiced. Now, however, it was what they had tentatively hoped for; a beautiful, homely place which smiled when you looked at it.

Fifteen years ago, it had been a slaughterhouse with a mean little cottage at one end. Now it was one long, low building with nothing to show it had once been divided. Impossible to believe, now, that the modern, gleaming kitchen and the comfortable, beautifully proportioned living room had once echoed to the disgusting and pitiful sounds of slaughter and fear.

Some villagers had hinted at ghosts and had said the Arnolds would never be happy there, but Clive said they were jealous because they had not seen its possibilities and bought it and anyway, it had not been used for slaughter for many a year. It had been a deep-litter house for cattle, then a workroom where the local blacksmith had made wrought iron gates and cartwheels for his customers, then his son had taken it over and used it as a garage to repair cars.

Clare could still remember her very first visit, when Clive

had brought her here in his little sports car. It had been autumn and the orchard had been heavy with russet and gold, the grass knee-high and white with drought. She had walked in and out of every room, in and out of the garage-cum-slaughterhouse, and had felt the first stirrings of certainty that this was a good place for them. Then, as now, the atmosphere had been nothing but friendly; any ghosts were well-disposed towards the young couple who had been so anxious, so desperately shy and eager to do the right thing by each other.

Clare began to cross the yard, not hurrying, despite the rain, when fearful howls from the kitchen made her smile and speed up. Tish would have heard the car and would even now be leaping up and down in an ecstasy of anticipation – and widdling all over the kitchen floor, unless Clare got a move on. Red setters apparently suffer from incontinence – and Tish was no exception. Excitement went straight to her butterfly brain and her bladder, and she was an easily excited animal. Right now, shrill whines, interspersed with shriller barks, reached a crescendo as Clare unlocked the door. She pushed it open and Tish flew out, widdling, and began to dance and lick and jump up, her eyes glowing with love, her long, feathery tail lashing from side to side, her mouth opening to let a mutter of doggy conversation emerge.

'Where have you been? I thought you'd forgotten me. I love you terribly – do you still love me?' Tish's greeting was always the same but none the less welcome for that, Clare thought, stroking the smooth auburn head and fondling the dog's long, soft ears.

She kept an eye on Tish's nether regions though and when the flood ceased, hurried her indoors. The rain was still falling steadily and she had no wish to get wetter than she already was, but Tish would not suffer her to go indoors without accompanying her and the kitchen tiles took enough of a hammering in the normal course of events without letting Tish wee all over them once or twice a day. The dog slept in the kitchen at nights and her morning greeting was apt to be as excitable – and as wet – as her evening one.

Now, with her nose actually touching Clare's calf, Tish trotted continently back into the kitchen, only her muddy feet sullying the cream and gold floor tiles. Clare dumped her things on the big pine table and then slumped down into her favourite chair, stretching her legs out and yawning luxuriously. Lovely to be home! Lovely to be alone for a moment, and to relax completely. Lovely to be able to appreciate her home again because, before she had started work, it had seemed more like a prison than the place she should be most at ease in.

Looking round now, Clare was glad she had never let Clive or her mother or anyone else persuade her to get to grips with the kitchen. It was a mess, she supposed ruefully, with all her old and battered saucepans hanging from hooks in the wall where Clive would have preferred to see neatly graduated copper or floral enamel. He had supplied her with a big sheet of cork to pin recipes up where she could read them as she worked . . . he had not bargained for her becoming attached to the recipes and refusing to move them, even when she nearly knew them by heart, and each one held food fragments, fingermarks and pencilled jottings as well as the original wording. Between the recipes she pinned photographs – Clive, holding Sally up to say good morning to a Shetland pony, she and Selina, flat-chested and bathing-costumed, on some forgotten shore, dogs and cats owned by the Carters and loaned for a quick spot of immortalisation. All dog-eared, all spotted with flying cookery, all familiar and therefore loved.

The kitchen windows were a good size, but the light they let in was subdued by greenery. Plants, mainly geraniums at the moment, crowded the wide window sills. She was always meaning to put them in the garden or simply chuck them out . . . but probably geraniums had feelings, too. Probably they would pine and sicken if they thought themselves ignored or unloved. Clare, who had been talking to houseplants long before it became fashionable to do so, knew she could never bring herself to throw out a geranium, no matter how leggy and barren.

They had always intended to 'do' the kitchen, but the rest of the house had come first and when Clive decided to turn his energies onto it, he met unexpected opposition. 'No fear,'

Clare had said loudly to his suggestion of proper work-surfaces, stainless-steel double drainer sink units and eye level ovens with invisible hot plates. 'I don't want any of that, I want a real kitchen.' When asked, mildly, what she meant by a 'real kitchen' she had given it a moment's thought and then said, with a belligerence foreign to her nature, that she meant a kitchen where she could burn things, drop eggs, and let the sink overflow from time to time.

'You mean the opposite of your mother's kitchen?' Clive had asked shrewdly and Clare, after a moment's thought, had nodded sheepishly and then burst into tears. Clive had hugged her, gone out into the garden, and picked a large bunch of the shaggiest and most ill-assorted flowers he could lay hands on. He had brought them in and put them in an old vase he knew Clare loved and stood it in the middle of the kitchen table. Then he had stood back to admire the effect, his hand resting lightly on her waist.

'There, how's that? You know, love . . . it's all been because I thought you wanted it that way – the living-room and the bedroom and all the rest. It is just the kitchen?'

She had known at that moment such a flood of overwhelming love and gratitude that she could have wept. Instead, she squeezed his hand and nodded.

'Just the kitchen. The rest has to be beautiful. But the kitchen must be . . . well, lived in. Scratched pans and wooden draining board, old recipes and too many plants. Even the chairs . . . I like them saggy, with cushions that don't match.'

'And the floor?' Clive said, eyeing the red quarry tiles with misgiving. 'I bet you like the little puddles where a tile is worn away, don't you? And you enjoy using a scrub-brush down to the wood every few days trying to get the dirt out of the dips and hillocks.'

'The floor's a bind, I admit,' Clare started, but got no further.

'Sweetie, if we can put down a new floor I'll put up with your dirty pictures and those relics from jumble sales that you call saucepans . . . I won't even try to persuade you to take a look at a decent cooker next time you're in the city. Is it a deal?'

It was, and Clare admitted that Clive had been absolutely right. The cream and gold tiles added a lightness, almost a glow, to the room which had previously been missing. They were easy to keep clean, a delight to look at . . . she hardly regretted the old red quarry tiles at all. And when Clive bought Tish and she saw her, stretched out asleep on the tiles in the morning sun . . . well, even Clare had to admit she would not have looked nearly so good on the old floor.

Tish's paws, landing with a thump on Clare's lap, brought her back to the present with a start. She looked at her watch and then relaxed again. Only ten minutes or so had passed, there was still plenty of time for a quiet sit-down before she must begin to cook something for Sally's evening meal. And Sally, bless her, was not difficult to feed. She would be quite content with something simple – eggs on toast, or an omelette and a nice fresh salad. There was ice-cream in the freezer, fruit in a bowl on the low table in the living-room, and cake, naturally, in the cake tin.

Tish, however, had not tried to get onto Clare's lap for nothing; she wanted a cuddle. A cold, wet nose thrust itself under Clare's chin and Tish gave a heart-rending sigh. Laughing, Clare cuddled her and let Tish climb casually right onto her lap and try, as she always did, to curl round there, like some gigantic great cat. The attempt usually ended in Tish falling heavily back onto the floor and tonight was no exception. Tish fell, Clare stood up, and the two of them crossed the kitchen to examine the contents of the pantry.

It was hard to see in there, so Clare switched the light on and as though it had been a signal the Aga grunted, clicked and puffed and then switched on. Hot water for baths would be simmering soon. She got a couple of lamb chops out of the freezer and scrabbled in the vegetable rack for some new potatoes. The salad was all very well, but Sally was a growing girl, and besides, Clare herself found that a cooked meal would be quite welcome. It was the rain, it made salad and an omelette seem inadequate, somehow.

Half-way through her preparations there was a subdued

but definite sound at the door, something between a knock and a scratch. Clare crossed the room, knowing that it was Gregory, her big ginger cat. She hoped that he would have nothing in his mouth but teeth – his own, for choice – so that she did not have the horrible task of trying to persuade him to release his prey if it still lived or to untangle it from his grip if it was dead. Clare loved Gregory but hated his habits and it took all her resolution now to go to the door and open it for him.

As soon as the door was an inch open Gregory shot a masterful paw round it to drag it wider, just as though she was in the habit, Clare thought crossly, of keeping him out in the rain when he wanted to come in. He entered, as always, like the lord of the universe he thought himself, head up, eyes blazing, tail straight up in the air until you reached the very tip, which curved ever so slightly, invitingly, like a walking stick handle. Sally had once grabbed him by it, when he was being really vile to a baby mole, and ever since, Clive swore, Gregory always flicked one ear backwards just as he passed you. He did it now and Clare laughed and made soothing noises – he had nothing in his mouth, thank God.

'Want some dinner, old chap? Well, let me get at the fridge, and you shall have something really good. How about beef and heart? It's your favourite. Here, don't crowd me . . . Hey, one of these days I won't realise and I'll shut the door and I'll have a headless cat!'

Gregory always entered the fridge when the door was opened; he was not one to hold back when opportunities were offered him on a plate so to speak. Many a time Clive had pointed wordlessly to a paw-print in the butter, many a time Gregory had been abstracted from the fridge just too late, with a satisfying chunk of chicken in his mouth. Clare knew the risk, Gregory knew the rewards, so it was really a test of character – and it said a lot for Gregory's that he had never yet been decapitated even slightly by a briskly slammed fridge door. On the other hand, Clare told herself, abstracting the tin of cat-meat from the second shelf and reaching for a clean saucer, Gregory had never hit the jackpot either and emerged with a whole chicken, so she was not quite as soft as he obviously imagined.

As soon as Gregory had settled himself in front of his food, Clare returned to her task. Once the potatoes were scrubbed and in the pan, the salad washed and tastefully arranged on a cut-glass dish and the chops ready to pop under the grill, she was able to get Tish's food ready. Tish, who had been hanging over Gregory salivating freely all over him but not quite daring to put her nose within striking distance of his too-ready claws, moved over to Clare with alacrity. 'About time too,' her expression said, as Clare tipped tinned dog-meat into her enamel dish and added milk and biscuits. 'Just because I'm too much of a lady to ask . . .'

'You're dribbling onto your own feet,' Clare remarked, picking up the full bowl. 'If Clive were here he'd pin up your ears, but I'm in too much of a hurry.' She bent down and put the bowl on the floor and Tish dived into it, ears and all. She was a noisy and enthusiastic eater; bits of biscuit and fragments of meat hurtled across the kitchen and speckled the tiles and within a very short space of time Tish's long, pink tongue was regretfully polishing empty enamel. Her ears, victims of her non-existent table manners, were hung with food particles. Clare, cleaning them, could see why Clive always fastened Tish's ears above her head with a clothes peg when he fed her, but that did not mean to say she approved, or would dream of emulating his tidy habit. How could the poor animal enjoy her food with her ears pegged into a floppy turban she asked herself, as she mopped. Not that anything would stop Tish from eating, of course. Even with her ears pegged up she ate with all her usual speed and sloppiness, finishing off with such a hearty headshake that the peg never had to be removed since it was always hurled across the kitchen at this point.

Having fed the dog and cat and checked that their own meal was cooking, Clare walked across the kitchen and dropped into one of the saggy armchairs. Immediately, comfort invaded her body and her eyelids drooped. It would be another twenty minutes before the potatoes needed draining, the chops need not start cooking until then. She could simply sit there and relax for a bit.

Relaxation, however, did not last long and that was because Clare knew very well what she ought to be doing. She ought to be seizing the opportunity of a few moments to herself to sit down at the kitchen table and write to Clive. She had quantities of frail airmail paper, a good many appropriate envelopes and plenty of stamps. All she lacked, indeed, was the will to write.

She had not written to Clive since she had started work at the caff, that was the trouble. Usually a devoted and ardent letter writer, she had found it impossible to explain on paper what had happened to her, how imperative it was that he should approve of her venture. The result was that she had simply not written, though she had sent a number of notes, all bright and hastily scribbled, all promising that a letter would follow in the course of the next few days.

Sally was getting twitchy about it, as she had told her mother.

'If you don't write and tell him I shall,' she had stated roundly only the previous day. 'I can't bear deception Mum, and besides, I'm no good at it. I'll give the game away and then he'll be hurt.' The two of them had been sitting side by side on the big, soft sofa in the living room, supposedly watching a comedy on television. Sally had put a coaxing arm round her mother's waist and rested her pointed chin on Clare's shoulder. 'Dear Mum, please write and tell Dad about the caff! How can you think he'll be cross? He only wants us to be happy.'

'I will . . . I'll write tomorrow,' Clare had promised unhappily. 'But I can't seem to find words to tell him, somehow.'

But the words, she knew, would have to be found. It was not as if Clive had forbidden her to get a job or anything like that. Indeed, even his disapproval had been more a general atmosphere than anything concrete. If I get the paper and start a letter now, I'll probably find the right words and then I can stop worrying, Clare told herself, not moving. Sally's right, wretch that she is. The longer I leave it the more difficult it will be to sound natural about it and besides, if I don't tell him someone else will and then he'll have a perfect right to be annoyed.

Gregory finished his food, walked over and examined Tish's empty dish with an air of dissatisfaction – Tish staring at him worriedly as he did so – and then made for the back door. Plainly he had business of some sort in the garden. Clare, getting up and letting him out, hoped devoutly that it was of a light-hearted nature unconnected with prey of any description. When she pushed open the back door rain blew in and Gregory stood still for a second, whiskers twitching slightly, one paw raised. He was obviously considering whether freedom was worth a wetting, but his decision was soon reached. He slid sideways along the wall of the house, reached the lilac tree and disappeared around it. Clare stood for a moment looking after him. Then with a sigh, she closed the door and walked back across the kitchen to the dresser. Her hand reached up, of its own volition it seemed, and took down a pad of airmail paper and a black, fine-point biro. She carried her materials over to the table, sat down and stared at the sheet before her. Presently, she began to write.

'Then he smiled at me, honest he did. Straight up into my face. I don't think Pamela saw, but you could tell he wouldn't have cared if she had. He really is the most . . . don't you think so, Em? Isn't Hutchinson the best of the lot of them? Ooh, when he looks at me I get the most peculiar feelings here.'

Sally clutched her stomach and Emma sighed in sympathy.

'I know, I'm the same. I followed him all round the city one day, and once, when I was looking in a window, standing beside him, he smiled. Not at me, mind. I'd have died! Just at a kid. But I got this curdling in my stomach . . . Don't you wish you were Pamela?'

'No, she's horrible,' Sally said with decision. 'But I know what you mean, Em. I say, are we in love, do you suppose?'

The two girls were sitting on Emma's bed in the room she shared with her younger sisters. It was not a large room but, crammed as it was with narrow, shabby beds, it appeared

downright minuscule. Not that such things worried Emma or
Sally; all they wanted at this precise moment was somewhere
quiet where they could talk without being overheard. Downstairs television reigned supreme, with assorted Carters
sitting intently before the set, watching a soap opera. In the
boys' room muted music and the occasional grunt or mutter
revealed that Lionel and Stan, the two eldest sons of the
house, were doing, or pretending to do, some form of
paperwork.

Now, Emma considered Sally's question, her pale, triangu-
lar face in its frame of light-brown hair, serious.

'In love? Oh, no, Sal! You've got to know someone
awfully well to be in love with them, we hardly know
Hutchinson at all . . . at least, I don't. You're so lucky, being
near the school at the caff. Is Pamela in love with him, do you
think?'

'Sure to be,' Sally said mournfully. 'When he touched her
hand . . . Well, I don't know how he can bear to, what with
her bossy ways and everything, but of course she doesn't boss
him. Anyway, as I was saying, when he touched her hand
. . . oh, I forgot, Dee saw him!'

'She did? Lucky Dee! What did she think?'

'Oh, well, you know Dee – she's awfully sophisticated,
and she's into much older men . . . but she thought he was
very good looking.'

'So he is,' Emma said fervently. 'Awfully. Did your mum
see him?'

'Yes, she brought out the coffee whilst I carried the cake.
She couldn't take her eyes off him . . . but then she stared at
Pamela quite a lot too, when I think about it. I daresay she
thinks they're a lovely couple,' Sally finished, her voice
loaded with scorn. 'You know what old people are.'

'Oh, yes . . . Not that your mum's old, Sal . . . she's
awfully young for her age as well. Much younger than mine.'

'Yours would appreciate Hutchinson, I bet,' Sally said,
having given the matter some thought. 'She likes John
Nettles, doesn't she? Well, I think he's quite like Hutchinson.'

'Do you think so? Now I think . . .'

A voice bawling up the stairs interrupted their conversation.

'Hey, young'uns, know what time it is? Time you weren't here, young Sally Arnold. And as for you, Emma, just you git your arse down here and give me a hand with the supper!'

'Gosh, I'd better run!' Sally slid off the bed and the two girls pattered rapidly down the steep, uncarpeted stairs and into the dim little front hall. 'Oh damn, you never heard my verbs . . . never mind, though, I'm sure they're engraved on my brain for the next day or two anyway.'

'Got a brolly?' a Carter voice enquired, as Sally stood for a moment in the kitchen doorway, struggling into her already damp blazer. 'You don't want to git pewmonia, young Arnold!'

'I int got a brolly, nor don't I want one,' Sally said, slipping into dialect without a moment's thought. 'I int made of sugar, boy Roddy!'

Roderick Carter laughed, stomping into the kitchen from the back shed. He was sixteen and worked on the land like his father but in a more technical way since he drove all the big machinery and was studying engineering at night-school. Sally grinned at him as he came across the room towards her in his stockinged feet, having left his boots in the shed.

'What, no brolly? Want to borrow Mum's, then?'

'No thanks, I told you, I'll be fine. I'll run so fast I shan't even be wet, time I get home. Night, all!'

Sally ran out into the rain, this time leaping the puddles on the bricks and getting cold splashes of water all up her legs. She swung the gate open, crashed it closed, and paddled and sloshed her way up the centre of the road. Nothing was coming and the verges were far too overgrown for walking on, so she kept to the middle of the road, her eyes ahead, watching for the first sight of her home.

She loved it. It meant Pegs, dreaming in the birch pasture, his chin resting on top of the dilapidated, mossy old gate. It meant Tish, dancing with joy at her coming, and Gregory, never deigning to show his pleasure but nevertheless pressing close, vibrating with purrs, brilliant eyes wide on her face.

And Mum, of course. Always there, always reliable. A light in the window in winter, a warmth, understanding.

She would be there now, getting them a meal, setting the table in the kitchen, waiting for Sally to come in with news of the great world.

Sally hurried up her own deeply gravelled drive, skirting the round rose-bed with the dark-red blooms heavy with rain and perfume. Under the lilac bushes Gregory sat, aloof, disdainful. He would not look at her but stared fixedly ahead, ears pricked.

There was a light on in the kitchen and a good smell drifted out of the half-open window. Food cooking.

Sally opened the door. Her mother sat at the table, absorbed. She was writing rapidly on a pad of airmail paper, her pen skittering, mouselike, across the page. She looked up as Sally entered, her gaze unfocussed, then smiled.

'Hi, there. Just dropping Daddy a line.'

Sally bounced across the room, avoided Tish who dived leggily towards her, and planted a smacking kiss in the middle of her mother's forehead.

'Three cheers for you . . . you've told him, haven't you?'

'I have.' Clare smiled again, stretched, then jumped to her feet with a squeak of dismay. 'Oh heavens, the chops!'

'Oh, Mum, have you burnt them? I'm absolutely starving!'

'No, not burnt . . . I haven't put them on yet, and the spuds will be nicely cooked . . . Be an angel, Sally and drain the potatoes for me whilst I see to the chops.'

The angel got to work. Thank goodness, Sally was saying to herself, as she busied her way over to the sink, thank goodness she's told Dad; now I'll be able to write to him about Dee and the caff . . . it's been awful, keeping half my life away from him!

CHAPTER
3

Mavis had been opening up at the caff for so long now that she could, she often declared, have done it in her sleep. Nevertheless, it was a different business, a more responsible one, now that Mrs Parnell was no longer just a short flight of stairs away, snoozing in the bedroom of her small flat. Then, if there was anything wrong all she had to do was to go to the foot of the stairs and call 'Mrs P, can you come 'ere a mo?' whereas now she was on her own from seven-thirty until nearly nine, when Clare and Deirdre joined her.

Not that she disliked it, mind. Not in summer, at any rate. In winter it might be a different matter, what with the dark early mornings and the car-park opposite and all. Still, Mavis told herself, stepping briskly off the bus and accidentally hitting a fellow disembarker quite a blow with her laden shopping basket, no sense in meeting trouble half-way. Summer was only just beginning and by the time autumn put in an appearance the chances were Mrs P would be fed up with her daughter and would be back in the flat.

Mavis lived in the city, but on the far side of it, so she had quite a little journey one way and another to get to work. Not like Clare, with her car, so she could thumb her nose at public transport, but not like Deirdre, either, who had to get two buses some mornings, if she was late up, like. Mavis left her terraced house, walked up her own road, down another, through a little brick loke between back gardens, and onto the main road where she caught her bus. The bus carried her to

Castle Meadow, and after that all she had to do was to cross the road, walk up the hill, and bob's your uncle.

Today, because it had actually stopped raining for a bit, she quite enjoyed the walk to the caff. Her veins, which by nighttime would be throbbing like a jazz band and shortening her temper by every minute she remained on her feet, were quiet and peaceful. The big one, which ran a circuitous route from her high instep (sign of breeding) to her crotch, was Mavis's deadly enemy. She alternately punished it with exercise and pandered it with rest but no matter which course she took it treated her with disdain, making her life miserable some days and ignoring her on others. No pleasing you, she told it severely as she climbed into bed last thing. Now don't you go moaning away all night or I'll make you sorry, come morning. One day, when she had the time, she intended to get it done. On the Health, of course, she wouldn't go private for a thing like that even if she could afford it, which she most certainly could not. No, she'd go on an ordinary ward and they'd slit her leg open and pull the monster out like rotten spaghetti and she wouldn't 'alf gloat when it was just muck in a bucket, instead of something that could darken her whole life.

Mavis reached the door of the caff and took out her keys. She fitted the first into the lock and glanced surreptitiously around, as she always did, hoping that someone would see her and believe her to be the proprietor, entering her property for the first time that day. There was a paper boy cycling down the hill, wobbly with the weight of the bag on his shoulder, and a postman walking up it. But no one was watching so Mavis unstraightened her shoulders, allowed herself to slump comfortably, and unlocked the dead-lock first and then the Yale. Then she pushed open the door and stepped inside.

The caff was cleaned down meticulously last thing, yet when you came in early it always smelt of food. Mavis, wrinkling her nose, shut the door behind her and then locked it.

'We don't open until eight,' she informed the uninterested

tables and chairs, 'and I'm buggered if I'm going to chance some old soak comin' in, not before I have to.'

She walked slowly down the aisle between the tables, being the proprietor again now despite a lack of audience. With Mrs Parnell away it felt just like her own place. She shifted a chair and centred a menu, then went through into the kitchen. Here, very rapidly, she would become Mavis again as she slipped out of her decent high-heeled shoes – which crippled her after ten minutes or so – and into the shabby flatties which were so much easier on the feet. She also took off her straight, pale green gabardine and put on her checked overall. Comfortable again, she let her stomach take its natural course instead of holding it flat, slopped over and drew back the kitchen curtains, and then headed for the stairs. It didn't do to leave Pocket and Hodge alone too long, otherwise they might leave little presents in dark corners. If they had been my cats, Mavis told herself, climbing the stairs, they'd have been shut out at night, not in, but that was Mrs P for you. Talked to those cats like Christians, she did, so what could you expect? Mavis's vein decided to object to the stairs and Mavis addressed it sharply, unconscious of irony. Just you dare set about me today, you bugger, she told it, and I'll keep them high-heels on for an hour after I get home, tonight. You won't like that, my fine fellow!

Mrs Parnell's flat was nice, if a trifle small. A miniature landing had four doors leading off; one was her bedroom, one her living-room, one her kitchen and one her bathroom-cum-lavatory. The cats, who could easily have been curled up asleep in their baskets, were both just the other side of the kitchen door. Mavis, who quite liked animals, opened it cautiously.

'Mind your toes, you little bleeders,' she said cheerfully, as the two furry faces appeared. 'Now what's it to be? Piddles first, or brekker?'

'Brekker? Righty ho.' Mavis tried to stick to Mrs Parnell's vocabulary when talking to Hodge and Pocket, although she did draw the line at copying Mrs P's indulgent tone. And Mrs P would never have addressed her darlings as little bleeders, either, but then, Mavis reasoned, she should not entirely suppress her own feelings just to keep two spoiled cats happy.

Not that she disliked her charges: quite the opposite in fact. She grew fonder of them the more she got to know them. They weren't like dogs, all over you and putting muddy feet where you least expected it, to say nothing of trying to make love to your left leg, the varicose vein leg, as her neighbour's Corgi did from time to time. Kick out she might and did, swearing beneath her breath, but that didn't stop the bloody little pervert from jumping her just when she was in her best nylons and her tightest skirt. Well, when she thought of its last assault, in front of a whole bus-queue of commuters, she got quite hot under the collar. The only good thing about it was that her kick had woofed the air out of the creature's lungs with such force that it had gaped like a hungry shark for five minutes afterwards.

'Here, then, get outside of this,' Mavis said, putting slabs of cat food into the two blue saucers in front of the sink and then pouring a judicious helping of milk into the two pink saucers. She reflected smugly that since animals love those who feed them, Hodge and Pocket would be getting mortal fond of her by the time Mrs P returned; they should positively dote on her already, in fact.

Not that they showed much interest in her once their saucers were on the floor. It was eyes down for a full house as you might say until the last smear of cat food and tongue full of milk had gone down the little red road. Only then did the cats turn to her, waiting for her to open the kitchen door, longing for release as ardently as, five minutes earlier, they had longed for food.

Mavis opened the door and followed as the cats progressed wildly down the flight, wrestling like a couple of kids as they bounced from stair to stair. Once in the kitchen she opened the back door for them and they erupted into the yard.

Knowing from experience that Hodge and Pocket would not be seen again for an hour or so, Mavis closed the door and went over to the big gas grill. She considered turning it on and making herself a couple of rounds of toast, then decided that as the day was quite warm she would use the little pop-up toaster instead. She also filled the electric kettle and dropped a couple of tea-bags into the teapot. A piece of toast and some hot tea would be nice and since it was only ten to eight there was no need to open up yet. Still, it would be as well to get the old coffee machine on the go and boil some milk. Breakfasts came in prompt at eight and several of them preferred coffee to tea.

Mavis turned the coffee machine on. Despite her having called it the old coffee machine it was really the very latest thing, a modern, hissing, fast-speed coffee dispenser. Beside it should have stood an equally modern, hissing, fast-speed milk dispenser but unfortunately Mrs Parnell's urge to get up-to-date had dwindled and died upon receiving the bill for the coffee machine, so a small bain marie set into the extreme end of the counter had to be filled with boiled milk every twenty or thirty cups. It did quite a good job of keeping the milk hot but unfortunately milk so kept tended to separate so that oily bubbles formed on the surface of the liquid after a while.

Clare worried about the bubbles. Mavis had noticed her sighing over them and trying to work out a cure or an alternative method of keeping the milk hot, but Mavis was used to it. Familiarity breeds contempt, Mavis thought now, just as the caff door reverberated to a blow. That would be the milkman with the day's delivery. He always crashed the crate against the door to let Mavis know he had arrived because once he had brought it early and ruffians had stolen the milk, or so he claimed when Mavis had rung up to complain of non-delivery. Mavis, of course, thought he had simply forgotten, so now he rammed the door and she came out at once and carted the crate back into the kitchen.

'Nice morning,' Mavis called to the milkman's retreating back. He was a well set-up fellow she considered, though she tried quite hard really not to notice men. It wasn't fair on Lionel, noticing men. But she might as well have saved herself the trouble of a civil word; the milkman merely grunted and continued to trudge towards his milk van.

'Pig,' Mavis remarked conversationally, carting the crate back into the caff. 'Oughter know better, a man with his looks.' She belonged to the school of thought which considers a pretty face reflects a pretty nature. To Mavis, eyes set close were sly, thin lips were mean and lobeless ears belonged, rightly, only to homicidal maniacs. Clare had pointed out that a good few of their most inoffensive customers had lobeless ears and apparently blameless pasts but Mavis was not impressed. A really good prejudice, she considered, should be clung to against all the odds.

'Give 'im a chanst,' she would say darkly. 'You mark my words, dear, 'is turn will come one of these days.'

The kettle boiled and the toast popped simultaneously but Mavis was ready for them. She fielded the toast with the skill born of long practice and slapped it onto a plate, then made the tea. Whilst it brewed she spread butter on her toast, jam on her butter, and then poured milk into a cup. She patted the teapot's fat blue side, then poured and made her way through to the caff, the plate of toast in one hand, the teacup in the other.

Settling herself at a window table, she reflected that the day was still comparatively fine so perhaps summer was about to. come at last. She also gave the big lorries lined up opposite, on the car-park, a cold and challenging glance. She knew them! Full of greedy, noisy, dirty lorry drivers they were, all waiting for eight o'clock to strike so that they could come clumping over in their great hobnailed boots, complain that she had kept them waiting, sully her floor with mud and her tables with fingerprints, and keep her dancing attendance on them until Dee came in at nine and took over the waitressing.

Sipping her hot tea and crunching her toast, Mavis saw a thin finger of sunlight slip between a couple of half-hearted clouds just as the city hall clock struck the hour. Opposite the caff a man swung himself down from the cab of his lorry, hitched up his trousers purposefully, and began to cross the road. Other figures followed suit. Mavis, her mouth full of toast, made crossly for the door. Them buggers knew full well she wasn't supposed to open until eight, but they made bloody sure that she was never a second late. A quick glance over her shoulder checked that the coffee machine was at full heat and, from the kitchen, the subdued tapping sound of the glass disc which she put into the saucepan to stop the milk from boiling over announced that the milk was ready, too. Mavis got the door unlocked just as the first-comer's foot touched the pavement. He reached out for the door handle and she snatched her hand back as though some infection might spread from his touch right through both handles and the door itself. The man grinned, shoved open the door and greeted Mavis cheerfully.

'Mornin', missus! A nice one, isn't it? Good to see a bit of sun, eh?'

'Good morning,' Mavis said, enunciating clearly to show him up. 'Full breakfast, is it?'

The man sat down at the window table she had just vacated, stretched, yawned, without putting a hand over his mouth, and nodded. He had a flushed young face, dust-coloured hair which he must have cut himself, employing a pudding basin by the looks, and round, surprised blue eyes. On the back of his head was an elderly cap, moth-eaten very like, Mavis thought, nose twitching. Cattle truck, she diagnosed. Very low. He wore jeans, faded but fairly clean, and enormous wellington boots.

'Tea or coffee?'

'Tea, I guess. Lots. What's on today?'

Mavis jerked her head to the board and then realised, with shame, that she had forgotten to change it from last night's dinner. Not that it mattered; breakfast did not vary. Still, if she had remembered to change it over she would not have had to bandy words with a truckie.

'Bacon, sausage, egg, tomato, fried bread, baked beans,' she gabbled now, as the door opened again to let in a small group. 'Toast and marmalade to follow.'

'That'll suit me,' the first man said. The others, sitting down with a good deal of chair scraping and boot crashing, made remarks suggesting that they, too would be satisfied with the full breakfast. Mavis, ignoring them, swept through into the kitchen. They would all be served in the fullness of time, let them wait for a bit until she had her first order sorted out. But despite such thoughts she got out the big pan and put a dozen sausages into it, then squeezed the bacon in beside them and reached for the loaf. Cutting it quickly into hefty slices, she let her memory tell her that she had seven customers, six of whom would drink tea and one who preferred very strong coffee. All seven would eat the full breakfast but one could not abide fried tomatoes so he usually got an extra sausage.

Moving around the kitchen putting out mugs, piling up plates and cooking breakfast for seven, Mavis was happy, though she would never have admitted it. It was natural to give a man breakfast and now that she could no longer feed Lionel every morning, what better than to feed, in his stead, seven hefty, hungry lorry-drivers? Rough and uncouth they might be – well, were – but someone had to feed 'em. Mavis slid an extra sausage onto the youngest feller's plate and salved her conscience by telling it to shut its face and leave her be, then began to martial her cutlery. She prided herself on getting them out in twenty minutes and today would be no exception.

As she and her laden tray re-entered the caff a few minutes later, Mavis thought that Mrs P would be quite pleased, if she could see her now. In the old days, before Clare (in Mavis's mind, B.C. ˙stood for before Clare), Mrs Parnell had always come down to do the cooking or the serving, depending on her mood, but now Mavis managed alone, as she had always maintained she could. She unloaded her tray quickly, returned to the kitchen, brought through the next lot of plates, went back behind the counter, hissed coffee into a mug, took it to the customer . . .

The sunshine outside crept a little further across the car-park and the leaves of the big tree directly opposite danced in a light breeze, dappling sunshine and shadow. Deep inside, Mavis began to sing a little song, only she wouldn't have dreamed of singing it aloud, in front of all these brutes of men. 'Pack up your troubles in your old kitbag and smile, smile, smile,' Mavis's soundless singing went. 'Keep your sunny side up, up . . .'

'It's a white shirt, Mum . . . you must remember it, my P.E. shirt, the one with the sprig of blue mistletoe on the chest.'

Sally's voice wailed down the stairs in the oldest tune known to schoolchildren. 'I need it today, I must have it or "Loopy-knicks" won't let me play tennis, you know what she's like. Wasn't it in the wash last week?'

'Darling, how can I possibly remember?' Clare, rushing round the kitchen trying to do ten things simultaneously whilst making her daughter's breakfast, tried in vain to recall the contents of the washing she had done last Sunday. 'Did you put it down for washing?'

'Yes . . . no . . . Oh Mum, it must be downstairs somewhere if it isn't in my chest of drawers . . . mustn't it? Oh hell, suppose I've left it in school? What'll I do?'

'Wear it, I suppose,' Clare shouted back, preparing to pour orange juice into her daughter's glass and juggling bread into the toaster. 'Do come down, Sally!'

There was a subdued thunder of feet and then Sally appeared in the doorway, hair on end, dress unbuttoned, shoes in one hand.

'Wear it? Mum it's dirty, I couldn't possibly! Oh, and that means no tennis and probably an order mark and of course death to my hopes of being on the team! Don't I have a spare?'

'Only last year's, and that was a bit small for you a year ago, and anyway I don't know where on earth it is. Now just sit down and . . .'

'I wonder if it's in the spare room? Or it could have been put in my wardrobe, I suppose, on a hanger. Half a mo, whilst I have a look.'

She disappeared again, ignoring Clare's injunction to remain, and could be heard upstairs, throwing open doors, slamming them again and finally thundering down the flight. She shot into the kitchen, waving a triumphant P.E. shirt at her mother, and slumped into a chair. Grabbing her orange juice she downed it in one swallow and began to butter toast.

'I can't think how I came to miss it first time round . . . but it should have been in my second drawer, not slung on top of all the books on my shelves.'

'Very true,' Clare agreed. She was trying to clear the kitchen of anything Tish might chew, scratch or indeed devour to her detriment during the long hours she would be left alone. She was also trying to drink a cup of tepid tea, stand her geraniums in water and drop various essentials into her handbag, and her slice of toast, buttered but unbitten, was growing steadily colder with every passing second.

'Did you chuck it there, Mum? Or did you ask me to take it up?'

'Does it matter?' Clare picked up her toast, took a bite, then laid it down again. 'Heavens, look at the time, we're going to be awfully late! You'll have to finish your toast in the car.'

Sally crammed the rest of her toast into her mouth, scuffed her feet into her shoes, dabbed at her hair with the nearest comb and bounded across the kitchen so that she could shove her P.E. shirt into her school bag before straightening up and grinning at her mother.

'I'm ready now,' she announced thickly. 'Have you given Tish water?'

'Of course. Darling, you are a sight – have you cleaned your teeth this morning? Washed? Changed your socks?'

'Don't worry, Mum, let's get moving,' Sally said, side-stepping any sort of reply. 'I'll comb my hair properly in the car.' She picked up Clare's toast, pulled a face at it, then doubled it over and made for the back door, taking a bite as she went. Tish, who had never learned to tell a departure for work from a fun-run, shouldered ahead of her, squeaking with excitement, trying to insinuate herself out of the doorway before anyone noticed.

'Tish, on your mat!' Clare ordered, putting firmness and a touch of bullying into her tone. Tish could take some catching once she got outside and realised that you were about to depart without her. 'Come on, away from that door.'

Tish's mat was a cream sheepskin which, for some reason, she had never attempted to destroy. Now, having tried to play deaf, she backed sulkily away from the door and cringed across to her mat. She thumped heavily down on it and lay watching them, her eyes rolling to show the whites, a picture of misery.

Clare and Sally got out of the door and slammed it just as Tish abandoned her mat and staged a last-minute attempt to join them.

'Mind her nose!' Sally cried anxiously, as she cried most mornings, but Clare slammed the door, locked it, and then pointed to the window. Like a large, exotic flower, Tish's face bloomed amongst the geraniums. When she saw mother and daughter looking at her she smiled at them, showing the enchanting little pearly white teeth in her bottom jaw, her eyes glowing with affection. Clare blew her a kiss and tried not to notice that Tish was bending two geraniums sideways at a dangerous angle, then swung open the garage doors.

'She's sitting on the draining board now,' Sally reported, as Clare backed the car out into the yard. 'Did you leave anything . . . ?'

Even with the engine running and the door shut, they heard the echo of a crash. Clare took her foot off the accelerator, frowned, then shrugged and headed towards the road.

'Let's hope it was only a couple of old mugs,' she said, turning the car neatly out of the gate. 'We can't stop and investigate anyway, we're far too late. Sit tight, Sal, I'm going into orbit presently.'

The car was nippy and Clare was familiar with every curve and bend in the road. They made good time in the lanes and better on the straight and Sally remarked, as they overtook a lorry carrying manure and then a tractor dragging a haycart, that she would be grateful if her mother did not kill them today as it was games later on.

'What's so wrong with being late, anyway?' she asked plaintively as the car whizzed past the thirty mile limit signs on the outskirts of the city. 'Do slow down, Mum, I'm too young to die.'

'Am I driving fast?' Clare said, conscientiously slowing. 'It must be because it's sunny, I suppose. Perhaps I'm feeling light-hearted and daring.'

'Or perhaps it's more as if a foul fiend did close behind your tread,' Sally said with unexpected shrewdness. 'Poor Mum . . . where's the letter?'

'Letter? Oh, you mean the one I wrote last night, to Daddy. It's not really finished, I put it in my bag but I'm going . . .'

Sally picked up the shabby red handbag which Clare had slung onto the back seat and opened it without apology, abstracting the letter. It was signed and sealed, the address written correctly, a stamp already in position. She waved it at her mother.

'It's all ready to go, so I'll post it for you. There's a box just outside the school drive, I can pop it in there in a second.'

'It's all right, Sal, I thought of something I should add . . .'
Clare drew the car into the kerb and Sally promptly leapt out, the letter still clutched in one hand, her school bag in the other.

'Oh, Mum, what a whopper,' she said cheerfully. She blew a kiss through Clare's open window but did not attempt to hand over her captive. 'Bye now, have a nice day!' Before Clare could say another word she had crossed the pavement, dropped the letter through the postbox's gaping mouth, and was engulfed in a crowd of other children all heading towards the school's gates.

Oh, well, Clare said to herself, as she drove slowly off. She would have posted it later, anyway. Probably. After all, she had been working in the caff for a month, she would have had to tell Clive sooner or later, and much later than a month you could not get.

Now that the letter was on its way, though, a sort of acceptance was setting in. Clive had never forbidden her to have a job, probably he would be quite pleased that she was working; after all he loved her and wanted her happiness. If she had never mentioned it – would that she never had – then she could have taken the job without a qualm and simply written to him telling him all about it.

Analysing the situation as she drove slowly along – all desire to hurry having left her, strangely enough, with the posting of the letter – she came to the conclusion that she was being silly. Clive could scarcely eat her, after all, just for having got herself a job. He had said he liked to think of her in the home they had created; so what was to stop him doing just that? She was still there from five or six o'clock each evening and all day Sunday! Gran approved, what was more, though Mrs Flower had made it clear that she would tell no one her daughter was now little better than a cook-cum-waitress in a third-rate caff. She had not mentioned her job to her mother-in-law, nor to Clive's brother Richard and his wife Rachel. She had no idea how they would feel about it and, on reflection, found that she cared not at all. She had always felt that Rachel disliked her and she knew, alas, that Richard . . . Her mind did one of its sideways twists and she forced it back on track. Richard fancied her, despite . . .

This time, she gave her mind its head and it promptly skated back to an evening many years ago, in her mad youth, when Richard had backed her into a corner and had tried to take advantage of her youthful eagerness to be considered an adult. She could still remember his hot hands, grappling with a slim-fit shirt, well tucked in to close-fitting jeans, and his mouth, hotly questing, whilst his body and the corner between them pinned her in.

She also remembered her knee, sinking into his groin, and the word he had spat at her as she twisted free . . . but it was a pretty crude word. She had spent the last fifteen-odd years trying not to think of it every time he hove into view.

Richard and Clive being brothers was a pretty odd thing, she had always thought so. Richard was slick and fast and dapper. Not the sort of man anyone would trust with his wife. Clive was sensible. Kind. Probably the better looking of the two, with his curly, light-brown hair and hazel eyes, the broad cheekbones and square, cleft chin. Richard had hair so dark it was almost black, dark eyes, a mouth that sneered more often than it smiled. He would laugh at her getting a job in the caff and then he would look at the idea to see how it might be turned to his own advantage. Despite the knee in the groin, he had made passes at Clare from time to time ever since, sometimes fairly openly, at other times so slyly that Clare had not realised just what he was suggesting until afterwards. The knowledge that Clive would half-kill Richard if he knew had not helped at all. With a husband far away in Saud it would have been manifestly unfair to have confessed that she had had trouble with Richard. Clive would have been powerless to do anything, and it would have hurt his relationship with Clare herself as well as destroying the uneasy truce between the brothers which just about lasted for the duration of Clive's home leaves.

Clive and Richard had never been friends. Richard was the spoilt darling of his mother's heart. Four years older than Clare and therefore nearly six years Clive's junior, he had been cossetted and clucked over all his life, though anyone less in need of care and protection would have been hard to imagine. Richard was pushy and self-confident, slick, with a narrow face and an even narrower smile. To Clare's constant surprise, however, he was popular with women and managed his frequent infidelities rather well, so that Rachel, though she surely must have suspected, never seemed certain enough to take action against either Richard or his women. As for the devoted and besotted Mrs Arnold senior, she admired her son's drive and never saw his ruthlessness, praised his single-mindedness and denied his selfishness, and was even pleased enough with his marriage to Rachel – a gel of good family, with money of her own – to pretend that she thought their childlessness a good thing.

As for me, Clare thought, driving along sedately in the early sunshine, the only good thing I ever did according to Ma-in-law, was not to marry Richard; you'd think she would have thanked me for that. In fact, when she and Clive had announced their impending nuptials, she was almost sure that there had been a gleam of relief in Mrs Arnold's cold, little, grey eyes before she began to suggest that it was all a bit sudden; that she and Clive had much better wait until Clare was a little older, a little wiser.

Ahead of her, the queue for the car-park was already forming. Clare drew the Mini into line and waited patiently enough, because she knew it would only take a matter of perhaps half a minute to get to the head of the queue. The park was empty still, but everyone always seemed to arrive together, hence the wait to creep past the attendant in the kiosk. Clare fished out her season ticket and held it against the windscreen, though goodness knew, after a month the chap ought to know her and the Mini by heart.

Inching along, she remembered Clive turning up at her home that evening, and finding the back door ajar and her mother deaf to his knocking, had simply walked into the room. Even from her position of disgrace – backed up against the sink with her mother's face no more than six inches from her own – she had not at once realised that Clive was in fact a knight in shining armour, turning up complete with white horse to rescue her from the dragon, or Mrs Flower.

'Who have you been with?' her mother had been demanding stridently. 'You little slut, don't waste your breath denying it, because I've been putting two and two together and I know, Clare, I don't suspect, I bloody well know!'

Clive's voice had made them both jump though only Mrs Flower had coloured. Clare, sick, terrified and shaking, had on this occasion at least done nothing to bring a blush to her cheeks. Having successfully got their attention however, by merely saying, 'Sorry to butt in', Clive had then gone on to do the real rescue bit.

'I did knock, darling, but no one heard me,' Clive had said, addressing Clare now and ignoring her mother completely. 'I've come to take you out for a drive, so go and slip a jacket on, in case it's cold later.' He turned to the still smouldering Mrs Flower. 'Is that all right? We'll probably drive down to the coast.'

Mrs Flower could not withstand Clive's easy assumption that his suggestion would be hailed with enthusiasm. She muttered something and Clive took it as agreement, bundled the ill and terrified Clare out to his hired car, and dumped her in the front seat. Clare, dazed by the speed and suddenness of his rescue, knowing that her stomach's churning augured ill, had barely managed to stutter two words before she was sick again, all over her own shoes and Clive's briefcase.

Clive swung over, parked, and put his arms round her. He had crooned and cuddled and soothed and miraculously, all desire to be sick again had left her. She had wept, scrubbed her eyes with her knuckles, been comforted. She let Clive wipe her face, clean her up with a box of tissues, and had not once explained why she was weeping, simply accepting his explanation that she had gone to a party of which her mother had disapproved. When her tears had dried and only the occasional dry sob shook her, he had lifted her chin so that she had to look into his face and said he thought she might do worse than to marry him.

She had been stunned, speechless. It had been odd enough when he had addressed her as darling – he had never even been in a room alone with her before and had always called her Clare – but to suggest marriage . . . well, he must have run mad.

She said as much, whereupon he laughed, hugged her and said that becoming though her modesty was, surely she had noticed how he had hung around her, last summer?

'Yes, but you were after Selina,' she had muttered. Selina, her dearest friend, was everyone's favourite. Tall, blonde, slow of speech but quick of wit; Clare had been constantly amazed at her luck in being Selina's chosen companion and confidante. She had assumed that Clive visited the Bothwells in order to see Selina; certainly she had not dreamed that Clive had even noticed herself. She had been fifteen and ordinary, Selina was eighteen and a golden girl . . . why on earth should Clive have stooped from his adult status to even notice her, especially when Selina was around?

'Of course I like Selina, everyone does,' Clive had said with commendable patience. 'But I don't want to marry her, I want to marry you. How about it?'

Clare had not told him about her condition. After all the years, the shame of it was still enough to bring heat to her cheeks. She had not told him about the party and what had happened there and why she was being attacked by Mrs Flower. She had simply stared at him and perhaps she had not seen him at all but an open door, through which she could escape to a normal life . . . a respectable escape from the misery of her condition and the fury of rage, scorn and derision her mother had been in the act of unleashing upon her when Clive had called.

She had not known for sure that she was pregnant. She had clung to that for months. Mrs Flower, coming upon her vomiting her heart up in the smart downstairs cloakroom with its blue toilet and little blue handbasin, had simply leapt to that conclusion. How could she have known, when it had been a mere three weeks since that dreadful, humiliating party?

Selina had gone away for a couple of days, up to London to see a show with a relative, and Clare had been left alone. Well, not alone, but without Selina, which was as bad. Only a month before, Mrs Flower had decided that she saw too much of Gran, and had stopped Clare going to Gran's for a meal after school and spending all her time there at weekends. She said it was too much for Gran, but Clare knew there was more to it than that. Her mother, who had never taken any notice of her, had suddenly realised that she had a nearly grown-up daughter on her hands, and had decided to do something about it. She had taken her out on clothes-buying expeditions, had introduced her to an elderly man who was, it appeared, something in the fashion business, and had told her that she was old enough, now, to be a companion for her mother as well as for Gran.

For a while, Clare had beeen too stunned and miserable to object, and then she had been invited to a party at which she had met a small, grinning boy called Toddy, who had attached himself to her for the evening and had then proceeded to take her about.

He was a friendly lad, too shy himself to go beyond kissing, a bit of neck-biting and the odd cuddle in the back row, but he had made Clare see that there was more to life than school and exams and her mother's censorious opinions.

She had kicked over the traces in the course of that month, but no one had known much about it. Selina, up to her eyes in 'A' levels, had not been available to discuss things and when the party invitation had arrived, from a friend of Selina's, it had been simple enough to say she was going with the Bothwells, and to get away from the house with no nagging by confirming that she would be spending the night with them.

She would have done so, too, had Selina not gone off to London. The girl whose party it was had assured Clare that she could spend the night with her – her parents were away on holiday, they would all have a great time.

They had. Drink had flowed, because the girl had found the key to her father's cocktail cabinet, and very soon boys began to disappear up to the bedrooms with girls.

It was a very large, very smart house. Richard was there, pursuing a little blonde girl called Shirley with a big bust and a very low blouse. Clare had known a good many of the other guests, but there were a lot of people she had never set eyes on before, all young, all hard drinkers. With no Selina to restrain her, she had mixed her drinks with all the ignorance and enthusiasm of extreme youth. At some stage in the proceedings she had passed out cold and had been carried upstairs and put to bed by her hostess's older brother, Tom.

She had woken to find someone else in bed with her; to be coldly factual, on top of her. Someone's knees jabbed and knelt on the soft parts of her inner thighs. Someone lifted and cuddled and persuaded her into bewildered compliance, and then muzzy with sleep and drink and incapable of even verbal protest, someone began doing things which she knew were wrong, which hurt, which . . .

Afterwards, there had been voices calling and shouts and laughter, and she had found herself alone again. Without a thought, merely glad that she was to be allowed to sleep, she had slept.

Next morning, she had been horribly ashamed of the bloodstained sheets; scarlet with embarrassment she had sneaked into the bathroom, soaked the stained cotton in the bath, and apologised to her inadvertent hostess for having started unexpectedly. She had forgotten all about the events of the night and was only reminded of them when she had got herself dressed and was descending the stairs. Why was she so stiff? Why did her legs hurt in front . . . and not only her legs, she hurt elsewhere as well!

Memory returned and with it, horrible fear. She had not got the remotest idea who had made love to her, if you could call it that. It could have been anyone – her hostess's brother Tom, Richard, even Toddy, though she was sure it had not been him. She left the house as soon as she decently could and hurried home. Her mother was out and she felt she could not go round to Gran's, not the way she was.

She took a bath, and spent about two hours scrubbing herself, as if by washing really thoroughly she could wash away what had happened. She examined herself, shrinkingly, and could detect no actual difference, but she knew what she had done – or what had been done to her – had been wrong, wicked, and feared punishment.

Then, nothing had happened. Selina came back from London a bit tight-lipped, and plunged back into her studying. Clare told her merrily about the party but found she could not mention the episode in the bedroom. If she told no one, she found herself reasoning, perhaps it would not be true, perhaps it would turn out to be a beastly nightmare, nothing to worry about at all.

Then she started being sick. Not morning sickness, which she had dimly heard about, but all-day sickness. Fear over the impending 'O' levels, they said at school. She believed them with part of her mind and the other part thought that it was a judgement on her for her behaviour. It did not occur to her once that she could become pregnant as the result of such a one-sided act. After all, she had not got any pleasure out of it, so surely she could not have a baby? She had read somewhere that it was impossible for a woman to get pregnant after her first impregnation anyway, so that did not worry her. It worried her that someone might find out and think her a fast, loose creature, that men might try to take advantage, but not that she might become a reluctant mother.

When her mother had found her vomiting over the toilet and had driven her into the kitchen, shrieking foul insinuations, she had been appalled. Yet even then, she had begun to think that Mrs Flower was right, that she was going to have a baby. She wanted to lay her head on her mother's lap and confess what had happened, explain that it had not been her ·fault or her wish and gain absolution, but this was plainly the last thing on Mrs Flower's mind.

And then Clive had arrived, out of the blue, and offered her escape. When she asked him why he had come, he had said, simply, that Selina had told him she, Clare, was being bullied by her mother. He could not bear to think of her being bullied, he had said. He had only had a few weeks of his annual leave, and had decided that he would like to spend the rest of it being married to her. What did she think?

'Are you sure, Clive?' she had said earnestly, staring up at him. 'Are you really sure?' She had not asked him if he loved her because she could not see how he could possibly love someone he scarcely knew; but when he said yes, he was absolutely positive, she had said she would marry him, then. And he had hugged her and kissed her on the mouth for the very first time, and driven her not home but back to Gran's, where she had scarcely had to do any talking or explaining.

'My love!' Gran had said. 'Oh, you poor little creature . . . go and change out of those clothes, have a nice warm bath, and then come downstairs. Clive will tell me what's been happening.

It took Clare an hour to get herself respectable again, and when she finally came downstairs, Clive had left. Gran bustled round, getting her a meal, and not asking any questions at all. Finally, when she and Clare were tucking into a lovely mushroom omelette with French bread and butter, she asked her first questions.

'Clare, love, are you sure you want to marry Clive? You aren't doing it because Mother was unkind?'

'I think he's super,' Clare had said, shiny eyed. 'He says he really wants to marry me; and I do want to marry him.'

'If you came back here to live . . . would you still want to marry him?'

Clare thought about it, then nodded vigorously.

'Oh, yes, Gran! Even when I thought he was Selina's feller, I had a terrific crush on him. And you see, he says it was always me, it wasn't Selina at all!'

It had gone on from there. The introduction to Mrs Arnold as Clive's bride-to-be, the scurry round to get the wedding off the ground so that they could have a honeymoon before Clive returned to Saud. It was not until they had been married for a month that Clare realised she was quite definitely going to have a baby, and that there was absolutely no way Clive could be the father.

He had left in August and come home at Christmas, because she was having a child, and he had never, by word or by deed, intimated that she had played him false. When Sally had been born he had accepted her as his and never made any sort of suggestion that she might not be his daughter.

People remarked on how like Sally was to her father, which made Clare shudder, because there was always the possibility that Richard . . . but she did not let herself consider that, not now. Now, she told herself that there was a possibility that Sally could have been of Clive's getting. Not a strong possibility, but a faint one.

Sally had been an eight-pound baby, plump and rosy and cooing. A nine-month child, one would have thought. But she could have been a seven or eight-month child, an especially well-developed baby, Clare supposed hopefully.

The only person she was ever tempted to confide in was Selina, and Selina had treated her tentative confession with the contempt she obviously thought it deserved. Or perhaps contempt was the wrong word; firmness was more like it.

'Not Clive's baby? Oh rubbish, love,' she had said. 'Just put that thought right out of your head. Sally's Clive's daughter, all right. Or are you trying to say you played him false after you were married?'

'Gosh, no . . . as if I would!' The eighteen-year-old Clare had been appalled by the mere suggestion. 'No, it was before . . . I started Sally very early, if you remember, she was born . . .'

'She's Clive's, you shouldn't ever think differently,' Selina said firmly. 'Even thinking such a thing is a kind of disloyalty, let alone saying it.'

That had stopped her short, and Clare had known that Selina was right. No matter who it was who had jumped on her in bed that long-ago night, the fellow had been totally unaware of the consequences of what he had done – perhaps he was also totally unaware of her identity – and must be left in ignorance. To the whole world – and that must include Clare herself – Clive was the father of her baby.

'Okay, love.'

The man in the kiosk acknowledged her season ticket with

the words and waved Clare through. Putting her ticket away in the dive she drove the Mini across the tarmac and parked it as she always did beneath the spreading branches of the plane tree. Then she got out, locked up and started to walk across to the caff.

In the whole of my life I've only done two things which were not absolutely conventional and expected, Clare told herself as she looked right and left and then crossed the busy road. Firstly, I got myself into trouble and married for some wrong reasons as well as some darned good ones, and secondly I got myself a job in the caff. Clive was so marvellous the first time – he made it all so easy for me, and so pleasant. Why, when all I've done this time is to get myself work, should I be so frightened of telling him?

But it was no good looking at it like that, because she had shrunk from telling him the first time that she was not a virgin, that there had been another man. This time, she had no choice, she had told him she had a job. The first time, it had been his decision to ask her to marry him, she had merely gone along with it. This time, he had said he did not want her to work and she had quite deliberately flouted his wishes.

Through the glass frontage of the caff she could see Mavis using the coffee machine and several men sitting at the tables, eating. She sighed and pushed the door open with one hand, and the caff came to meet her; the familiar smell of food and floor polish, the warmth, the friendliness which would flower as soon as Mavis looked up and saw her.

What she had done the first time had been wrong, because she had deceived Clive, but what she was doing now was fair enough. She was a woman now, not a frightened child, she was entitled to have a life of her own.

Nevertheless, as she greeted everyone and walked through into the kitchen to change her pearl-grey mac for her checked overall, she was conscious that by deliberately going her own way and defying Clive, she had taken a step away from him, possibly even a step away from Clare as she had always been.

She thought of her behaviour over the last fifteen years while buttoning her overall, slipping off her high-heeled shoes and scuffing on her flatties. It was, she concluded, about time. No woman of character wanted to be nothing but a wife and mother, surely? She had done wrong fifteen years ago but ever since she had made up for it. She had been meek and good, she had stayed in her home and brought up her daughter and she had never done anything to upset Clive. She had even turned down an invitation to go and visit Selina in her glamorous London home, because Clive had made it plain he would prefer her not to go. She and Selina had grown apart, though they still exchanged long letters two or three times a year, but she would have loved to visit Selina, grow close once more.

'Clare? It's Dee's tech. day . . . can you come and give an 'and with the breakfasts?'

'Yes, of course,' Clare called back readily. I'm more of a person now, she told herself, carrying a tray of cups through to the coffee machine. Clive should be glad I'm working, I'll be able to contribute much more to our marriage!

She was not, however, convinced that Clive would see things in this light.

CHAPTER
4

Outside the shelter of the shack, the heat was intense, so intense that Clive could see the sand actually undulating, or appearing to do so, as the heat rolled upwards.

It was not exactly cool in the shack, either, though at least you got an illusion of coolness from the shade and from the grunting little pig of an air-conditioner which did its poor best to make life bearable, at least in its immediate vicinity.

Outside they were drilling. Of course. What possible reason could any civilised human being have to spend the heat of the day out here in the rolling nothingness of the desert, save that there was oil beneath one's feet? The Saudis, who owned this oil and exploited it, had more sense than to do the actual work on it themselves. They left that to technologically intelligent Englishmen, who were willing to put up with the un-put-up-with-able conditions in order to earn vast sums of money for themselves and thus for their government's economy.

Clive glanced at his wristwatch. Solid gold, of course, because you might as well have something good to take home with you when you went. You could smuggle gold into Britain, because gold was cheap out here – Clive had taken quite a bit back, one way and another, for Clare and Sally – but since it was so cheap, most of the men wore it on wrist and occasionally round neck or finger. However gold it might be, though, his watch still did not show that it was time to get back into the jeep and make for comparative civilisation again, so Clive sighed, pushed his fingers up into his sweat-soaked hairline and told himself that he must have a haircut soon, for comfort's sake if for no other. Some men, in their forties, lost hair, but his toffee-coloured curls still grew as thickly as ever, so far as he could judge.

In front of him, a half-filled sheet of figures waited to be completed. It was stained with sweat and also with dirt from the sand. He picked up his biro – gold again, naturally – and forced his mind to concentrate on the latest calculations. He made his mind's eye see into the dark, so that it was like watching an animated cartoon; the drill, the pipes, all the business of fetching out the oil, the depth of the sand, the rock, and then, black and gleaming, the lake of oil far below. He looked at the scribbles in his hard-cover notebook, and then at the picture in his mind, and then began to write. Neatly, despite the conditions, the way the biro slipped in his sweaty fingers. Presently he became absorbed; flies buzzed, touched his skin and hair, tentatively settled. He swatted them, but absently, without serious irritation. They moved more confidently. Clive worked on.

A yell from outside brought him back to earth just as he finished the last figures. He leaned back in his rickety chair and sighed, then put the papers down, capped the biro, and stood up. He walked over to the doorway and peered out. Jim and Simon were getting into the jeep; he went over, papers in hand, and joined them. Both men grinned at him, a flash of white teeth in faces darkened and creased with the fine desert dust.

'Hi; finished figuring? We thought we'd have a couple of beers back at the base, then go into town. There's a party at the hospital. One of the nurses is twenty-one, she's asked a few of the lads up to her place. Coming?'

Clive sighed and climbed into the back seat of the jeep. It was an open vehicle, though the top was canvassed. They would drive back more slowly than they would have liked because of the dust which rose chokingly at any sort of speed.

'No, I won't bother, though I wouldn't say no to a beer or two. I'll get myself showered and cleaned up though, and if I'm feeling sociable by then I'll join you.'

Jim, short, red-headed, cheerful, made a rude, disbelieving noise and hit the horn with the heel of his hand to let everyone know they were leaving as they drew away.

'Huh! You never feel sociable, or not if there are women around, anyway. What's your wife got that mine hasn't?'

'Me, I suppose,' Clive said shortly, and leaned back in his seat. He was lucky to have Clare, he knew it, even if he had got her by a trick of sorts. Would she have married him if she hadn't been scared out of her mind, he wondered, as he had wondered so many times before. Selina had wised him up about it. 'She's terrified of Mrs Flower,' she had said, when he had asked after Clare. 'She went to one of those wild parties . . . I don't suppose much happened, but she's been quite ill and Mrs Flower's got her living at home full-time, she's not allowed to go round to her Gran's.'

He had gone round to the house on the off-chance, and had heard Mrs Flower's tirade as soon as he got near the front door. He had not then thought about marriage, he had simply wanted to rescue Clare from her persecutor. But then, in the car, with the poor kid looking so desperately scared and sick, his protective instinct – and another, older and less selfless one – had reared up. He had wanted to take care of her, not just that evening but for always. And not only to take care of her, he admitted to himself now. He had wanted her.

Wanting Clare had started a year before, when she had been only fifteen, a slim, shy, schoolgirl with a mop of dark curls, a pale little face, and eyes such a dark blue that one looked twice to check the colour. Even then, she had had a great attraction for him – greater than all the Bothwells, even Selina who was the best looking and the most intelligent of a very handsome and clever family.

Selina had liked him; he knew it and had taken advantage of it but the more he had seen of Clare the more he longed for a closer relationship. Her hair was very fine and soft and silky, her skin was pale, blue-veined. Her body was supple rather than buxom, her breasts slight, little apples compared with Selina's mature, statuesque beauty.

In the strange way that one has at a particular age or a particular time in one's life, Clive knew that he was ready for

61

marriage and a strong emotional relationship, and that Selina, too was ready. Equally, he knew with all his senses that Clare was not. Oh, she wanted kisses and cuddles, wooing and admiration, but she did not, yet, want to be sexually aroused. Odd, then, that it was Clare who filled his thoughts and dreams and not Selina, particularly as Selina was beautiful and Clare just young and full of promise.

He had married Clare, then, and never regretted it. He had tried not to frighten or disgust her with demands she could not fully share, and he thought, most of the time, that they had a good life, a good marriage. The idea of Clare taking a job he had dismissed as soon as he could. She did not need to work and besides, he could not bear the thought of her in some office, being told what to do by any fellow other than himself. Because he was only home once a year and had what he supposed was an average sort of sex-drive, he burned for her. He supposed, vaguely, that she, too, must miss his lovemaking. If she was in the constant company of other men, suppose she made good the loss? He felt heat rush over his body just at the thought; he could not bear to risk losing even his dreams of her, moving quietly round the house and garden, waiting for him. Losing the reality would be awful to him. Still, she seemed to have accepted that working was a foolish idea. Thank God for that!

'She's a lucky woman, your Clare,' Jim remarked, as they turned in the direction of the base camp. 'Never known you look at another woman – not that there are many chances, out here.'

He had looked at another woman, though. More than looked. Guilt over his relationship with Selina was long dead, but not forgotten. He had treated Selina shabbily, let her down hard, but she had forgiven him. It had spoiled her relationship with Clare though, that long, close friendship which he had once so envied. Selina had once tried, tentatively, to start it all up again and though he had been ashamed afterwards, at the time he had acted swiftly and decisively, killing the hoped-for intimacy stone-dead. It was best, he told himself now. It would have led, in the end, to heartbreak.

'You could come to the party though, Clive,' Simon said, breaking his silence for the first time since the jeep had started. 'Look at me, I never chase nurses but that doesn't mean to say I shut myself up like a hermit, and I'm not even married.'

'I'll see,' Clive said.

Simon was not married any more, but he had been married once, to a warm and loving woman who had reared his children, taken care of his home, and then got herself a very good job as personal secretary to the head of a big building concern. She had subsequently left Simon for her new boss, 'a full-time husband being more my style than a part-time one,' she had written.

It had, naturally, reinforced Clive's desire to know that Clare was safely at home, and had made his urge to keep her there stronger still. He had never met Simon's wife but had seen photos and read many of her letters. She had looked and seemed a homely body, not pretty or smart, certainly not above average intelligence, yet her boss had been glad enough to marry her and Simon had taken his loss hard. The bitterness and pain the divorce had engendered had, Clive was sure, made all the men edgy, less sure of themselves and their own relationships. Part-time husbands one and all, they found they had no desire to follow Simon through the morass of pain, uncertainty and loneliness which might well result in a wife finding herself another man.

Looking back now, Clive was comforted to remember that Simon, for all he talked of not chasing nurses, had been the sort of fellow who could never keep his hands to himself; squeezing, touching, insinuating, had been his natural follow-up to an introduction to any female. Now, wounded by experience, he seemed to have lost the urge, and he lost any woman's interest very speedily by talking constantly about what his wife had done to him. Even the plainest and most highly sexed of the nurses would think twice before having a night out with a guy who spent all the time moaning about the way he'd been treated by another woman!

'Here come the night-shift,' Jim remarked, as they saw, over the furthest ridge, the lights of the city.

They saw also, coming towards them, the familiar armada of cars. It happened every evening. As dusk fell and the burning heat drained away the city people, the rich oil sheiks, got into their big American cars and headed for the wilderness. Plotting, scheming and conniving all day, Western-seeming to their fingertips, they were nevertheless children of the sands still. When the desert was cooler and the breeze had got up they would bring their children and womenfolk out here, to play at being Bedouin again, as they had once been in earnest. They would camp out on the sands and brew strong, sweet coffee and open cans of Coke for their kids, and they would talk about the past, tell tall stories and breathe in their inheritance of freedom. But before the cold dew of dawn spangled the sands they would drive back to their palaces in the city, to their air-conditioning and convenience foods and colour telly, and they would sleep in their soft beds and wake to a good and plentiful breakfast, Westerners once more – till the next night fell.

Clive had scoffed at them once, as most of the young men did, but now he felt he understood, for he, too, could not entirely accept the world to which he had been born, the world of England.

He had promised himself long ago that when he was forty he would retire from the game and go home and raise pigs or do a small job in a large office, working from nine till five and leading a normal life. He had dreamed of weekends in the garden, tennis in summer and golf in winter, Christmas morning with snow on the windowsill and a turkey in the fridge for cooking later.

When he was living at home he could make love to Clare gently, cuddling her in bed seven nights out of seven instead of having the hectic six-week sexual marathon which his leaves tended to become. He always felt, and assumed she did, that they must pack into those six weeks all the loving and the lust which, in other circumstances, would have taken them a contented twelve months to enjoy.

Yet his fortieth birthday had come and gone, unregarded, and here he was still, working in the Kingdom, earning his huge salary the hard way, grumbling about it, talking and dreaming of home . . . yet doing nothing to change the way things were.

Why? He had a delightful wife and he was as in love with her now as he had been when they were first married. His daughter was pretty and adorable. His home was everything he had always wanted.

The reason, he suspected, was quite simply that he was not sure he was capable of being a full-time husband, sustaining a normal, full-time relationship. Clare was wonderful, but suppose she found him boring, when their marriage was for always instead of for six weeks? For the past year or two, if he was honest, there had been nights at home when he had seriously played with the idea of going straight to sleep; only shame and the memory of his lonely bed in the base camp, with the Saud stars big and bright in the dark arc above, had brought him up to scratch. He told himself that other men, full-time husbands, did not expect a nightly hard-on, but for all he knew he could be totally wrong. It might be only he who contemplated a cuddle, some kisses and then sleep for possibly as many as five nights out of seven.

He was not a group type, never had been; a loner, they had said at school. So he had very little idea whether his urges were slowing down in a perfectly natural and understandable way, or whether he was peculiar. When he first arrived back home after ten months total abstinence, he only had to raise a hand to touch Clare's cheek and other things rose too, as naturally as a level crossing barrier at the departure of the train. It was quite often a work of considerable difficulty to get up the stairs and into the bedroom before grabbing her . . . And the event, so long awaited, was then frequently so short, sharp and sweet that he was ashamed of his greed, his lack of control, and sure that he was cheating Clare who must have been as anxious as he for the delicious, sensuous business of love-making to begin.

But Clare never showed disappointment, only deep fulfilment and purring pleasure in his love-making. When he cuddled and caressed she curled up in his arms, responding enough but never suggesting, by so much as an ill-timed wriggle, that he was too slow, too fast, or simply out of step with her.

So why not chance it? Why not go home and stay there? He would miss the work, the companionship, and oddly enough, the desert itself. But he was ninety per cent sure that once he was settled in the village he would be happier than he had ever been, and would look back only in pitying astonishment at those years spent in another man's land, searching for another man's minerals.

Would Clare be happy, though? Or would she pine for those ten months of managing alone, being mistress of her own home and above all her own body? With no one to make claims on her, with only herself to please? Or would she expect the honeymoon effect of a six-week stay to continue throughout the year?

He could be sure, now, that he wanted nothing more than to spend every night making love, but he was equally sure that this was only true in the absence of any possibility of being expected to do so. He even wondered, fearfully, whether he might discover at the end of six weeks that he had simply run out of steam, as well as sperm, and would have to spend the rest of the year recharging his batteries . . . and things. A grisly prospect.

As if he could read his thoughts, Jim swivelled round to face him, a less dangerous act out here than it would have been, for instance, driving up the M.1, but still fraught with peril when half Saud was bearing down upon you in holiday mood.

'Well, old sport? You coming to give the nurses a thrill, if you'll forgive the euphemism? Or going to sulk in your tent like the Arab in the poem?'

Clive heaved a sigh. Perhaps he should mix more with people, particularly women. Perhaps, then, he would get some inkling of how it would be to be a full-time lover.

'I'll go to the party, for a while, anyway,' he said half grudgingly. 'I'm feeling depressed for some reason, probably because of the time of year. Usually round about now I'm looking forward to my leave.'

'Uh huh. You went early this year, I remember.' Jim

nodded, facing front once more. 'Why was that? Not bad news from home, I hope?'

'No, everything was fine. It was just an urge to see the spring come back . . . you know, leaves and buds and the new grass coming, that sort of thing.'

Jim nodded and even Simon gave a grunt of agreement. They did understand, of course, no matter how much they might pretend to be indifferent to England and her seasons. Simon had been here twenty years, Jim a mere five, but they both knew the strains of only going home for the briefest of visits in order to keep the money rolling in and their own positions as invaluable workers, who spoke good Arabic, constantly to the fore. Most of the men who worked in the Kingdom had developed extravagant tastes which only their present inflated salaries allowed them to indulge. It was easy enough to talk about going home, but when it came to it, most hesitated.

'I did that . . . went home in April . . . once,' Simon said dreamily. 'I was getting myself accustomed to it. Still am. That's why I had a Christmas at home just before Anna left me. I'll start doing it again soon, I think, so when I decide to stay . . .'

Clive nodded wisely and wondered whether Simon would really go back to the U.K. for good. If he was a bit nervous over the idea how much worse it must be for Simon, with nothing really to draw him back. No wife, half a dozen children all grown away from him, a mother sick and resentful. No home even, his wife had sold it and Simon had been too far away to do anything about the high-handed action.

I'm bloody lucky, Clive told himself not for the first time, all I've got to do is mention it to Clare and she'll back me every inch of the way. I'll put in for Christmas leave and tell her I'm retiring, she'll be delighted to have a full-time husband, bound to be.

The nearest limousines came alongside. Air-conditioning or no air-conditioning, every window was down, hands waved at them, voices shouted, but above all the din the car radios blared out. The dust they made was appalling so until they were past no one spoke, then Simon turned and addressed Clive.

'Tell you what, old boy, when you go home for good I'll do the same. Shall we shake on it?'

Clive, shaking Simon's proferred hand, knew that Simon would never have made the suggestion had he suspected that he, Clive, was on the very point of retiring from the game. In fact, he guessed that Simon would use the 'pact' as a good excuse for lingering on.

'I'd go tomorrow, old boy,' he would roar back at the base, 'But I've got a gentleman's agreement with old Clive here not to go until he does.'

What a shock for him, then, when Clive announced his own decision to leave as, naturally, he shortly intended! Poor Simon, forced to take a decision he feared because of a silly, meaningless handshake!

The jeep clattered through the gateway in the walls and into the city itself. I'll go to the party, Clive decided abruptly, and not just for half an hour either, to show willing, I'll go properly, and stay till the bitter end. Better see just what it is that makes people want to get together in little groups, drink illicit alcohol and giggle, because somewhere in my make-up that urge to congregate was left out and if I'm to become a full-time husband, at least I'd better try to behave like everyone else.

It was not until very much later, when he was showered and changing into a lightweight suit, that it occurred to Clive that perhaps Clare might not want a normally gregarious husband. After all, she had not married one!

The thought comforted him throughout an otherwise boring and comfortless evening.

Mavis left the caff in good time despite the fact that it was Dee's tech. day, which meant that she and Clare had to do all the clearing up between them. In fact though, Tuesday was a quiet day and since Sally had come in from school earlier than usual they had whistled through the teas, the squashes and the chocolate biscuits quicker than they expected and had then cleaned down briskly and slammed the door right in the face of a would-be customer, a lazy good-for-nothing called Ned who slept rough all summer and consequently smelt.

Now, Mavis was heading homeward with a nice piece of pork for her tea in her basket as well as three potatoes, a handful of string beans and an almost untouched drumhead cabbage.

Clare had brought her the string beans because she had grown them in her garden and Mavis had happened to mention she was fond of them. Ever so young and tender they looked, Mavis thought fondly, remembering the curly shape of them and the soft fuzz of green which made them cling together in the bag. Then she had given Mavis the pork because she said it would not go another day, the cabbage for the same reason, and Mavis had nicked the potatoes just to complete the meal.

Not that Mavis told herself the potatoes had been nicked, of course. She was no thief . . . the potatoes had been liberated, more like. Else they'd have got made into chips, which were devils for putting on weight, or they might even have been boiled. Boiled potatoes were not popular with the caff's hungry customers, so when Clare insisted on boiling some spuds they often went to waste. Which was what might easily have happened to these particular potatoes had Mavis not decided to take a hand.

Her conscience clear, Mavis's new high-heeled shoes stepped out, and she was soon at the bus stop. Her legs ached a bit but not as much as they sometimes did and the sunshine which had heralded the morning lingered still, brightening the red-brick façade of the Royal Hotel and catching the trees and grass on the Castle mound, gilding leaf and blade. What was even better, there was a goodish queue at the bus-stop which meant that she had not just missed one. Joining the end of the queue, Mavis promised her feet a rest in a moment or two, and then gave the fish-eye to a young man who looked enquiringly at her – as if she'd address a total stranger, and one in a dirty red tee-shirt, what was more!

The bus came and Mavis boarded it and managed to get a seat, which was not always easy. Her feet and legs gave an almost audible sigh of relief as she sank down and she patted her thigh consolingly; it had done well by her today, it deserved a rest.

As the bus trundled along, Mavis considered her day. It had been quite a good day, one way and another. Clare had been a bit absent-minded but perfectly friendly and though Deirdre had been off at that so-called course of hers, they had managed very well without her.

I'll write to Lionel tonight, Mavis told herself. I might even write to Sondra an' all. Tell her about Clare and that feller, the dark one, the one who always sits up the corner by the window and reads while he eats. Daft habit. But the way he looked at Clare and she at him . . . you'd have thought they was old friends, though when he'd gone out and she'd asked, Clare had said she'd never clapped eyes on him before. And Clare, unlike some Mavis could mention, was a truthful sort of gal.

He was an odd sort of bloke, though. Mavis called him Coffee and Book. Dee called him Rambo, because of his muscles. Mrs P used to call him 'that Indian', because he was so dark and had longish hair. Not that he was, naturally; English as meself, Mavis assured Sondra in her mind. Mrs P might have done better to call him a gypsy . . . now that she thought about it, Clare had said, 'Chief Sitting Bull wants another coffee,' so it was probably Red Indians Mrs P had in mind when she'd christened him.

Nothing wrong with Red Indians, Mavis consoled herself; not like real Indians . . . now them she couldn't abide. Last time she'd visited Sondra up at Earls Court scarcely a corner-shop but had some foreign name over it and some little darkie behind the counter. Mavis sniffed at the recollection. Good thing she and Lionel had got out and come down here years ago. Lionel might not mind darkies handling his food but she, Mavis, would be afraid of what she might catch. All sorts of foreign diseases they could pass on to you, she knew that. She'd read somewhere that AIDS came from abroad . . . it didn't surprise her, of course, plain as the nose on your face that something as horrible as AIDS would be brought in, like Dutch elm disease and that Mixie as our rabbits got off them European bunnies.

Still, it wouldn't do to say that to poor Sondra, living hutched in by 'em, as you might say. She wouldn't mention Coffee and Book's resemblance to an Indian, then, she'd just say as how he'd gazed at Clare and given one of his best smiles . . . Dee wouldn't half have liked to get a smile like that . . . and then changed his mind about moving on and ordered another coffee.

That was pretty surprising, now she had the leisure to think about it. I do know customers, Mavis told herself now, and he was ready for the off, you could tell. He'd had a piece of fruit cake and a cup of coffee and he'd eaten and drunk with his eyes on his book, as usual, only shooting glances across at the car-park every now and then, to where his waggon was parked. Then Clare had seen he had finished and had gone across to clear the table . . . he was getting out his money, closing his book . . . he was off, no doubt about it . . . and he'd looked up, seen her, and re-ordered.

Sondra would think it ever so romantic – love at first sight she'd call it – but it wasn't like that at all, of course. It was just . . . Mavis struggled to put it into words . . . just kind of . . . abruptly, she got it. Recognition! They had both recognised they were . . . what? The same type? But Clare, whatever her faults, was a real little lady. You couldn't say that of a feller who drove a waggon, wore breeches and wellington boots and read paperback books whilst eating his dinner. Possibly they were both country people. Yes, that must be it. Still, it made you think, gave you something to wonder about on the bus ride home. Better than dwelling on the fact that she couldn't remember shutting the kitchen door on Hodge and Pocket, which might well mean they'd do a dirty in Mrs P's immaculate little lounge and if there was one thing Mavis hated first thing, it was clearing up a cat's dirty.

Lionel might be interested in Coffee and Book, though, now she thought about it, and Lionel wasn't interested in any of their other customers; he thought they were low and wasn't afraid to say so. Which meant . . . Mavis's mind, unused to such contortions, winced at the work it was being forced to put in . . . which meant that Coffee and Book might well be more Clare's type than she had at first supposed.

Exhausted, Mavis abandoned the topic and decided to suggest to Sondra that it might be nice if they had a weekend together. Sondra might not be too keen on trekking all the way down to Norwich on the train, not with the two lads, but Mavis would not mind going up to London on a Weekend Special ticket, doing a bit of shopping and spending time with Sondra and her beloved grandsons.

Lionel would approve too. He loved his daughter and her children, though he was constantly puzzled by little Rupert. With his looks, he lamented whenever the subject came up, and with his grandfather's training, Rupert could have been anything, done anything. Yet Rupert seemed to have no inclination for the game and absolutely no interest in people. What was worse, despite his cherubic looks people had no interest in Rupert. Mavis could not understand it, and nor, of course, could Lionel. He felt sorry for Desmond, who at eight was plain as a pikestaff with nibbled-looking mouse-brown hair, a squint and a wide confiding grin which revealed gappy and uneven teeth, but of course Desmond would have to find some occupation other than following in his grand-father's footsteps.

'Good looks,' Lionel had said instructively last time he and Mavis had met, 'good looks are imperative! When you are in selling it is yourself and your appearance which the buyer buys, even if he thinks he's purchasing a twelve bore shotgun or thermal underwear. Now Rupert . . .'

'Th'Artichook!' the driver called out, bringing his vehicle to a juddering halt alongside the pub of that name. Mavis, climbing down onto the pavement, could still remember her astonishment that any pub, anywhere, could be called after a vegetable and a foreign one at that, but Lionel, who had been born and bred in Norwich and was, when all was said and done, merely returning to his roots, had assured her that the pub was an old one and the artichoke a common vegetable to the Norvicensians and not some new-fangled word used to impress.

Mavis, a Londoner then as now, though she had taken on a

good deal of protective Norfolk colouration over the years, had pretended to get used to it, but in thirty years of living within a stone's throw of it, she still privately considered it an outlandish, even heathenish, name for a pub. However, it was a sign that she was getting closer to home and as such she welcomed it, for her feet were telling her crossly that much though they had enjoyed the bus ride, it was not enough; they wanted to be up off the floor pronto or they'd make her sorry.

Accordingly, Mavis hurried along the main road, dived down the loke and turned into the first, long road which led home. As she went she planned her evening. Letters first, then a nice watch of the telly, then possibly a hot bath, followed by a small gin and finally hot chocolate and bed. Or perhaps it would be better to have a small gin, then write the letters, then have another tiny, tiny snifter and then have a bath.

Musing happily on the endless computations possible once the words 'small gin' had entered the field, Mavis scarcely noticed as the paving stones passed rapidly beneath her clicking shoes. She did not drink much, particularly alone in the house, but the gin would lubricate the stiff wheels of her letter-writing, and cause the words to flow in a way which otherwise would have given her a good deal of trouble. Besides, Lionel liked to think of her having a drink when she wrote, he had said so. She would drink to him . . . and to Sondra, of course. Perhaps she might drink to Clare too, and that feller of hers, stuck out in Arabia or some such.

Her and me's two of a kind, she thought, as she put her key in the lock. Grass widows the pair of us. I really oughter ask her round for a meal, one night. We could have quite a time of it, she's a good sport, is Clare. We might nip along to The Artichoke and have a laugh and a jar. Not that gin comes in jars, but Lionel always says he's going out for a jar . . .

It was quiet and chilly in the small front hall and there were two letters on the mat, both bills by the looks. Mavis skirted them, giving the Gas Board's offering – which she recognised by the way they spelt her name in that window thing – a contemptuous kick as she passed it. She went into the kitchen and at once the warm smell of the casserole which she had not quite finished last night and the chirping of her budgerigar, Cheepy, made her feel at home and welcomed, though the kitchen itself faced north and might not have appeared cosy to anyone else.

'Hello, my lovely boy,' Mavis said, pressing her sharp nose against the bars of Cheepy's bijoux residence. 'Mummy's home . . . Is my lovely boy going to give his Mummy a kiss?'

Cheepy sidled along his perch, chattering away in his tiny, sinister voice which, despite its gravelly tones, was still noticeably Mavis's and made quite convincing kissing noises against her cheek. Mavis rubbed his small green and yellow head, said 'Love 'im!' in her most doting tone, and plonked her bag on the floor and her bottom on the saggy cane chair nearest Cheepy's cage.

'I'll 'ave five minutes, Cheepy my son,' she remarked, kicking off her shoes and watching her feet swell gratefully before her eyes. 'Then you and me'll start on our tea.'

'After I've had my grub, Mum, I'm going to rush down to Em's and we'll do our homework together, then I'll come home and write to Dad.' Sally slumped inelegantly down on the edge of the kitchen table and craned her neck to peer into the saucepan Clare was gently stirring. 'Is that okay? By the time my letter's in the post, Dad'll have read yours, so I can tell him about Dee and the caff, can't I?'

Clare turned and surveyed her only child, long and gangling, with a smudge of biro on her cheek and hope in her eyes. She laughed and poked Sally with the handle of her wooden spoon.

'How you can stay so skinny when all you ever do is eat beats me, but yes, you write to Dad and say what you like. I never asked you to lie to him, Sal, now did I?'

'No, of course not,' Sally said readily. She slid off the table and took the spoon gently from her mother's hand. Carefully, she dipped it into the cheese sauce that Clare was stirring, blew on it, tasted, and then smiled seraphically.

'Golly, dee-licious. So it's cauliflower au gratin and crusty French bread, is it? Where was I? Oh yes, writing to Dad.

Well, you didn't say to tell lies, naturally, but you did say try not to talk about it until you'd told him, which meant I couldn't say about Dee and that, could I?'

'No, I suppose not. Well, feel free to write in full now, then. As for supper, it's cauliflower and crusty French bread, but with a couple of lean pork slices each. So you won't starve, not tonight.'

'Super,' Sally said contentedly. She began to bustle round the kitchen, laying the table, whilst Tish followed her hopefully, always on the alert for an extra little something. 'I say, Mum, who was that man, the one in the corner table?'

'Big Chief Sitting Bull? I don't know who he was, except that Mavis said he was a regular customer.'

'Oh. Then Dee will know him, I suppose.'

'Probably. Yes, of course she does, Mavis told me she called him Rambo.'

Sally snorted.

'Honestly, Rambo . . . that girl's got a one-track mind, hasn't she, Mum? I liked his smile, though.'

'Did you? I thought you were probably attracted by the smell of horse which hung about him.'

'Oh, it was him, was it?' Sally came out of the pantry, her arms full of condiments, and decanted them vigorously – and untidily – all over the table. 'Yes, there was a stable sort of smell; I thought it was that little toad up by the counter, stuffing himself with strangled yeggy.'

Strangled yeggy was Sally's baby-talk, now so much a part of the Arnold vocabulary that Mavis, too, had started using it.

'He did smell a bit, but Mavis said he was a cattle drover, so he was smelling of cows, not horses,' Clare said vaguely. 'Fancy you noticing a feller though, Sal . . . things are looking up!'

'I don't see why you say that, I notice all sorts of things and people, but I don't happen to keep falling in love with them, like Dee does,' Sally objected. 'Do you wish I did, Mum? Would you like it if I told you Big Chief Sitting Bull had the bluest eyes and hair like . . . like elderberries? Or would you rather I noticed someone smelt of horses?'

'His eyes are very . . . Help, the pork slices!' In considerable confusion over nearly having given herself away, Clare dived for the grill and rescued the perfectly cooked meat from beneath it, pretending to examine the pork for signs of scorching. She stood up, patted her chest in mock relief, and began to dish up. 'One for me and a couple for you, you growing girl you! Be a dear, Sal, and serve up the cauliflower; I haven't had time to pour the sauce over and then put it under the grill, you'll have to have it pale but interesting, tonight.'

Presently, with the food before them, she and Sally got down to the serious business of eating and then all too soon, Clare felt, Sally was jumping to her feet and promising fervently to do the wiping up when she got back from Em's, if only she might go now, before the Carters settled down in front of the telly and Em's chance to do her homework in her room was gone, because the little ones would be in bed.

'Right, off you go,' Clare said, trying not to feel hurt because Sally would rather do her work up in Emma's cramped little room instead of in the comfortable, quiet living-room with her mother reading a book but on hand to help if needed. 'Don't be late, there's a good girl.'

'I won't.' Sally blew her a kiss, seized her satchel and whistled Tish, who leapt for the back door like a lifer when the prison gates open and disappeared in the direction of the road.

Left alone, Clare began to pile up the dirty dishes and then, with her red plastic washing up bowl full of hot water and suds, to wash them. As she washed, she mused on Sally's remark. Fancy her noticing the chap in the corner, though – it really was unusual and it just went to show that he was an arresting sort of bloke. She did not have to think hard to recall his features – the thin, high-bridged nose, strong, cleft chin and the dark eyes set slightly aslant under thick, winged eyebrows. He was, she supposed, one of those people who are immediately fascinating; he had a dangerous sort of face, or perhaps that was not quite what she meant. He looked as though he must live a dangerous life, which was really being quite absurdly fanciful, especially when you considered his breeches and wellingtons, to say nothing of a waxed jacket slung carelessly on the back of his chair and the well-worn brown sweat-shirt with the sleeves rolled up which adorned his lean, muscular person.

Clothes like that – and the smell of horses – meant only one thing in the caff. He was a horse-waggon driver, she supposed with a small shudder of distaste; for even seven weeks of working in the caff could not reconcile Clare to such an occupation. Of course it was possible that he was driving a horse-box for some more innocent reason but the chances were, in this day and age, that he was carting horses to slaughter, either in Norfolk, or over to the Continent where good prices were paid for horse meat.

She might not have noticed him, or no more than she noticed any other customer, had it not been first for the smell of horse which hung about him and second for the electric encounter between them which she was still at a loss to interpret. She had gone to his table to collect his used plate and cup and as she bent over he had looked up. Eyes, unfathomably dark, had met hers and just for a moment it was as though he had touched her, or spoken some secret language known only to the two of them. She had felt hot colour invade her face and had been astonished to see a darkening of his lean cheeks. But then he had ordered a second cup of coffee in a quiet, deep voice and she had hurried into the kitchen to get a clean cup. Mavis, making a cheese and tomato roll at the counter, had given her a sharp look, but it had meant nothing. When presently the two of them were in the kitchen Mavis had merely remarked that Dee called the fellow Rambo and that he was in quite often. She had followed this up, later, by asking whether Clare had ever met Coffee and Book before.

Clare assured her that she had not, for by and large she did not serve the customers personally, leaving that to Mavis and Deirdre, but the small encounter remained with her, intriguing her, though she was not in the habit of giving any customer a second thought once the door of the caff closed behind her.

Later, she asked Mavis casually whether Chief Sitting Bull

77

was a farmer and Mavis had shrugged and said it was possible, except that so far as she could remember he did not usually come in on market day, which led her to suppose him merely a waggon driver.

Now, Clare finished the washing up, put the dishes away and then, without noticeable enthusiasm, began to prepare the kitchen for the next morning. She stood bread by the cooker, put cereals and the covered sugar bowl on the table, then pulled the kettle over the hot-plate and made herself a cup of coffee.

Taking it through into the living-room she was about to settle in front of the television when she heard a peremptory tapping at the window and, looking across, met Gregory's cross-eyed, furious stare. He seemed to have difficulty in actually looking through glass but that did not mean he was unaware of Clare's presence. What made him so cross was that he knew she could see him, so why on earth did she not immediately fly over to the window and let him in? Clare teased him for a few moments by continuing to sip her coffee then got up, pottered over to the window and pretended to draw the cream-coloured curtains across. Poor Gregory stood up at her approach, arching his back, preparing to step graciously across the sill, and then saw her hand on the curtain. His tail began to lash but at the same time such an expression of bafflement crossed his face at his own inability to communicate that Clare took pity on him and opened the window. Immediately he stepped in and feeling possibly the tiniest degree of gratitude for her action he stayed for a moment on the wide sill, on tiptoe, pressing the top of his broad ginger head against the underside of her chin and purring like a motorbike.

'You really are a darling,' Clare said, touched by this rare show of affection. 'I'm glad someone still loves me – Sally's gone out and left me alone without even Tish to keep me company. Never mind though, you can stay and watch telly with me if you like.'

She was quite prepared to have her offer flung back in her face as Gregory stalked majestically out to examine his dish in the kitchen, but plainly tonight the cat was sensitive to her and also he had possibly dined recently. Clare remembered that in the past, when Gregory had been particularly beastly and cruel to some unfortunate rodent, he would be extremely affectionate towards her afterwards, as though he felt such a chap as he could afford to unbend a little. Now, as she sat down, he leapt lightly onto her lap, examined her face earnestly for a few moments whilst she struggled not to laugh – Gregory hated to be mocked – and then proceeded to knead and pummel her skirt into what he obviously considered the right state of submission before suddenly descending into a crouching position, facing the television, ears erect, purr reverberating.

They had barely watched five minutes of the programme before Gregory sighed, yawned with much flashing of milky fangs, and curled into a tight ball. He was clearly settling down for the night.

'Oh Greg, I'll have to move you in a few minutes when Sally comes in,' Clare said distractedly. Gregory hated being moved once he had settled and could make his feelings known with his excellent set of claws. Her tights were new and her skirt, now covered with a fine patina of cat hair, was also quite a nice one. 'Would you rather move now, get yourself comfy on the couch?'

Gregory opened one eye and glowered greenly through the slit, then closed it again.

'You wouldn't? You'd rather I sat here all night and nursed you? Well, old boy, I'm sorry to disappoint you . . .'

'Kick him off, Mum, don't let him bully you!' Sally's voice had Clare leaping a foot out of her chair to say nothing of what it did to her heart. 'Show that cat who's boss!'

'I do – he is,' Clare said breathlessly. 'You gave me an awful fright, darling. Couldn't you have made a bit more noise as you came in?'

'I did, but the telly's so loud you wouldn't have heard a Regiment of Foot doing drill in the kitchen.' Sally threw herself violently onto the couch and it skidded a yard, screeching. 'Do you know I'm starving? Can I go and scrounge something from the pantry? Bickies? Chockies? Bread and dripping?'

'If you've marked the parquet I'll kill you,' Clare said, trying to see just what damage the castors had done to her gleaming wood block floor. 'As for being hungry again, I sometimes wonder if you've got worms! However, there's wholemeal bread in the crock and cheese in the fridge . . . If you're getting yourself some you might as well get some for me as well, I'll have pickled cabbage with it . . . or would I prefer onions?'

'Sure.' Sally sloped out of the room and returned presently with a loaded tray. She had brought a jug of coffee, two mugs, a hunk of cheese, half a loaf of bread and one jar of pickled cabbage and one of onions. She stood this offering on the small table between her mother and herself and then sat down, a little more carefully this time, on the couch.

'There you are, Mum, how's that for service?'

'Wonderful; what would I do without you? Which I seem to be doing most of the time, right now.'

The complaint was carefully worded but as Clare helped herself to bread and cheese and two of the largest pickled onions, she was glad to see her daughter look a little self-conscious.

'Oh, Mum, I did have to do my homework, only of course we chatted.' Sally hacked cheese and bread off their respective wholes, forked a couple of pickled onions out of one jar and cabbage out of the other and poured two mugs of coffee. Then she took a big bite of bread and cheese and spoke through a full mouth. 'I told Em I wanted to spend all the hols going round the horse-shows, just to accustom Pegs, you know.'

'Oh, do you? Well, I want you to work in the caff, actually, Sal. You'd be earning yourself some money and you'd be with me a bit more, because it's bad enough at the moment, we only seem to meet for ten minutes before bed and ten minutes after breakfast as it is.'

She did not know quite how she expected Sally to take this, but her daughter sighed, took a pull at her coffee, and then answered quite cheerfully.

'Yes, I'd like to work in the caff and the money would be

nice, I probably need some clothes, but most of the shows are at weekends. I could fit both in, couldn't I?'

'Yes, of course you could. And as for clothes, love, you've never shown much interest but if there's anything you want right now, we could go shopping when the caff's quiet, just you and me. I'd love to buy you some nice bits and pieces.'

Sally gave Clare the sort of look she was more accustomed to receiving from Tish when the poor creature was in mid-puddle in some anti-social spot, such as the goatskin rug in the spare bedroom. It was the guilty, oh-God-this'll-upset-her look which children turn occasionally on a loved parent. Clare squared her shoulders and prepared to be rebuffed.

'That would be great, Mum . . . but there are things I'd like to try on and perhaps even wear which . . . which . . .'

'Sweetheart, I understand. Your taste isn't cast-iron, like mine, you want to find out for yourself what suits you and what doesn't. That's fine by me, I was being silly when I suggested shopping with you.'

It hurt; children amputate one piecemeal, Clare thought painfully, smiling brightly at her child who was struggling to emerge from the chrysalis and wanted to do it alone. I'm losing the growing-up Sal before I even had her! But it's all part of being a parent, I suppose.

'You're a wonderful woman, Mrs Arnold,' Sally said in a transatlantic accent. 'You sure are a wonderful, generous, giving kinda lady, Mrs A!' She changed back briskly to her own young, unaccented voice. 'Don't worry that I'll put safety pins through my ears or have my hair spiked or buy see-through dresses, because I'm not into that kind of thing. But there are some pink jeans which I've seen in Elliott's and there's a leather jacket in Breakers . . . well, anyway, I wouldn't mind trying them.'

'Yes, sure, darling,' Clare said brightly, trying to stifle an urge to point out that Breakers catered for young male motor-cyclists and that the clothes in Elliott's were blown together by a very young ape unaccustomed to working with its hands.

She succeeded in stifling the urge, and crushed another one to suggest that a stroll round Miss Selfridge or a wander

round Debenham's might bear better fruit. I mustn't interfere, she told herself crossly. Selina and I used to spend
months of our lives, probably, trying on clothes in tatty little
shops all over the city. Only – only the shops sixteen or
seventeen years ago hadn't been tatty, they had been exciting
and fresh and daring.

'More bread and cheese, Mum? No? Me neither, so if you
don't mind I'll take a cup of coffee and this abominable
animal up to bed with me. Don't wake me before you have
to, will you? I like to lie there savouring the sound of you
getting up and starting breakfast, I pretend its the holidays
and I'm not getting up for hours!'

Sally headed for the door, Gregory draped over one
shoulder like a particularly fat and well-groomed fur stole.

'Oh . . . well, if you don't mind sleeping with Greg I
suppose it's all right, but if he wakes at 3 a.m. and wants to go
out you're to let him, understand? That means take him all
the way downstairs, unlock the back door, eject him, and
lock up afterwards. I will not have him trying to dig his way
under my door at around dawn and ruining my night's sleep.
Clear?'

'Clear as mud,' Sally said cheerfully.

She heaved Gregory off her shoulder, to the detriment of
her fawn school cardigan, and turned him upside down in the
crook of her arm so that he lay as a baby might, except for the
thunderous expression on his face. Sally tickled his chin with
her spare hand, then seized his paw and flapped it up and
down. Gregory sneezed. 'Say goodnight to Mum, honeychild!'

'Honeychild' gave a bad-tempered mutter which made
Sally laugh, then the two of them disappeared and Clare
could hear Sally bouncing up the stairs with scant regard for
Greg's dignity or comfort.

Alone again, she tided the living room, went into the
kitchen and washed up and tidied in there, filled Tish's water
bowl, locked up, switched off lights and made her way up to
bed. Another day done . . . In three more days Clive would
get her letter and probably in another week she would receive
his reaction to her news. Whatever he said she would have to

face up to it, as she was having to face up to Sally's newfound maturity and desire to be anywhere but at home. She was not looking forward to it but who knew, Clive might surprise her by giving his unqualified approval of her new venture.

In her room Clare turned on the bedside light and undressed, washed at the pink washbasin, cleaned her teeth, then jumped into her half of the big double bed with its white broderie anglaise duvet and matching pillows. Cuddling down, she told herself that she was glad to be alone in the bed, so that she could concentrate on making up menus for the weeks to come, because the customers liked variety, but in fact she was foiled by her own tiredness. She was asleep within five minutes of pulling the quilt up round her ears.

CHAPTER
5

The letter came eight days later, when Clare had almost stopped worrying and wondering about it. Almost, but not quite. And of course the postman arrived at the gate in his little van just as she and Sally were about to escape to the city. Only he was blocking their exit and took no notice of her desperate pip on the horn but jumped out, shoved a bundle of mail through the window, and then drove off with a sprightly wave.

'It's the one from Dad, isn't it?' Sally said brightly, holding out the familiar airmail envelope with Clive's neat, decisive writing on the front. 'Shall I open it for you and read it out?'

'No,' Clare snapped. The letter was the sort of letter that needed time, quiet and solitude, she had no intention of opening it with Sally near at hand, let alone allowing her to read it aloud.

'Oh, all right. I just thought you'd rather know than not,' Sally said, plainly rather offended. 'I don't care what he says, he's too sensible to mind about the job.'

'Yes. Sorry. Over-reacting,' Clare said, and then started to chat on other, safer subjects, but all the way to school her heart was thumping and her mind was only half on what she was doing. Once she had dropped Sally she could have drawn up by the roadside and read the letter but it would have made her late, or so she reasoned. So she parked the Mini and then crammed the letters, all of them, into her handbag and hurried across to the caff. Later will do, she told herself. I'll read them later, when I'm having a coffee break.

'Morning Clare,' Mavis said cheerfully, as she hurried in. 'Dee beat you today. She's making pancake batter, Gawd knows why. Not a bad day, eh?'

Clare, who had scarcely noticed the sunshine, murmured agreement and went past Mavis, who was slapping butter on a round of toast with a prodigality which would have turned Mrs P's hair white. She made a determined effort to drag her mind off pointless conjecture, tossed her anorak onto the nearest object, and walked over to Dee, who was using the electric whisk on a large bowl of batter. Dee looked up and smiled, then switched the whisk to low in order to explain herself.

'Morning, Clare, we did pancakes yesterday at tech., so I thought I'd do some lunchtime. What do you think? Ever such fancy ones you can make with a bit of pie filling or thickened fruit.'

'Sure, make a change.' Clare peered at the batter, sighed, and went to hang up her anorak. After all the things she said to the others about keeping clothing in its proper place she had best watch her own behaviour.

'That's what I thought,' Dee shouted above the high speed whine of the whisk. 'They said you had to leave the batter to rest though, for a coupla hours; that's why I come in early, to give it a chance to rest.'

'Yes, I remember doing that when I was at night-school,' Clare agreed. She went over to the sink and began to run hot water into the bowl. 'I'll start washing up, shall I?'

Deirdre, absorbed once more in her work, did not answer, but since it had been a rhetorical question anyway, Clare proceeded to wash up, still trying to concentrate on what she was doing rather than what was in the envelope. Her handbag, hung on the hook above her anorak, might have hidden a tarantula or a viper the way she kept casting glances at it. What a fool you are, she scolded herself, either open it or forget it, don't let it rule your morning! But she did not believe in letting her personal life interfere with work; it would have to wait for her coffee break.

It was one of those days, though. At around the time when she, Dee and Mavis would normally have snatched a break the caff was buzzing. At lunch-time they were nearly slack enough for a quiet read, but just as she was thinking she would nip over to the Mini or up to the flat on some pretext and open the letter, a coach-load of tourists came down from the Castle, spotted Dee's pancake notice, and came flooding in. They filled the place to the eyebrows and every man jack of them had a pancake of some description.

By the time she had finished their orders Clare wished she had never heard the word pancake, and Dee was saying bitterly that their teacher would hear a thing or two next Tuesday. Mavis, frantically opening tinned pie fillings, heating them and serving the pancakes, was so tight-lipped that Clare thought it would need minor surgery to get her to speak again.

When at last the coach-load left, and Mavis was cleaning down, Deirdre went out and wiped the word pancakes off the board, then came back in, slipped in a puddle of spilt batter and clouted her wrist against the cooker. Even beneath the make-up you could see the colour flee from her face, and for a moment Clare thought the child was going to faint. She abandoned her pan of sausages and rushed across the kitchen, nearly following Dee's example as her foot met the wet and slimy patch.

'Dee, love, are you all right?'

Dee murmured that it 'ad bloody hurt, whereupon Clare turned and shouted to Mavis to come and clean the floor, for God's sake, before someone broke their neck.

Mavis stumped in, bright spots of colour in the middle of each cheek and her eyes burning with righteous wrath.

'And just what do you mean by that?' she enquired, visibly bristling. 'This floor's clean enough to eat off of, and well you know it.'

'If you fancy pancake batter raw, you're right on target,' Clare said with rare sarcasm. 'Dee slipped in it . . . look at her wrist.'

Her wrist was already swelling fast and turning a delicate

plum colour. Mavis looked, sniffed, and then went and brought the mop out of its corner.

'Am I to blame because the silly little creature throws batter about?' she enquired righteously. 'Is it my fault if . . .'

Dee cut her short.

'It's all right, Mave, it was all my fault,' she said faintly. 'It serves me right – it hurts like hell, though.'

Mavis finished mopping and came over to where Dee was sitting on the kitchen stool whilst Clare supported the injured wrist.

She looked judiciously at the pair of them, sniffed again, then went out into the caff. Half a minute later she returned, triumphant.

'Git your coat, gal, I'm taking you up th'hospital, git you x-rayed. You'll be awright Clare, for a half an hour, won't you? After all,' she added, her tone heavy with injustice, 'After all, if I'm here I'm liable to let the floor get mucky and perhaps next time it'll be a customer what hits the dust.'

'I'm sorry, Mavis, I shouldn't have made it sound as though you were to blame,' Clare said, suppressing a desire to scream. 'Look, you stay here, I'll run Dee up in the car. You're right, she should get it x-rayed. I wouldn't be at all surprised if it was broken, or sprained at any rate.'

'Naw, you stay 'ere. Mrs P's cousin Pammy's in the caff, she says she and her Albert'll run us,' Mavis explained, donning her light mac and kicking off her scuffies in favour of her navy court shoes. 'Come on, Dee, we haven't got all day, gal.'

Dee, obviously past protesting, stood up and allowed herself to be led out. Clare watched as cousin Pammy, a massive woman who looked as if she had been poured into her cream and magenta striped dress, helped Dee and Mavis into an elderly station waggon driven by, presumably, her Albert. From behind the counter it was not easy to take in detail, but if what she could see was any judge the car was fully loaded merely with Albert and Pammy aboard. What the extra weight of Dee and Mavis was likely to do to the station waggon's springs she shuddered to think. Mopping down the long counter and watching as a group of mothers left the caff, Clare hoped that either Mavis or Dee would return in the fullness of time. It was quiet now, all right, but around four o'clock they usually had a rush. Being in charge was all very well, but no one, no matter how efficient, could cope with the cooking and the customers without help, or not at four, anyway, when customers tended to rush in, in droves and to expect immediate attention. However, Sally would be in round about rush-time, which would be a help; I'll probably manage, Clare told herself, and was about to start setting cups and saucers out when she remembered the letter.

Like a sleepwalker she crossed the kitchen, rummaged in her handbag, and produced the familiar envelope. A glance at her wrist-watch showed her that it was still the quiet, middle-of-the-afternoon time, when the most she could expect in the way of customers would be a couple of tea and scones or possibly a Pepsi floater.

She crossed the empty caff and took a seat by the window. Outside, the city dreamed in the rare sunshine. Traffic seemed to have decided to give it a rest for once and even the leaves of the plane tree hung quiet in the warm air. She looked up towards the Eastern Counties Newspapers building and saw that the unfamiliar quiet extended that far, too. Usually the long steps bustled with people; now only pigeons cooed and strutted. She looked to the right and there was no sign of bustle around the television centre, either. On the car-park a lorry moved, wheeling into an empty space, but otherwise, nothing. No one.

Clare slit the envelope open with a convenient knife and fished out the flimsy airmail paper. She glanced at it, then away. Oh heavens, it was only a letter, after all, what harm could it do her? She unfolded it, smoothed out the first sheet, and started to read.

She got to the end before she allowed the tears which had stood in her eyes to overflow and trickle down her cheeks. Oh God, it was worse when he was hurt like this than angry; anger she could have faced and probably conquered but his palpable dismay and distress, his bewilderment, were another matter. Why on earth had she done it when she knew how he felt about working wives? He had more or less begged her to stay at home . . . why could she not have taken up voluntary work, with the W.I. or the W.V.S., if she was bored? He knew he was old-fashioned but she had never wanted for anything; why could she not have thought about Sally and the long school holidays? Sally wouldn't want to be a latch-key kid – certainly he could not bear to think of Sally being at home without her mother.

That was bad enough, but the next page was worse. Clive said he was definitely going to take extra leave at Christmas, preparatory to giving in his notice and coming home for good. Or rather, he had been going to do so, but there was little point in his returning if she was working six days a week!

'I want your companionship when I come home,' he had pointed out. 'Do you think I'll be happy at home whilst you work in the city? And what about my leave? I suppose I'm meant to amuse myself whilst you cook and serve meals to total strangers!' He had erroneously supposed that she worked late, which she could easily put right when she next wrote, but even on that point his tone of a man wronged was not easy to dismiss lightly, or not easy for Clare, at any rate. He ended with what amounted to an ultimatum.

'I'm sure you don't realise how you've hurt me, my darling,' he finished. 'But when you do, surely you'll change your mind? Give in your notice? Now you know how strongly I feel, I mean. I long for my leaves, I count the days, mark off a calendar in my office and another in my room. Don't let me down, pet – I can't imagine coming back to a working wife who isn't even in the home we've made together.'

Clare read the letter through once, then again. And then she put her head down on her arms and had a good cry. She loved her job, Clive was being foolish beyond anything, she would not just meekly stop work – but oh, what difficulties lay ahead if she followed that path! Clive and her mother would combine against her, Richard and Rachel would pity Clive for having such a headstrong, selfish wife, all Clive's colleagues would feel sorry for him . . . and what was worse, he would not come home to live permanently and would blame her for forcing him to remain in the suddenly uncongenial Kingdom!

The abrupt opening of the caff door acted on her like a pin stuck in the bottom. She leapt to her feet and scuttled for the counter, muttering as she caught a glimpse of a tall figure coming in, 'Back in a moment.'

In the kitchen, she grabbed a tea-towel and scrubbed at her eyes with it, not letting herself consider what she would have said to Dee or Mavis if they had behaved in such a way. Glancing at her reflection in the round mirror beside the door, she saw that her eyes were still red and that streaks of dirt were smeared across her cheeks. A quick dash to the sink, a splash of cold water, another application with the tea-towel, and she decided she would have to do. She picked up a waitress-pad from the working surface nearest the door and went through into the caff, trying to make her mouth smile, her face look normal, though heaven knows, she thought ruefully, no one could feel normal so soon after a hearty bout of tears.

'Can I help . . .' the words died on her lips. The man sitting at the window table was Coffee and Book, or Rambo, or Big Chief Sitting Bull, and for a moment he did not look up at her, because he was, as usual, reading.

Clare glanced down to see what he was reading and gasped; he was quite calmly reading her letter! Only the back page, thankfully, since she had scrumpled up the others in her hand as she flew from the table, but that was quite enough. She leaned over and took it – snatched it, really – out of his grasp. Colour had flooded her cheeks and she felt like forgetting he was a customer and slapping his head for him. How dare he . . . how dare anyone . . . read someone else's private correspondence?

He looked up at that. 'Sorry, someone's left a letter,' he said quite calmly and cheerfully. 'I was just reading through it to see if I could find a clue as to the receiver, but no hope, it's the last page. Still, if you . . .' he seemed to notice, for the first time, Clare's flushed cheeks and over-bright eyes. He smiled, a quick amused curl of the lips.

'Yours?'

'Yes!'

But his words had been so natural, so easy, that all Clare's indignation was oozing away.

She said stiffly, 'I didn't notice I'd left a page, but you shouldn't have read it, you know.'

He raised lazy brows. He still looked more amused than repentant.

'I'm sorry, I didn't realise the owner was still on the premises or I wouldn't have, of course. But you shot off in such a hurry I didn't really see which table you'd been sitting at.' He picked up the menu and made a pretence of looking at it, then abandoned even that and looked up at her again. His dark eyes were shrewd. 'Boyfriend making you cry, is he? Come on now, what's so terrible? Lover's tiffs weren't made to be taken too seriously, you know.'

To her shame and horror, Clare felt tears begin to gather in her eyes once more at even the suggestion of sympathy. She swallowed and stared down at the menu, laying on the table between them.

'It isn't . . . I'm married, Clive's my husband. He doesn't think wives should work . . . and Dee, she's the YTS girl, fell against the cooker and did her wrist in. Mavis took her up to casualty so I read the letter . . . it's just been one of those days.'

'I see.' He looked startled. 'Who's Mavis?'

'The other one.'

He looked amused again and Clare, feeling foolish, said briskly, 'The one who isn't Dee or me, there are only the three of us as I dare say you've noticed.'

'I hadn't, but . . .'

If it was possible to go redder, Clare went. What an idiot she was, to assume that he would have noticed the staff of a little caff which he visited perhaps a couple of times a month! He must think her conceited to the point of egomania.

'No, of course, I'm . . .'

He cut across her stammered attempt at an apology.

'I've noticed you, and a couple of youngsters. Look, why don't we have a cup of coffee and continue our discussion over it? After all, you were sitting down when I came in, so presumably it was your off-time or whatever you call it. I'll buy the coffee, of course.'

'It's very kind of you, but I couldn't, I'm supposed to be working.' Clare was itching to get back into the kitchen again and see just what Clive had said on the last page; offhand, she simply could not remember. She wrote 'One coffee', firmly on her pad and turned towards the kitchen.

'I see, no fraternising with the enemy, eh?' the man said. 'What if I have a slice of cake as well? Doesn't that entitle me to company?'

Clare turned to shake her head and found herself laughing. She tried to pull her face into sobriety but it refused to go – and anyway it wouldn't hurt her to sit down, it would be just about the first time today what with one thing and another.

'All right, but I'll buy my own coffee and if a customer comes in I'll leave you without an apology and at the speed of light; understood?'

'Sure, fine.'

'I'll just get the coffees.'

She was in mid-pour when he got up from the table and lounged over to the counter. It occurred to her that he walked a bit like a cowboy in a Western, she almost expected him to produce a gun and start twirling it round one finger or possibly to tell her that Wyatt Earp was in town, but his remark was far more mudane.

'Which is the best cake? Are they all home-made?'

'They're all home-made, and they're all equally delicious,' Clare said, not to be drawn. 'There's coffee and walnut, chocolate fudge and pineapple surprise today. Which do you prefer?'

'Hmm, a good question. What's the surprise?'

'The surprise? Oh, well I suppose it's the fact that the cake's made with whole pineapple rings.' He smiled and she added crossly, 'I only made the cake, I didn't christen it.'

'In that case I'll do without the surprise and have a piece of chocolate fudge. Is it that one? Yes, it looks pretty substantial.'

'You don't have to have it,' Clare pointed out, cutting a

wedge. 'On the other hand, after eating it you won't want much else for a while.'

She pushed the cake over the counter and he took it in one hand and dived the other into his pocket.

'What's the damage?'

Clare told him, he paid, and they returned to the window table with the last page of the letter still unread in Clare's pinafore pocket. But she was no longer thinking about the letter at all, her mind was firmly on . . . Rambo? Big Chief? Coffee and Book?

They settled themselves and Clare took a cautious sip of her coffee. If he wanted to talk, let him, the onus of conversation with a relative stranger was far too taxing for one who had recently been howling her eyes out.

'Well, Clive's wife? Are you going to tell me why Clive doesn't want you to become a working woman? Or is the bit I read his explanation? That he wants the little woman to be waiting whenever he returns?'

'My name's Clare, and I suppose he's entitled to want me at home. Only . . .' She hesitated, leaning forward on her elbows, gazing earnestly into the dark, spare face before her. 'Only I've not had this job long and I like it so much, I can't bear the thought of giving it up, at least not until he's really come home for good.'

'One thing at a time, Clare. I'm Oliver Norton.' He held out a thin, brown hand. Clare shook it; they smiled.

'Hello, Oliver.'

It occurred to her that they seemed to have skipped most of the preliminaries to a normal acquaintanceship but it was a bit too late for regret now, and anyway she was not at all sure she did regret it. She could scarcely explain to Sally how Clive felt, nor to her mother or in-laws. She could tell Gran, but then Gran was always on her side. She needed to tell an impartial person and gauge their reactions to what Clive had said and how she herself felt.

'Well? Spit it out.'

'What do you think? Should I give it up and sit at home waiting?'

'This job? Certainly not – how can I come in here and have

a coffee with you if you're miles away? I take it you don't need the money, then?'

'It's lovely to have a bit of independence but strictly speaking no, I don't need the money.'

'And you've no kids?'

'I've got a daughter, you've seen her in here, probably, she was in last time you were at any rate.'

'One of those girls, your daughter? Good God! No more hidden away?'

'What, children? No. Just Sally.'

'Then I can see no earthly reason for you not working, if you're lucky enough to get a job. You must have been bored to tears until you came here.'

'I was,' Clare said eagerly. 'I really was! We live miles out of the city, right in the country, and I don't have neighbours near enough to go round for coffee or anything like that. Clive's old-fashioned, that's the trouble; he can't understand a woman working because she wants to and actually enjoying it.'

'Army, is he?'

'No, he's an engineer, he digs oil wells out in Saudi Arabia. He comes home for a couple of months each year but that's it. So I can't help it, I get . . .' She was about to say lonely when it struck her that she was behaving like a woman on the cop, as Dee would have called it, for a feller. For a moment she was struck dumb, too embarrassed even to look at him, and then she adroitly changed the sentence ending. '. . . I get fed-up and depressed and go rushing round to my family for days on end.' It was not true but right now it sounded a lot better than the truth would have done.

'You've family, then? What do they think?'

'About the job? They don't know much, to tell you the truth, just that I'm working.'

'You've not asked them for their opinion?'

Clare hesitated, then took the plunge.

'No. Because they'd be prejudiced, you see. Either in my favour or in Clive's. I felt I wanted an outside view.'

'Mine, eh? Well, for what it's worth I think everyone should have a life of their own, particularly if they want one.'

He took a big bite of chocolate fudge cake, savoured it, swallowed, then smiled at her as he picked up his cup. 'Though if your man wants to keep a cook like you to himself, who can blame him?'

Clare smiled back, but uncertainly. Ought she to pretend that Dee had made the cake and squash any similar compliments? But then being complimented on one's cooking was not exactly likely to turn one's head! She was used to a certain degree of surprise when she admitted to being Sally's mother but that was due to her youth at the time of her child's birth; more blush-making than complimentary when you thought about it. And anyway Oliver had merely said 'Good God!' when she had spoken of Sally which could mean more or less anything.

'So having this job is just having a life of my own? Then you think I'm justified in keeping it despite Clive's feelings?'

She expected an easy affirmative but Oliver finished off his cake, took another sip of coffee, and then shook his head.

'Well, no, I couldn't say that, not without a bit more knowledge. Why, for instance, did you wait for so long without apparently needing or wanting a job? Or have you worked from home?'

'Clive said that too,' Clare admitted. 'When we first married and I had Sally she was very demanding, little babies are, and then there was the house and the garden all needing no end of work. Only you see Sal's a big girl now, she's got friends and a life of her own, she doesn't need me the way she once did. And the house doesn't need much work, just the usual tidying sort. You can't cook all day, not just for yourself and a daughter who's out most of the time, and even gardening can be boring when you're the only one doing it. Mind you I love gardening and I do most of it, but there are times when I can't, in winter, or in spring when the bulbs are out and the weeds haven't really got going.'

'So you've grown up, like Sally, and want to feel more of a person. But that doesn't mean to say that Clive's point of view doesn't matter. After all, he isn't here to see you when you're alone, if you'll forgive a crass remark, and probably in his imagination things haven't changed all that much. So don't just dig your heels in and tell him hard luck, and don't lie to him, either. Explain. Tell him you're going to give it a try for three months. Let him see you do understand his point of view even if you find it hard work.'

'I wouldn't lie to him,' Clare said earnestly. 'I never have and I won't start now. Only when he came home last I told him I wanted to work and tried to explain why and he didn't seem to understand at all. Well, I don't think he listened properly, to tell you the truth.'

'He was probably thinking about you and not about your words,' Oliver said. 'He's got to sit down and concentrate on a letter, so do it that way.' He finished his cup of coffee and leaned back, narrowing his eyes to stare into Clare's. 'The way I see it . . .'

The door opened and Clare only stayed to smile at him before getting to her feet and picking up her own coffee cup and his empty plate.

'Sorry, thanks for the advice, I did warn you,' she said, turning towards the kitchen.

The customers were a couple of motor-cyclists but behind them Clare saw Mavis, solicitously ushering Deirdre into the caff ahead of her. Dee's right arm was in a sling and her cheeks were still interestingly pale beneath the layer of blusher, or paler, or whatever concoction she had spread on her face that morning. Clare hurried forward, telling herself it was a natural anxiety for the child and not merely a suddenly overwhelming desire not to be caught sharing a table with a customer who was both virile and interesting.

'Dee, what are you doing back here? You should have gone straight home, love.'

Deirdre pointed proudly to her sling.

'It's a sprain, Clare, a bad one. They say I shan't be able to use my arm for a coupla weeks at least!' She sounded thrilled by the whole thing and Clare, with a vision of a whole fortnight with only two of them doing the work of three, tried to bear up.

'Oh dear, but I dare say we'll manage,' she said with what brightness she could muster. 'Perhaps we can get someone temporarily from the Job Centre, just to see us through.'

Deirdre, however, was having none of this. As the three of them made for the kitchen she said airily, 'Oh no, I'm coming in don't you fret! I'm left-handed, for a start, and there's lots of things I can do which won't need both hands. I can use the grill and serve drinks one at a time and dry up if I'm careful . . .'

'Dry up? With one hand? How on earth will you manage that? No, love, best get it properly healed and then we'll talk about you working again.'

But Mavis, slipping on her scuffies and casting her mac onto the peg by the backdoor, shook her head reprovingly at Clare.

'Just you listen to 'er, anyone 'ud think we didn't need the gal here! Thing is, Clare, she can use the right 'and but she mustn't slip off the sling for a week at least. So she can 'old cutlery in that 'and, or a plate or whatever, provided she's careful. See?'

Very clearly indeed, Clare saw that Deirdre had no desire to hang about at home being bossed by her mother, and that Mavis, a disliker of new faces, had even less desire to find yet another feckless teenager (as she would have phrased it) wished upon her. She felt that she should have put her foot down and insisted that Deirdre went sick but perhaps it was fairer to see just how useful she could be before taking a firm decision. She said as much, whereupon Dee promptly picked up a pad and rushed into the caff. Clare, following more slowly, remembered not only the motor-cyclists but Oliver; would he still be there, expecting her to return to their discussion once she had seen to her staff? But he was not. He had gone, leaving a small pile of silver by his coffee cup. Dee shot over, picked it up and dropped it into her overall pocket, then returned to the motor-cyclists. She looked a bit awkward writing down their order but was plainly enjoying the challenge. Clare had heard her informing the young men proudly that she had a sprained wrist even before the more usual 'Can I help you?' had been voiced.

Clare watched for a moment, letting her eyes stray a couple of times from Deirdre to the car-park; there were several huge lorries parked out there. She wondered which of them held

Oliver, or indeed if any of them did. Today she had not noticed the smell of horse . . . he had talked to her like a sensible man but that did not preclude his driving a horse-waggon, of course. People did all sorts of things these days.

Returning to the kitchen, she asked Mavis whether she really thought they could manage with Dee as she was, more as a conversation piece than because she was terribly interested in Mavis's opinion which she already knew to be prejudiced by her dislike of strangers. Mavis said Dee would be just fine and then proceeded to give Clare a blow-by-blow of the hospital visit.

'They expected us to wait, but I wasn't having none of that,' she said, roaring hot water into the sink and plunging a pile of plates into the foam. 'Told 'em we was running a caff full of customers, said we'd left a slip of a girl in charge . . . pushed Dee right to the front I did so's we could get back here before the rush. And that doctor! Black as your 'at . . . I said to the nurse it wouldn't be so bad if you could understand a word 'e says, I told 'er. I wasn't none to 'appy when 'e said it was a strain . . . more like a break I thought, with Dee being so pale an' all . . . but the radio bloke was as white as you or me and 'e said a strain, so that's all right. No bandage mind . . . old-fashioned they said bandages were, just that sling and a lot of talk about what she could and couldn't do, that's all they gave the gal. Still, the nurse told 'er to take aspirin if the pain got bad and come back if 'er fingers turned blue, which I'm bound to say sounds sensible enough.'

'It does. And did er . . . Pammy . . . wait for you?'

Mavis turned from the sink for a moment to fix Clare with an affronted stare.

'Naturally; you don't think I'd let 'em sneak off, do you, leaving me with the gal and no means of getting back 'ere? I don't say it didn't pass through Pammy's mind when she saw the queue but "just let me 'andle it," I tells 'er, "and we'll be out before the cat can scratch its ear". Which we were, as you're me witness. Have many in, did you?'

'No, only one. Fortunately the rush was over and they'd not started on teas, though I dare say . . .' she glanced at the clock over the cooker '. . . they'll start coming in any minute.'

Deirdre, entering the kitchen, took Mavis's mind off Clare's solitary customer, or Clare hoped she had. Dee looked pleased with herself.

'Got it! Writing's a bit funny, but that's all down on paper.' She held out the pad, then read it aloud. 'Beans on toast with sausage on the side twice, and tea now with two of them sticky buns.'

'I'll make the tea,' Clare said automatically, while reflecting on the fact that young males of the species seemed unable to wait ten minutes for a meal without something in their mouths. Either they got out cigarettes and puffed away, even in the face of Mavis's disapproving sniffs, or they ordered tea and buns to while away the minutes until their main order arrived.

Whilst she set out cups and then poured, Clare decided she had been undeservedly lucky. Neither Mavis nor Deirdre had noticed Oliver's presence or her own proximity to him. If they had, how they would cross-question, giggle, exclaim! But fortunately Deirdre's sprain had been uppermost in their minds to the apparent exclusion of all else. It was not like Deirdre to let any man go unnoticed and Mavis was almost the same about customers; she seemed to take either an instant liking or an equally instant dislike to everyone who came through the doorway, so all in all Clare felt favoured by fortune. She passed the tray of tea through to Deirdre, who took it cup by cup across to the customers and then returned to do the same with the sticky buns.

'See?' She said triumphantly to Clare after performing this feat. 'I can manage quite well, in a day or two I bet I don't need to use me right hand!'

Clare murmuring qualified approval, thought to herself that it would take more than two teas and sticky buns to prove the point but in the event, when the tea-time rush was over, she had to agree that Deirdre had managed very well indeed and would probably get through her fortnight of one-handedness without being forced to go sick.

'I'll run you home tonight, though,' she insisted, when

they were all ready to finish for the day. 'It's been pretty tiring, Dee, what with rushing off up to the hospital and everything. Tomorrow, find out the times of an earlier bus and I'll get the car out and nip you straight to the nearest stop.'

'Are we going home with Dee?' Sally beamed. 'That's great, Mum, that's really sooper! Can Dee and me sit in the back and talk whilst you chauffeur? We'll feel like royalty!'

But Dee, who either had an untapped reserve of understanding or, more likely, wanted to ride in the front seat, told Sally it wasn't on.

'A right fool your mum would look, drivin' half across the county with us two giggling in the back seat,' she said severely. 'It in't manners, young Sally.'

Sally was crushed, but only momentarily. As they made their way out to the car, having been told brusquely by Mavis that she was quite capable, thank you very much, of dealing with any late customers and of closing the place up, and she'd be very sure that the kitchen floor was even cleaner than usual due to Clare's fear of industrious accidents . . . Clare kept a straight face without much difficulty since Mavis's frosty eye was upon her . . . Sally swung her satchel and chattered and Deirdre tried to tell them both that one of the porters had been real cool. Clare saw Deirdre into the front and Sally into the back, waved gaily to the caff, though Mavis was in all likelihood in the kitchen and so unable to see the gesture, and drove off.

The day, which had begun so badly with the arrival of the letter and gone on worse, when you came to think about it, had taken a decided turn for the better. Oliver . . . he looked like an Oliver, though Goodness knows what she had previously thought an Oliver looked like. Perhaps it was because she knew no other Olivers, so she was not seeing an existing person in her mind's eye. She wondered, vaguely, whether their brief chat would mean that he would avoid the caff in future or whether he would come in more often. She did not intend to sit around with the customers when the staff were in . . . anyway, he was a bird of passage, probably next time they met they would both smile politely, he would take out his book and that would be that.

He had advised her to sit down and try to explain properly to Clive what the job meant to her. He had said she ought to say she was going to do it for a trial period. It was both sensible and fair, she supposed, to do just that. After all, Clive was not a Victorian, even if he seemed to believe he could behave like one. If she explained rationally and calmly why she wanted a job then the least he could do would be to explain as rationally and calmly why he preferred her to stay at home. She would not find it hard to promise him that when he came home for good she would abandon the job . . . though when it came to actually doing it she thought she might well regret the promise.

On the other hand . . . I've got as many hands as an octopus when it comes to getting my own way, she thought ruefully . . . On the other hand Clive had been saying for four years that he was going to quit the Kingdom but he hadn't shown the slightest sign of actually doing it yet. Her heart, usually such a reliable organ, dared to lift at the thought of Clive staying in Saud and she felt so ashamed and disgusted at herself that she began to drive too fast and had to speak quite sternly inside her head before she steadied up once more.

'You all right, Mum?' Sally's voice showed that she had noticed both the sudden jerkiness of her mother's driving and also the deliberate slowing down.

'Yes, I'm fine.' They were entering Deirdre's village now and Clare slowed down even further. 'Dee, you'll have to direct me from here; straight down the main street, is it?'

'Yes please, Clare. We're through the village and turn left . . . I'll tell you when we get nearer.'

The left turn looked, at first, as though it led nowhere, but in fact after passing across a couple of still-green cornfields they came to a rash of council houses. Each one had a long, well-kept front garden and most had vehicles of some sort in the short drives. Deirdre's, when they reached it, was the exception to all these things. Its garden was a wilderness, the only thing on the drive was a broken pram and an ancient, rust-covered lawnmower. Clare, however, stopped the car at the gate and got out, going round to give Deirdre a hand if she needed it. Sally jumped out as soon as Dee was vertical and went over to open the gate. Since it had no latch and no apparent hinges this was a lifting job, but Dee, obviously an old hand with the gate, simply entered her home through a gap in the hedge and Clare followed suit. Sally promptly abandoned the gate half-open and skipped after them.

'I'll just see you to the door,' Clare proposed, but Dee was having none of it.

'That you won't!' she said roundly. 'After bringin' me all the way you gotta have a cuppa, at least. Anyway, you in't met me Mum, have you?'

'Well, no, I don't think . . .'

'There you are then.'

They had ignored the front door and taken the scrubby little track which led round the side of the house to the back. The back garden was covered in what looked like wire cages and indeed a closer look confirmed that each cage contained an animal of some sort. Dogs, rabbits and even a couple of cats stared at the visitors through various sizes of chicken wire. Chickens, on the other hand, were free to roam where they would as Clare saw when they entered the kitchen to find a fat Rhode Island Red frantically trying to get out of the doorway before it was trapped.

'Mum!'

Deirdre's shout brought a woman through into the kitchen. She had a cigarette dangling from her lower lip and her fringe was twisted into metal curlers. She smiled at them brightly, however, revealing big, strong white teeth with a noticeable gap in the middle.

'Hello, both,' she greeted them. 'You'll be Clare as we've heard so much about and this'll be Sally.' She looked at her daughter with a fond maternal eye. 'What've you bin an' gone and done this time, you gurt fewl?'

.'Sprained my wrist on the cooker,' Deirdre said briefly. 'Can I put the kettle on, Ma? Clare brung me home special.'

'That's just boiled.' Mrs Spooner waddled across the kitchen . . . she was heavily built though not exactly fat, more muscle-run-to-fat, Clare decided . . . and began clattering tea-bags into a pot and then water onto the tea-bags.

'Well, I'm too bad, Clare, I in't never interdooced meself! Alice Spooner, and many thanks for bringin' the gal home.'

'That's all right, Mrs Spoo . . .' Clare began, but was promptly corrected.

'Alice to you, my dear. We don't stand on ceremony here, this is Liberty Hall. Now Dee, get you out to the back and show Sally the animals whilst Clare and I have a sit-down and a bit of a chat.'

'I didn't know you had so many pets, Dee,' Clare said rather desperately, hoping to put a stop to a tête-à-tête. Her hope, however, was in vain.

'Pets? They in't pets. That's Mum's boarders,' Dee said cheerfully, vanishing through the back door. 'Come along, Sally, do you'll miss feedin' time.'

Left alone, Clare took the chair hospitably gestured at and also the cup and then settled down to be chatted to, telling herself that she really ought to be glad of the opportunity to get to know her staff. Mrs Spooner, it soon transpired, knew a good deal about Clare already and being a talker, as she would readily have admitted, intended that by the time Clare left she would be equally *au fait* with the Spooner household.

'Well, Clare, when we come here, Reg and me . . .' Clare was glad to be informed of Mr Spooner's existence since she could not recall Dee mentioning a father . . . 'We both worked, Reg on the farm acourse, me up at the big house. But then Dee come along, and our Jason, and there was no way Reg 'ud let me scrub floors and light fires, not with a coupla littl'uns needin' me. So I just stayed here . . .' an arm gestured comprehensively '. . . and kept the place decent, fed 'em and so on.'

Clare hoped that her expression remained one of lively and comprehending interest and did not reflect the horror she felt; if this was the Spooner household when it was kept decent, what on earth must it have been like when Mrs Spooner was working? However, she had no need to speak, Alice Spooner plainly enjoyed the sound of her own voice.

'Now like you, my woman, the day come when there

weren't enough to keep me busy here, things being as I wanted 'em, more or less. And as you can see, we're miles away from factories and such, where I might've got work. So I sat me down and thought; bed and breakfasts, I thought? That's a good idea, I know that, but who'd come by here? So that horse didn't run. Then I had a mind to go cleaning, only them at the big house don't want no one, and for why? Because it's been made into them flat-things since my time. Field work's all very well, but that's hard on a woman and seasonal, which in't ideal. But we've a damn' gurt garden, as you may've noticed . . .?'

The pause plainly called for a comment. Clare said, faintly, that she had noticed the garden and added that she herself had a good deal of land and found it quite hard work.

'That that is,' Mrs Spooner said profoundly. She took a couple of swallows of her tea. 'Yes, you're right, Clare, gardening can be quite hard work. Not that I do a lot, nor did; acause I can't abide it, that's why, and no more can my Reg. But as I was saying, we've a damned gurt garden so I thought why not use it? Why not make some money out of the garden? But I didn't fancy gatherin' peas or diggin' all day and every day, might as well go for a farm worker, so I looked about me for something which 'ud fit into that patch o' ground. Been thinking of bed and breakfasts as I said, so I thought, "People won't come by, acos that in't on the way to anywhere pertickler; but they'd come if they was bringing something just to me. Now what could they bring to me what I could charge 'em for?" And then I got it, like a lightning flash. They could bring their animals when they went off on their holidays, I thought. They could bring 'em Christmas, when they've got people visiting; they could bring 'em summer, like I said. They could even bring 'em if they were old and lonely and had to go in hospital. So I put a little old advert in the *Evening News* and Reg built me a dog-house and a run. Nothin' happened for ten days and I was thinking the money was gone and wasted when the first woman come. She brung a parrot . . . imagine that? A parrot! But I kept her old Cap'n Flint . . . that was the parrot's name, seemingly . . . for a week, charged her fair, and after that they all come. So now you see, I'm in business. Just like yourself, Clare.'

'Yes indeed,' Clare said hollowly. 'Only of course you own your business, so perhaps you should compare yourself with Mrs P rather than with me; I'm only managing for her, you see.'

'I'm the boss here, you're the boss there,' Mrs Spooner said decisively. She drained her cup and slapped her thigh. She was clad in a floral print blouse, a much-darned grey cardigan and a vast pair of brown trousers with the zip missing, so someone had threaded a black shoe-lace across the gap to make her respectable, more or less. Glancing covertly at her as she heaved herself to her feet and began to pour more tea, Clare noticed that her thick untidy hair was touched with grey and that her face, which was really amazingly like Dee's, was beginning to sag below the chin and to wrinkle around the eyes. Her neck, which showed from the back because her hair was caught up in an extremely untidy and inefficient bun, could have benefited from a wash.

'More tea, Clare? Go on, my dear, don't hold back,' her hostess urged hospitably. 'Dee tells me you're a lovely cook – I int so bad myself, truth to tell, though I'm generally too busy to cook much. As for cakes and fancy things . . . puddings and so on . . . I can't be bothered to mess with 'em. But give me a good joint of beef and some spuds and I'll make a meal I'd defy anyone to better.'

'I like cooking a roast,' Clare said. 'No thanks Mrs . . . Alice . . . I won't have another cup. Sally and I will be late getting home already, I don't think we ought to detain you much longer. We've got a dog of our own and a cat, to say nothing of Sally's pony and they all need feeding and letting out and so on. But it's been so interesting . . . I'll just give Sally a call . . .'

She was at the back door in an instant, calling her daughter's name, but then Sally emerged from one of the tumbledown sheds so Clare needed no additional excuse to leave the house and hurry up the garden path, if such it could be called. In fact, it was a cinder track between the wire netting.

'Come on Sal,' she said as soon as she was near enough. 'It's high time we were on our way, Tish will be getting desperate.'

Sally came gaily out of the run, bending down to give a final pat to a high-spirited little Welsh terrier which bounced hopefully up at her and then put its front paws on the wire and whined, head cocked.

'They're all lovely, and so happy,' she was saying over her shoulder to Dee. 'I'm surprised you can bear to go into the city each day to work; wouldn't you rather stay here and give your Mum a hand?'

'That I wouldn't,' Dee started. 'Quite honestly, Sal . . .' she broke off to look guiltily over Clare's left shoulder. Clare glanced back too and saw that her hostess had followed her out and was beaming at the two girls.

'There, now you've seen everything, young Sally,' Mrs Spooner exclaimed. 'Come you on outer there, the pair of you, so's Clare can get back to her own supper. Now if ever you want that dog of yours kept somewhere safe and friendly, where the food's good and she'll have plenty company, you know you can send her here; special terms for friends.'

'That's awfully good of you, Mrs Spooner,' Sally said earnestly. 'Tish would love it . . . but we don't go away very often because of Pegs, and when we do, Gran always comes to stay and takes care of things and Tish takes care of her.'

This however, did not prevent Mrs Spooner from accompanying them to the car and talking all the while about the advantages of her homely surroundings when you wanted a pet taken care of.

As they drove off down the road Clare heaved a sigh of relief, then shot a cautious look at Sally; you could never tell how the young would take things. But on this occasion at least, Sally was thinking along the same lines as her mother.

'Dee's mum's weird, isn't she? I mean why curlers at this hour in the afternoon?' Sally shot a cautious glance at her mother's face. 'I don't want to sound like a snob, but I never

106

thought Dee's place would be like that. Did you?'

'I don't think I gave the matter any thought at all, but I suppose I thought her mother would be a bit more like Dee . . . you know, clothes conscious and pretty neat.'

'Yes, I thought so too. Did you get to see the front room?'

'No, just the kitchen. Why?'

Sally sighed and wound the window down so that the freshness of the breeze lifted her hair and blew it across her face. She struck her fingers into it, trying to trap it behind her ear as she spoke.

'Well, there wasn't much furniture, but there were heaps of clothes and a big cauldron thing full of cooked scraps. We went and got some to feed the dogs with. There was a telly though.'

'People live differently,' Clare said vaguely, feeling that as a mother herself she probably ought to defend Alice Spooner. 'Material possessions aren't everyone's cup of tea.'

'Things, do you mean? I know that, Mum – look at the Carters! But what they've got they keep nice, their front room's lovely, as good as ours. And you should see Dee's bedroom, she keeps it beautifully tidy, a lot tidier than I do. And she's buying furniture, too. She's bought a duvet and a dressing-table with three mirrors and her clothes are all on hangers from the picture rail. I didn't see the bathroom, but I bet it isn't up to much.'

'What about the kennels though, sweetie? Were they in good repair and so on? Were the animals happy, do you think?'

'They ponged a bit, but they were probably all right,' Sally observed after some thought. 'Dee thinks it's all dreadful though, I could tell.'

'Oh I don't know, love. She had no call to invite us in, I did try to refuse only I couldn't without seeming rude.'

'Yes, I wondered about that. I don't think she sees anything wrong with the kennels and probably it's just me . . . I've never been in a kennels before so I'm probably not a good judge . . . But she's not too proud of her mother, I could tell that.'

'And are you proud of me? I thought you had all sorts of reservations . . .'

'Hmm.' This was plainly a new idea and Sally turned in her seat to stare speculatively at Clare. 'You aren't such a bad old thing . . . but I see what you mean in a way. I hate it when you wear that awful mini-skirt thing and when you turn up at parents' evenings in jeans. Mind you, I'd rather jeans than curlers!'

'We all have our faults,' Clare said placidly, slowing to a crawl behind a homeward-bound tractor. 'And when you look at her surroundings, you realise what a triumph Dee's appearance is.'

'Yes, I was thinking that myself,' Sally admitted. 'Look how easy it is for me, and yet . . .'

'Precisely. What'll you do, pet, if Dee asks you to go home with her though, over the summer holidays?'

'I'd go, just for an afternoon,' Sally said. 'Dee's herself, it's her I like. I'd just have to get used to her family.'

'What if she wanted you to stay?'

'Couldn't. Not with Tish and Pegs depending on me,' Sally said virtuously. 'I'd like Dee to stay with us, though.'

'Any time. Aha, at last.' The tractor swung into a farmyard and the Mini shot past with a toot and a twirl of the fingers. It was not until she was driving into her own garage, though, that another thing occurred to Clare.

'Sal, love, I've just thought; this is going to slow Dee down quite a bit no matter how much she protests. Would you like to come in and give us a hand on Saturday?'

She expected a prompt and enthusiastic response but instead, Sally looked hunted.

'Oh, Mum, not Saturday, Emma and I thought we'd start training Pegs for the jumps and generally practising for shows. Besides, you said in the hols and it isn't the hols for another three or four weeks.'

Mindful of the fact that her daughter's time with Emma, during the term, was never sufficient, Clare sighed and agreed that they would manage somehow. But she felt a bit hard-done-by, especially when, immediately upon finishing her pudding, Sally headed for the back door.

'Where are you going, young woman?' she asked rather sharply. 'Don't forget the washing up!'

But Sally was above such minor strategems to keep her indoors.

'Oh Ma, I must see Emma, she won't know what happened to me otherwise! I'll take Tish, which will save you walking her, and I won't be gone more than twenty minutes or half an hour.'

'That's all very well . . .' Clare began, but she was addressing empty air as well as a gently but firmly closed back door. With her spoon poised over her own dish of yoghurt and peaches, she considered jumping to her feet and ordering Sally back but after all, why should the child not go round to Emma's? As for exercising Tish, whose long legs devoured the miles, she might as well let Sally take some of the bounce out of her before the long evening walk.

But the enjoyment had gone out of her pudding. Sighing, she got up and went over to the sink. She might as well get the washing up over, and once that was done at least the evening, such as it was, stretched before her, an empty canvas for her to fill.

It did not take long to wash up and then Clare went through into the living-room and switched on the telly. She had not been watching for more than a few minutes, though, when boredom made her jump to her feet and switch the set off. She glanced out of the window; the sunshine was still pleasant . . . and the big bed of roses in the middle of the drive was sadly in need of weeding.

Presently, on her knees in the grass busily pulling up groundsel, it occurred to Clare to let her mind wander to Oliver once more. It would be rather nice, she thought almost wistfully, if he lived near here, so that they could enjoy a chat in the evenings, occasionally. It was lonely here with Sally off somewhere. In order to visit Gran she would have to get the car out again for though Gran had lived in the village for years she had moved nearer the city a couple of years ago. Clare's mother, of course, had been in a small house in Norwich for even longer, not that Clare would voluntarily have visited her for a friendly chat!

She had cleared a big patch and was actually beginning to enjoy herself when a car slowed, tooted and turned into her drive. Clare sat back on her heels and pushed her flopping hair off her forehead, then struggled to her feet. Oh curses and damnation, it was Richard, with Rachel in the passenger seat. What on earth did they want at this time of the evening? But she smiled and dusted soil off her hands as she went towards them. Richard was Clive's brother, after all, and Rachel her only sister-in-law.

'Hello, lovely evening,' she called brightly across the intervening space. 'I'm afraid Sally's out, but I can offer you a cup of coffee and some walnut cake if you'd like to come in for a minute.'

Richard nodded his narrow head but Rachel was more forthcoming.

'Walnut cake? You've been busy, Clare; lucky you, not having to watch your figure! We wondered whether to come over and risk you being out, but it was such a lovely evening . . .'

Clare, preceding them into the kitchen and putting the kettle on, wondered uneasily whether they had visited the house during the day hoping to see her, but it seemed unlikely since neither of them had mentioned it. Rachel's high, rather whiny voice, which always made Clare think of mosquitoes, was complaining over hairdressing charges of all things and Richard was mooching, picking things up and putting them down again, whilst whenever he thought Rachel's attention was elsewhere he stared hard at Clare's face. Clare ignored him, cutting cake, pouring water, stirring coffee, and at last they went through with her into the living-room and sat on the comfortable couch and drank their coffee and ate their cake.

Sally came in, only an hour later than she had promised, and Rachel shrieked when Tish shook herself and covered everyone with specks of saliva and mud droplets. Presently they left, and Clare and Sally prepared for bed. Clare, preoccupied with the reason for her in-laws turning up unannounced, was quieter than usual and Sally, aware that she had stayed out later than she had said, was quiet too. Just as they climbed the stairs and reached the top landing though, she spoke.

'Mum, does Auntie Rachel know about the job?'

'I haven't told her, so I don't suppose so. Why?'

'Well, you know when you took Tish for a quick run round the yard just as they were leaving? And I went over to the car to say cheerio?'

'Yes?'

'Well, Uncle Richard was saying, "It was her, Rachel, I'm sure of it. She was wearing a pink blouse, not the shirt she's got on now, but it was her." '

'Heavens! Well, they couldn't have meant me, poppet, since I don't own a pink blouse.'

'No. But Mum, you do wear a pink and white checked overall and from a distance . . .'

'Oh heavens, that's torn it,' Clare said, dismayed. 'If they know it'll be all over the city in no time. Oh God, I'll have Granny Arnold round tomorrow, ticking me off and tutting at me. Oh Sally love, I do hope you're wrong!'

CHAPTER
6

After Clare, Sally and Deirdre had left, Mavis took in the board and put up a notice saying tea and cold snacks only. Then, secure in the knowledge that they rarely had customers between five-thirty and six, she began to clean down.

She enjoyed cleaning down. First she put all the chairs on top of all the tables, which allowed her to have a real go at the floor, then she took the chairs off again and went over them with a wet cloth and a good deal of elbow grease. The counter came in for a scrubbing with bleach and water, then the bain was dismantled and taken through into the kitchen. When it was reassembled the meat slicer was reduced to pieces of metal in the sink and when that, too, was back where it belonged Mavis emptied the fryer, cleaned it out, put fresh oil in and closed the lid. Only then did she cross the caff, bolt the door, put up the closed sign and think about going home.

Home, of course, did not have the same attraction when Lionel was not in it, yet when she considered it, home in the course of their marriage had contained Lionel far less frequently than it should have done. How long was it since he had last lived at home? She did the calculation whilst totting up her overtime – any hours she worked when Clare was not present counted as overtime – and found rather to her dismay that in the thirty years of her marriage Lionel had probably lived at home for only about ten of them. My, a third of that thirty years had been spent apart then, worse almost than Clare and Clive.

Still, no use repining and he was retired now, or would be next time he returned to the city and consequently to her arms. Retirement in his job was not perhaps quite the same as retirement in other jobs, but he had promised and Lionel kept his promises. Or he did when he made them to her at any rate.

'Had enough of it I have,' he had announced six months ago, as he and she faced each other across the bare deal table. 'I've got a little nest-egg put by, then there's your job and I can get something similar myself . . . we'll manage, Mave, dear heart.'

She had smiled and patted his hand, well pleased. Ever so fancy Lionel could talk, but that didn't mean he was insincere, it was just his way. Part of his charm, you could say. And she was luckier than most, a good few men with Lionel's charm would have turned it on women, but Lionel had never been that way inclined. He'd picked Mavis out of the crowd thirty years ago and never looked at anyone else since, she told herself proudly now. Made a home for her, given her the best daughter in the world, stood by her through thick and thin, same's she'd stood by him, and made sure she got her share of whatever was going, even if, strictly speaking, it wasn't his to give.

Startled by her last thought, Mavis metaphorically slapped her own wrist, finished her calculations and propped the piece of paper up against the drum of salt so that Clare would see it first thing next day. The day she criticised Lionel's career had not yet come and would not, either, she reminded herself severely. She had known on the day they walked down the aisle together that anyone who was in selling needed their wits about them; if Lionel's wits were sometimes a good deal sharper than the unfortunate buyer, whose fault was that? Certainly not hers, even more certainly not Lionel's. Still, it would be nice to have him home for good, nice not to have to listen for a knock on the door and even nicer not to feel sick with apprehension each time you picked up a newpaper when some clever-clever newshound decided to do an exposé of this or that.

Not that Lionel minded; Esther Rantzen was a favourite of

his. 'We're in the same game, me and her,' he had announced one evening, sitting in front of the screen. 'If it wasn't for the likes of me, what could she do, poor gel? Besides, it's good for the lot of us, keeps me on my toes and one jump ahead.'

Secretly, Mavis had been a bit upset. Lionel didn't go taking the savings of the old or sick, he didn't cheat young newly weds out of their honeymoons or anything of that nature. All he did – ever so quickly and cleverly too – was to start up little companies, recruit workers and apply for grants, and then sell shares. Or that was what she thought he did, she had never really worked out Lionel's exact job. All she knew, come to think, was that Lionel's little businesses didn't really exist, his flourishing staff training schemes employed no staff, his premises, scattered all over London, were as much myths as any dodo or dinosaur.

Esther, bless her, had never got on to Lionel because that really would have been embarrassing. She might have done, in the old days, when Lionel had been in a bigger way, but not now, when he was semi-retired and taking things easy. Once, he had sold old London buses to American tourists. Well, the idea of old London buses, at any rate, since the buses were no more his than the garage he had discovered them quietly rotting in, like elephants in some long-forgotten elephants' graveyard. But the tourists had loved the idea, and had paid Lionel considerable sums of money before someone put the cops onto him and Lionel had been forced to move on.

Not that there had been anything illegal about it, of course. Lionel had actually bought one of the old buses; the only slightly doubtful part was the number of buses he had sold to the eager Americans. And the fact that he had sold them as reconditioned running. And possibly his behaviour in taking the tourists on bus trips and letting them believe they were riding in vehicles reconditioned by his firm . . . that had been less then truthful. Still, it had clearly not been illegal or anything of that nature, since Lionel had not gone to prison for it, to the best of Mavis's knowledge. Which was proof positive, she maintained, or would have maintained had she been questioned on the subject, that her husband had merely

114

been selling dreams which was no worse than what them book writers or film makers did.

Having satisfied herself in her own mind that Lionel's inventiveness was something to be proud and not ashamed of, Mavis changed her shoes, put her high tea in her bag, and set off for the bus stop. As she went she let her mind dwell on the weekend to come. On the Sunday she would visit Lionel – she always loved that – and then she would stay with Sondra for a day or so. She had Monday and Tuesday off this week and though it annoyed her to think of poor Clare and poor little Deirdre having to put up with that awful Lizzy Treece she could not help being thrilled at the thought of a long weekend in London.

At the bus stop she met a neighbour and they shared a grumble about the crowded state of the buses, the way the warm weather brought more folk into the city like bluebottles round a ripe leg of lamb, and the fact that the city fathers made no provision for such sudden overcrowding of public transport. When the bus came, however, Mrs Burt was separated from Mavis by the push of people so Mavis crammed herself onto a seat near the door which by rights should only have held two and allowed her mind to return to her weekend.

Bus was cheaper, but train quicker. She could be sure of a seat on the bus but not on the train. Lionel, however, did not approve of her travelling by bus, he thought it low. So had she better get herself a cheap day return at Thorpe Station and book a seat for an extra few bob? Mind, they were a friendly crowd on the buses these days and there was a lav and all at the back of the bus so you didn't have to cross your legs for miles. Served refreshments too they did . . . but then it took all of four hours.

The journey passed quite pleasantly with such thoughts. Mavis got off at The Artichoke and waited for Mrs Burt, then the two of them walked slowly home together, on account of Mrs Burt's arthritic knee. Mavis never mentioned her varicose vein but that didn't mean she was unaware of it.

'Me and you'll have words when I get home,' she told it in her mind as it stabbed and throbbed and made itself felt, 'just because I've got me 'eels on, doesn't mean you can play me up without a word said.'

Mrs Burt hobbled up her path and Mavis continued, her heels tap-tappeting along with a pretence of briskness because Norah Burt was not going to see that Mavis, too, had problems. Give her five years any day, Mavis thought rather obscurely as she turned thankfully into her own gate. Give her ten on a good day.

She unlocked the door and went into the cool dimness of the front passage. Down it and into the kitchen, kicking off her shoes, over to Cheepy's cage for a quick word, then her bottom and the cane chair met and a long sigh came from Mavis's lips. It was good to sit down, stretch out her legs, have a word or two with Cheepy. Tonight she'd have chips, cheese on toast and a tin of baked beans for her tea, with a wedge of Clare's fudge cake for afters. If Clare noticed it was missing next day, of course Mavis would own up that she'd taken it and pay up as well without any fuss because Clare was fair on them and never overcharged. But if she didn't notice . . . not my business to offer money, Mavis decided, eyeing the damp patch on the bag where the rich fudge filling was beginning to melt in the warmth. Noticing, after all, was the name of the game.

By the same token, Mavis wondered whether Dee had noticed who Clare had been sitting with when they entered the caff. Coffee an' Book, that's who it was, sitting bold as you please in the corner by the window, with that wicked dark head of his only inches away from Clare's.

He's smelt her out, Mavis thought, half satisfied, half annoyed. Come round like a dog sniffing for a bitch and smelt Clare's dissatisfaction and vague, unformed needs with just as unerring a nose as Lionel showed when he decided which section of the public would most like to buy a London bus, or a share in a chocolate factory, or a piece of a grouse moor in Scotland.

If there's one thing I do know, it's customers, Mavis decided, fishing out the fudge cake and breaking off a bit for Cheepy and another bit for herself. Wonder if he's married, Coffee and Book? Wonder if he knows Clare's married, or if he simply doesn't care because what he's after doesn't depend on married or not married, it depends on something much more basic.

Mavis had noticed before that when lads come in after a girl they could usually tell which girl had come in after lads and which were merely passing the time. Clare and me, we're in the same position but we're quite different, Mavis told herself now, delicately eating fudge icing. Clare's young and she isn't getting it, I'm older and I'm not getting it either. But for some reason Clare's got a banner out and I haven't. Wonder why? Is it because I'm that fond of Lionel that I don't want anyone else? Nah, can't be, because Clare's fond of that Clive of hers, even if he does annoy her, times.

Cheepy got his beak stuck into the fudge icing and panicked when it clung; he bounced about his cage, lashing his beak at the bars, the cuttlefish shell, the wheel with the bell in it. Mavis got creakingly to her feet and tutted lovingly at him through the bars.

'Who's a silly feller, then?' she asked him dotingly. 'Give us your beak, Mum'll soon clean you up.'

The following day, Clare saw Richard as she made her way across to the caff. It annoyed her; she felt spied on and ill-used but she simply pretended to have noticed nothing, which was just as well. When she was serving a group of women with coffee and cake later on, the door opened and Richard came in. He was not alone. He had a man with him of about his own age and they came in talking at the top of their voices.

'So if you'd gone in earlier, old boy, you'd probably still . . .'

Fortunately, before Clare could even think again, let alone say, that Richard was spying on her, she realised what she should have realised right from the start. Richard was an advertising agent and the TV studios dealt in advertising. What more natural – or unfortunate – than that he should park his car on the nearest car-park and walk down the hill to the studios when he was selling space or whatever he did? And what more likely that he should notice his little sister-in-law, for whom he had had a letch for fifteen years, working in a caff situated just about opposite where he parked his car? Being Richard, of course he had not mentioned it to her, he had waited, as she had known he would, to see what was in it for him before making a move.

'Good morning, Richard,' she said now, coolly, wiping the table he had chosen down with a cloth despite its surface being entirely clean and untouched by human customer. 'Another nice one I'm glad to see.'

'Ah, Clare; Rachel said you were working here,' said Richard. He let his eyes slide hopefully down to the vee of her overall but since she was wearing a tee-shirt and had therefore no skin showing they slid disappointedly up to meet hers once more. 'I did take a look last evening but I couldn't be sure. You never mentioned it.'

'I've not been here long,' Clare said, still coolly. 'Two coffees, is it?' Richard was notoriously mean; he would eat cake eagerly when he was her guest but not, she imagined, if he was to be asked to pay for it.

'Coffee for me; Nick?'

'Sure, coffee for me as well.' Clare had not spared a glance at Richard's companion but she looked at him now because of his accent. American? Or possibly Devonshire. But not local at any event. He had a heavy face with prominent, swimmy blue eyes and a double chin but he was at the same time attractive. He smiled at her. 'Do you have any fresh-baked scones, honey?'

'Yes, I've only just got them out of the oven,' Clare said truthfully. 'Would you like one? With jam and cream or butter?'

'Butter, I guess.' The man called Nick turned to her brother-in-law. 'What about you, Dick? Care to join me?'

Clare could almost see the wheels turning and the figures clicking in that narrow head. He was fond of scones but would he end up paying for both or would the other man offer? And if Nick offered would it be politic, in the end, for Richard to refuse to be persuaded to allow the other to pay? She did not know which argument won, but Richard sighed and nodded grudgingly.

'Yes, why not? Two scones then please, Clare.'

Whilst she buttered the scones and made the coffee, Clare wondered about the American. Client? Friend? Whoever he was it must be a fairly remote relationship since Richard had not attempted to introduce her, or perhaps it was not done, in the circles in which the two men moved, for a waitress to warrant an introduction.

But in this at least she was proved wrong, for when she returned with the coffees and scones Richard stood up and took them from her, then performed the introduction.

'Nick, this is my sister-in-law, Clare Arnold. Clare, my client, Nicholas H. Bernstein, known as old Nick the length and breadth of Tennessee.'

Clare smiled and murmured something and would have returned· to the kitchen, but Richard caught her arm, restraining her.

'Just a sec, old girl. Look, Rachel and I want to take Nick out for a meal tonight, somewhere decent where he can see a bit of life; on the Broads for choice. If you'd care to come along as our guest we'd be delighted. Make up a foursome, see? Clive wouldn't mind, not with me and Rachel along as well. What do you say?'

'I couldn't possibly, but thanks all the same,' Clare said primly. 'There's Sally for one thing . . .'

'Oh come on, she left you last night, why not leave her tonight? It isn't as if we'll be terribly late, you can get Gran to keep an eye on her or your mother I suppose, and then pick her up on your way home.' He gave her what he no doubt believed to be a charming, rueful smile. 'Be a sport, Clare . . . Nick would be far more comfortable in a foursome.'

Clare was in the middle of another, even firmer, refusal, when to her astonishment she hesitated. Last night had been grim, with Sally off the first moment she could, the washing up to do, the gardening all alone . . . and yet a dinner with her in-laws she could most definitely do without. On the other hand, Nick seemed quite a pleasant, fatherly sort of fellow, it might easily be an interesting evening and at least it would be a jolly good excuse for not sitting down and marshalling her arguments against giving up her job, putting them into a letter for Clive.

'I'd take it kindly, ma'am.'

The soft transatlantic voice sounded like something from a soap opera but even so, it sent a little tingle of appreciation along Clare's spine. It would be rather pleasant, for once, to be courted, possibly even complimented. It would be nice to eat a meal she had not cooked, sit at a table she had not laid, drink a glass of wine she had not poured. It would also, she told herself with wry humour, be nice to look out over a garden she had not planted and ride in a car whose good performance she was not concerned over.

'We-ell,' she began, and was immediately interrupted by Richard.

'Atta girl, I knew we could rely on you! What time do you finish here?'

'About six, but I'll have to get Sally home, or to Gran's, depending. And then I'll have to change, I can't very well come out to dinner in a pink and white checked overall.'

'Right. I'll book the table for eight and pick you up at half seven. Will that be all right?'

To her own considerable surprise, Clare felt a pleasant glow of anticipation start in her toes and tingle up all over her. It would be fun to go out on the town, laugh and talk, look her best. She would enjoy it, even in the company of the wretched Richard and his disapproving wife. She smiled at both men, but saved the warmth of her glance for the American.

'Yes, that'll be fine. Thanks very much. See you at half-past seven.'

By half-past seven, of course, doubts were almost crowding out anticipation. She would be bored, poor company, taken somewhere which was too posh. She would be overdressed or underdressed, she would see people staring at her, thinking her a country bumpkin . . . or a city slicker, depending on whether she was overdressed or underdressed of course. But when the bell rang she hurried to the door, her oatmeal jacket over one arm, the oatmeal dress with its wide, dark-brown belt and matching high-heeled sandals looking as good as it could.

Richard stood there. His eyes slid over her and then returned to her face and she could see his slightly startled approval. Of course for years he had seen her in jeans and shirts, or in summer dresses. Never dressed up, because she and Clive did not dress up for family occasions and she and her husband simply did not go out with her brother and sister-in-law.

'You've settled Sally? Jolly good – you look stunning,' he added, leading her out of the house with a possessive – and unnecessary – hand cupping her elbow. He made Clare feel like a prisoner, as though he had to keep his fingers on her or she would run off, but she tried to smile graciously and keep up a flow of light conversation as she sank into the passenger seat and Richard joined his wife in the back. It would not do to start the evening off by showing the antagonism she felt, she realised that.

'Hello, Rachel,' she said, having greeted Nick Bernstein. 'Gosh, this is rather posh . . .' she turned to Nick. 'Is it yours? I know it's not Richard's.'

'Nor mine; I hired it,' he explained, but before he could say anything further Richard was addressing him.

'All set? Good, good. Turn left when you reach the road, Nick, and then keep straight on until I tell you to turn again.'

'Gran! Lovely to see you!'

Sally kissed Gran, gave her a hug and then darted past her into the small flat's pleasant living-room. It was odd, she reflected, as Gran bustled through it and into the kitchen with Sally following, how completely Gran had managed to convert a modern place into the cottage she had left. Once inside the door it was the cottage, the place her mother had been more or less brought up, even though outside the front door there was merely flat, officially shared grass, then the pavement, then the service road, and beyond it the roar of main-road traffic which Gran seemed to find exciting and interesting rather than a nuisance.

'I lie in bed and I can tell by the sound of the engines

121

whether it's a ten-tonner or a delivery van or a motor bike,' she had told her great-granddaughter on her last visit. 'No one can be bored here!'

Not that Sally could imagine Gran ever being bored. She was too full of life and energy for that. She was seventy-six now but her hairrwas still dark red, her eyes hazel-green, her skin pale as paper. Softer now, perhaps, delicately crumpled, but still astonishing for a woman of her age. Sally's friends, brought up on white-haired old ladies, were always amazed over Gran; they guessed her hair was dyed – Sally knew it was, having several times assisted Gran in the putting on of the dye around the back of her hairline – but they took the attitude that even dyeing it was amazing, a sign of a rich and unrepentant eccentricity which not even age could fade.

'Well, darling?' Gran's deep, musical voice always had the power to charm Sally, to make even the most mundane remark seem exciting. 'What's got into your Mum now, then? Going out with that wretched brother-in-law of hers after the things she's said about him! What a turn-up for the books!'

Slang delighted Gran, she used it all the time, sometimes with wild inaccuracy. When she heard someone decrying it she was at her most brisk. Nonsense, she would say, an enrichment of the language, that's what it is. Only the truly dull would want language to remain stationary.

But now Sally put her right.

'She's not going out with Richard, Gran, not really, he and Auntie Rachel have got a Yank staying with them and they've invited Mum to make up a four.'

'Yes, so she said. But once, Clare wouldn't have wanted to spend two minutes, let alone a couple of hours, in Richard's company, nor Rachel's for that matter. If you ask me, love . . .' here she turned from the sink and wagged a finger knowingly at her great-granddaughter, '. . . if you ask me, your Mum's reached a turning point. She's done more than just take a job . . . By the way, you must tell me all about it.'

'It's a nice job,' Sally said positively, as Gran made two tall glasses of lemon tea for them and selected a plate on which to set out her interesting biscuits. No ordinary rich tea for Gran, if she served biscuits they were liable to be foreign and exotic.

Today they were brandy snaps and what looked like tiny pyramids of nuts and chips of chocolate. Sally carried the plate through into the living-room and they both sat down. Gran sipped tea and Sally nibbled and thought about the caff. Of course Mum had told Gran about it, but obviously not much and so far Gran had not turned up there to see for herself.

'Nice? Do you mean the work's pleasant or the people are interesting or what? I need more information than that to build a picture.'

Gran was always building pictures, which bore no resemblance to what had been described to her. Sally frowned and then reached for her glass of tea.

'Well, Mum seems to enjoy the work, the people are great, even the customers are mostly all right, and the caff itself could be worse. Why don't you go and take a look for yourself, Gran? I think you'd like it, really I do, or I wouldn't say go there.'

'Hmm, maybe I will. Told Dad yet, has she?'

'Yes, ages ago. He's written back and everything.'

'Does he approve?'

Sally considered this question for the first time. She assumed by the fact that her mother was still working that Dad had approved, but now that Gran had put the thought into words, she realised it didn't follow. Mum wouldn't let Mrs P down, that went without saying, so perhaps she was only working off a month's notice or something like that. Sally frowned uneasily, than her brow cleared; of course it must be all right or Mum would never have suggested that she, Sally, work over the summer holidays. She said as much to Gran, who shook her head in a knowing fashion.

'That doesn't mean Clive approves, sweetheart, it merely means that Clare's decided to keep the job come hell or high water.' She looked gratified at having managed to fit in an expression which pleased her and repeated, 'Come hell or high water,' thoughtfully.

'I suppose you could be right, except that Mum wouldn't do anything to upset Dad,' Sally pointed out. 'She never has, at any rate.'

'Well, when she came in here earlier to see if it would be all right to bring you over – as if it could ever be anything but all right, silly girl! – I noticed a difference in her. Yes, a real change. Not that I object to change, as you know, and it's about time Clare asserted herself. That job's doing her good, I told myself. That job's making her satisfied instead of hollow. No, I don't mean satisfied, exactly, or perhaps it's hollow that I don't mean.' Gran thought it over, chin on hand, then leaned back in her chair once more. 'A couple of months ago she wouldn't have gone out with Richard and Rachel, I grant you, but even less would she have joined them when a stranger was making up the party. And earlier, there was something about her . . . I know! She's ripe for mischief!'

This was said so triumphantly that Sally giggled.

'Gran, you know how responsible Mum is, and how sensible, she doesn't even want to be mischievous I'm sure.'

'She didn't, but she does now,' Gran said firmly. 'Pass me a biscuit, darling – not one of those dreadful barbed wire entanglements, they get behind my plate, one of the nutty ones.'

'Take the dogs out, Dee, there's a good gal!' Alice Spooner's powerful voice rose easily above the whine of the power drill which her husband was using out in the shed and pierced even the vibrant notes and the shriekings and gurglings which were being emitted by Deirdre's record player. Deirdre shouted back that it was about time young Jason took a turn but nevertheless she descended the stairs and made for the back door.

'Just the big 'uns?' she enquired as she passed her mother, more as a matter of form than a regular question, since it was always the big 'uns who needed the exercise. Jason, spoilt little rat, got to take the miniatures out for a ten-minute waddle last thing, it was always Deirdre who landed for the wolf hounds, German shepherds and daft, leggy, untrainable setters.

'That's it, gal. There's two retrievers and a collie,' her

mother said lazily. 'A mile or so'll do 'em, they're been out today earlier.'

'A mile! They'll be lucky,' Deirdre growled, going out of the back door and shutting it more forcibly than was strictly necessary.

It was not fair! She worked hard all day, her arm was in a sling, any other mother would have been urging her to rest, but not her mum. Her mum just handed out the jobs like she always did and took in the money come the weekend.

Some of the dogs could be walked without a lead but not many of them. However, the collie was fairly good and the retrievers, being litter brothers, were used to a double lead, so Deirdre got down the lead for them and merely unlocked the collie's run and whistled him. He came like a bullet from a gun which made her uneasy for a moment, then she reflected that if he ran, he ran, and her mother could take the consequences. Serve her right, she thought vindictively, sending me out with my arm in a sling. She clipped the leads onto the retrievers, checked that they were secure, and then set off, the collie roaming ahead. It was an elderly dog, well used to staying with the Spooners. Rolf, it was called.

Outside the gate she hollered hello to Neddy Byrne up the road who was digging in his garden and then turned left, away from the houses. With three dogs, it might not be a good idea to walk through the village as she otherwise would have done. The collie was all right really, a good-tempered beast enough, but there was no point in courting trouble. Three dogs can make an awful mess of one dog if it comes to a fight, and the collie and the retrievers, whilst not by any means aggressive, had already shown that to their minds the post office's pug ought to have been dead and buried long ago.

It was a fine evening. As she walked, Deirdre's mood began to mellow. The balminess of the air made her believe summer had really come at last and that conjured up thoughts of seaside holidays and trips to the lavender fields on a coach.

Not that Deidre had ever had a seaside holiday but her mind was set on it this year; why not, she was earning and had a bit put by. She had friends, too, who might easily go with her. She would have liked best to go with Sally, only she couldn't see Sally being voluntarily parted from that horse of hers, so she would have to fall back on Beverley at tech., or possibly even on Mavis, who had made remarks which led Deirdre to believe she might take at least a long weekend down Yarmouth and see a bit of life come August.

The road to the right led, eventually, into deep country where she might easily be able to let the dogs off the lead for a bit, but Deirdre fancied a bit of company; if she turned off the road down a deep little loke she would come to the pond. It wasn't really a pond, more a lake, and strictly speaking it was on private property, but all the village lads fished it when they had nothing better to do, and Reynold Butler, who owned it, seemed resigned to their presence. It might be a laugh to go down the pond Deirdre told herself vaguely, you never knew who might be there. If any of the fishermen had a motor bike he might be prevailed upon to go down the chippy and buy everyone chips . . . yes, she'd visit the pond tonight.

She reached the pond with only a couple of minor mishaps. Goldie, the larger of the retrievers, decided to drag behind whilst Glitter, the smaller, tried to hurry on. This led to some discomfort for Deirdre who was forced to keep pushing Goldie with one knee because she could not swing out briskly with her injured arm, but they got to the pond eventually, Rolf well ahead, and Deirdre scrambled up the hazel-clad bank and dragged her charges after her until she reached the small group of village youths intently staring at the still pond waters, when they weren't covertly eyeing the village girls, that was.

'Hey up, Dee,' one of the lads said. 'Christ, gal, keep them dogs outer the water, will you?'

Since both retrievers were dancing on tiptoe at the sight of their favourite element this was no idle request but Deirdre lashed the double lead tightly round a sapling, bade her charges sit down and shut up, and then wandered over to Eric Dolman, commonly known as Quack for a reason so lost in the mists of time that no one, including Eric, could remember it.

'Hey, Quack,' she greeted him. 'Any luck?'

Quack shook his head slightly and looked at her under his brows. He was an extraordinarily attractive youth, she considered, with long, luxuriant browny-gold curls to his shoulders, dark-blue eyes fringed with incredibly long, black lashes and a spare, broad-shouldered body in the obligatory tee-shirt and patched and faded jeans. Quack, however, was notoriously indifferent to females and only tolerated Deirdre's friendship because she had sat next to him in school for several years and made no demands on their relationship. Even his recent acquisition of a motor bike had not brought Deirdre whining to have a go; her stock, at the moment, was high and Dee had more sense than to lower it with importunate demands. 'Softly softly catchee monkee' was her present attitude to Quack. When he was ready for a girl, she wanted his mind to pick on her, that was all.

'Anyone caught anything, then?'

'Naw. Too warm ... too bright ... too dry.' The comments came from more than one throat but Deirdre's eyes never left Quack's.

'Well, that means more for tomorrow evening, then,' she said practically. 'Anyone gone for chips?'

Mandy Edwards, sitting on a low branch and swinging her feet over the water, shook her head.

'Not yet, gal Dee; why, thinkin' of volunteering?'

'I don't mind, but someone'll have to keep an eye on a coupla dogs for me. I've done my arm in, can't manage all three of 'em through the village, far less carry stuff.'

'What you done, Dee?'

Deirdre told them, omitting no interesting detail, and when she'd finished Quack heaved himself to his feet.

'I'll go on the bike,' he said. 'You're had a rough day by the sound, young Dee.'

He lounged over to the group sitting along the branches of the willows on the far side of the pond, collecting money and orders. Presently he returned to where Dee sat by his rod.

'Keep an eye on it for me?'

At her nod he nodded too and climbed the hazel bank. Dee scrambled half up it and looked down on him as he sat astride the bike, revving desperately. The bike's hoarse,

127

hiccupping roar reminded her of Quack's voice which had only fairly recently gone from a boyish tenor note to its present deeper tone. She was a bit disappointed that he had not asked her what she wanted though and very nearly shouted after him, only remembering at the last moment that this would ill accord with her planned strategy of being no trouble whatsoever. In the event, furthermore, it was not necessary. Quack returned twenty minutes later and the first person he served with chips was Deirdre.

'There y'are,' he said gruffly, pressing the newspaper packet into her hands. 'They're vinegared.'

'Great. How much . . .?' Deirdre knew very well how much, but it was only polite to ask. Quack, however, shook his handsome head and his curls bobbed across his broad, tanned brow.

'No, I bought 'em for you; make up for your wrist. Got a bottle of pop, too. We'll have drag and drag about.'

He left her before she had done more than stammer thanks and proceeded to deliver the rest of his purchases. Deirdre, almost speechless over his generosity, could only stare after him, her heart in her eyes. Who cared for a bit of pain in the wrist if it meant Quack would take more notice of her! She ate a chip; he had vinegared it exactly as she like it. Perhaps he would take her home on the back of the bike because of her wrist . . . oh damn, but there were the dogs, they could scarcely all get on Quack's pillion.

The gang stayed by the pond until the light had all drained from the sky and then they started for home. Quack gave his friend Bert a ride and Deirdre saw them disappearing into the dusk sadly, though she was glad he'd chosen a feller and not a girl.

She made her way along the darkening lane alone but for the three dogs. They all sauntered, the retrievers now hurrying, now lagging, now spending an inordinate length of time apparently glued, leg raised, to a tree or a bank. She was only half way home when she saw someone coming down the lane towards her, a dark figure approaching purposefully.

'It's only me.' She would have known that voice anywhere, of course, though she would never have admitted it.

'Oh, hello, Quack. Forgotten something?'

'Didn't think you oughter walk home alone, not with that arm.'

Deirdre's heart nearly burst. So much for Rambo . . . She would never think about him in the same breath as Quack, appealing though the older man was; Clare was welcome to him. Oh yes, she had seen the two of them earlier in the day, their heads close over the window-table, and she had wondered then just what they were up to, though of course she had not let on to Mavis, who was such a busybody that she would likely put all sorts of interpretations on what might, after all, have been the most casual and unimportant of social meetings.

A picture of Rambo sitting opposite her, looking deep into her eyes, was fading fast already. How much better if Quack would unbend towards her, even the littlest bit! Older men were boring, that was the truth of it. But she must show none of this or Quack would shy away and never come back.

When Quack put out his hand Deirdre's anticipation almost let her down and she very nearly slipped her fingers shyly into his, but in fact all he was doing was taking the retrievers' lead from her. Fortunately she realised in time and so did not make a fool of herself; instead, they walked amicably home, chatting quietly.

At her gate, she would have asked him in for a cup of cocoa or something, but one moment he was there, the next he was striding up the road, just a dark figure in the dusk. Never mind, Dee consoled herself as she went round the back and put the dogs back into their runs, there'll be other nights. Poor Clare would probably never see Rambo again, or if she did it would only be in the surroundings of the caff where neither could start anything. Whereas I, Deirdre reminded herself hopefully, can see Quack seven nights out of the seven if I care to look around a bit and some day he'll decide he wants a girl, same's they all do.

Indoors, she watched as Jason brought in his yapping, dancing protégés and actually helped him to kennel them without being asked, then she made hot drinks and then she took herself off to bed. Dreaming would be easy tonight, she told herself exultantly, undressing in her small room and planning her outfit for the morning as she did so, her usual practice. Quack was at tech., in the city, but now that he had the bike perhaps he'd pop into the caff some time, especially if she casually suggested it.

Jeans tomorrow, then. The tight pink ones. And her checkered shirt. She would have to change once she got to work of course but you never knew, Quack might pass the bus as it took her into the city. Or he might walk home with her from the bus stop in the village the following evening, because Clare had said to catch an earlier bus.

Things are looking up, Deirdre told herself exultantly, as she cleaned her face with cold cream in front of her dressing-table with its multitude of mirrors. Yes, things are definitely looking up!

The meal was good and Nick Bernstein an attentive and interesting dinner partner. Richard behaved himself and Rachel was more relaxed than usual and Clare found that the caff was good for a topic of conversation and that anecdotes which she had previously shared with no one for the simple reason that she was still unsure who would find them funny, turned out to be very amusing indeed.

They went to a restaurant called the Look-out, and sat on a wooden balcony actually built out over the Broad, eating delicious and well-cooked food, drinking an expensive wine and chatting as the sun flamed down the sky and sank in the west. Richard watched her a lot but she did not let it worry her; he frequently watched her anyway, and the fact that he did so now may merely have been because he wanted her to be good company for his client.

During the course of the meal Clare managed to ascertain that Nick was over in England to buy certain products – she did not manage to find out which – and wanted the English advertising to be used for the States, though with certain changes so that, although it would still be English, it would also be completely understandable to the American audiences.

'Surely we all speak the same language?' Rachel said at this

130

point, to be howled down by the two men, who immediately began to give her various words or phrases which had, in their time, nearly been the downfall of the teller.

'So how will the advertising have to change?' Clare said when they'd finished. 'Just the words, or the action too?'

'Oh, just the words. We'll pay actors to dub in rather than do the work again,' Nick said easily. 'Richard here is arranging it now. So I shan't go back home until that part of the job's done.'

'You'll wait for the work and take it home with you?' Clare asked. At his nod she added, 'Then you'll be here for a week or two yet, I suppose. What will you do? Go up to London and live it up or stay here in Norwich and sight-see?'

'Stay here, I guess; I know London fairly well but this is my first trip to Norwich.' He smiled at Clare with a good deal of charm. 'Fancy showing me round? I'd sure appreciate it.'

'Sorry, I work,' Clare said, smiling back nevertheless. 'This is my first evening out in ages and I'll be tired tomorrow because of it. Catering's an exhausting business, as I'm beginning to discover.'

She had already told them, only half truthfully, that she had taken the job in order that Mrs P might go off to stay with her married daughter for a few weeks. It had eased things with Richard and Rachel though, making her action seem less eccentric. Anyway, Clare told herself now, eating small spoonsful of something creamy, light and delicious, for all I know I might be speaking the absolute truth. Mrs P did say she might want to come back on a job-share basis, if she decided that a mere two day a week job was not enough for her. Come to that, Clare thought, Mrs P might easily simply come back and expect her replacement to move on and if she did there could be no argument; she was, after all, the boss.

'You work evenings?' the American asked. Knowing the answer quite well of course, Clare thought bitterly.

'Well, not evenings, no, but it's quite late by the time I get home and then I have family responsibilites.'

131

'Sure, I understand. Say I ask you and the little girl to come out with me?'

'She's studying for exams,' Clare said and then, seeing the smirk of Richard's face, added, 'but we'd be delighted if you'd come round to us one evening, have a meal, see a bit of country living.'

She regretted the words as soon as they were out of her mouth and heard his lively acceptance with dismay. But it was done now, all she could do was hope that she and Sally between them could cope with the ebullient Mr Bernstein.

CHAPTER
7

The first thing Clive saw as he emerged from the souk, clasping his purchases, was a half-built block of flats or offices. The workers swarmed over the uncompleted walls like ants, black against the brilliance of sky and concrete. He stopped in the shade of an immense fan-palm, glad to rest for a moment, and stared upwards. The Yemeni workmen, in loincloths with rags tied round their heads, seemed indifferent to the height at which they were working. It certainly did not seem to cross their minds that there was any danger. As he watched a man stepped from one half-completed piece of wall to another, over a three-foot gap. Had he missed his footing he would have fallen five or six storeys, to end up as strawberry jam on the rubble below.

It had been hot in the souk but out here a breeze blew softly and it was cooler. The sun was sinking and within an hour it would be dusk. Right now it seemed a good idea to Clive to rest a moment, let the sweat cool, before he returned to his Land-Rover, so he wandered over to the nearest fountain.

There were several fountains in the city but this one, overlooking the new office block – or flats – would enable him to go on gazing curiously upwards. Clive perched on the rim, beneath the shade of another palm, and watched the acrobatic antics of the workmen. They had no nerves, he concluded after a moment, but he supposed that their ancestors had been Bedouin, and from what he'd heard the

133

Bedouin were all brave as lions and held life cheap. Not that that was particularly praiseworthy, because their lives had been nothing to write home about, not until oil had been discovered in the Gulf. Here in Saud the Bedouin had had few pleasures, even food had been boring in the extreme, coarse bread, camel's milk and blood when times were good, God knew what when times were hard. It was existing, not living. A man would own, if he were lucky, a woman, a black goat-hair tent, and a camel. He would live for fighting, the occasional taste of meat when he slaughtered a beast, and the hope of heaven after he died. Not a lot to lose; no wonder it didn't worry the workmen up there when they found themselves perched on top of ill-made cement walls a hundred feet up. Probably, Clive thought sourly, they got their Imam to promise them a dozen houris each if they died on the job. That would account for their airy indifference to the giddying height.

But that was a sceptic's view and not one which Clive held in all seriousness. Although the Kingdom was fortunate on the whole, with the oil sheiks so rich that they could buy up huge areas of London and New York, the imported Yemeni tribesmen, who did all the manual work, were poorer than the poorest Englishman.

But the comparison meant very little in real terms, because the oil sheiks, though mean as hell with wages, had time for their people. Food was plentiful and the richest man would send the remains of his huge banquets out to feed the poorer citizens. It had to be said that banquets were always vast, even when only half a dozen men were invited, which ensured that the uninvited ate well and frequently.

Clive had been looking up at the workmen, but now a movement on his own level caught his eye and deflected his gaze. A man strode past, dressed in European fashion and well-dressed too – Savile Row, probably, Clive reflected with the indifference of one who wore the same dark suit for all formal occasions and had done so for fifteen years. The man was followed, at a discreet distance, by a woman. All in black, her face hidden, her head a little bowed, she hurried along, robes flapping, sandalled feet flapping too, in the dust of her master's progress. Clive caught a glimpse of a gold-enamelled toe-nail, saw the flash of dark, lustrous eyes as she passed him, and then the man called something over his shoulder and she broke into a trot, answering breathlessly as she went. Her voice was muffled, but he still heard the English words panted out as she hurried along.

That was one of the drawbacks, of course. Women had a hard time of it here, though they were treated well by some standards. No man would doubt a woman's word, but since she was rarely seen and almost never heard that did not mean much. Harems still existed of course, women's quarters were sacrosanct and purdah was so much a part of life that Clive felt uncomfortable when he first arrived home and saw bare faces in the streets.

Of course it was different at the base, but there were very few women there and they did not stay long. It was no life really, forced to stay indoors unless you were with a man, having to keep all your skin surfaces covered in this breathless heat, with a headscarf over your head in case the sight of naked hair drove some poor Saud wild with desire. Here, a woman could not drive a car, must never sit in the front passenger seat, and when walking with her husband in the street was forced by law to keep two steps to the rear of her companion, just like the Englishwoman who had just passed him.

He had never wanted that for Clare. It was no place for a woman, especially one like Clare, and then there was Sally. Sally would have been sent home to school and Clare would never have abandoned her child to relatives whilst she stewed out here.

Because it had happened naturally, by a simple progression, he allowed his thought to turn to home and Clare, although after getting her last letter he had been so hurt and angry that he had avoided thinking about her at all. He had answered the letter too quickly, that was the trouble, and had bared his heart and soul, but in retrospect perhaps that was not a bad thing. At least she could not pretend that she had not understood his feelings. His annoyance at finding she had taken a job in spite of knowing he did not approve had been natural, surely? So it seemed to him equally natural that she should give it up once she knew how hurt and upset he was.

Yet, despite telling himself now that Clare would not keep the job he did not, in his heart, have much faith in the supposition. She had changed. The old Clare would not have wanted or needed a job, she had been too involved with her home and her child. Then the Clare of even a year ago would never have dreamed of doing anything which was directly contrary to his wishes. He remembered how she had agreed not to go up to London to see Selina when he had asked her not to embarrass him by starting the old friendship up again. He reminded her that his friendship with the Bothwells had abruptly terminated on their marriage, and pointed out it was possible even Selina believed he had used his friendship with the family to further his courtship of Clare herself.

Clare had loved Selina, had looked up to her. Clive would have understood, even to an extent, sympathised, had she insisted on seeing Selina but she had not. She had bowed to his wishes and had, in thus doing, ill-prepared him for her sudden rebellion – and over such a thing! Over going out each day to do a doubtless rather boring and hard little job, missing out on the lovely summer weather, the beauties of the countryside, the companionship of her daughter, once the school holidays started. He could not understand it, no matter how he tried.

Which was why, when you came down to it, he had come into the city when his work out at the well finished for the day.

'Remember that cute nurse you talked to when Major and Mrs Trett asked us for drinks? She'll be at the party, she's bound to ask for you.'

That had been Simon, full of the milk of human kindness, intent on getting Clive into a better frame of mind.

He had not said he would go to the party, though. He had grunted. And then, when he got back to base and back to his room to change for dinner, he had remembered that he needed supplies, anyway, and had driven in to the souk. He had seen a bracelet . . . not expensive but extraordinarily pretty . . . and had bought it. For Sal? For Clare? He had no idea, he had simply bought it. And now, sitting on the rim of the fountain with the little packet in royal blue tissue paper in his pocket, he admitted to himself that he had bought it because he thought he would probably go along to the party, after all.

It would be a nice gesture, he told himself, to give his hostess the bracelet. Then he shook his head crossly at his own powers of self-delusion. He had bought his hostess a bottle of whisky and a spray of white, sweetly scented orchids and these gifts would be perfectly acceptable. The bracelet would not. The bracelet was . . . but he refused to analyse his reasons for buying the bracelet, because he suspected they were not very nice reasons.

Somewhere in his subconscious he wanted to punish Clare for upsetting him, he wanted to show her – though she would never know – that he could be appreciated by others, even if his wife had proved herself less than discriminating. So he had bought the bracelet and now he sat on the rim of the fountain, wondering whether to go back to the Land-Rover and drive back to base. There was a film showing tonight which had quite interested him, and if he returned at once he would not miss more than the first few minutes. Not everyone was off to the party, furthermore, there was good company to be had if one went into the bar for a beer.

Up above his head, the workmen continued to scuttle heedlessly over the half-constructed building. The sun was sinking quite fast now, though. Only the upper parts of the walls were in the golden glow, the lower parts were in dark, dramatic shadow. One of the great black and silver Cadillacs driven by the oil sheiks and their chauffeurs hummed passed, its tyres squeaking as it turned into the courtyard in front of a palatial block of flats. From where he sat Clive could see the car's reflection in the great marble slabs which paved the frontage, so highly polished they looked like a lake, the car floating on its own image like a lily on water.

Clive stood, stretched, and then began to walk back towards the souk; whether or not he went to the party he needed a meal. It would be pleasant to eat out in the city, it was not something he did often, he would treat himself.

There was a new restaurant, several of the men had been to it and considered it well worth a visit. He would go there, dine well, and then in all probability return to the Land-Rover and go back to base and his own bed.

But even as he ducked under the canopy of the first stall in the souk he knew he lied; he would go to the party.

It was an enormous room in what he afterwards discovered was a borrowed house in the middle of the city. The approach was probably awesome to one not in the habit of visiting the palaces of the royal household, but Clive was not awed; nevertheless he appreciated that his host and hostess must know all the right people to have been lent the dwelling.

The approach was, naturally, marble-paved but the tamarisk trees, the flowering exotics, the lawns and fountains, were considerably more than most foreigners merited. There were coloured lights in the trees shaped like Chinese lanterns and they cast their glow indiscriminately on beds of what looked like scarlet, pink and white peonies, on the soft green of the lawns and on the great gleaming cars. Clive swung his Land-Rover away from the porticoed frontage round to the side, where he found several similar vehicles bashfully hidden. Then he walked back to the front door, clutching his offerings. The bracelet – intended, of course, for Clare or Sally or possibly his mother – nestled in its protective wrapping in his pocket. Well, he could scarcely leave it in the Land-Rover! And anyway he had forgotten it. Almost.

The front door was open but guarded by a slim Arab in European dress who asked his name and passed him along to another man, this time an Englishman, a secretary or something to Major Trett or so Clive understood from his muttered introduction. He was led into the enormous room, chandeliers sparkling above his head, marble flooring gleaming beneath his feet, and immediately pounced upon by Mrs Trett who accepted his orchids with a coo of pleasure, waved the whisky away with the secretary after slightly more formal thanks, and immediately seized Clive's arm the better to tow him around with her for the obligatory five minutes, introducing him to people he had known either officially or by sight for the past five years at least.

The room, despite its size, was still crowded, both with party-goers and with the type of furniture which a rich, confused man may buy to fill one of his several houses. Gilded sofas and day-beds, round Persian carpets which should, in Clive's opinion, have hung on walls rather than be thrown down on the marble floor, cabinets made in fifteenth-century China and cabinets made in twentieth-century New York elbowed each other whilst the guests, impervious to their surroundings, talked, shrieked with amusement, and drank.

'Do you know Bob Reynolds, Clive? He has a charming wife . . . she's somewhere about . . . oh, and you'll love to meet Freda Ulnovich, one of her husbands is a Russian . . . or should it be was? . . . we're bound to catch up with her presently, she's wearing the most divine dress in black and gold, with a dear little jacket . . . ah, Tony's calling . . . will you be quite comfortable, dear boy, if I leave you here?'

Clive nodded reassuringly into Mrs Trett's round-eyed, pink and friendly face and watched as she trotted off in pursuit of the mysterious Tony. A nice woman, in her sixties, with her white hair cut short and curled so that the first thing you noticed about her was the shape of her small head and the last thing, her rather short neck. Right now, that neck was hung about with diamonds and diamond drops hung from her ears, yet Clive could still see she was a home-loving sort of woman, ill-at-ease out here yet enjoying the strangeness of her surroundings, the friendliness and interest of men far from home eager to meet new faces.

He wondered how she got on with the sheikhs, if she had met them, and how she got on with the wives, too, if she had been invited into the harems of course. Most women were asked to a harem if they were out here for very long and Mrs Trett had been in the Kingdom for the best part of a year now, moving around to be sure but always coming back to the city.

But right now, there was one woman in particular who interested Clive, and so far as he could see she was not present. However, in the far corner of the room, or rather on the far side of it, he could see a knot of women in European dress, almost hidden by the mass of men around them. If she was anywhere . . . not that he was bothered, he was a married man after all, and even if Clare had been thoughtless and selfish, gone against his spoken wishes, behaved in a way which offended all his sensibilities as the bread-winner of a family, even then, he was too aware of right and wrong to simply make a play for another woman. Even one as pretty and sweet as Della Knighton.

He made for the group, nevertheless, and on arrival hovered hopefully. A gliding, soft-footed servant brought a tray of drinks and canapes and Clive helped himself and stood nibbling something made of flaky pastry and containing some sort of meat and a sauce, he would commit himself no further than that. He sipped his drink, which was orange juice, and was narrowly contemplating the back of a head which might quite possibly belong to Miss Knighton when someone caught his arm.

'Well hello, Clive! I was beginning to wonder whether you were a mirage, like dying men see in the desert, because since meeting that time at the Trett's first place I've not seen hide nor hair of you.'

A heart-shaped face just about level with his shoulder and a thick shining cap of golden-brown hair. Very light-blue eyes with a dark line round the iris set wide apart. A neat nose and a large, smiling mouth. Della.

'Hello! No, you wouldn't have seen much of me, I'm out at the wells most of the time or I hang around back at base.'

She was wearing a white dress which showed off the golden tan of her legs and arms and was clipped at the waist with a blue velvet ribbon. She wore blue sandals too, with high-heels, and now that he was close enough to see her properly he saw that her eyelids were coloured a pale, misty blue as well. He smiled down at her; she reminded him of Sally's friends, and of Selina, long ago. There was a childlike quality about her, an innocence. He knew, or course, that she could not be as young as she appeared since she was a staff nurse at the big city hospital, but of her innocence he was entirely convinced. Now, she was smiling at him, clinging to his arm, offering him a sip from her glass.

'Just orange juice,' she said triumphantly. 'Do you know all the time I worked in London I felt foolish when I asked for a soft drink, but here it seems perfectly natural. And it's better for my complexion, of course . . . better for my liver as well. Why don't you follow my good example, Clive?'

'I'm drinking orange juice too,' Clive said, putting his own glass up to her nose. 'Go on, sniff . . . I'll pay a forfeit if you can smell liquor.'

She wrinkled her small nose and then smiled up at him, nodding her approval.

'So you are, so that makes two of us with a bit of sense. Do you believe what they say here . . . that there's less crime and less adultery and so on because of no alcohol?'

Clive laughed.

'Myself, I think having your head cut off for adultery and your hand for theft may have something to do with it,' he said solemnly. 'But if you believe it's because the whole of the Kingdom is on the waggon, who knows? Perhaps you're right.'

'Except that they aren't,' Della said. 'I say, it's awfully warm in here now that so many people have arrived. Is it allowed to walk in the gardens or are they just for show?'

'I'm sure it's allowed,' Clive said easily. 'Would you like to go outside for a bit?'

'Yes, I think I would,' Della said. She put her hand into his elbow, then changed her mind and slid her arm round his waist. Not to be outdone, Clive followed suit. Like rather uncomfortable Siamese twins, for the difference in their height was considerable, they made their way out of the big reception room, through the hall and into the garden.

'It's been a lovely party, Mrs Trett, I don't know when I've enjoyed myself more.'

Clive shook his hostess's hand then kissed her cheek. Beside him, Della echoed his remarks.

'Most of the other nurses are making their way back to the hospital now though, so I'll have to be going,' she added.

'Clive's giving me a lift since I came with Mr O'Reorden and he won't be leaving for a bit by the look of him.'

'Thank you both for coming,' Mrs Trett said warmly. 'Especially you, Della dear, because as Clive would be the first to tell you, men outnumber women out her by goodness knows how many dozens to one, so every nurse who comes to my parties ensures a little more success for me as a hostess.' She turned to Clive and patted his arm. 'You'll see her right into her apartment block won't you, dear? These young things . . . they don't take into account how inflaming it must be to the local lads to see skin and hair and faces and things, instead of just a big bundle of washing.'

'I'll take great care of her,' Clive promised. 'Thanks again, Mrs Trett.'

'My dear boy, you must call me Elsie; everyone else does,' Mrs Trett said, crossing the hall with them and then standing on the top step to wave as they made their way round the side of the house. 'Don't do anything I wouldn't do!'

Clive helped Della into the passenger seat of the Land-Rover and then drove through the quiet of the city streets towards the apartment block where Della and her fellow nurses lived. The district which held the Tretts' borrowed mansion was a rich district and from several of the huge houses as they passed they heard faintly the sounds of music. Sometimes a door opened and Arabs in *mishlahs* and *ghutras* floated down the steps and into the street; sometimes Arabs in European suits and shoes but with their traditional head-dresses emerged, calling thanks and respects to their hosts as they crossed the threshold.

'It seems terribly romantic at this time of night,' Della said softly as the Land-Rover moved steadily onwards. 'But in the daytime . . . well, it's a far cry from the *Arabian Nights* isn't it, Clive.'

'Mm hmm, you're telling me. And out at the wells it's even worse. But as they say the money's good. I suppose it's the same for you? Though you won't be keeping a home and family going with your salary I don't suppose?'

'No, that's true. I'm saving up to get married, though. I'm engaged, more or less, to a fellow back home. He's a trainee

142

accountant which means we can't really get married whilst he's studying and so on, so we decided I'd apply for a job out here, stay here for a couple of years, and then go home rich enough to buy a small house or something. And I'm getting awfully good experience this way too, better than I'd get in England, probably.'

'You look too young for getting engaged, let alone married,' Clive said as the Land-Rover turned into the forecourt of the nurses' flats. 'Now I'll stay and watch until you get into the building.'

'Oh don't do that, come in for a nightcap,' Della urged, as he came round the vehicle and helped her tenderly to alight. 'I'm on the fourth floor, I'm scared of the lift and I'm always afraid of being attacked on the stairs.'

'Well, that just proves you've not been here long,' Clive said chidingly. 'Still, thanks for the invitation, I'll come up for a few minutes providing the nightcap's a cocoa.'

'It'll have to be; whisky's not a drink women take to much when they're living alone,' Della said, leading the way into the apartment block. 'Lift or stairs?'

'Stairs, I think,' Clive decided. He did not have a great deal of faith in local lifts. 'If I'd known I was going to be asked back to your place I'd have bought some biscuits to go with your cocoa.'

Della, walking beside him up the flight, laughed and took his hand, giving his fingers a squeeze. A faint flutter of unease moved in Clive's breast, but he dismissed it as unworthy. She was engaged to a fellow and he was happily married – a comradely squeeze of the fingers meant nothing, after all.

'I've got plenty of biscuits, thanks very much!' They reached her door and she fished out a latchkey on a chain round her neck, unlocked and ushered him in. 'Now do you want to sit in the living-room whilst I make a drink or will you slum it in the kitchen?'

'The kitchen,' Clive said promptly, following her. 'It's a decent sort of place, this. Do you share or is it all yours?'

'It's all mine.' Della switched on the cooker and got dried milk out of a cupboard. She found the cocoa and set out biscuits on a plate. 'Well, isn't this cosy? Now why don't you tell me all about the home and family you're out here to keep going whilst the kettle boils?'

'There isn't much to tell, but actually I'd like your advice on one matter which has bothered me a lot over the past few days.'

'Advice?' Della turned to look at him, her eyes rounding. 'Oh, but I'm not awfully clever, Clive!'

'You don't have to be clever,' Clive said broodingly. 'Look, Della, when you go home to your fellow and he's a fully qualified accountant, how would you feel about continuing to work?'

Once he had started, the story poured out. In the kitchen he told Della all about their house and garden, the way they had worked to get it right and make it the sort of home they had dreamed of possessing. He told her about Sally and Pegs, about Tish and Gregory whilst they sat on the couch and drank their cocoa and ate some rather good biscuits. As they talked, or rather as he talked, Della got closer and closer, her lids drooping, cuddling up to him like a sleepy child.

She really was a darling, he concluded. She was so sympathetic and understanding over the way he felt because of Clare's job. He just hoped her fellow back home appreciated what a little gem she was. He put his arm round her and gave her a brotherly squeeze. A thoroughly nice girl!

Three hours later Clive came down the stairs, walked out of the front door and climbed wearily into the Land-Rover. He turned it for home and drove more slowly than was his wont.

He tried to keep his mind interestingly full of ordinary, everyday subjects, but his mind was not very obliging and he was forced, in the end, to write imaginary letters to Clare in his head to stop himself from either falling asleep or simply turning the Land-Rover round and driving back to the flat he had just left.

When he reached the base he parked his vehicle and made for his quarters where he undressed slowly, flinging his clothing haphazardly down as he did so. It was not like him and for a moment he considered hanging his jacket up properly and checking the pockets for the bracelet, only then he remembered the bracelet was not there. The bracelet was on Della Knighton's wrist.

Clive sighed, got into bed, buried his face in the pillow, and fell heavily asleep.

As though to prove it had only been fooling them, the day after Clare's trip to the Look-out the rain started again and what was worse it was accompanied by a cold and unseasonally strong wind.

It was the sort of weather to make everyone snappy and difficult. Sally was annoyed anyway because she had counted on spending the night with Gran but Clare, needing a chat, had called for her just as she had promised and taken her home to her own bed. Because she felt hard-done-by, Sally had scarcely spoken to her mother as Clare got breakfast, tidied round and pleaded with Gregory not to spend the day out in the rain. When Gregory gave her mother his most offensive look, Sally felt pleased and showed it.

By the time Clare had dropped Sally at school, parked the car and walked to the caff she was soaked and every bit as cross as her daughter had been. What wretched weather, no month could have been more ill-named 'flaming June' than this one! The thought of Clive probably lying on a beach somewhere was almost more than she could bear. Not that she would change places with him, but right now, she could not imagine why she had been so keen to get a job. The caff looked dreary in the rain, Mavis would spend most of the day muttering because of the mud the customers brought in, and business would of course be brisk because of Deirdre's sprained wrist which would mean that Clare herself would be run off her feet for the next eight hours or so.

However, it was no use repining; she had got the job and she would do it to the best of her ability. She opened the door and dripped across the tiled floor, calling a cheery 'Good morning!' to Mavis for the worst possible reason – she knew that a display of good spirits was the best way to put Mavis's back up on such a morning – and then went through into the kitchen.

Deirdre was already there. She was washing up with one

hand, and despite the weather and the awkwardenss of her task she was humming quite cheerfully. She looked round at Clare's entry.

'Morning, Clare! Don't forget it's bin day.'

Clare groaned and hung her jacket on the hook by the door. She hated bin days as they all did because the bins, well-filled to the point of obesity, had to be half-dragged, half-carried out onto the roadway since there was no means of access to the yard save through the caff itself and the dustmen, for some obscure reason, would not enter the premises for the purpose of bin-emptying.

'Damn and hell,' Clare said. She would have to manage by herself today, presumably, or with a bit of half-hearted help from Mavis. 'Mavis doing breakfasts?'

'Not so's you'd notice,' Deirdre said, clattering plates. 'She's got the board indoors, she's going to try rigging a cover over it, she says.'

'And you can't very well help with that wrist of yours,' Clare supplied. She opened the back door and the wind swirled into the kitchen bringing a good deal of misty rain with it. Hastily Clare shut the door and went over to her coat. It might be wet but at least it would stop her overall getting soaked as well.

'You could ask a customer to give you a hand,' Deirdre suggested, walking over to the back door. But Clare, head down, eyes half-closed, was grappling with the first bin. She rolled it across the yard, picked it up and staggered across the kitchen with it, and dropped it noisily just behind the counter in the caff. Mavis, tongue protruding and eyes squinting, was writing on the chalk-board and took no notice so Clare heaved the bin up in her arms again and charged across the caff. A large male customer who looked rather like a dustman himself grinned at her and continued to drink tea, but a girl with her hair plastered to her skull and both hands round a cup got up, held the door open, and then went back to her table too soon, so that the door caught Clare's bottom a resounding blow as she hesitated for a fatal second in the doorway, reluctant to face the driving rain and wind until the dustbin was securely gripped in both hands.

146

It was not the sort of thing to improve one's temper. As Clare brought the fourth and last dustbin out onto the pavement and crashed it so hard into the other three that one of them went sideways, spilling unmentionable nastinesses onto the pavement and into the road, a voice behind her said, 'My word!' and she turned in a blaze of temper to find herself almost nose to nose with Nicholas Bernstein.

'Oh! What on earth are you doing here?'

It was not a gracious remark but then Clare did not feel gracious. She felt that fate was dealing her unkind blow after unkind blow, and she failed to see why she should pretend that she was enjoying herself. The American, however, did not seem ruffled by her aggressive tone.

'Well, ma'am, I thought I'd have a cup of coffee . . .'

'Then go in and order it,' Clare snapped. 'I'm rather busy, as you can see.'

'Sure I can.' He bent over the horizontal bin, righted it and began trying to kick the contents into a heap. Clare wanted to scream.

'It's all right, I'll do it, I'll go and get some rubber gloves. Do go inside, I'm just . . .'

Because he did not at once abandon his attempt, Clare reluctantly began to help him, scuffing the tea-leaves, cold rice pudding and empty tins into a pile and then, shrinkingly, beginning to put them into the once more upright bin. Having started her off, Mr Bernstein then stood back and watched, presumably approvingly, as she made order out of chaos. When she had finished he hurried over to the caff doorway and held the door open for her, which at least prevented her from having to handle it with her now gooey and disgusting hands. Because it was his fault that she was in such a mess though, Clare swept past him without a word and into the kitchen. There, she cleaned herself up, took off her coat, put on her overall, and only then did she return to the caff. The American sat himself down at a table and smiled at her. Clare smiled tightly back, glad to see that one of his well-polished black shoes now had traces of rice pudding and potato on the toe-cap. Serve him right, the interfering old bugger, she thought vengefully. However, he was a customer.

'Good morning, Mr Bernstein, thanks for your help with the bins. And now that I'm clean and tidy and in my right mind, how can I help you?'

'Oh, sure. I'll have that coffee, please, and . . . have you any hot rolls, or orange juice?'

'We've got both,' Clare said, busily planning to get a couple of bread rolls under the grill as soon as she got back into the kitchen. 'Which would you prefer?'

'Oh, a coupla rolls and a big glass of juice.' Mr Bernstein said. 'Say, it's quite a place you've got here.'

'Thank you,' Clare said, heading for the kitchen. 'Shan't be a tick.'

She had barely begun to get the orange juice out of the fridge however, and assemble rolls, butter and plates, when Mavis followed her through.

'I done the board,' she said briskly. 'Who's the Yank then, Clare? Someone you know?'

'He's a client of my brother-in-law's,' Clare said, pouring orange juice into a slender glass. 'I went out to dinner with them last night. Why?'

'Oh, I just wondered.' Mavis headed for the sink, snatching a tea-towel off the clothes maiden on which they were hung as she passed it. She began to dry up. 'Not often we see a Yank in here.'

'True, though being so near the TV studios I suppose we might easily get stars of the silver screen and so on. Doesn't it happen?'

'Nah,' Mavis said scornfully. 'They've got a canteen, didn't you know? Otherwise they go to the pub, they don't come here.'

'Well, perhaps they'll start coming here now we're doing a different sort of cookery,' Clare said tactfully. But this did not suit Mavis. She turned to give Clare a long, hard look.

'Different? What d'you mean?'

'Well, we make different cakes and things,' Clare said vaguely. Mrs P had got very set in her ways and though she, too, had always made at least fifty per cent of the food sold in the caff it had tended to a regular pattern of chocolate or coffee cake, plum or apple pie, ginger or lemon biscuits.

Mavis sniffed. Clearly, the miserable weather had already brought a deepening of depression or whatever the weatherman on the telly called it, to her libido as well as to the general outlook.

'I don't see it. New-fangled's all very well but if you ask me, we'll lose our regulars. They like to sit down to a feed, they don't want a lot of fancy cooking.'

This was so different from what Mavis usually said that even Deirdre, up to her elbow in the sink, turned to stare but Clare took it in her stride, recognising it for what it was – wet day blues. She assembled her cutlery and crockery on a tray and headed for the grill. Over her shoulder she put her point of view.

'The only regulars we're likely to lose are the truckies and the layabouts and I thought you didn't approve of them!'

'You always say you like the new cakes and things,' Deirdre pointed out with a total lack of tact. 'Mavis, you said my coconut layer cake was the nicest thing you'd tasted in years.' She had swivelled round from the sink and was staring at her helper with astonishment. Mavis snatched another plate from the rack, dried it viciously and slung it onto the working surface.

'Ho, yes, some of it's quite nice,' she said in a lugubrious tone. 'I'm not saying it isn't tasty . . . well, some of it's very tasty and that's the truth. I'm just saying folk don't always like new things and even if we get the odd Yank now and then, that don't make up for losing regulars.'

Clare rescued her bread rolls from the grill before they became toast and headed for the doorway with her now complete tray. Fizzing coffee into the cup, she decided that the day might well turn out to be better than she had at first thought – Deirdre was plainly in a happy sort of a mood and old Mavis, when she had the grumps, could be quite amusing as long as you didn't take her seriously.

But of course when she delivered the hot rolls, orange juice and coffee Mr Bernstein had to spoil it all by asking her out again, explaining that he had desisted the previous evening in case she was diffident about agreeing to be entertained because of the presence of her brother and sister-in-law.

'It's very kind of you, but it's out of the question,' Clare said with good humour and patience. 'However, if you'd like to come and have a meal with Sally and me on Sunday evening we'd be delighted to entertain you.'

Mr Bernstein seemed about to demur but Mavis heading towards them changed all that. Hastily, he accepted her invitation, agreed to arrive at about seven o'clock, and began to tuck into his hot rolls. Considerably grateful for Mavis's opportune arrival, Clare smiled at him and headed back into the kitchen where she spread out her cooking things and began to make a gooseberry cobbler.

At the sink, Deirdre made mournful noises because try though she might she could not peel potatoes. Mavis, having cleared the tables from the two breakfasts she had served earlier came back into the kitchen, shooed Deirdre away from the sink and started to peel potatoes herself. Presently, in a tone both huffy and slightly apologetic, she admitted that the weather was enough to get anyone down after a couple of days of sunshine and all, that she was feeling a bit low on account of seeing that her long weekend was about to be spoiled by the weather, and that in fact she enjoyed all Clare's cooking and thought it gained them more customers than it lost.

Touched by this magnanimity, Clare unburdened herself about her outing the previous night and told Deirdre that not only did she not mind if Deirdre went out and took Mr Bernstein's money so's she could get a look at him, she would be downright grateful. They all had a laugh, and Deirdre dealt with the few customers who trickled in, soaked and cross, during the course of the morning.

'What'll you give that Yank to eat, Clare?' Deirdre asked as the three of them settled themselves at a table to eat their lunch around two o'clock, when the rush, such as it was, had been and gone. 'Something special? Typical English or typical American?'

'Something special it'll have to be,' Clare said, having thought the matter over. 'Not too elaborate, but something really nice. You see I was, in a manner of speaking, his guest the other night, even though I think it was Richard who engineered the whole thing and probably paid for it as well, or rather his firm did.'

'What, then? Steak and salad, with a fresh strawberry shortcake for afters?'

'Tell you what, we'll plan it out later, with a cookery book,' Clare said, visited by inspiration. 'Then I'll tell you how it goes down when I see you on Monday. It'll give us something to talk about with Mavis far away in the big city.'

'Huh! Hif you get a word in edgeways with Lizzie Treece trying to bend your ear all the time,' Mavis said disapprovingly. 'I wonder if I oughter go? It'll be me first bit of time off since you come though. All you've got to do is remember Lizzie's a cleaner and not much else then you can't go wrong.'

'Oh you go, Mavis,' Clare said easily. 'I've met Lizzie, though we haven't worked together so far. But I'm sure we'll cope, even with poor Dee handicapped.'

'Well, I can't hold your hand for ever,' Mavis agreed. 'And Monday's quiet, quieter then Tuesday I'd say. Yes, you'll manage I'm sure.'

The rest of the day passed uneventfully. Deirdre and Sally put their heads together at four o'clock and came up with a plan for Saturday, when neither Deirdre nor Mavis worked at the caff because the Saturday girls took over. Clare herself sometimes considered having a Saturday off but realised she could not do so yet, not until she had found a sensible woman to replace her. She had nurtured hopes of Mrs Treece but from the way Mavis talked about her they were vain hopes. Never mind though, Mrs P had given her *carte blanche* to find a responsible replacement for the next few weeks so that she, too, could take a day off occasionally.

I'll put an advert in the window, Clare decided, as the afternoon passed almost customerless, thus enabling her to plan her dinner-party menu, do a mound of cooking for the following day and to instruct Deirdre in the art of making meringue cuite, an activity which positively demanded plenty of time and concentration. After all, Mrs P got me through an advert so perhaps I'll get my Ms Right as well.

'So you and Deirdre are having a day out, I gather,' Clare said as she and Sally climbed into the Mini after having checked that the cats were indoors, their cat-trays newly charged with absorbent litter, and that the caff was as ready as it could be for the following day. 'Where are you off to, may I ask?'

'Just into the city,' Sally said vaguely. 'We're going to mooch round the shops and have lunch out . . . that sort of thing.'

'Lunch out, eh? At the caff, I presume?'

A quick glance sideways showed Sally looking shifty; Clare laughed and leaned across to squeeze her daughter's hand.

'Don't worry, pet, I'm kidding – you go wherever you want for your lunch; I'll give you some money.'

'Thanks Mum. Only it wouldn't be much fun for Dee, sort of coals to Newcastle, eating at the caff. And besides, we want to go to the sort of place where you go to see . . . well, everyone.'

Clare slowed to let a big waggon pull out of its place on the car-park and saw, in the cab, a vaguely familiar face, or thought she did, but then she chided her thumping heart for making an idiot of her over a fellow she had only ever spoken to once, and that at no particular length. Was it Oliver in the cab? But she couldn't be sure, only the man had half-raised a hand, a gesture which looked as though it had been cut off short when he realised that she had someone with her in the passenger seat.

The waggon was ahead of her now though and infuriatingly it turned right so she was not even treated to a second glimpse of the driver. She craned her neck, then the vehicle behind hooted, bringing her back to a sense of her surroundings and she obediently indicated, turned left and was heading home whilst beside her the oblivious Sally chattered on.

'. . . so it depends who you want to see,' she was explaining seriously. 'The people from Dee's village go to MacDonalds but our lot prefer Tweedledums, so probably we'll go to both.'

'One for coffee and one for lunch, I suppose,' Clare said, remembering her own youth, but Sally laughed and shook her head.

'Not specially, we'll just turn up at both some time. I did wonder about asking Em, but I don't think I shall; three's such an awkward number. By the way, you know when we drove out of the car-park?'

'Mm hmm?'

'Wasn't the fellow in that waggon like Big Chief?'

'Big . . . oh, you mean Coffee and Book! Was he? I can't say I noticed particularly.'

Clare put her foot down and the Mini surged past an elderly man in a BMW and then fell into line behind a Land-Rover. After a few more miles they reached a straight stretch and she went through all the motions of taking off once more . . . edging out so that she could see the road ahead past the vehicle in front, indicating, keeping a wary eye on her mirror . . .

She was half-way out when she saw, two vehicles behind her, what looked very like the waggon which she had seen on the car-park. From this distance she could not see the driver, save as a dark-haired male, but nevertheless the glimpse spoiled her concentration. She hesitated, squeezed a bit harder on the accelerator, got hooted at by the driver directly behind her who wanted to pass as well, and saw a red sports car approaching her too fast for her hoped-for manoeuvre. Sighing, she drew back into her previous place and saw her chance of getting ahead of the queue in front diminish as the road returned to its squiggling progress through two villages.

After that, nothing could have been more exemplary than Clare's driving. With one's eyes constantly flickering to the rear view mirror forward motion has to be exemplary, and she was intrigued by the possibility that she and Oliver might by sheer chance be on the same road.

She missed another couple of opportunities to overtake and then her turning came up and she could delay no longer. She indicated, pulled over, and dived down into the village street. She glanced into the mirror again just to see what had happened to the big waggon but so far as she could tell it had gone past whilst she was still turning.

She drove sedately through the village and then, at the gate, speeded up, to dash in fine style into the drive and stop abruptly, with the usual satisfying spray of gravel. Sally was laughing and climbing out of the car when, out of the corner of her eye, Clare saw a big waggon pass by. It was going only moderately fast but even so she could not catch more than a glimpse of the driver.

'Here, Mum, don't forget your cauliflower!'

Clare picked the cauliflower off the back seat and waved to Tish, who appeared to believe that leaping up and down on the draining board and knocking everything near her onto the floor constituted the best, the only, greeting of long-lost relatives. Was it just a coincidence that the waggon or a waggon very similar to the one which had been following her along the main road had just gone by? It was not as if their road led anywhere, save to a number of small farms.

'Mum, I'm feeling rather mean about tomorrow,' Sally said as they headed for the back door. 'Do you think I should pop down to see Em and explain, when we've had supper? Or now, if you think it would be best.'

Clare was about to tell Sally she could jolly well wait until they'd eaten when another thought crossed her mind. The lane did not lead anywhere in particular . . . if the big waggon had missed its way or if it had simply come down here to see precisely where she lived . . . well, it was absurd, Oliver could have come into the caff and asked her where her home was if he was that interested! . . . still, if either of those things had happened the waggon would presently retrace its steps, or rather its treads, and would appear, briefly, in the lane outside.

'Yes go off now, love,' Clare said, therefore. 'I'll walk down with you.'.

But half-way to Em's, she squeezed Sally's hand, told her not to be long, and turned, cauliflower in hand, for home and Tish, whose anguish at being apparently abandoned would have resulted, by now, in a lake the size of Michigan. And sure enough, scarcely had she turned the corner before the house when a big waggon bore down upon her, its driver so intent upon staring at the gateway through which she had disappeared five minutes before, that he nearly ran her down.

Nearly but not quite. Clare shouted and waved, and the driver looked, shouted too, and applied his brakes. He also opened the door of his cab and jumped down.

'And what might you be doing here?' Clare said severely. 'Or did you just happen to be passing?'

Oliver grinned.

'Trying to buy a cauliflower for my tea.' He pointed. 'Is that one for sale, lady?'

'This one is going to be transformed into cauliflower au gratin for Sally's and my supper,' Clare said primly. 'Seriously, Oliver, what are you doing here?'

'I went down to Brett's place to ask them whether they'll be selling their spare hay, come October. Why?' He looked hard at her, his expression suddenly knowing. 'You didn't think I was searching for you, did you? Because if so, remember I didn't have a clue where you lived.'

'Well, no . . .'

'However, since I now do know, and since of all my favourite things cauliflower cheese right now is tops, why don't you invite me in to share your meal?'

'Because there's only enough for two,' Clare said. 'Besides, it's very rude to invite yourself to supper with someone you hardly know.'

'True. And in any event, my passenger wouldn't think much of it.'

They had been standing in the road, Oliver holding onto the door of his cab, Clare holding onto her cauliflower. At his words, Oliver had jerked a thumb to the back of the big lorry and Clare, remembering what she thought he probably did for a living, gave a small shudder.

'Where are you taking it? Not to . . . to . . .'

'My stallion? Home actually. He's been serving a mare out near Acle but now his job's done and so I fetched him back.'

'You own a stallion? And he's at stud? But surely the mares come to him, don't they?'

Oliver climbed back into his cab and then leaned out of the

open window. It had stoppped raining some time back but the sky was still thick with cloud and the wind fretted and tugged at Clare's skirt as they talked. Burdened by the cauliflower and with rain all too evidently about to start at any moment, Clare found herself almost wishing that she had asked him in. At least she could have concentrated on what he was saying, instead of giving at least half her attention to preventing her skirt from blowing over her head.

'Yes, it's more usual, but when it isn't convenient for an owner to bring a mare to me, then I can always take the stallion over to them. And of course, being experienced with moving horses and having a number of decent horse-boxes, I'm quite willing to pick up mares and take them home to my place for a short stay of a few weeks, just until I'm sure they've been covered.'

'So that explains it,' Clare said, and grabbed at her skirt as a gust of wind tweaked it above her knees. 'Oh damn it, I'll have to go in, the wind's wreaking havoc with my dress. Nice to have met you. 'Bye!'

She turned and left him, hearing the waggon's deep growl of an engine start up as she went. Wrestling with the back-door key, the cauliflower and Tish's moans and whistling whimpers, she neglected to hold down her skirt and was enveloped in its folds, but she slid quickly through the opening, heart banging, cheeks hot with embarrassment, and hoped that Oliver had driven off before the incident.

Once in the kitchen, she was diverted by stepping straight into Tish's latest contribution and was forced to eject the still widdling creature so that she could at least finish out of doors. A mop, vigorously wielded, half a bottle of disinfectant and a good few muttered curses rescued the floor. Then Clare let Tish in, suffered herself to be knocked into a chair and covered with frantic wet kisses before staggering off up to the bathroom to clean up and change out of her skirt which, what with Tish's muddy feet and the vigorous moppings, looked as if it had been undergoing a steam bath and a mud-pack simultaneously.

Once upstairs, Clare decided to go for the definitive beauty treatment and ran herself a bath. Luxuriously soaking with half a bottle of bath oil tipped into the water and her very best talc standing by awaiting her pleasure, she remembered Sally, supper and her responsibilities without much guilt or enthusiasm. Sally was quick enough to whip off down to Emma's and happy enough to have her meal deferred if it suited her. Well this evening her meal would be deferred because it suited Clare, and that did not seem a particulary terrible arrangement for once.

Dreaming in the bath had always been one of Clare's vices, and this evening she allowed herself the luxury of all sorts of fantasies before she decided the water was going cold and forced herself to abandon the tub.

Beautifully clean and warm, with her hair hanging in wet ringlets and a silk bathrobe her only clothing, she padded downstairs presently and looked with disfavour at the cauliflower. Tish, sitting pointedly by her dish, seemed to indicate that she would personally guzzle every scrap of the cauliflower if she was not fed soon, so Clare, with a sigh, opened tins, sloshed milk, mixed biscuits and put the resultant dog's dinner on the floor for Tish's delectation. Tish leapt upon it, hoovered it down, polished the dish and then turned to gaze hopefully once more at the cauliflower, the only edible item within sight, unless you counted the bar of carbolic soap which Clare had used to scrub the floor and which, in her green youth, Tish had devoured if not with pleasure at least with a good appetite.

'You aren't having it, but neither are we,' Clare murmured, putting the cauliflower in the vegetable rack just inside the pantry and scanning the shelves with a lack-lustre eye. What could they eat which was quick and convenient yet which would fill Sally and be at least fairly nutritious? There was always beans on toast, or eggs on toast, or spaghetti on toast, but if she put that in front of Sally she would feel she had taken the first step on the slippery slide into culinary sloppiness. Just because she had been cooking all day she should not shower Sally with convenience foods, junk foods which she had always thought she despised – now she was not so sure. What was wrong with a couple of eggs on toast, anyway?

157

However, she remembered the freezer and a brief skirmish produced a bag of frozen chips and two really proteinous (was there such a word?) pieces of 'Frozen Cod in Crispy Crumb' as the label on the box put it. Clare heated oil, divided it into two saucepans, tossed the chips into one and the fish into the other and then, feeling thoroughly sinful, made herself a large mug of strong coffee, sweetened it with two sugars, and slumped in the easiest of the easy chairs, a cookery book open on her knee so that she could pick out some menus but her mind a good few miles away. Thinking it over, she realised that if Oliver had really been calling on the Bretts to ask about the hay he had done so in a remarkably short time, in fact, he must have hollered out of the window of his cab, because he simply had not been gone long enough to allow him to walk up to a farmhouse door let alone ask a question which called for any sort of an answer.

When the back door rattled she was still wondering whether she had been taken for an idiot or whether Oliver really had visited the Bretts only to find them out, or really had been able to get an answer to his question from a farmworker.

But she got to her feet, letting the cookery book crash to the floor, and padded barefoot across the tiles saying as she did so, 'I told you not to stay outside on such a filthy morning, you awkward old devil you! You won't take advice and now I dare say you're soaked and cold and cross, and serve you bloody well right for being so righteous and pig-headed!'

She flung open the door, her eyes naturally at Gregory-level, only to find herself contemplating not a ginger cat but a pair of gingerish walking shoes with laces neatly tied and topped by dark-brown slacks. Unbelievingly her eyes slid upwards. Oh! Oh, hell! Oh dear oh dear oh dear!

'Good evening, Clare my love. Can I come in? My, what a revealing gown!'

Richard's polished black hair gleamed above his narrow face, his eyes were fixed on the outline of her breasts, clearly visible through the thin silk. He was moving forward, in another moment he would be in the kitchen and Clare would find herself most uncomfortably situated. She had always been so careful to avoid meetings like this with Richard, especially with Sally out . . . Oh God, what should she do?

'Oh, hello, Richard. I got drenched . . .'

Without being truly rude, Clare could not have prevented her brother-in-law's entry to her kitchen but in any case he moved her aside and stepped past her. However, all was not lost. Tish, who had been in the very act of stealing a piece of buttered bread, carelessly left by Clare too near the edge of the table, turned round wildly, thought herself caught, and tried diversionary tactics.

Barking on a high, hysterical note, she launched herself at Richard, obviously shouting 'Burglar! Rapist! Thief!' at the top of her voice though with a wary eye on Clare in case her mistress should order her to stop making a fool of herself and welcome her visitor.

Richard was probably very fond of dogs but he was even fonder of his dark-brown trousers. He fended Tish off, laughing, trying to tell the dog to get down and shut up. Clare made ineffective grabs at Tish's collar and devoutly hoped the din would bring either help in the shape of Sally or at least a cooling of the ardour she thought she had seen in Richard's eyes as they rested on her imperfectly concealed figure. And then rescue came, though not quite as Clare had hoped.

'Clare, what on earth's going on here? My dear, right down on the road I could hear that dreadful animal . . . ' The speaker stopped short, obviously realising that there was more than one person in the room. 'Good gracious! Is that . . . Richard!'

'Oh hello, Mother,' Clare said a trifle breathlessly. 'Tish, don't start again, it's only Granny Flower! Look, I'll shut her up in the living-room until she's calmed down a bit.'

She towed Tish out, struggling against hysterics. Richard had looked exactly like the Lord of the Manor confounded when he had seen Mrs Flower surge into the room, all heather tweed suit, medium-heeled brogues and a hat with a bunch of violets resting on the neat little brim. And her mother, who had obviously entered with the intention of telling her daughter off in peace for the awful row Tish had been making, had suddenly bitten off a real tirade in deference to a stranger, only to discover that it was Richard, a man she disliked but wanted to impress.

Tish and Clare tumbled into the living-room and Clare knelt down with her arms round Tish, gave her a hug and a kiss on the bumpy bit on top of her head, and then told the dog in a giggly whisper that she was a good girl, a proper little mummy's saviour. Tish showed signs of wanting to kiss back though, so Clare got to her feet and returned, as slowly as she dared, to the kitchen. Out there, Richard and her mother faced each other, Mrs Flower making polite conversation about the weather in a mincing sort of voice, Richard being very suave and rather cold.

'I'm awfully sorry,' Clare said as she came through the door. 'I'm afraid Tish got rather over-excited. As you can see I got soaked to the skin earlier, and I left the poor old lady rather a long time down here whilst I bathed and changed, and then when I came down . . .' she crossed her fingers behind her back at the awful lie she was about to tell, '. . . when I came down she wanted to be fed, naturally, so just as I was about to feed her someone knocked, and it was Richard and she just went bananas . . . She can't bear to miss her meals.'

'Very understandable,' Richard said in an unbelieving sort of voice. 'And who did you think I was, Clare? You were talking to someone as you answered the door!'

'I thought you were Gregory; he usually knocks a bit like that,' Clare explained. 'He will go out in the rain . . .'

'Gregory? Who on earth . . .'

'If you were expecting a guest, Clare dear . . .'

Mrs Flower and Richard spoke in unison. Clare fought successfully against her urge to laugh and said, in a voice which shook only slightly, 'Oh, Mother, you know very well who Gregory is! He's the cat!'

'Yes, of course. I do think it's a silly name though, Clare, for a cat, I mean. Now perhaps you'd like to go upstairs and dress in something a little more formal . . . I'll keep Richard company whilst you're gone.'

But this, however, was going too far for Clare. She did not know what her mother thought she had interrupted, but she was certainly not going to get dressed again just so Richard could tell her whatever he'd come to tell her and then depart. She began to say something of this when, perhaps fortunately, she smelt burning. She dashed over to the cooker and whipped off the chips. They were beyond help. As she lifted the lid blue, stinging smoke filled the air and Richard opened the back door but not before they had all begun to cough.

'Clare really . . .'

'I'm sorry . . .' Clare began, and then rallied a little. For goodness sake, she had been in full command both of the situation and of the chips when her uninvited guests had put in an appearance. She drew herself up to her full height, carried the saucepan to the open kitchen door, and stood it down outside where it could pollute the fresh air rather than make the kitchen uninhabitable. She did the same with the saucepan full of fish, then she turned to Mrs Flower and Richard.

'I'm very sorry, but I'm trying to get supper. What do you want, Richard?'

'Oh nothing much; just a word. It'll do another time . . .' Richard, at this straight question, seemed to have lost a little of his formidable composure. Clare was delighted, but merely gave a dismissive little nod towards the kitchen door.

'All right, then perhaps you can pop in some other evening? Only do give me a ring first, so that I can shut Tish away. Now, Mother, what can I do for you?'

'I thought I'd see how you and Sally were . . . it's a good while since we met,' Mrs Flower said. 'Are you off now then, Richard? So nice to have seen you . . . give my regards to your wife.'

Richard left, leaving mother and daughter eyeing one another cautiously across the still blue-misted kitchen. Clare broke the silence.

'Mother, I simply must eat and Sal will be back in a moment. Have you had a meal? I'm afraid I've ruined the fish and chips but I'll do some poached eggs on toast in two shakes, if you'd like to share it with us.'

'Poached eggs . . . do you have any low-calorie bread though? I'm trying to lose a little weight . . .' Mrs Flower patted her tightly packed tweed skirt at about hip level, '. . . or perhaps I could just have some boiled eggs? Lightly boiled with a crispbread.'

'I'll do you some eggs,' Clare said. 'Sally and I don't go much for crispbread, but if I cut the bread and butter very thin . . . and I don't see why you're slimming, Mother, you've go a very nice figure.'

'Well, I eat carefully,' Mrs Flower agreed. She moved over to the round, speckled glass which hung above Tish's mat and examined her reflection closely.

Clare could see her giving herself a satisfied little smile, opening her mouth to check that there was no lipstick on her teeth, closing it again and examining the matt finish of her make-up, the delicately applied light-brown mascara, the smooth, pale-pink lipstick. She is a handsome woman, and she's got a good figure for fifty, Clare told herself, trying to whip up some daughterly pride in herself and failing dismally.

Her mother had always eaten with care, dressed with care . . . you could say she lived with care. Widowed when Clare had been only months old, she had worked all the time Clare had known her and had never, to Clare's knowledge, let go. Every morning, even Sundays, she got up, bathed, dressed, made up her face and emerged to greet the day. Her hair was permed every twelve weeks, set every Friday in the hairdressing establishment situated on the top floor of the store in which she worked. She planned her holidays a year in advance and always went somewhere fashionable, even if it meant having to stint herself in other directions. She drove a small car which she changed every six years, and before sitting in the driving seat she swapped her high-heeled court shoes for a pair of flat brogues.

It went without saying, Clare thought now, as she got out a saucepan to boil a couple of eggs, that her mother kept a special box in the dive of her car with small change in it for car-park fees, and always knew to the last penny what money she had in her bank account.

I don't know why I sneer at her for being neat and

organised, which is really very laudable, Clare told herself as she broke eggs for herself and Sally into the poacher. Perhaps it's because I'm so different. Mother would never have forgotten the fish and chips, she would have dealt with them first, then Tish, then Richard. Only of course she would never have owned a dog to start with, let alone an incontinent, over-excitable beast like Tish, even now whining dolefully from the living-room and attacking the door with sharp, impatient claws.

'What on earth . . .?'

Sally's voice brought Clare back to her surroundings and sent Mrs Flower over to the back door, a greeting on her lips.

'Sally, my dear! Mother had a little accident with your supper . . . all my fault for coming in unexpectedly I dare say . . . but she's poaching you some eggs this very minute and I'm about to make the toast to go underneath them.'

'Hello, Granny Flower,' Sally said without too much warmth. 'I didn't know you were coming over this evening.'

'Really, Sally!' Mrs Flower's finely arched brows rose. 'Do I have to announce myself before I visit you? A fine thing, and you my one and only grandchild!'

'No, but you usually do,' Sally pointed out. She came into the kitchen, hung her wet anorak up by the door, and glanced around her. 'Where's Tish?'

'Oh, in the living-room. Could you let her out now, love? Richard was here and for some reason Tish decided she didn't care for him, but I'm sure she'll be all right now it's just family.'

'Yes, and you can feed her, dear,' Mrs Flower said firmly. 'Mother was just saying Tish was starving, that's why she made such a noise and a fuss.' She laughed, the artificial titter which Clare privately stigmatised as her Duchess laugh. 'I wonder if Richard thought she'd eat him, in lieu of dog biscuits?'

Mother and daughter laughed dutifully and Sally went over to the pantry and got out a tin of dog food whilst her grandmother put sliced bread under the grill and Clare tipped the boiled eggs out into cups.

Presently, the three of them sat down at the table. Tish, her

163

eyes wide with astonishment, had accepted and eaten her second meal in half an hour with no apparent diminishment of her usual appetite and now she sat demurely, paws together, tail out straight, by Clare's side and fixed the poached eggs on toast with a hopeful and greedy eye.

Mrs Flower, meanwhile, was coming round to the reason for her visit. She commented on the weather, the likelihood of Wimbledon week being rained off, the state of business in the store. And then she turned to her daughter.

'And what about you, Clare dear? You've joined the working world, I believe. How is your little business going?'

'The caff, do you mean? I wouldn't have described it as my little business at all, really, I'm just an employee.'

'Well, Clare, since you haven't seen fit to mention it to me I'm in no position to pick my words, am I?' The smile which accompanied what Mrs Flower plainly thought of as a damning statement was sugar-sweet. Coals of fire, except that they have no heat, Clare thought wryly. 'News gets round, though – a friend popped in and said she thought it was you but couldn't be sure – said you were in the kitchen at the back and she only caught a glimpse.'

'I haven't said anything in case I didn't like it and decided to leave,' Clare explained. 'But I love it, and I've no intention of leaving, so I'd have told you when we next met.'

'Would you? Well, well, since I know . . .' Mrs Flower took a mouthful of egg. 'I might come in on Monday, we're quiet on a Monday. Just to take a look at the place, you know.'

'You won't like it,' Clare said at once. 'It's very small and rather . . .' She did not want to say 'common', which was what Mrs Flower would call it, but could not think of a suitable alternative.

'Now don't make my judgements for me, please,' her mother said decisively. She sprinkled salt into her egg. 'As a matter of fact I'm impressed. It's about time you did something other than bring Sally up, I'm very much in favour.'

Clare's astonishment was such that her mouth fell open,

but she hastily filled it with poached egg and swallowed before she spoke, to give herself more time.

'You are? Jolly good. Sally, be a love and pour the tea, it's brewed for quite long enough.'

After Mrs Flower had left, with promises to come into the caff on Monday and bring either her friend Mrs Samuels or her current escort, Clare could not think of him as her mother's man-friend, she and Sally stared at each other before finally succumbing to unworthy amusement.

'Can you see your grandmother sharing a table with the pigman or the old lady who drinks her tea out of the saucer?' Clare gasped presently, recovering a little. 'She's so fastidious, and she thinks plastic tables are really grotty.'

'She wouldn't if she had to clean down each night,' Sally said, grinning at her mother. 'I wonder what she'll think of Mavis, though? She'll probably offer her lessons in how to apply make-up!'

'I don't know, I think she's mellowing with age,' Clare said, starting to wash up. 'At one time, young Sally, she'd have swept in, forbidden me to do such a menial job, reminded me of the money she'd spent on my education, made me cry, and swept out again.'

'It isn't only her, then,' Sally remarked. 'Perhaps as she's mellowing you're un-mellowing. At any rate, she hasn't made you cry for ages!'

Clare made some non-committal reply but Sally's words caused her to think. She was quite right; Mrs Flower did not have the power to wound that she had once had and nor, it seemed to Clare, did she worry so much about what others were thinking.

It's having a job, she concluded, piling the last of the cutlery into the drying rack and turning away from the sink. It's being responsible for the running of the caff and the people who work there. It's doing me good!

As she was climbing into bed that night she realised that she had scarcely given Clive, and his reaction to her job, a thought all day. Nor had she begun to dread an evening spent entertaining a strange American. Nor was she agonising over

165

her mother's promised – or should it be threatened? – trip to the caff.

If I'm un-mellowing, then it's a good thing, she concluded, shrugging the sheet up over her shoulders. Perhaps it's time I tried to be a bit more like my mother, instead of expending all my energy on being different from her.

It was a totally new thought, and it occupied her until she slept.

CHAPTER 8

After all her heart-searchings Mavis finally caught a coach, because with the money she saved she could take her grandsons out somewhere a bit nicer than she would otherwise have been able to afford. And the coach journey was all right, anyway. Relaxing. She sat quite near the front so's she could watch the driver, and a real lady sat next to her. She and Mavis got on fine. Mavis told her all about the caff – it was scarcely her fault, she told herself, if she had, quite inadvertently, sounded like the proprietor – and the real lady told Mavis all about the cafe-cum-gift shop she ran out at Beccles, with afternoon teas a speciality and the gifts all of the home-made, hand-turned, artistic sort.

The coach stopped twice despite having a dear little toilet compartment in the back, which Mavis thought was a good thing. As she said to her new friend, it was not everyone who could perform in a bucking, swaying coach roaring down a motorway at eighty miles an hour. My insides like a bit of stability, she said, and the tea-shop lady said she quite agreed, and wasn't it nice to see the countryside looking so green after all the recent rain?

At the first stop they had a rather gritty but otherwise much-needed cup of coffee and in Mavis's case an Eccles cake, in her companion's, a French fancy with pink icing. They went into the gift shop and had a good look at what was on offer, and then the tea-shop lady said it was a lot of trash and not to be mentioned in the same breath as her handmade lace and cottage pottery. Mavis agreed, hastily withdrawing her hand which had been hovering covetously over a really quite nice mock-tapestry dressing-table set which would have done for Sondra as a thanks-for-having-me gift on leaving. Still, there would doubtless be opportunities during the course of the long weekend. Just because I'm her mother, Mavis reminded herself, that doesn't mean I can take Sondra for granted. A little gift is always appreciated.

At the second stop the tea-shop lady said she felt a snack wouldn't come amiss so she and Mavis headed not just for the snack bar but for something called 'The Eaterie', where they paid an exorbitant sum for a gravy pie, a handful of gólden chips made out of pressed potato and a few suspiciously green peas. It was now Mavis's turn to inform her companion that she wouldn't have given the stuff house-room at her caff, not she!

'Our chips is real spud,' she said impressively, 'and our steak and kidney pies is crammed with meat.'

The tea-shop lady, who had been tucking in with a will, pushed the rest of her chips to one side and agreed it was certainly not value for money. Then they both had a big slice of chocolate fudge cake – a proprietary brand, Mavis said – and washed the food down with a pot of tea each. Mavis eyed the bar thoughtfully – The Eaterie was licensed – but decided not to suggest a little nip to keep the cold out, especially as the coach-driver kept looking in at the doorway in a suggestive manner.

The journey was the slow one and took getting on for five hours, but what did it matter when you were on holiday, as Mavis said to her companion, and the tea-shop lady agreed completely. She was not really on holiday though, as she was quick to point out; she was staying with her sister for a few days and doing some buying for her shop.

'Well, I could say the same,' Mavis hastened to assure her, 'since there's things you can get in London – flavourings, foreign stuff – which I'll be buying in the course of me stay and taking back for my girls to use.'

By the time they reached Victoria they were in good charity with one another. The tea-shop lady would be going back to Norwich on the eleven-thirty on Tuesday; when would Mavis be travelling?

Mavis had wondered whether to get the flyer rather than this slower coach, for all it was pricier. But as the tea-shop lady pointed out, if you took the slow you could consider it all part of your hol . . . your trip, and as it was cheaper the money for a meal was not difficult to find. Besides, the tea-shop lady said, I can show you a few of the things I've bought, and you can tell me what business you've done; it'll make the journey pass in a flash.

The coach drew in to its stop and the two women got off, having agreed to catch the eleven-thirty and to sit together. Mavis watched the tea-shop lady, who was thin and bespectacled, approach the taxi rank, take a look at the size of the queue and head, instead, for the underground station. Mavis walked slowly over to the end of the queue, stood in it until she was sure her erstwhile companion had disappeared into the bowels of the tube system, and then crossed the road and waited for a bus to Earls Court. No point in a taxi when you know your way fine by bus, she was telling herself as she lugged her case past the driver, pushing her money into his hand and telling him that she wanted a stop two earlier than she did so's to save the extra money another stage would have cost. Anyway, Sondra might meet the bus . . . or she might not, since she had no idea which one her mother would be catching, but even so, why waste money on taxis?

Although in her heart Mavis did not have the slightest expectation that her bus would be met, she was wrong. It drew in to the stop, Mavis got off, struggling with her suitcase, and had it whipped from her hand with enough speed to make her give a startled 'Hi!', but it was only her grandsons. Rupert had got her case and Desmond was clutching at the handle and trying to help with its weight and both boys were beaming proudly at her.

'Hello, Nan! We've met two buses and no luck and then there you were!' Desmond's small, plain face was split by a gigantic grin, his eyelids creased with it. 'Mum said we could, it's quite all right.'

'You're good boys,' Mavis said. 'Isn't that case too heavy for you, though, Rupe? I can manage it you know.'

'You can't, you're not as strong as me,' Rupert said indignantly. 'Women are the weaker sex, my teacher says.'

'Okay chick, you take the case and I'll foller on behind.' Mavis dropped back and Desmond abandoned his attempt to help and dropped back too, putting his grubby little hand into his grandmother's. 'Me and Des will keep each other company,' Mavis added, raising her voice. 'But you're to say if the case gets you down, Rupe . . . understand?'

Rupert nodded impatiently but continued to stride lop-sidedly ahead so Mavis concentrated on Desmond.

'Well, me lad? Had a good day at school, have you?'

'Not bad, Nan. Me teacher, she give me a star for readin'. She likes me, I can tell. She let me clean the board, yesterday.'

'That's nice.'

Mavis was feeling tired now though, and anticipating her arrival at Sondra's with real pleasure. A sit-down, a cuppa, and then a nice long chat. You couldn't have better than that.

'Yes. Tomorrer's not school though, is it?'

'No, not tomorrow. Tomorrow I go to see your Grandad.'

'That's right. Can I go wiv you, Nan? Aw, go on, say I can . . . Grandad 'ud like to see me, I can tell ya.'

'No, son, not tomorrow. Tomorrow's for me and Grandad, your Mum and you can visit anytime. I only get a chance every now and then, otherwise it's letters.'

'Well, we can't go each and every week, Mum says. But once a monf, we can go once a monf. Only she takes Rupert usually, I has to stay at home wiv Auntie Flo from round the corner.'

By this time though, they had reached the house. It had a tiny patch of dog-abused grass in front of it but no hedge or wall. Once, there had been a hedge but acid rain or neglect had reduced it to nothing years before. Still, it was a house, not a flat, and that was something to be pleased about up here, with property such a price. Rupert stood the case down and reached up to the knocker; he was red in the face but smiling after his suitcase-carrying feat. Sondra came to the door, kissed her mother, took the case and they all trooped in after her, Mavis even following her upstairs, though her legs – particularly the left one – objected pretty strongly to such unnecessary exercise. Her legs would much have preferred to take her through into the living-room, to the couch opposite the brand-new colour telly she had glimpsed through the half-open door. Then they could have hoisted themselves up on a level with the rest of her and the blood in her vein could have slowed down a bit, instead of pumping and aching the way it was doing now. Still. She wanted a word with Sondra whilst the kids were jockeying for position down by the set.

'Sondra, love . . . when did you last get to see Father?' Lionel had always insisted on being called Father rather than Dad, it showed more respect he said, but Mavis loved being a Mum and would have been very hurt had Sondra showed such respect to her.

'Must be a month,' Sondra said. She reached the spare room and turned to face her mother.

She was a sight for sore eyes, Mavis thought fondly, smiling at her. Shoulder length blonde hair, light eyelashes spiky with black mascara and blusher adding emphasis to the smooth oval of her face, she wore a slim-fit pair of dark-blue jeans and a pink, clingy top with a scoop neckline which showed off her creamy skin. Before her marriage Sondra had modelled for photographers and even now she sometimes sat for artists and others. Mavis thought her the most beautiful woman alive and even Lionel agreed she was a little cracker. Which made it all the odder, really, that she'd married that Vincent . . . nasty little pimp, Mavis thought viciously now . . . with all her chances.

Still, Vincent had gone long since and Sondra managed pretty well without him. She had fellers from time to time, Mavis was not stupid enough to imagine a beauty like Sondra would be celibate, but they none of them treated her bad, not like Vincent had. They spent money, took the boys about, paid for things . . . and then disappeared when she'd had enough of them. Despite her own long and happy marriage to Lionel, Mavis could see that Sondra had men taped and admitted her single-mindedness with regard to the opposite sex. She would have preferred to see Sondra happily married to a good bloke, but since she didn't seem to meet the man of her dreams, her own way with the fellers was best. 'Love and leave 'em' that seemed to be her motto, and 'only love 'em if they can afford you'. It wouldn't do in Norwich, Mavis told her sometimes, you'd get a bad name down Norwich. But up here, where nobody seemed to know anybody else, why not?

Now, however, Mavis could not help a little frown creasing her brow, even whilst contemplating Sondra's breathless beauty. Sondra and her father had always been close, like as two peas in a pod in many ways, so why had Sondra not visited him for a month?

The answer was not far to seek.

'Look, Mum, I know what you're thinking, but Father goes on so! He wants Rupert to be something he just ain't, and when we go, and he sees the poor lad can't improve, he gets very low and depressed, which ain't no more good for him than it is for Rupe and me. See?'

'I know,' Mavis said gloomily. 'He just can't see as how a lad with Rupert's looks can't have that extra something. I've told him over an' over to let the lad be, but . . . well, you know Father. I'll have another word with him, you leave it to me.'

'Thanks, Mum,' Sondra said gratefully. 'What's more, I've got a new feller – you'll like him if you get to meet him. He's different from the others; steadier, more reliable. But he likes me to be here, weekends, and I've not said anything about Father yet.'

The spare room was a very pink sort of room. Now Mavis, looking narrowly at her daughter, was at a loss to decide whether she was blushing or merely reflecting; for the pink walls, the deep-rose curtains and the fuchsia of the bedspread were all powerful colours. What was more, Sondra did not stint her blusher.

'Like 'im, do you?' she asked shrewdly. 'Want to make a good impression? So you've kept away from Father lately?'

'No! You know it ain't that! I'm dead fond of Father, always have been. But we haven't known Russell very long . . . oh Mum, try to understand! If Father didn't nag about Rupert, if I didn't feel all the time as if it was my fault the lad's no good at the game, I'd go more often. You talk to 'im.'

'I shall. Come on, dearie, I'm gasping for a cuppa, let's go down to the boys. And don't worry about Father; I'll have a word. Come to that, why don't you take Dessie when you goes? Father just says Desmond'll be a vet when he grows up, acos of the way he likes animals, so there'd be no harm in that.'

'Well, perhaps you're right. I take Rupert because Des is easier to leave with people. Flo's real fond of him and he talks just like a little old man when he's with her, but Rupert's more difficult, more of a handful, like.'

As they talked, the two women had descended the narrow stairs and now they crossed the dark hall and went into the kitchen. It was a bright, practical little room this, with a backdoor leading out to a tiny cobbled yard. The kitchen, all done out in yellow and white, always had Mavis sighing with envy and today was no exception. Her daughter had acquired from somewhere a number of brilliant posters and these, Blu-tacked to the walls, gave it a touch of what Mavis decided was class. She stood stock still in the doorway, regarding the room admiringly.

'Them posters! They raise the tone no end, Sondra. Where d'you get 'em?'

'Oh, Russell give 'em to me.' Mavis knew her daughter well enough to recognise unerringly the pride behind Sondra's laconic utterance. She went into the kitchen and closer to the poster nearest her. A brilliant view of a tropical paradise, the sky and sea bluer than seemed possible, the sand whiter, the figures browner. There was no doubt about it, Russell had laid his hands on some good stuff.

'He did? Hmm . . . wonder if he could get a couple for me, eh?' Mavis pointed at the one over the fridge. 'That's real nice . . . artistic.'

'Yeah, well, that's Russell that is – artistic, I mean.'

'What's he do, then? For a living, like.'

'Oh, all sorts. He's in the travel business, that's how he got the posters; works as a courier sometimes. He's got quite a business in photography, too . . . does a lovely wedding album, Russell. He paints, too. Not lavs and windowsills I don't mean; pictures!'

'An artist is 'e?' Mavis's interest flagged, then started up again on a recollection. 'Did you say he was a courier? Ain't that just another word for a spy?'

'Oh, Mum!' Sondra had put the kettle on; now she began to make the tea and to fish out from a cupboard a tin of biscuits and what looked like a Battenburg cake. Mavis was extremely fond of marzipan. Just like Sondra to lay in my favourite, she thought affectionately. There was no doubt about it, Sondra was a good girl.

'Well, if he isn't a spy, what is a courier, exactly?'

'I dunno, something to do with the travel business; he goes off to Paris and that, picks hotels for the firm . . . speaks lovely French he does, and Spanish, a bit of Eye-tie . . . there isn't much Russell can't do.'

'Sounds a bit of all right,' Mavis said, keeping her secret fears that her daughter's latest was both a big'ead and a ponce to herself for once.

The sort of feller Sondra favoured didn't usually paint pictures or talk French, quite the opposite in fact. Sondra usually went for wealthy businessmen, what Lionel called the 'successful nouveau-riche', or for fellers who were lucky on the dogs or the horses, bookies, smart-alecs, fast movers. Still. Russell sounded all right. Mavis would see what Lionel thought and perhaps she'd have a word with young Des, whose head was screwed on all right even if he wasn't particularly handsome nor particularly fetching. She had noticed more than once that young Des could pick a wrong'un. Still. Didn't do to make snap judgements and this Russell certainly seemed to be making Sondra happy. You never knew, Mr Right could come in all sorts of guises and from what Sondra said he must be quite well heeled, which was always a help to oil the wheels of romance.

'Yeah, Russell's special,' Sondra was saying dreamily now, cutting into the cake. 'This is 'is favourite cake . . . like a bit, Mum?'

Mavis stiffened. So the cake had been bought not for herself but for Russell, had it? Then she relaxed. What did it matter, after all? Sondra had bought the cake for love, that was what mattered. She helped herself to the biggest piece.

'My love!'

'Oh, dearest, how I've missed you!'

It was not easy flying into someone's arms with a third party always present, especially when the third party, uniformed and correct, did not take his eyes off of you for the first ten or fifteen minutes. The warder thought, presumably, that if a woman of her age hugged a man it was merely in order to pass him a file or some fags . . . little does he know, Mavis thought, giving the screw her coldest and most malignant glance. Us old 'uns have a lot of good tunes yet to play on our fiddles.

The thought had come out confused, but Mavis's own feelings were crystal clear. She sat down opposite Lionel and looked at him long, hard and lovingly, since the look would have to last for possibly as long as six weeks until her next visit. He was much his old self but a bit thinner and the fine, sandy-blond hair which covered his head in thick, boyish curls and waves was looking more blond than sandy . . . there was a considerable quantity of white in it now, Mavis saw. Out of clink, Lionel would soon have dealt with that – white hair was becoming, he informed her but pepper and salt hair was repelling so until his hair turned completely white it behoved him to keep it brazenly gold.

Not that it mattered much where he was, but the day would come, and it was coming closer with every hour that passed, when he would be released into the world once more and then, even if he had decided to retire, he would need a little job for the sake of their old age and that would mean a good appearance. But Lionel was returning her long look, his own eyes fond as always, his mouth curving into a reminiscent smile.

'Mave, my little sweetheart, you're lovelier than ever. You didn't bring the lad?'

'Who, Rupert? No, dearest, nor yet Des. I told 'em they can come any week, but I'm only able to come once in six and that means when I do come I want Grandad all to myself.

175

They understood . . . though Des did remind me Sondra hardly ever brings him, which I'm bound to admit don't seem fair.'

'No, perhaps not. But Des is a good little chap and easy; the neighbours don't mind keeping an eye, whereas Rupert . . . well, he's a lively one.' Lionel smiled again and nodded his head judiciously. 'Aye, a lively one, that's my Rupert.'

'That's as maybe.' Mavis felt mean to speak sharply, but she must keep her promise to Sondra. 'Look, love, Sondra feels bad about not coming to see you more, but worse about coming, because of the way you treats Rupert. You expect too much, love, the lad's only eight, he's got no natural apti . . . no apter . . . he ain't no good at the game, so why can't you accept it, eh, and let things rest?'

'I can't believe a grandson of mine . . .' Lionel began, and got promptly jumped on.

'Ho, now that's a lot of rubbish, dearest, because you know full well our Sondra never took after neither of us and we didn't care a jot, did we? You want the lads to be themselves, not just like us. So forget Rupert, will you? Just concentrate on the fact that you were top of your trade, don't yearn for Rupert to go one better, because he won't . . . can't, if we're honest. Promise now? Eh?'

'Oh, well . . . if that's why Sondra hasn't visited, I suppose you're right – as usual, dear heart – and I'd better leave it alone. Though personally I thought it was this Russell who kept her from me.'

'Yes, Russell. What do you think of 'im from the sound, Li?'

'From the sound, quite highly, my dear. She's not told him about me yet, but if he loves her half as much as she loves him, my present misfortunes won't tell against me. Now enough of them . . . tell me about the caff, your new boss, the cats . . . tell me all the things you hinted at in your letters.'

Mavis stuck her elbows on the table, half-closed her eyes and began to talk. By a certain amount of gabbling she managed to recount almost all of her life for the past six weeks before the warder called 'time' and parted them. Lionel drank it all in, too. He asked after Cheepy, recommended that she get Clare to give her some recipes so that she, Mavis, might practise cooking them against his own return and told her that she should certainly go off for a week or so with young Deirdre and have a bit of a holiday.

'Why not? It's not much holiday for you in Earls Court with our Sondra besotted over a new young man and the boys too young for long journeys,' he said a trifle gloomily. 'Next year . . . but that's a long time off. This year you get whatever pleasure you can on your own, and write me all about it.'

'I wouldn't go abroad,' Mavis assured him, anxious that he should not think she would enjoy a holiday without him too much. 'But just down Yarmouth for a few days . . . I'd like that and it'ud be company for Dee. I've got a bit put by,' she added, in case he might think she would dream of using their savings. But this, apparently, was the last thing on Lionel's mind.

'Dear one, you're welcome to spend as much as you like,' he said earnestly, though lowering his voice as the screw's eyes swung round to their part of the room. 'We've always been savers, the pair of us; when I come out we'll be spenders, I think . . . why not? We've reached years of discretion, I'd say, wouldn't you?'

'We certainly have,' Mavis agreed fervently. 'Now tell me, Li, what do you think about Clare and Coffee an' Book? Does a man know when a woman's . . . available? She's a good girl, Clare, I don't think she knows she's putting out them signals I told you about. Should I warn her? That man of hers, he's kept from her, just like you my love . . . it doesn't seem right that she should get involved with anyone else.'

'Nor it does, nor it is,' Lionel said earnestly. 'But don't interfere, dear heart, because one is never thanked for it. I should know, indeed I should, for when I've been tempted to drop a word, keep a friend out of trouble, that's when my best schemes have turned round and bit the hand that thought of 'em, so to speak.'

'I'll remember,' Mavis said.

The screw came towards them, starting to say, in a falsely jolly voice, that all good things must come to an end, so Mavis grabbed hold of Lionel, gave him a big squeeze and then headed for the door. The tears in her eyes threatened to run over and cry in front of a prison warder she would not, so she stayed, facing the door, until she heard the other door, the one which led back to the cells, click shut behind her. Then she turned, looked through the veil of tears at the now empty room, and then, with dignity she told herself, left with the other visitors.

Lionel, back in his cell, lay on his bed and contemplated the ceiling, but his mind was full to bursting with all that Mavis had told him and he knew he would spend several happy days thinking about the richness of the life his beloved was leading and their eventual reunion.

He wondered about the girl, Clare, though. Poor creature, her man imprisoned, as he was, and God knew for what offence against the State or the Powers that Be! Probably the poor fellow fell from grace more by carelessness and the vice of others than any wrong in his own nature, as I did, Lionel told himself.

Was it not a strange coincidence though, his musings went on, that Mavis and the girl Clare should find themselves working in the same small caff, with more in common than they had dreamed – both with a man doing 'porridge', as the saying went. Still, they could support each other in their hours of need. Better that than some stuck-up bitch who would look down on Mavis because of his own position. Not that he would care to be in the shoes of anyone who looked down on his lady-wife. No fear, no sirree! Lionel could just see her, feathers ruffling, eyes cold, if anyone dared to consider her the worse for being married to an inmate of Her Majesty's Prison, or indeed to pity her for her plight. You had to hand it to Mavis, she was a strong-willed and passionate woman; just as much a little cracker as her daughter.

Thinking of Sondra turned his thoughts naturally to her new boyfriend. Lionel just hoped this Russell was good enough for his one-and-only, because Sondra deserved the best just as Mavis did. But there's only one me, Lionel thought humorously, so Sondra must do the best she can. And if I get out and find Russell's leading her a dance it'll be the worse for him, he added to himself. Prison introduces you to some violent men and even if you never become violent yourself you certainly know where to find someone to do your violence for you!

Mavis had a marvellous weekend. She took the boys to the zoo and young Desmond was so charming to one of the keeper's wives who happened to be visiting that day that she prevailed on her husband to let Des go into a closed house whilst the inmates were fed. Mavis, with a thousand horror movies behind her, did trust that the animals were not about to be fed on Grandson. But all too soon Des was darting out of the door with touching descriptions of being allowed to hand bananas to baby monkey and of being given two free tickets for next weekend, besides an invitation to visit the keeper's wife at home whenever he was in the vicinity.

She took the boys and Sondra out to lunch in the West End and they went all round the Swiss Centre. Desmond was so impressed by the marvellously creamy chocolate that he went and congratulated the lady behing the counter and was given a tiny nest of sugared almonds, all with babies' faces delicately drawn in icing on each nut, lying in a nest made of Swiss chocolate. He told the lady earnestly that it was far too beautiful to eat whereupon she bestowed a bar of chocolate on him as well. Desmond and Rupert had polished both babies, nest and chocolate off before they had gone six yards from the place, but Mavis and Sondra agreed that no matter how plain Desmond might be, people certainly took to him.

It was the same wherever they went. People would exclaim over Rupert's good looks but there was something in Desmond's monkey face, his gappy grin, his horrendous hair which stuck up where it should lie down and lay down where it should curl, that attracted people and Desmond, perhaps realising in the way a child will that he was not pretty, reacted by being genuinely friendly and genuinely interested in whatever was at hand. Rupert was often bored, Desmond never. Rupert could be both rude and disobliging when his own interests were at stake, Desmond could not bring himself to upset anyone, not even when they deserved it.

After three days' close association with her grandsons Mavis had to admit to herself, although she would have died rather than admit it to anyone else, that Desmond was rapidly becoming her favourite. After four days, Mavis decided that she might as well own up to her feelings if challenged, since Rupert was high favourite with Lionel and even seemed to have an edge over Desmond with Sondra. Not that Sondra did not adore both boys, but she did rely on Rupert, him being fourteen months the older and more liable to sympathise with Sondra's problems.

Unfortunately, Russell was away in France, so she never actually clapped eyes on her daughter's paragon lover, but Sondra assured her that if she definitely contemplated taking Russell on full-time, she would bring him down to Norwich to be looked-over and approved.

'Because you will approve, Mum,' she said earnestly, as she and the boys stood at Victoria, seeing her off. 'You couldn't not – he's so gentle and loving, so generous . . . he loves the boys already . . . well, I just know you'll love him like we do.'

Mavis sniffed but she was, nevertheless, touched. If this feller meant so much to Sondra she would simply have to like him, whether she did or not. She was trying to say so without actually putting it into words when she saw the tea-shop lady waving to her, and the coach was getting full so she gave Sondra a hug, kissed the boys, and climbed aboard.

'I love you, Nan,' Desmond roared. 'Give Cheepy a cuddle for us! Give Dee a big kiss! Tell Clare we fink she's a great cook!'

Mavis was so amused by this that she turned back for a moment to tease her little grandson.

'Dessie, love, you've never even met Clare, let alone tasted her cooking so how can you say she's a great cook?'

Desmond looked genuinely puzzled.

'But don't she like to hear people say she's a great cook, Nan?' he asked, his simian forehead wrinkling into a deep frown. 'I fought she'd like to be told that!'

Mavis reassured him and got back on the coach. She sat beside the tea-shop lady and they exchanged experiences and the tea-shop lady said that she'd taken a rare fancy to the tiny boy . . . not the pretty one, delightful though he was, but to the tiny one . . . and what a pity she'd not had time for a few words. But there was a sample in her bag . . . she fished it out and held it in the palm of her hand . . . which would have been the very thing for him, and perhaps Mavis might like to pass it on?

Mavis looked at the little carving in the tea-shop lady's fingers. It was a tiny monkey carved out of some dark grained, reddish wood. Even as she was taking it, thanking her friend, remarking that it was a lovely thing, probably far too good for a child only she knew Desmond would value it, a most extraordinary thought went through her mind. Lionel had once said that in his game, caring was really important and the chaps who thought it wasn't were real fools and would never make the grade.

'You've got to be genuine,' he had assured Mavis, his whole being radiating genuineness. 'You've got to mean what you say, believe every word even if you know in your heart that it's not exactly the whole truth. You've got to be able to pull 'em all in . . . and you've got to pull yourself in too, Mave, my love, otherwise you won't ever hit the big time.'

She had tried hard to understand and had succeeded, at least in part.

'You mean you've got to be a man what owns the Tower o' London?' she asked at last. 'Like an actor say, or a fillum star? You've got to pretend so hard it's real?'

'That's it, that's it exactly,' Lionel had encouraged. 'By God, we'll make a con-artist out of you yet, girl!'

So was it possible that for all Lionel said it was important, looks and appearance did not really matter all that much? If so, was it equally possible that Lionel had been making a bad mistake all along, when he had only considered Rupert as his heir and successor? Had they all been wrong? Was it plain little Desmond who was destined for greatness? When he had been sending his message to Clare he had wanted to please her and had used the very words, if the truth were known, to do just that, though he had only instinct to guide him.

Instinct. That was half the battle, Lionel said. The instinct which tells you unerringly who will believe what – who wants to believe what. And if you ask me, Mavis thought jubilantly, Desmond's got that instinct rooted in him. He don't need to have it cultivated and he don't need to be taught; if all Lionel told me about the game is true, it's Desmond who's the natural!

The thought of telling Lionel and hearing his incredulous disbelief turn first to realisation and then to unbounded joy kept her happy all the way home in the coach, even when she was forced to admit to her tea-shop friend that she had been so busy enjoying the company of her daughter and grandsons that she had quite neglected to visit a single delicatessen!

CHAPTER
9

On Monday it was Clare who got in early, opened up, let the cats out and fed the breakfasters because, though Lizzie Treece might be as capable as Mrs P thought her or as careless as Mavis implied, she, Clare, was still in charge and must make up her own mind.

Accordingly she woke Sally at seven, reminded her that she was catching the bus, put a pile of small change on her bedside table and ran down to the kitchen. She enjoyed the drive in even more than usual; early sunshine which would undoubtedly later turn to rain cheered her, the emptiness of the roads meant that she could exceed the speed limit without fear of being copped or of hurting someone, and she felt her cup of happiness was full when she drove onto the park opposite the caff to find the kiosk still shuttered and empty. I'm parking free, she said to herself gleefully, which was pretty stupid since she had a season ticket but that happened to be the way she felt. It was like blackberry pie, a pippy and probably wormridden treat, which she always adored because it made her feel self-sufficiency was just round the corner.

Up in the flat, feeding Hodge and Pocket, she found herself thinking of the telephone in the flat's tiny living-room. She seldom used it save for ordering supplies but she could leave the appropriate money by it and just ring home to make sure Sal was getting up. After all, they had both been later to bed than usual the previous evening owing to entertaining Nicholas Bernstein to a meal. It had gone off well, too, she mused, dialling her own number and listening to the rings, counting them, watching, in her mind's eye, Sally getting groggily out of bed, stumbling down the stairs, locating the phone, pushing Tish down . . . Aaargh, she had not let Tish out for a wee since the dog had still been moribund when she tiptoed through the kitchen. What a good thing she was ringing, she could remind Sally of her duty to the dog.

At the sixteenth ring she decided that Sally must be taking Tish out right at this very moment and she would ring back later. At the twentieth ring however, the receiver the other end was lifted, she heard heavy breathing, and then a voice still thick with sleep and sounding resentful to say the least, said, 'Three-five-seven-five . . . 'lo? Zat you, Ma?'

'Yes, it's me, darling. Are you up . . .' she laughed. 'Sorry, silly question, but you'd better get washed and dressed and so on now, or you won't have time to take Tish out for a run round the orchard before you catch your bus.'

'Oh, right. G'night.'

'No, Sal, not goodnight, you're getting up, remember!'

There was a long pause before Sally's voice, sounding much more alert, said, 'Yes, of course. Get down, Tish! Okay Mum, I'm awake. I'll get ready right away . . . what's the time?'

Clare glanced at her watch.

'Seven-forty . . . heavens, I must go love, but promise me you won't crawl back to bed!'

Sally laughed. 'I promise. See you fourish.'

The two receivers went down and Clare hurried back to the kitchen. Hodge and Pocket were finishing up so she left the door open and went quickly down the stairs and back into the caff. She turned the coffee machine on and then boiled some milk. She then had to stop for a moment to release Hodge and Pocket, who were sitting miaowing by the back door, but after that it was all go. At eight, when she rushed across the room and flung open the door, there was a small queue of truckies on the doorstep, all good-tempered and jocular.

'Here's a nice change,' the first chap in said, narrowing his eyes against the smoke from a cigarette apparently glued to the corner of his lower lip. 'Where's the lady with the frown, then?'

'It's Mavis's day off,' Clare explained, hurrying back to pick up a pad. She returned, pencil at the ready. 'Is it full breakfast?'

'Sure is.' The customer counted laboriously. 'Six, seven, eight . . . that'll be eight with tea and one with coffee. Oh, and one of the eight don't eat tomatoes so frowner usually give him a coupla sausages.'

'I see,' said Clare, uneasily aware of the uselessness of her pad and the general air which pervaded amongst her customers that she would know, presumably by osmosis, all about their likes and dislikes. Still. Eight breakfasts with everything and one without tomatoes wasn't too complicated; she should be able to manage.

'Dee! Bless you, you wonderful girl, you're half an hour early but how glad I am! Can you do the tables near the counter for me? I don't know how Mavis manages as a rule honestly I don't, they've been coming in in droves for the past half-hour . . . I blush to admit I didn't know the full breakfast included two rounds of toast . . . we've run out of marmalade and someone complained the marge tasted funny and when I told him it was butter I could see he didn't believe me.' Clare stared in a hunted fashion round the untidy kitchen. 'Oh, Lor, we're almost out of sausages . . . how does Mavis manage?'

'She never have a crowd in, for a start,' Deirdre said, donning her overall and heading purposefully for the caff. 'What's got into 'em? Look, you cook and I'll serve, we'll get through quicker that way.'

Presently, returning with another order for Clare's smoking frying pan, she was able to enlighten Clare on the sudden increase in breakfasters.

'That's an agricultural machinery show, out Costessey way,' she said, pinning the order on the counter top with a wet milk jug. 'Seems the chaps all brought their stock in, found no one intended to supply 'em with a cheap breakfast,

185

and hightailed it back here. Seems to me we've got a week's customers all in at once.'

'Crumbs . . . I wonder if Mavis knew?' Clare chuckled. 'Not that it matters . . . can you tell 'em when you take the food back that I've run out of sausages but they've got extra bacon and beans instead?'

'Sure. They won't care, so long as they get plenty,' Deirdre said sagely. 'I shouldn't think Mavis knew . . . she would have got in extra sausages I bet.'

'Yes, you're right, I was being uncharitable,' Clare said remorsefully, spooning hot fat over a nest of fried eggs. 'Open a couple of tins of beans would you, Dee?'

In the middle of all this frantic activity Lizzie Treece appeared. She was a plumpish, middle-aged woman with beautifully set grey hair, well-groomed hands, nails covered with dark-red polish and what Clare soon realised was a very good opinion of herself and thus an air of condescension which was difficult to take. She greeted Clare typically.

'Hello! You must be Clare . . . I saw your little car on the park so I guessed you were in early, this morning. Now, what can I do?'

She was wearing a powder-blue linen dress with a wide white belt, and a pair of extremely high-heeled court shoes in a deeper shade of blue. Around her neck was a deep-blue chiffon scarf and diamante earrings shone from her lobes. She looked nicely dressed for a wedding but most unsuitably clad for a day of washing up greasy dishes.

'Well, there's heaps of washing up . . .' Clare began uncertainly. 'But perhaps if you'd just slip Mavis's spare overall on . . .'

'Oh no, my dear! That little overall is so . . . anyway, I've brought my own.' She produced from a blue shopping bag which Clare had not previously noticed what looked like a small but elaborate ball-dress but when she put it on it was indeed an overall of a sort. It had wide frills round the top which went over both shoulders and the front was another frill with a flat piece in the middle. It was white and the most unsuitable garment for washing up in that one could imagine.

'I think you'd be better off in Mavis's,' Clare dared to

comment as Lizzie Treece turned to the sink, but this remark was swept aside.

'Don't you worry, Clare, dear. If I splash my dress what does it matter? I've plenty more. It's different for Mavis of course, poor girl, with her Lionel in that dreadful place, but I'm really only doing this to oblige my old friend. The money's neither here nor there.'

'But you try underpaying her by so much as a penny and she'll be on you like a ton of bricks,' Deirdre muttered under cover of the customers' badinage as she and Clare cleared tables and carried through last cups of tea. 'In't she awful, Clare? Such airs . . . and don't you let her make so much as a slice of toast, do she'll burn it. Not that you'd believe it to hear her talk – she offered to do your job you know, only Mrs P had more sense.'

As the day wore on, Clare began to miss Mavis more and more. Her sharp tongue was as nothing compared with Lizzie's, only Lizzie did all her digging under the guise of friendly interest which was, somehow, very much worse.

Lizzie did not come in as Mavis would have done and say caustically, 'Bloody 'ell, chuck that burn't muck away gal, and I'll toast you fresh.'

She said, 'Have we had a little accident? Ah well, if you've had my experience . . . but then you're doing your best I'm sure, Clare. I daresay the customers will understand . . . after all, you are new to it, allowances have to be made . . .', and so on and so forth until long after the event, so that it seemed to Clare that a gentle but perpetual monologue of constant criticism was to be her lot.

'You just close your ears to it,' Deirdre advised, when the two of them were seeking respite in the caff itself. 'That's what I do, when she's in.'

But Clare decided that she would have to show her mettle, otherwise Lizzie would simply ride roughshod over her. She had already swanned out to the caff and apologised – gratuitously – to an old woman who had been asked to wait five minutes for an omelette whilst Clare and Dee dealt with more straightforward meals.

'She's new,' she hissed at the old woman, who looked

187

justifiably both bewildered and terrified. 'Just a replacement, that's all . . . don't hold it against her, even a little place like this takes some getting used to.'

When Lizzie swanned back, Clare told her crisply that her place was in the kitchen or at the sink, not chatting to the customers. Mrs Treece's smooth cheeks actually went a shade darker. She tossed her head.

'I thought it right to explain,' she said, not troubling to hide her annoyance. 'After all, Clare dear, you've only been here a week or so; I've worked as relief for several years.' She smiled forgivingly. 'So we'll say no more, shall we?'

'We'll say a lot more unless you stay in the kitchen,' Clare said crossly. 'I can't have you undermining my work like that, Mrs Treece. If you're simply reflecting the way you feel I think it might be better if you didn't come in tomorrow. I've a . . . a cousin who would give me a hand with the washing up if I asked her.'

In fact for all her annoying ways, Clare knew very well that Lizzie Treece was as good at her job as she could be, provided she stuck to washing and wiping up. She was fast, she was efficient, and the pans shone after her ministrations just as they did after Mavis's. Deirdre, with the best will in the world, could not do as well even with two hands, with one she was next to useless. So it was a brave thing really to stand up to Lizzie . . . but as it happened, it paid off.

'Clare, my dear, you've only to say the word . . . the last thing I meant to do was to undermine your little position . . . I'll certainly keep my nose to the grindstone if that's how you prefer it. My, I wouldn't let you down by walking out of here even if I wanted to, because that would let down my old friend Mrs P, and I couldn't do that.'

Fortunately, Lizzie finished at four so Deirdre and Clare were able to tell Sally all about the horrors they had suffered when she came in after school. It did them good and as Clare said, Lizzie's reign was already half over since Mavis would be back bright and early on Wednesday morning.

'It just shows,' Clare remarked to Sally as they drove home, 'that getting on together is the most important thing in business. If I'd come here at the beginning and found Lizzie

188

in command over the sink, I wouldn't have lasted ten minutes.'

'You would, Mum,' Sally said stoutly. 'You'd have tamed her. Just remember how difficult you found Mavis, at first. She made you wild several times.'

'Did she? Odd, all I can remember now is how good she was when I made mistakes. I always liked Dee, of course, but she's simply got nicer and nicer and more and more useful. Now that Lizzie . . . I can't imagine liking her if I lived to be a hundred.'

'It's a good thing you won't need to, then,' Sally remarked. 'Because you know Mavis – she hates being away, she might miss something! But what if Mavis and Dee take a week off together? Dee was saying they might go down to Yarmouth for a few days on the razzle.'

'The razzle? Heavens, I can't imagine Dee's razzling and Mavis's coinciding, can you? Anyway, what about Cheepy? Think of the heart-searchings last week.'

It was true that it had taken a lot of persuading for Mavis to hand Cheepy, cage and all, over to Deirdre for her mother's careful kennelling and Clare was sure that Mavis's first words, on Wednesday, would be for her 'boy'. Deirdre had promised to bring him in on the bus with her early in the morning and in the end, because nothing better was suggested, Mavis had gloomily bowed to the inevitable and sent Cheepy into durance vile with many kisses and twitterings. Mavis, it must be said, had provided both the kisses and the twitterings since Cheepy had been stricken dumb by the bus journey and sulked in the back of his cage all day without saying a word to anyone.

'Yes, that's true. Only I suppose we could have him, at a pinch,' Sally said rather gloomily. 'They aren't much trouble, budgerigars, not like blooming great dogs. You should have heard Dee going on today about having to exercise her mum's inmates. You'd have died.'

Clare turned the car in at the gate, drew into the garage, and got out with Sally following suit with great alacrity. She had not said a word about being dropped off at Emma's. Perhaps in view of the fact that the two of them had spent the entire day together on Sunday she felt she could wait an hour or two before flying up to the Carters' place tonight.

'Glad it isn't raining,' Sally said as they let Tish out for her usual run round the back yard. 'We were lucky with the weather last night, as well. Whatever would we have done with Mr Bernstein if it had rained, Mum?'

'He wasn't that difficult, not really,' Clare objected. 'I suppose we'd have taken longer over our coffee and chatted and so on. He's quite a pleasant bloke, didn't you think?'

'Boring, boring,' Sally chanted, opening the back door and suffering herself to be danced over and licked. 'When you told him that the river wasn't too far off I thought you were going to suggest he went and jumped in it, but even showing him round was better than sitting at home trying to find something to say.'

'Hey, he wasn't that bad,' Clare said, walking into the kitchen and going straight over to the Aga to put the kettle on. 'You're right, mind you, the trip out in the car did make conversation easier. Anyway, I felt I'd done my duty by Richard's business, not that I care a jot whether your uncle Richard sinks or swims, incidentally. But he did take me out to dinner.'

'I had more fun at Gran's,' Sally said. 'Mum, what have you planned for supper? Because if it's going to take long, shall I run down to Em's now? There's something I need to tell her.'

'Really? You mean a moment slipped by unrecorded by the two of you yesterday? Oh all right, poppet, if you must, you must. But before you go just check that there's no post, would you?'

The postman delivered through the letter-box in the almost unused front door, so Sally came back with a handful of mail. She put it down on the kitchen table announcing laconically, 'Three for you, one from Dad and one from Dad to me, as well. Shall I read mine now, see if he says anything about your job?'

'No, love, you go up to Em's for half an hour. But don't be late, please, because this evening we really are going to have cauliflower au gratin before the wretched thing goes off. Oh, can you do Tish's dinner before you go? And you could put Greg's saucer on the fridge with his food in it, then all I'll have to do when he comes in is stand it somewhere where he can reach it and Tish can't.'

'Rightyho,' Sally said briskly.

She got the tins out and a pint of milk, then heaved the enormous paper sack of dog biscuits onto the table. Then she opened her letter from Clive, read it whilst making passes at the tins with an opener, and finally shoved it back into its envelope without comment.

Clare meanwhile, opened her own missive. She had written to Clive explaining more or less what Oliver had suggested she explain, and half-hoped, half-feared, that this would be Clive's answer. But it was not. He did not seem to have received her letter, this was just a chatty, friendly note, talking about a party he had attended, the people he had met there and a film he had recently watched at the base cinema. The sting, if such it could be called, was in the tail, right at the end of the letter.

'By the way, I've made some enquiries about coming home with a view to finishing over here,' he wrote. 'Nothing definite yet, but thought I ought to let you know it really is on the cards.'

Sally finished making the dog's dinner, slid the cat's saucer up onto the fridge, and headed for the back door.

'Shan't be more than half an hour, Ma,' she called. 'I'll give Em your love!'

Left alone, Clare began to make a cheese sauce, then changed her mind and cleaned the cauliflower and put it on the stove first. All the while she was saying to herself, 'You're pleased he's really going to come home at last – pleased, do you hear me?' Because of course she was pleased, it was what she had always longed for. So why, for heaven's sake, had her heart dropped like a stone into her sandals when she read that bit of the letter?

Gregory head-butted the door and she opened it for him, watching him streaking over to where his saucer usually stood with amusement, especially when he saw it was missing – not just empty, missing! – and turned to wither her with a glance.

191

'Okay, old boy, it's not far away.'

Clare got it down from the fridge and put it on the ground. Greg crouched over it, a lion over its prey, and Tish, finishing up her own meal, strolled over to him. Greg turned his head and fixed Tish with a steely and threatening eye and Tish sauntered away again, her long tail between her legs. She was totally uninterested in cat food, her rolling eyes seemed to say; and anyway that cat was aggressive!

Clare worked quickly after that, and the meal was on the table by the time Sally reappeared, right down to crunchy French bread and pats of dewy farm butter. Sally came in a bit preoccupied though and sat down without a word, for once. Clare waited a few moments and then asked what had got into her garrulous daughter.

'Who, me? Sorry, I was thinking.' Sally began to eat, slowed, stopped, and turned a worried glance on her mother. 'Mum . . . am I being mean to want to see more of Dee now and then? Is it not fair to Emma? She's been my friend for ever, only Dee terribly wants me to go and stay with her, just for a weekend, and I would actually like to.'

'You would? Well fine darling, but what about Pegs?'

'It's summer, he'll be okay. And anyway it's only for a weekend, I can ride him in the evening if you say I can. Actually, it's this weekend, the one coming.'

'Well I don't see why not, if you can square it with Emma. Suppose you ask Emma if she'll exercise Pegs for you – wouldn't that reconcile her to you going off without her?'

'Mm, perhaps. Thanks anyway, Mum, for not nagging about it. And you'll be all right here without me for the whole weekend? I'll go home with Dee Friday evening, you see, and go straight to school from her place Monday morning. If that's all right.'

'It's fine. Goodness, I might actually go out myself, I could stay with Gran for a couple of days,' Clare said without the slightest intention of doing any such thing but wanting to make it easier for Sally. 'You go off and have fun, love. And then in a week or two, you can ask Dee back here and the three of you can be together.'

'Oh Mum, you are lovely!' Sally jumped up, hugged Clare

192

perilously across the table and sat back down with a bump
'Will that Bernstein chap have gone back to the States by
then?'

'Good Lord, I've no idea – does it matter? Even if he's still
in England he's very unlikely to come here!'

'I suppose not, only I wouldn't want you pestered.' Sally
hesitated, then said with some diffidence, 'Gran said you
were ripe for mischief, whatever that might mean ... I
wouldn't want to leave you to that fat old bore's tender
mercies.'

'Ripe for mischief? Gran's going senile,' Clare said decidedly, feeling rather annoyed. Fancy Gran worrying Sally,
because Sally must have been worried to raise the matter.
Still, whatever Gran had meant by it she most certainly had
not been thinking of fat elderly Americans on the loose in
England for a few days! 'Forget it, Sal, she must have been
teasing you. You aren't worried because of the job, are you?
Did Dad say anything which upset you about me working?'

'No. You can read the letter if you like,' Sally said
disarmingly. 'He talked about coming home for good though
– that 'ud be nice, wouldn't it?'

She did not sound certain. Clare was glad that the thought
of a full-time father was not an immediate cause for rejoicing
with Sally any more than a full-time husband had been for
her. I've made my life on the premise that Clive will be away
for ten months of the year and so has Sal, she found herself
thinking. The new order will cause both of us a certain
amount of trauma before we can accept it.

Somehow, this made her wickedness in not feeling unreser-
vedly pleased at the thought of Clive's imminent return less
blameworthy. Clare finished her meal with a good appetite
and then washed up whilst Sally wiped. Then, in perfect
accord, they went and watched a very silly comedy on the
box, wrote half a letter each to Clive and joined them up with
Sellotape and lots of daft little pictures, just like the old days,
and then went peacefully up to bed.

Mavis came back on Wednesday as arranged and Lizzie
Treece departed whence she had come, though she promised,

archly, that she would be waiting eagerly for Clare's next summons.

'We had a good time, didn't we girls, in the little cafe,' she said gaily, folding her frilly pinny up and putting it into today's bag, which was red leather and expensive. 'Now don't forget, if you're busy I'm always glad to oblige.'

Mavis, clamoured at on Wednesday morning never to go away again leaving them in Lizzie's clutches, smiled grimly, said she had told them so, and promised to think of someone else, come her holidays.

'Even the cats missed you,' Deirdre assured her. 'Pocket wouldn't go out on Monday morning until she was thrown, and Hodge did a dirty on the upstairs landing . . . it's all right, we found it right away and cleaned it up.'

Mavis sniffed.

'Cats don't miss people,' she said, but she smiled as she said it. 'How's my best boy, then? Was he a good little feller, then? Did he talk to Dee in his best little voice?'

'I wasn't there, mostly,' Deirdre pointed out. 'Saturday I spent the day in the city with Sal . . . we had a high old time, didn't we, Clare? . . . and Sunday I was with my mates down the Rec. But Mum said he ate all right, and chattered away to 'er hours together.'

'Well, there you are.' Mavis chittered to Cheepy and the little bird chittered back. 'Now just you be a good boy today and then come this evening we'll go home and you can have something real nice, yes you can!'

'I wonder what a budgerigar considers a treat?' Clare asked Deirdre when Mavis was out the front changing the chalk-board but Deirdre, despite her mother's pet-minding service, did not know and confessed she cared less.

'I never look at the birds,' she admitted. 'Dogs need exercising, so they're different, but parrots and that leave me cold.'

It was a quiet day, a middle-of-the-week day as Wednes-days so often were, and at lunch-time, having snatched a sandwich, Clare decided to go shopping and leave the other two to manage, which they were well able to do.

'I shan't be long, I'll be back well before Sally rolls in,' she said, standing in the doorway with her light coat on and her shopping basket over one arm. 'You'll be okay?'

'Get me some kidneys would you?' Mavis said instead of replying to a question she plainly considered foolish, if not downright insulting. 'I just fancy 'em in a nice sauce with rice.'

'Sure. What about you, Dee?'

Dee shrugged. 'Don't worry about me, Clare, I've got all day Sat'day to get my shopping. You have fun.'

Fun! As if shopping could possibly be fun, Clare told herself, but nevertheless she felt light, airy, with a skip in her step. She went down the hill, past the television studios and into Castle Meadow. From there she dived down the steps into Davey Place and headed for the open-air market. It was odd, she reflected, that what had for years been a rare treat – a trip to the market – should now be the natural place for her to shop.

It was easy to get Mavis's kidneys at a butchery stall, but once she had got them it was a case of wander, poke, pick, purchase – the sort of shopping, on reflection, that she most enjoyed. She bought a string of garlic cloves to hang in the kitchen, two lemons, mainly because they were so big and fat and juicy, a couple of grapefruit for the same unworthy reason and then more ordinary things. Tomatoes, a Webb's lettuce, half a cucumber and some radishes. On another stall which specialised in wholefoods she got spaghetti, some vine leaves for fun, and large bag of Bombay Mix which she and Sally considered a gourmet's delight and which Clive thought disgusting and kept referring to as Indian mouse droppings; this could easily have put her off, except that it was so delicious.

Right at the back of the market was a second-hand bookstall, and that was her next destination. Always greedy for books she bought a wholefood cook book, a cook book which specialised in bread and other dough products, and two whodunnits. By this time her shopping basket was full to overflowing so she accepted the offer of a carrier bag from the stallholder, bought two more books which looked interesting, both straight novels, and turned to leave.

She walked straight into the browser next to her and was in the middle of a mild apology when he straightened, book in hand, and grinned at her.

'Hello, Clare!'

'Oh! It's you!'

'That's right, Oliver Whatsizname . . . Coffee an' Book.' He flourished the volume he was holding under her nose. 'This is where I go first when I come into the city, the next place is your place, for a quiet cup of coffee and a read. You going back now? If so, I might as well walk with you.'

'You'd better pay for that book first,' Clare suggested. 'No, look, I'll go ahead of you, you're still choosing.'

But he shouted to the man behind the counter, threw the money across and then took Clare's basket from her in a very no-nonsense fashion.

'Rubbish, and that looks heavy. I'll carry your books, Miss!'

'The books are in the carrier, and they aren't heavy at all in any sense of the word,' Clare said severely, falling into step beside him and accepting the inevitable. She might not like it but she was about to walk into the caff beside Big Chief Rambo. 'However, my fruit and veg. are heavy and I'm grateful for the loan of your arm, though what the girls will say . . .'

He cocked a quizzical eye at her.

'Do you care? Why should they say anything? If you'd rather I'll give you back the bag fifty yards or so away and you can enter in the singular.'

'That makes it look as though I'm doing something I'm ashamed of,' Clare objected, having thought the matter out. 'No, I'm at liberty to let anyone carry a heavy bag if I want to, so thanks very much you can bring it all the way.'

'Good.'

They crossed the walk companionably, then went back to the caff the way Clare had come, only a good deal slower since it was now uphill and they were burdened with shopping.

'Have you written to your husband yet?' Oliver asked, as

they passed the television studio. 'Or more to the point, has he written back?'

'Yes to the first and no to the second. Or rather he has written back, but he did so before receiving my letter, which doesn't count. But actually, the whole thing may have done a great deal of good, since he's now talking about coming home for good.'

'Really? Soon?'

'He didn't say, but I imagine he'll probably finish the year. He did mention Christmas . . . but that's a good way off. No, I shouldn't think he'll come back this summer for instance. You see he came back for two months earlier, April and May, so he really isn't due even for normal leave this quickly.'

'Well, you'll have plenty of time to get used to the idea, then,' Oliver said. He took her elbow and steered her across Cattle Market Street right opposite the caff and Clare saw, with resignation though not with surprise, that Deirdre and Mavis were both standing behind the counter, staring blankly out. Oh, well.

They entered the caff, Oliver ushering her inside first. Once in, she took her bag back, smiled her thanks and headed for the kitchen. Oliver, on the other hand, went straight to his usual table, but this time, instead of immersing himself in his book, he spoke to Deirdre and Mavis.

'Good afternoon, ladies. I think I'll break with tradition today and have buttered toast for two and my usual cup of coffee.'

'Oh? And who's your friend? The invisible man?' Deirdre asked, tossing her head and looking at Oliver out of the corner of her eye.

Clare, watching through the open kitchen door as she took off her coat and put on her overall, could not prevent herself from smiling. He was a charmer all right, when he put his mind to it . . . Mavis was smiling down at the coffee machine as she manipulated it, Deirdre was smiling at Oliver as she laughed at his reply. But before she had time to wonder what had been said Deirdre came into the kitchen, still with a smile on her face, and picked up the thick-cut loaf.

'Rambo wants toast for two; he says he's hungry. And then he said if one of us would share it with him, he'd have toast for four! He's a card, in't he, Clare?'

'He's certainly coming out of his shell; I didn't know he ever talked when he came in,' Clare said, less than truthfully. But Deirdre took the remark at its face value.

'Oh yes, sometimes he does. I'm going to ask him what sort of waggon he drives.'

'Yes, why not?' Clare made a dive for the oven and examined the contents. 'Dee, my love, when did this quiche go in? It looks . . .'

'Oh my Gawd!' Deirdre exclaimed, snatching up a tea-towel and pulling the dark-brown quiche out of the oven. 'Oh damn, it must have been in an hour or more. I'm that sorry, Clare . . . I clean forgot it what with Mavis telling me about her weekend and all. Wonder if any of it's okay . . . say I skim off the top?'

'You can take it home for your tea, but we can't sell it to customers,' Clare said regretfully. All those eggs, all that bacon, to say nothing of the mushrooms, red peppers and onion which had gone into the creation of the quiche. 'I'll have to charge you a bit, love, but only cost of course. And you'd better make another . . . sorry, I know it's a bore but Thursdays can be quite busy.'

'Yes, of course.' Dee turned to put the quiche on a working surface and Clare had to dive across to the grill to rescue the toast before that followed the example of the quiche. However, it was perfectly all right, brown but not buggered she thought thankfully, so she just buttered it, put it on a plate and handed it to Deirdre.

'Don't you want to take it through? As a sort of thank you for him carrying your bag?' Deirdre asked. Clare laughed but shook her head.

'I don't think it's necessary really, Dee . . . besides, he might expect to get it free and I wouldn't do that! You take it, there's a dear. I'll start the pastry for the quiche case.'

It took quite a lot of resolution, actually, not to return to the caff just for a moment. There were so many things she wanted to say to Oliver, including asking him a question or

198

two about his trip to the Bretts'. But it behoved her not to get too friendly with the customers, especially the younger and more attractive ones.

At four o'clock Sally came in, full of stories about a rounders match in which the unworthy Pamela Forbes had been run out and knocked flying by First Post, but she spared a good few glances and giggles for Oliver, now sitting quietly in his corner reading his book, eating his toast and occasionally sipping his coffee. Clare wondered whether he intended to stay there until they closed so that he could have a word with her and resolved to work late and to get Sally a meal in the caff to save going home and cooking, but when she went into the caff later on with sausage and chips for a customer, the corner table was empty. Coffee and Book had gone.

'He left me a fifty pence piece!' Deirdre said, as she saw Clare's eyes go to the table in the corner. 'Fancy that, for tea and toast!'

'Who did?' Clare said involuntarily, and Deirdre sighed and rolled her eyes in a manner which would have been downright rude had Sally done it. 'Oh, you mean Ol . . . the chap Sal and I call Big Chief! That was nice of him.'

'Yes . . . but I wouldn't call him old anything,' Deirdre objected, having obviously misunderstood Clare's slip. 'He's even better close to than from a distance, and when he smiles . . .'

'Oh, yeah? I thought Quack was the only man you cared about,' Sally said tauntingly. 'Gee whizz, Spooner, you're so fickle!'

'That I in't! But Quack's not here,' Deirdre said, rather flushed. 'Anyway, I like Rambo the way I like film stars; Quack's real.'

'Yes, I get that,' Sally said. She accompanied them into the kitchen and picked up a tea-towel. Mavis was at the sink, getting through the washing up at a great rate. She glanced up as they came in, then continued to work briskly, a slight frown on her forehead.

'Are you okay, Mavis?' Clare said. 'Would you like me to have a go at the sink for a bit?'

Mavis, however, shook her head.

199

'That's all right, Clare, I'm fine. But to tell the truth I'd like to leave a few minutes early, if that's all right by you. I don't fancy taking Cheepy home on the usual bus, that gets so crowded you wouldn't believe. Would it be all right?'

'Tell you what, if you don't mind hanging on whilst I lock up and put the cats away, I'll run you home. Probably that would be easier for Cheepy and for you as well.'

'It 'ud be great, if you wouldn't mind,' Mavis said at once. 'Thanks ever so.'

So another evening did not follow the usual pattern. Clare and Sally bustled round whilst Mavis cleaned down, they put the cats upstairs and filled the trays, they set out the ingredients for breakfasts so that Mavis could lay hands on them easily next morning. Then the three of them — for Deirdre had caught her earlier bus long since — set off for the Mini and for Mavis's home.

Mavis sat in front in the passenger seat, her handbag clutched on her knee, her feet, in honour of getting a lift, still in her old scuffies.

'I'll have to remember to put 'em in me bag tomorrer,' she said as Claire drew up outside her house. 'Come in for a mo, will you? I'll get you a cuppa.'

But Clare said regretfully that they were late already, bade Mavis take care of herself, and let out the clutch. Whether she had half-expected to see Oliver lurking in the car-park or not she could not have said, but no one followed the Mini out through the city and no one picked her up once she hit the road home.

I don't want the chap following me around, Clare told herself unconvincingly as she put the car in the garage and headed across the yard. Heaven knows life is complicated enough at the moment without that! But the evening seemed oddly flat and she even found herself regretting that Nicholas Bernstein had gone away and that Richard and Rachel never visited.

That thought brought her up with a jerk. But you hate Richard and you don't have much time for Rachel either, she reminded herself. What on earth's got into you, Clare Arnold? Don't say you're lonely! But she knew that she was.

When Sally went blithely off to Emma's for an hour or so after their meal she could have screamed. She actually went to the phone and rang Gran, just to hear her voice, and then she decided to write to Selina. After all, what harm could there be in a friendly letter? But she knew, as she put pen to paper, that she would suggest a meeting, and she was certain, in her heart, that Selina would jump at the chance.

After all, she reasoned as she began to write, with Clive really coming home for good, if he was, her whole life was going to change. For some reason which he had not attempted to explain properly he had stopped her going to see Selina eighteen months ago; when he was home for good he would undoubtedly scotch any attempt on her part to see her old friend again. So now, right now, might well be her only chance.

As soon as the letter was finished she sealed it into an envelope, put a first-class stamp on it and slipped it into her bag.

As she did so she was struck for the first time by the change in herself. How long ago was it that she had written to Clive, in fear and trembling, and then not dared to post it herself? It seemed like a lifetime but it was probably not much more than a couple of weeks. Now, for no reason that she could fathom she was preparing to defy him again, go directly against his expressed wishes . . . what was the matter with her, for God's sake? How could she behave like this all of a sudden? You could not blame Clive for being surprised . . . but he had better get used to it, she decided, suddenly defiant. Quiet, meek little Clare had disappeared at last whilst she had need of a firmer and more resolute will for her job. Clive should be glad that she was happy, mixing more, giving more to life as well as taking more.

But somehow, she had her doubts as to Clive's gladness. It would be tempered with unease, she was sure.

Nevertheless, she knew she would post the letter.

Clive had opened Clare's second letter with trepidation; suppose he was right? Suppose she simply refused to give up the job? But it was nothing so straightforward, as he realised after a second perusal of the letter.

She was so calm all of a sudden, so bloody reasonable! Her first letter had been a nervous, contradictory explanation full of half-finished sentences and wild attempts at self-justification, but the second was quite different. She set out plainly and simply her reasons for taking the job in the first place, then she told him equally simply how good it was for her, making her take control, giving her natural flair for cooking a chance to be appreciated. Then she assured him that, should he decide to return home for good, she would of course hand in her notice immediately though she could not, as he would be the first to understand, let Mrs Parnell down by simply leaving before she had found someone else to take her place.

She ended as sensibly as she had begun, by saying that she loved the job right now but might easily find it grew boring as she became used to it – if so, she would hand in her notice. On the other hand her employer only intended staying in Scotland until the autumn so it was quite on the cards that when September arrived she might find herself only working a four or even a two or three day week. In those circumstances he must see that she would still be very much a full-time wife and mother and a very part-time worker. She supposed that he would be quite happy with this?

Clive sighed and laid the letter down on the table. He was in his own tiny apartment, eating what was supposed to be his favourite English breakfast of cereal, toast and marmalade and coffee. Only the milk was dried and the butter tinned, which took the edge off it, somehow. And now the letter, propped up against the marmalade pot, was turning the morning sour before it had properly begun. Clare was right in a way, he could see that now. She had only taken the job to see whether she could do it, and whether she liked it. If she found herself competent and enjoyed it as well, who was he to lay down the law and demand her immediate resignation?

A much longer description of the caff had helped, too. It seemed the staff were all female and the customers, from what he could gather, were either young toughs on motor bikes or farm labourers or young wives with schoolchildren on their hands. Sally's letter had made it even clearer; she had told him about her friend Dee, one of Clare's waitresses, and about various customers. She talked about the pleasure of being allowed to help to serve, and of how Mum was teaching the girls to make all her nicest cakes . . . She never even implied that Mum was not around when she needed her, nor that Mum was even slightly interested in any sort of social life either apart from or connected with her new job.

Clive picked up a round of toast and buttered it thoughtfully, then took a bite. The trouble was, having made his wild statement about giving up the job and going home for good, he was not at all sure that he wanted to do it. True, they had bought their house, paid for Clare's car and had a good deal of money in the bank, but they were still both fairly young and he had no intention of lowering his standard of living, far less that of his wife and daughter. It was all very well to talk vaguely about getting a 'small job' but that would mean getting a small salary as well. His enquiries so far had been dismaying to say the least; if he went home, he would take a cut in salary not merely of a few hundred pounds a year but many thousands. And what was worse, from what they had been able to tell him at Head Office, jobs for his particular speciality in Great Britain were hard to find and fiercely contested for if you did find them.

'Most of the chaps work until they're say, fifty, and then they can afford to do part-time work or they've enough capital to start a small business of their own,' the executive who advised him had said. 'Of course, you may be the thrifty type – do you have enough saved to start up in an advisory capacity, for instance? Or a family business? Some fellows farm . . . buy small hotels . . .'

Clive said ruefully that he had never given the matter much thought. He had assumed he would get a job easily, being a practical sort of chap. The executive, smiling, had not quite. managed to hide his obvious feeling that for a practical chap, Clive had acted in a highly impractical way and Clive was forced to give his adviser best. He had not been sufficiently interested, when it came down to it, to apply his mind to exploring job prospects in Great Britain, he had simply thought of himself as a rare commodity in the market place, and as such had assumed that rare meant precious.

Clive tipped the coffee pot into his cup and frowned as a mere trickle emerged, then got up and went over to the cooker to make a fresh supply. Coffee helped him to think. If he had not known Clare's style and writing so well, he would have thought someone had helped her to compose her letter to him. As it was she must have talked it over with Gran, or perhaps with a neighbour or someone from work, and that had helped her to get her ideas sorted out and put her case properly. So perhaps he ought to do the same?

Oh, not over the wretched job, she had quite cut the ground from under his feet by her swift promise to give it up should he return home for good. But it might be a good idea to have a chat to Della about going back home, see what she thought. Having come out so recently – she had only been in the Kingdom six months – she should have a much clearer idea about the job possibilities for engineers than he himself had. As for Mr Brownlow, it was pretty clear he had no desire to lose yet another of his best workers and one way of keeping men in Saud was impressing on them the impossibility of getting work back in England.

Someone rattled on the door. Clive shouted 'Come in!' and hastily slopped coffee into his cup and drank it on his way across the room. Simon opened the door six inches and said, 'Ready?' and Clive, still swallowing, nodded and grabbed his folder. The two of them made their way out into the comparative freshness of the morning.

CHAPTER
10

When the telephone rang Clare was in the middle of filling the washing machine, a pile of dirty clothing at her feet, more in her hand, and water hissing into the tub. Cursing, she dumped everything on the floor and ran into the living-room, putting out her hand to the receiver just as the bell hesitated and stopped.

It is useless to pick up the receiver and speak into it in such circumstances and equally useless to hurl it back onto its rest as a punishment for dumb insolence, but Clare did both. Equally foolishly she hung around straightening the rug, feeling the earth in the plant pots and waiting for it to ring again. It remained silent. There was no sound until she was once more immersed in the task of sorting the light wash from the medium and dropping the garments into the filling tub. Then the shrill note rang out. Parkinson's law. This time, however, Clare was ready for it. She tossed washing willy-nilly into the suds and set off at an Olympic sprint for the living-room.

'Hello?' she panted. 'Oh, I mean three-five-seven-five . . . hello?'

A warm chuckle greeted this display of panic.

'Dear Clare, I couldn't mistake you for anyone else in the world; thanks for your letter, or should I say for your novella? It was long enough for printing, I'm sure.'

'Selina!' Clare gasped breathlessly. 'How lovely to hear your voice! Was it you just now when I didn't quite make it?'

'Who else? I thought perhaps you were still at work so I rang off, then I checked with your letter and had a second try.'

'Gosh, it's lovely to talk to you . . . why didn't I think of ringing you?'

'Possibly because you don't have my number,' Selina said practically. 'Look, love, I gather you aren't averse to a meeting any more, or rather that it was not you but your lord and master who thought it unwise to rake up the past. Do you still feel that you'd like to meet? Because if so, how would you like a visitor for the weekend?'

'Lina, I'd love it. I'd have to leave you alone all Saturday though, or could you come on Sunday? I'm hoping to take Mondays off in future to give myself a proper break.'

'Sunday would suit me fine but would you mind if I came on Saturday and spent the night? With the removal of the entire Bothwell clan from the area I don't have a Norfolk base any more, otherwise, believe me, I'd never have let our beautiful friendship dwindle to a few letters at Christmas and birthdays.'

'Of course you can come Saturday, or even Friday! Sally will take care of you whilst I'm working, she's a good kid . . . oh, I almost forgot, my dauntless daughter's weekending with a friend. Still, you won't lack things to do, knowing you. Care to give a hand in the caff? I could do with another adult person in there, good though the Saturday girls are.'

'In that case I'll come Friday evening, and go home late on Monday,' Selina said. 'One thing — I gather from what you said in your letter that Clive's thinking of coming home for good — you and he haven't quarrelled or anything, have you? I don't mind if you want to weep on my shoulder, I just like to be prepared.'

'We don't see one another often enough to quarrel much,' Clare confessed. 'He didn't approve of my taking the job but I think he's come to terms with it. If you're wondering why I wrote properly, instead of just standard-type keeping in touch letters, it's because I rather resented him telling me not to go and visit you in London, and also more or less telling

206

me not to invite you back here. Not that he ever forbade me, of course, he just made it plain he'd rather I didn't.'

'Hmm. Well, let's not waste time now trying to catch up, we'll do all that at the weekend. Will Sal be home on Monday?'

'Goodness, yes; Sunday evening, possibly, if she knows you're going to be here. You haven't seen her since she was tiny, have you?'

'I saw her at the Openshaw wedding when she was eleven; that was the last time,' Selina said. 'She is my god-daughter, so if Clive objects you can tell him I was making sure she was being brought up in the way of God. Will you be a darling and meet my train? I'll catch the one that gets in at half-six, so you can come straight from your beloved caff and we can have a meal out at my expense, somewhere really nice.'

'Oh Lina, I shan't know how to wait . . . not for the meal, just to see you again, and natter,' Clare said honestly. 'When I think about the last fifteen years I wonder how on earth I existed! Perhaps you ought to wear a pink carnation in your buttonhole, otherwise I might not recognise you!'

They laughed, then Selina said, 'Till Friday then, poppet,' and put the receiver down. Clare followed suit and walked slowly back to the kitchen.

Selina was actually coming for a whole weekend . . . a long weekend, furthermore! They would be able to talk as they had not done for fifteen years, or rather as Clare had not done for fifteen years. Selina, living in London, doing an important and interesting job, must have found plenty of friends who could take Clare's place.

It had been different for Clare. She had always been shy, rather unsure. Shopping, taking Sally to and from school, going to parent-teacher meetings, she had still never tried to make a close friend amongst the women she met. She had never cared for whist drives or bridge fours, and because Clive was away so much she had never gone to parties or dances save for family ones.

Selina had been married two and a half times . . . the half was when she had merely lived with a fellow . . . and she had borne no children, so naturally her life had been crammed with the sort of opportunities which had been denied to Clare.

Clare was fishing the finished clothing out of the machine when the back door banged open and Sally and Tish barged in. Naturally it had been raining heavily so they brought quite a lot of mud in with them as well as a lovely smell of wet grass and dripping clothes and coat. Sally started talking as soon as the door opened, temporarily preventing Clare from telling her own good news about Selina but when she did manage to get it out Sally was gratifyingly pleased, though not for quite the reason which Clare had imagined.

'Selina, coming here? Oh, that's absolutely great, Mum, because then you won't mind if I go home with Dee Friday evening and go straight to school from hers on Monday morning. It'll save an awful lot of to-ing and fro-ing and it means Dee and I will have three whole evenings to talk in.'

'You must see Selina before she goes home, though,' Clare said firmly. 'She's your godmother, love, and she's not set eyes on you since you were ten or something.'

'Eleven, actually; at that posh wedding where I drank champagne,' Sally reminded her. 'Well, all right, if I must I'll come home Sunday night then, only you'll have to call for me, the buses on a Sunday are awful.'

'I'll bring Lina over with me.' Clare was hanging as much washing as she could get in her drying cabinet. The kitchen felt stuffy as a result and humid from the damp, but beggars couldn't be choosers; there was no other way to get the washing dry until the rain let up and it didn't look as if it ever intended to stop again. 'I take it you did your homework at Em's, and also explained about the weekend?'

'Mm hmm, sort of. All right if I go to bed now, Mum? I'm knackered.'

'Gracious, yes, look at the time!' Clare bundled the rest of her washing onto the wooden slats and went over to bolt the back door. 'I'll come up with you; thank heaven Mavis is back and I don't have to start until nine!'

It was a couple of days before Mrs Flower actually kept her promise – or had it been a threat? – to go into the caff, and when she did so she was rather disappointed in the size of the place and the obvious inferiority of its customers. However, she had no wish to quarrel with Clare because she had sensed, the last couple of times that she had been with her daughter, that Clare was no longer quite as easy as she had once been. Not as caring, Mrs Flower pondered ruefully, making her way, under her smart navy and red umbrella, down across Bank Plain.

She had kept Clare polite, respectful and amenable towards her for most of her adult life largely by not seeing too much of her and by insisting on her daughter at least respecting Mrs Flower's own high standards whilst in her company. Strangely enough though, she found herself almost preferring this new, self-confident Clare to the meek little creature who had always done as she was told.

Of course, Clare had not always done as Mrs Flower wished, but she had been adept at appearing as an obedient daughter and that had been sufficient, taking into account their not very close relationship and the fact that Clive was both a good son-in-law and a slightly dictatorial husband.

So now, in the caff, she had kept her criticisms to herself. To be sure she had advised Clare to wear something other than the pink and white gingham overall, so that a customer could see at a glance who was the manageress and who the cleaner. But when Clare had said, quietly, that the customers seemed to have few doubts and that perhaps it was better, with such a small staff and in such a small place, not to stress differences, she had been forced to see the sense of it.

The rain pattered on the umbrella and Mrs Flower tap-tappeted along the pavement, neatly skirting puddles and apologising when her umbrella nearly decapitated a handsome young man, striding along in the opposite direction, rain-beads glinting in his dark hair. Now that she was old . . . more mature . . . she could admit an attraction in the opposite sex to which she had been blind for many years. Ever since her honeymoon, in fact, when the startling and brutish behaviour of her chosen partner had caused her to ban him from her bed . . . too late, as the subsequent arrival of Clare had proved.

Since then she had never seriously considered a liaison with any man. After all, Edward Flower had seemed a pleasant enough person and look what he had done! But now she had actually caught herself thinking, a couple of times, that it would be pleasant to have someone else to chat to occasionally in her spotless home. Nice, perhaps, to share things. A trip abroad, a candlelit dinner, an excursion to London to see the shops and watch a show.

Then there was Grosvenor. He wanted marriage, which was out of the question, quite impossible, but she could see no reason why she should not share her home with him on a purely business basis. Or perhaps a purely platonic basis was what she meant. At any rate he could pay his half of the household expenses, have his own bedroom, come and go as he pleased just like a lodger. Only they would be . . . friends.

She had hinted at it already and Grosvenor had seemed to take the point. She had no desire to spell it out for him – so embarrassing – but even less desire to find herself struggling with an amorous lodger some dark night, so obviously she would have to make her position very clear before she and he got down to the practicalities of sharing a house.

Mrs Flower turned left, paused at a zebra crossing until the traffic had slowed and stopped, then stepped out briskly, knowing that she would get back into the store just in time to shed her wet things, touch up her lipstick and return to her position behind the counter, if she kept up a good pace. Her second in command, Milly O'Donnell, was engaged to be married and consequently had her head in the clouds half the time and was no longer the tower of strength that she had been.

It was not as if Milly were a young girl, either, Mrs Flower told herself, aggrieved, as she hurried along the pedestrianised precinct which led through to her place of work. Milly was in her late thirties, old enough to know better. All that sex business would come as an awful shock to her, Mrs Flower was sure. She had tried to warn the poor creature without actually saying too much – not easy – but Milly, about to give her all to the rabbit-like Tod Napier in the sports department, had just tossed her head, giggled, and assured

210

Mrs Flower that she knew what it was all about and simply couldn't wait!

How different from myself, Mrs Flower had mourned, looking back down thirty-odd long years to that other person, Anne Forsyth, who had thought marriage would be 'nice'. She had known nothing of what was about to happen to her, had been totally unprepared for it, unlike the young of today, who seemed to spend their teenage years practising what poor little Anne Forsyth that-was had not even preached. Her mother had told her nothing, or perhaps that was being a little unfair since she distinctly remembered Gran trying twice to tell her about marriage. On both occasions she had been sharp, terrified that her freely-spoken, indeed outrageous, parent would say something coarse.

If you come right down to it, most of it was Mother's fault, Mrs Flower told herself now, as she entered the store and, looking neither to right nor left, made for the staff changing room. If Mother hadn't gone and given way to that G.I., then I would have respected her, instead of being ashamed of her all the time. And then she wouldn't marry, wouldn't say yes to any of the nice young men who had tried to make an honest woman of her. And it follows that if I hadn't been so ashamed of her, I'd have let her tell me what she kept trying to tell me – that marriage was . . . well . . . intimate. If I'd known, perhaps I wouldn't have been so upset by it all, wouldn't have made a fool of myself that first morning in the hotel, wouldn't have told Edward he must sleep in a separate room. And of course if you carried this to its logical conclusion, Mrs Flower's thoughts continued, perhaps Edward and I would have been together still, living in loving harmony, and I wouldn't even have to give Grosvenor a thought.

But she had never seen Edward again after that disastrous honeymoon, and by and large she had been glad of it. He had sent money for the first few years and she had spent it on her home and on the child. But then he must have grown tired of continually giving and never receiving, for the cheques had stopped coming and she had quite philosophically accepted that she was unlikely to see him again.

She always referred to herself as a widow and probably she was; Edward had gone to outlandish places, followed outlandish careers. She reckoned she was entitled to widowhood, as entitled as Clare was to consider her father dead if she considered him at all, which was unlikely. Mrs Flower had never mentioned him, had let her own Mother tell any wild story she liked to the young Clare. It was only now, because she was contemplating sharing her house with Grosvenor, that she had begun to wonder, just a tiny bit, what had happened to Edward.

Brisk and capable, Mrs Flower adjusted her crisp, white blouse with the frill under the chin, made sure it was tucked neatly into the waistband of her navy skirt, reapplied and blotted her lipstick, smoothed her hair with a comb, dusted imaginary dandruff from her shoulders and set off for her counter.

The first honeymoon breakfast! She had been so young, so unsure of herself! It was the breakfast, of course, which had set her so against Edward, had precipitated the row which had caused him to blast out of the hotel.

They had looked at the menu, herself still shaking internally after the ghastly experiences of her wedding night, and she had decided that cornflakes were too noisy to eat with a comparative stranger seated opposite and porridge too slimy. She had chosen prunes. Imprudent girl, she chided herself now with an indulgent smile for her youthful folly. Why on earth had she not considered the stones?

She only considered them, in fact, when she popped a prune into her mouth, chewed and swallowed the flesh, and found herself still in possession of the stone. Hopefully, she looked at Edward. Munching cornflakes – and making a great deal of noise in so doing. Typical. She looked around her. No one else had taken up the offer of prunes. She had been desperate. How on earth did one transfer the stone from one's mouth to the side of the dish without spitting it out? The sheer horrid vulgarity of the action made it out of the question, of course.

So she swallowed it. And the next. And the next. She swallowed every single stone in every single prune, and there were quite a number of them. And then Edward had looked at her plate and had somehow divined what she had done with the stones.

How he had laughed! How he had roared and pointed and dismayed the trembling, scarlet-faced Anne Flower! She could never have forgiven him for that, never, not if they both lived to be a hundred. Change the name but not the letter, change for worse but not for better, someone had chanted at her, when she had been telling them what her new name would be. Superstitious nonsense, she had thought disdainfully. But how true it had proved! Sitting at that table, the prune stones heavy and cold in her stomach, her whole body still sore and shaken from the dreadful things Edward had done to her the previous night, she had known what an awful mistake she had made.

The rest of their week's honeymoon was a disaster, of course. And when they left Edward had driven her back to Norwich more or less in silence, had spent one night in their brand-new little house, and had gone off to the railway station to return to the North of Scotland, where he was working with a big firm building bridges, or roads, or some such thing.

'See you in six weeks,' he had called.

She had never seen him again. Oh, the cheques had come, sometimes even with notes attached in his handwriting, but Edward Flower had never darkened her doorstep from that day to this, had never set eyes on his daughter, never knew he had a granddaughter.

If he was alive – which she doubted – he was probably abroad. She suspected that he was married with a dozen or so children; he must have enjoyed that dreadful business a good deal, she reflected bitterly, to have fought so hard to ravish her on their wedding night. No doubt he had taken a mistress within weeks of leaving her, and had been grunting, heaving and sweating over some other unfortunate woman ever since.

At the time she had been rather proud of her own stiff resistance and her chief feeling when she had realised Clare was pregnant was horror that her daughter, an unmarried girl, a child, had clearly consented to some man's interference. Had probably enjoyed it – done it more than once!

But Clare had behaved well in the end. She had married Clive quite happily, had produced the child without a murmur of complaint, or at least if she had complained Mrs Flower had not heard tell of it, and had brought Sally up with complete dedication to the task.

I was not a good mother, Mrs Flower remembered, tidying her 'Big Girl' brassieres with a shudder of sympathy for any woman so mammarily well-endowed. In fact, a maternal instinct seems to have missed a generation. Her own mother had been over-sexed and over-maternal, and that had resulted in herself being possibly a little short of both counts. Now here was Clare taking after the older generation . . . true, she had only given birth to Sally but it had not been for lack of trying. There had been a distressing series of miscarriages at one time . . . but it was no use dwelling on that. Sally was a happy, lucky little girl and Clare had settled down very well to being almost a one-parent family, and to having an only child.

'Er . . . I wonder if you could possibly . . .?'

Mrs Flower immediately banished all thoughts of a personal nature from her mind and leaned slightly forward over the glass top of her counter. Her face lit with spurious interest, her mouth curved into a practised, deceptive smile. She saw her customer's hesitation give way to confidence. She was a large, untidy looking woman with a bulging, untidy sort of figure. Just the sort of person who needed the Mrs Flowers of this world to set them on the path to corsetted righteousness.

'Can I help you, madam?' Mrs Flower cooed. 'Did I notice you glancing at the "El Cid" range? I think you might find them a little lightweight – for the fuller, deeper figure a trifle more support, even restraint, can be more comfortable, such a help . . . it gives a youthfulness to one's bustline which . . .'

The customer listened, comforted. Mrs Flower, well into her stride, glanced with seeming casualness at the other woman's overflowing, ill-cached breasts and reached, in her

214

mind, for the style of brassieres her unrepentant juniors called the girder-range. Talking constantly, understandingly, she led the way round the counter towards the stacks of waiting lingerie. Another sale was as good as in the bag.

Friday dawned rainy, of course, but to Clare's astonishment and delight the sun came out at noon and stayed out, albeit rather waterily, so that when Sally came in and when she and Dee took their departure, giggling mightily and obviously longing for their coming weekend, it was into an afternoon of pale sunshine with the prospect of the weather actually remaining quite good over the weekend.

'Be good,' Clare shouted after them, rather conscience-stricken over the happy way she had let them go, because had it not been for Lina's arrival in a few hours she would not have felt nearly so light-hearted.

Sally had gone away from home before, but never to stay with someone not related. Still, Dee was a dear, her mother was friendly and very probably not nearly as sloppy and sluttish as she seemed, and a weekend with them would do Sally a power of good. It might even make her appreciate her own well-run and well-furnished home.

Mavis, standing sentimentally by and waving as the two youngsters disappeared, remarked that it reminded her of when Sondra had been no bigger than Sally was now.

'Always gaddin' off she was then,' she said, turning away from the door and giving the nearest table a valedictory wipe. 'If she weren't with some lad it'ud be with her mates, as she called 'em. Always a great one for making friends was our Sondra. I'd come home, some nights, and you couldn't see the kitchen table for gals perched on it.' She sighed, walked through to the kitchen and continued as she ran her cloth under the hot water tap. 'Happy days, eh? Still, I wouldn't change things.'

Not quite knowing how to reply, Clare merely mumbled an agreeing sort of mumble and began drying up. An odd customer or two came in and she dealt with them but it was not until Mavis was in her high-heels and ready to go that the caff door opened and Oliver lounged into the room.

215

'It's Coffee and Book!' Mavis hissed in a penetrating whisper, though Clare had already recognised the shape of him against the sunshine. 'I'll serve 'im, shall I? You don't want to be here alone with him, do you?'

'Oh Mavis, he won't eat me,' Clare said, rather amused. 'And he won't want feeding – well, only toast, or possibly a slice of cake. You go off and get your bus.'

'Oh, I don't mind . . . there's only Cheepy waiting,' Mavis said with unconscious pathos. 'I'll hang around for a bit.'

'Right. Then you take a menu out whilst I finish off here. Is the coffee machine still switched on?'

'Bound to be.'

Mavis seized a menu from the pile by the door and clicked across to the corner table. Clare could hear her greeting Oliver, handing him the menu, repeating his order. Then she reappeared in the doorway.

'Two rounds of toast please, Clare. I'll do the coffee.'

Clare made the toast, buttered it and carried it through just as Mavis was doing the same with a mug of coffee. Oliver thanked them both and then grinned at Clare.

'Sorry I'm late, hope I'm not inconveniencing anyone. I've just delivered a mare to Inverness and coming home I thought I'd pick up some paperbacks and have a snack, so I dropped in. How are you?'

'Fine, thanks,' Clare said. Oliver nodded to the chair opposite his own and hospitably handed her a round of toast. Clare laughed but shook her head. 'How kind you are, but I won't, thanks. I've got quite a bit of cleaning up to do before I can go home, so I'll have to get on.'

'I'll give you a hand when I've eaten this delicious toast and drunk this equally delicious coffee,' Oliver said. Mavis sniffed and he turned to her. 'What's the matter, Mavis? Don't you approve of men in the kitchen?'

'That I don't, not cutomers,' Mavis said. 'You get that lot eaten, then we can all go home.'

'I can't, I'm here for a bit, so there's no need to hurry,' Clare said, earning a dirty look from Mavis who was clearly determined to protect her from Oliver's fairly harmless presence. You could not consider him entirely harmless, she

reflected, when he sat there looking so dangerously attractive.
'Look, Mavis, you're going to miss your next bus as well if
you don't get a move on.'

'On your own head be it,' Mavis muttered. She returned to
the kitchen for her coat then reappeared in the caff, bag in
hand. 'Rightyho. I'm off, then. Goodnight, all. See you
tomorrow, Clare.'

'Thanks very much, Mavis,' Clare responded. 'See you.'

Mavis, however, still lingered.

'Don't forget to put the trays out, upstairs,' she instructed.
'And shut the kitchen door, won't you? I hate finding things,
first thing.'

'Don't worry, I will.'

'And I'll be in first thing, as usual. Want me to give you a
hand with them pots, before I go?'

Oliver bolted one of his two pieces of toast, grabbed his
coffee cup and drained it, then headed for the door. He was
grinning.

'All right, Mavis, you've outlasted me. Shut up shop,
Clare, and thanks for the hospitality. See you!'

The door swung shut behind him. For a moment Clare just
stared, then she turned crossly to Mavis.

'You do know you were terribly rude, I hope, not only to
O . . . Coffee and Book, but to me? You made it look as
though the moment you were out of here he was going to try
to rape me . . . and you made me look as though I wouldn't
have raised a finger to stop him! That isn't on, Mavis. You've
probably lost us a regular customer, do you realise that?'

Mavis, true to form, sniffed.

'Huh! All I did was offer to give an 'and with them pots.
Any road, you don't want to be left alone with a customer
like 'im, do you? As for losing 'im, what's a coffee and toast
once a week, eh? And I didn't do nothing to put 'im off,
anyway. Only looking out for your interests, I was.'

'Well, don't do it again.' Clare said, trying to sound severe
and not succeeding very well in the face of Mavis's obvious
indifference. 'I dare say you're right and he didn't mind what
you said. He probably had to go anyway.'

'That's right,' Mavis said, obviously only half listening. She

217

picked up her shopping bag and opened the door, then stood in the doorway for a moment. 'Huh; gone, has he? Why's his waggon still there, then?'

'He's probably gone into the city for something,' Clare said rather crossly. 'Or he's sorting out the horse in the back. I don't know. See you tomorrow, Mavis.'

'Huh, gone into the city? At this time o' night? Oh all right, all right, I'm just leaving.' She went off, her back very straight, her nose in the air, and Clare returned to her tasks about the caff. She was just about to go through and lock the door so that she could see to the cats when the door was pushed open by an impatient hand.

It was against Mrs P's rules to go through and say 'We're shut', she said that if you were shut the door must be locked, so Clare, cursing, picked up a menu and an order pad and went through, devoutly hoping that it was not someone after a full meal. But one glance through the doorway set her mind at rest on that score. It was Oliver.

'Alone at last,' he said as she smiled at him and leaned on the counter. 'Where's my toast?'

'In the bin. Whatever did you go off for?'

'If I hadn't your poor old Mavis would have stood there until I did and I didn't want her to miss her bus,' he smiled seraphically at Clare. 'I wouldn't put Mavis out for the world!'

'That was kind,' Clare said sarcastically. 'Do you really want more toast? And another coffee?'

'We-ell . . .' he looked at her quizzically across the counter, walking towards her as he spoke. 'What are your plans for this evening?'

She was startled and showed it.

'My plans? What do you mean?'

'Do you plan to close at five forty-five, or at six . . . half-past? I'm not usually in so late so I've no idea when you normally shut up shop.'

'Oh,' Clare said. She was half relieved and half disappointed that his question had been so innocent; not a proposition at all, in fact, as she had at first thought. 'Well, I'd planned to stay open until six or until the last customer left, and then to stay on for a few minutes as I usually do to settle the cats for the night and so on. You see I'm meeting a friend off the 6.30 from Town, so there isn't much point in going home, I'd have to turn straight round and come back.'

'Well in that case I'll have a round of toast and a coffee, but why don't you lock up whilst I eat it so that you don't get yet more late customers in? It seems sensible. Here, I'll come round the counter and eat in the kitchen, then everyone will think you're properly closed.'

'There's no need for that,' Clare protested, going into the kitchen and turning round, found him at her elbow. 'Hey, I'm not sure our insurance covers kitchen-customers!'

'I'm casual labour,' Oliver said. He went over to the loaf, took a slice and popped it into the toaster. 'I'll make it myself for a small reduction.'

'All right, but I'll make the coffee,' Clare said. 'It'll have to be instant, I'm afraid. I don't want to have to get the machine heated up again and there's no hot milk ready anyway; I've cleaned down the bain.'

'If it's instant, I could just as well make my own,' Oliver informed her, putting another round of bread into the toaster. 'I'll have two, I'm starving. Look, you go up and deal with those cats, won't you? Or are you afraid I'll rifle the till in your absence?'

'I've cashed up,' Clare said, laughing. 'Not that there was much to cash . . . it's the rain, it stops people coming into the city in the morning and when it clears up it's too late. Are you sure you don't mind making your own? I won't charge you.'

'Sure I'm sure.' Oliver was putting coffee into a cup and touching the side of the electric kettle with the backs of his fingers. 'It's already hot, it won't take long.'

Clare hurried up to the flat, put out the cat tray on its newspapers, checked the food, tipped it into two saucers and then hurried down again. Oliver was sitting on the kitchen table, eating toast. He waved a bit at her.

'This is Cordon Bleu toast – want me to make you a bit?'

Clare was starting to refuse when she thought how long it would probably be before she and Selina actually ate, so instead she nodded.

'Please, if you wouldn't mind. I shan't be long.'

She opened the back door and called, at the same time rattling two saucers suggestively together. Hodge appeared first, his green eyes glinting, black fur wickedly immaculate. He was actually a placid, good-natured creature with none of Gregory's dictatorial ways but his total blackness, save for a neat white triangle just below his chin, gave one an impression of a cat sophisticated and suave, devilishly inclined. He advanced purposefully on Clare now, purring loudly, and twined himself lovingly round her ankles whilst the two of them waited for Pocket, who came belting across the yard with no thought of her dignity and skidded to a halt by Clare so that she might miaow fetchingly and stand on tiptoe for a carry up the stairs. She was an affectionate little thing and obviously missed the cuddles which Mrs P had handed out each evening.

'Nice cats,' Oliver said as Clare and her charges passed him and made for the stairs. 'Or should I still say kitten to the tortoiseshell?'

'She's just small, she's about five or six years old I believe,' Clare called over her shoulder, mounting the stairs. 'Mrs Parnell said she had a deprived childhood and never has grown much.'

Oliver's laugh followed her.

It was the work of a moment to feed both cats and put milk out, but then it occurred to Clare that it might be difficult to get rid of Oliver now that he was ensconced in the kitchen with his toast and coffee. Still, she should be able to manage without hurting anyone's feelings – he did know she had a train to meet, after all.

In the event it was no problem. She rejoined him when she'd finished with the cats and shut them in, and ate the round of toast he had made for her. He remained sitting on the table whilst she cleared up and put on her jacket, then he went ahead of her through the caff and held the door open.

'All set? Shall I walk you to the station, ma'am?'

'I'm driving, thanks,' Clare told him. 'See you some time.'

They went over to the park together, then he waved a careless hand and she climbed into the Mini, started the engine and drove off. Her last sight of him was as he stood by the open door of his cab, apparently contemplating the offside wheel which he suddenly seemed to decide he disliked, since he aimed a vicious kick at it. Clare strained her neck to see what he would do next, but the man in the car behind her hooted indignantly and she was forced to face front and continue down the road and by the time she was at the lights and could legitimately glance round again Oliver and his waggon were hidden from view.

Not that it matters what he was doing, Clare reminded herself as she drove down Prince of Wales Road, because he's nothing to me. And any moment now I'll be seeing Selina again!

CHAPTER
11

'Come in, and mind Tish,' Clare said, opening the back door much later that night. 'She's as good as gold really, but she'll be dying for a wee, and she does rather tend to dive out.'

'I didn't know you'd got a dog,' Selina said, as Clare threw open the back door and Tish, yapping frenziedly, darted past them, to squat, tail still wagging, in the middle of the yard. 'I say, she's a big one, isn't she?'

'Red setter,' Clare said. They went into the kitchen, blinking as their eyes tried to accustom themselves to the brilliant strip lighting. 'Well, Lina, that was a marvellous meal and many thanks, but I could still do with a cup of coffee. How about it?'

'Sure thing,' Selina said readily. Immediately at home, she went over to the cooker and picked up the kettle. She glanced round her as she filled it. 'This is a marvellous room – the last time I saw it, it was a bit different, as I recall!'

'Was it? Well, there were quarry tiles I suppose and the walls were cleaner,' Clare said rather vaguely. 'You went to university quite soon after Sally was born, so one way and another you didn't see as much of the house as you might have done, but we've made an awful lot of changes.'

'We?'

Clare laughed. 'Clive may not have done the actual work, but most of the ideas were ours, not just mine, and of course he paid for everything. I just had to put up with the workmen, and choose colours and things like that. Do you want a polite little cup or a rude great mug?'

'Oh a rude mug, definitely.' Selina walked over to the cork board and peered at the photographs. She pointed to the one of herself and Clare on the beach. 'Gracious, fancy you keeping that old thing! What a skinny little rat I was – and you another, I might add.'

'Well, you certainly couldn't be described like that now,' Clare said, eyeing her friend with affectionate approval.

Selina was lovelier than ever, she thought, her golden hair a richer, deeper shade, her sky-blue eyes as clear and bright as ever whilst her waist seemed unaccountably to have got smaller, her long legs more slender, whilst her figure retained every generous curve which had once had her labelled junoesque.

'Nor you.' Selina took the proferred mug of coffee and perched on the edge of the kitchen table to drink it. 'Who was he?'

Clare, startled, stopped in the middle of crossing the kitchen and slopped coffee onto the floor. Tish, entering the room all of a rush, licked it up in passing and went over to make Selina's acquaintance. But though Selina obediently fussed her she still continued to fix Clare with her bright gaze.

'Who was who?'

'Oh come on, Clare, as if you didn't know! Who was the dark chap who followed us into the restaurant, walked past the table, and then went straight out again.'

'Oh, him. He's a customer. Drives a horse-box.'

'Really? What luscious customers you have! What's his name?'

'Selina, you don't know customers by their names, it's not like that at all! The girls call him Coffee and Book, because he always drinks coffee and always reads whilst he's drinking it.'

'Really? What do you call him?'

There was a moment's silence whilst Clare contemplated lying and rejected the idea. She gave a shamefaced giggle.

'Oh damn you, Lina, don't try and make a mountain out of a molehill! His name's Oliver. Oliver Norton.'

'Oliver. Yes, he looks like an Oliver. Do you see much of him?'

Clare put her hands to her hot cheeks. This was ridiculous – and worse, despite her own total innocence she was beginning to feel guilty over Oliver, who had never so much as touched her hand!

'No, I don't. He comes into the caff about once a fortnight and has a coffee, and once ... once, mind you, Lina ... he carried my shopping basket from the market to the caff because it was heavy and he was coming in anyway for a coffee. Satisfied?'

'If I were you I wouldn't be,' Selina said frankly, opening her eyes very wide and grinning wickedly. 'He's a dish! And of course he's after you.'

'After me? You must be crazy, I've told you...'

'My dear girl, didn't you see him at Thorpe Station? I saw you and there he was ... you'd been together, surely?'

'He was at the station? Oh no, Lina, you must be mistaken,' Clare assured her. 'He was in the caff earlier, that's true, but he only had his coffee and then went. Why on earth should he be at the station, unless he was meeting someone as well. Was he? Well, he must have been.'

'He was alone, and he followed us out,' Selina said positively. 'The only reason I noticed him – apart from his looks, of course – was because he was standing just behind you and he didn't take his eyes off you. Even I didn't get much of a look in, and I'm not exactly easy to miss, am I?'

'I can't imagine anyone looking at me if they could look at you,' Clare said honestly. 'You mark my words, you made a mistake, it couldn't have been Oliver on the station.'

'What about Clive? My dear girl, you managed to get Clive right from under my nose ... that was quite a feat for a quiet little thing! Because I thought for ages, you know, that I'd probably marry Clive.'

'Did you? Oh Lina, I thought you'd got bored with him, or that he'd never really meant anything to you,' Clare said, distressed. 'You ... you didn't love him, did you?'

It was Selina's turn to colour and look awkward.

'We shouldn't be talking like this, you've been married to

the guy for fifteen years! I thought I loved him, of course, or I wouldn't . . .'

The sudden breaking off of the sentence, the silence that followed, spoke louder than Selina could possibly have wished. She began to speak, to change the subject, but Clare flapped a hand at her, frowning, trying to cast her mind back.

'Lina? Did you? With Clive?'

'Does it matter? It was all such a long time ago . . . oh dammit, the habit of telling the truth and being frank makes one such a poor liar when you need to be able to lie slickly! Yes, I'm afraid Clive and I did sleep together. I was a little idiot, girls of eighteen frequently are, but I wanted to know what it was like, whether it was as fantastic as men kept telling me it was, and Clive . . . well, he was in a position to gratify my curiosity without anyone being any the wiser, you see.'

'Then you only did it with Clive because you could keep it quiet? You weren't wildly in love with him, or anything like that?'

Selina beat the heel of her hand against her brow and gave Clare a hunted look. She was very pink now.

'I can't believe this! We're discussing me sleeping with your husband as though it was an academic exercise! When you and he got married I tried to steer clear of you because I was afraid you might guess, or ask a question I didn't want to answer and now, fifteen years later, I let a cat out of a bag which, dammit, should have been dead for years!'

'When you slept with him he wasn't my husband, though,' Clare began, then turned and looked straight into Selina's eyes. 'Was he? Lina, you must tell me the truth!'

'What a question! Of course he wasn't your husband, girl, what do you take me for? Look, I'd better tell you the whole story or you'll make up something for yourself and face Clive with it when he next comes home. No, don't shake your head, let me get it off my conscience and then perhaps we can both forget it.'

She told Clare all about it. How she had gone up to London on a course and had met Clive by previous arrangement. How they had booked into a small hotel as man and wife and had, for three nights, consummated their imaginary relationship with increasing pleasure, on her part at least. How, on the fourth evening she had mentioned a big party in the village the following evening and had gone on to tell Clive that she was worried about Clare going to such a party without her.

'I told him you'd been forced to live with your mother again, and were miserable, so had jumped at the chance of a party at the Forbes's place. I even said I was worried that you'd get in with that set because Tracy drank a lot more than the rest of us and had some pretty wild friends. Clive was going back to Scotland the next day – he'd come down for an interview for the job in Saud but even if he got it he had promised to work out three months' notice – and he said he might pop in and see you, then continue on to Scotland and try to get back to London for another couple of days before my course ended.

'Well, anyway, he changed towards me from that time. We'd had a lovely three days, or rather three nights, because my course occupied my days, and I was looking forward to seeing him again before I had to come back to Norwich, but he didn't return. He sent a telegram just saying return impossible see me at home sometime, so I finished my course and then I got that holiday job – do you remember me writing to you about it? – in the design department of a big clothing factory, and when I got back to Norwich again you and Clive were getting married. It was all cut and dried, and of course I'd met Dan in the design department so I wasn't interested in Clive any more, or not in that way. I'm terribly sorry I told you, chick, but remember, Clive was twenty-seven, you couldn't have thought you were his first woman – I certainly wasn't.'

'Don't be sorry, you had a perfect right to sleep with Clive,' Clare said, sipping her coffee and trying to face what her mind was telling her.

Selina never lied; but she had lied tonight. Clare had been looking straight at her when she denied having slept with Clive after his marriage and Clare, who had once known Selina almost as well as she knew herself, had seen the quick recoil, the decision that truth was too painful, and had recognised the humanity which had denied the painful fact. Clive had undoubtedly slept with Selina since their marriage. Had it been often? Was there a lively affair going on? She knew, even as she tried to tell herself that it was her imagination, that she would have to find out.

'Are there any bickies? I'd love one before I go to bed.'

Selina's question was straightforward; also a declaration of intent. She was going to bed, there had been enough questioning for one night. Clare got up, fetched the biscuit tin, then put it on the table beside her friend.

'There you are. Take as many as you like, but there's one thing you must tell me before you go up. Don't lie to me, Lina. Are you still sleeping with Clive now, from time to time?'

'No! Good God, Clare . . .'

'I accept that. Selina, you're a rotten liar, I knew as soon as you said you'd not slept with Clive since we got married that you were just being kind. I care, I'd be a liar too if I told you differently, but Clive's been so good to me, he's accepted Sally completely . . . look, will you just tell me, please? Once I know that'll be that, I'll make myself forget all about it, I swear to you . . . only tell me, don't leave a lie between us.'

There was a long silence. Around them, the kitchen seemed to settle back as if it, too, was waiting to hear the story. Tish sat in front of them, for Clare was perched on the table too now, and eyed the biscuit tin with unashamed lust. Now and then a thin rope of saliva dangled from her jowls, to fall on the floor with a tiny plop. Selina had closed her eyes and now she put her hands up and knuckled them, a childish gesture, then sighed, opened her eyes wide and began to speak.

'All right. All right. Perhaps it's best. Certainly I've never believed in lying about anything important. First though, love, you must accept that it was entirely my fault. From beginning to end Clive was simply drawn into something he didn't understand and couldn't help with . . . or not in any way other than . . . than the way he did help.'

'Did it help? To sleep with my . . . with Clive?'

Selina closed her eyes again. She nodded, her mouth

trembling, and Clare was horrified to see tears squeeze
themselves through her friend's dark gold lashes and trickle
down her cheeks. She would have liked to put her arm round
Selina, comfort her, but it seemed, at his moment, an
unwarrantable intrusion. Instead, she just waited.

'It helped. That was why I got in touch with him ...
because I was so unhappy, so cut-up, I needed someone to
tell me I wasn't ... that bad. It was after Dan walked out on
me.'

Dan Carruthers had been Selina's first husband.

'I see. And did Clive reassure you?'

Clare had not meant to sound cold, but that was the way it
came out. Selina, however, opened her eyes suddenly, threw
back her shoulders and let out her breath in a long whistle.

'Phew! I wish it hadn't happened but yes, he was a great
help. I rang you up – remember? – and told you I'd caught
Dan with another woman. Surely you remember?'

'Yes, of course. And I told you Clive was coming home, I
was meeting him off the 2.35 the following day or I'd have
rushed straight up to London, only he had been a bit difficult
about our friendship and anyway Sally was only four, I hated
leaving her, couldn't really take her ... Oh Lina, I should
have gone to you, you sounded so unhappy and dazed.'

'I was,' Selina said flatly. 'You asked me earlier if I loved
Clive and I said I thought I loved him but as soon as I met
Dan I knew Clive wasn't the man for me. I worshipped the
ground Dan walked on, I adored him. And to find him in our
flat, in our bed, with ... well, it was a blow which knocked
all the breath out of me. We worked in the same design
department too, which meant I couldn't rush in to work and
tell everyone, I couldn't face work at all just then. I'd walked
the streets, pretty well, for twenty-four hours after I'd found
Dan and before I rang you. And then you said Clive was
coming home and I thought at least he'd be someone I could
tell, and I thought he might have gone to the hotel he and I
had used, not for old time's sake or anything like that, but
because he'd said he often went there. So I got a taxi straight
to that hotel.'

She smiled, the tears still standing in her eyes. 'I must have looked a sight, uncombed hair, face blotched with tears, still in the shirt and jeans I'd been wearing two days before, when I'd walked in on Dan. I asked at the desk for Clive and they rang for him and he came down ... he looked tired but excited ... it wasn't until much later that I realised he thought it was you, come to meet him for a surprise. I just sort of fell into his arms and he took me up to his room and I told him all about it.

'It took me hours, I kept bawling, you see, and when I finally got it all out I was so sleepy. You wouldn't believe how sleepy I was, I just wanted to lie down and sleep for ever and never wake up. Clive tucked me up into his bed ... I took off my jeans ... and I fell sound asleep. I woke up after ages, it felt, and squiggled around a bit and found Clive's back and put my arms round his waist ... I felt safe and warm and as if none of it had happened, not Dan, or the woman, or being married. I felt as if I'd turned the clock back five years and Clive and I were both free and sex-starved. Not that he was, you understand, he was simply sound asleep. So I cuddled him and ... well, woke him up.'

She stopped speaking. Clare waited.

'And then he woke,' she prompted, since Selina seemed disinclined to say more. 'And then you and he ...'

'Yes,' Selina said with a snap. 'That's what happened and that's how it happened and I'll swear on the Bible if you like that it never happened again, and never would have happened then if Clive hadn't been three-quarters asleep and easy to ... well, to seduce. I promise you, Clare, that I haven't set eyes on Clive from that day to this, and he hasn't set eyes on me.'

'Or anything else,' Clare said demurely. 'It's all right, Lina, I understand now. Shall we go to bed?'

She slid off the table, opened the tin of biscuits and offered it to her friend. Selina selected a handful, then picked up her almost empty mug.

'Will friendship stretch to another cup of coffee? I'm parched after all that talking.'

'Yes of course, but I think we'd better have hot chocolate, otherwise we won't sleep. And whilst I'm making it, Lina, I'd like to say I'm sorry I forced you to tell ... sorry for you, I mean, because it must have been awful to talk about it. But don't think it'll change things between Clive and me, because it won't.'

Selina looked shrewdly across at Clare as she spooned chocolate into two mugs.

'It won't? My love, I hope you mean that because I'd hate to think that something I did in a moment of despair spoiled one of the best marriages I know.'

'If anything spoils my marriage, it won't be one tiny slip which probably meant no more than saying "there, there," when someone's hurt. But I won't stand by another time and let Clive tell me who I can be friendly with and who I can't. He had no right, Selina, to stop me visiting you for fear I'd find out ... what I have found out.'

'No, you're right there. I didn't realise he disapproved of us continuing to ... oh damn!'

'What's the matter? Here's your drink, can you manage it? Then I'll bring you a cup of tea to wake you up as I'm going to work in the morning.'

'The matter? Clive will find out I've stayed here and ask me if I told,' Selina moaned. 'You said yourself I'm a bad liar ... oh dear oh dear, whatever shall I do?'

'You aren't that bad a liar, it's just that I know you too well,' Clare explained. 'Just open your eyes very wide and let your mouth drop open a tiny bit ... then pause ... then say, "Oh Clive, for goodness sake, what do you think I am?" and he'll never guess the truth.'

'You're a really horrid girl,' Selina said appreciatively, as Clare bade Tish goodnight, turned out the light and closed the kitchen door on the dog's anxious face. 'Fancy more or less teaching me how to lie to a man!'

'Oddly enough, I don't want Clive hurt any more than you do,' Clare said, heading for the stairs. 'What's more, if he knew I knew, whether I cared or not would be beside the point. His sense of guilt would be quite enough to wreck half a dozen marriages, you know it would.' On the upper landing she stood for a moment outside Selina's door to finish off what she was saying. 'Just remember, I know all about guilt; Clive never reproached me for Sally, never once.'

She turned to go into her own room but Selina stopped her, a hand on her arm.

'You've said that before; what on earth do you mean by it?'

'For Goodness sake! Don't you remember the party, and ...' she stopped short, almost unable to believe what she was about to say. 'Lina, don't say you don't know about Sally ... and me and Clive? Don't say you thought what everyone else thought for all these years?'

'Tell me or I'll scream,' Selina threatened, gripping her mug handle with whitened knuckles. 'You are the most annoying creature!'

'I thought you knew ... I tried to tell you once and you cut me off short,' Clare grumbled. 'I went to that party, the one your friend Tracy gave, and I got drunk and someone ... well, someone raped me. I don't know who. Anyway I got pregnant with Sally and Clive was so sorry for the way Mother was bullying me that he asked me to marry him. I never told him I was pregnant because I wasn't sure, not till later, and I never told him then either but he must have known. Sally was born when we'd only been married seven months. Everyone else thought she was Clive's, they didn't think back, you see, but of course Clive wasn't at the party, he was in London, applying for that job in Saudi Arabia, but everyone thought he was in Scotland. So whoever Sal's father was, it wasn't Clive.'

Selina was staring at her. There was a funny look on her face.

'And it never occurred to you to ask Clive? To ask him whether he could possibly have been the father?'

'No, of course not. I told you, he was miles away.'

She looked at Selina. Selina was shaking her head from side to side, a decided negative.

'Oh no he wasn't, pet. Didn't you listen to what I told you? He had been in London with me, but I was nervous for you, sure you were unhappy and afraid you'd get into deeper water than you could cope with at the Forbes's place. So I asked Clive to pop into the party, make sure you were all right. Only I swear to God I thought you knew; I thought he

231

came back and told you and asked you to marry him. I thought ...'

'You thought he was doing the decent thing by me,' Clare said blankly. 'Making an honest woman of me. Which I thought as well, only I thought he was even more decent. A hero, really. I thought he was prepared to accept another man's child as his own. I thought ... I thought ... Lina, you've made a mistake, he couldn't have been in the Forbes's place that night.'

'He was, love. He wrote, you see, after he telegrammed. He said he'd been to the Forbes' place and seen you, he even said you were drunk and that he intended to take care of you from now on. So of course I thought you'd slept together at the party and then decided to get married. It never crossed my mind, love, that he married you because there was a baby coming. People don't know that soon! Was it ... were there several men with you at the party? Is that why ...'

'No. There was just one.' Clare was beginning to shake. She tried to stop herself, tried to think calmly and rationally, but her world was turning upside down and shake she must. 'Just one man. Got into ... bed ... on top of ... me. It c-could have been ... anyone.'

'But love, have you no eyes in your head? Sally's the image of Clive, she was as like him as a child can be to a fellow when I last saw her and I'm told she's still the image.'

'I thought she might be Richard's,' Clare mumbled, her hands gripping the mug so tightly that all the blood had left them. 'Lina, I can't believe it, I can't! He c-couldn't have let me believe it was s-someone else, if it was him, no one could be that cruel! I knew the fellow knew, of course. It was just me ... I lay there and someone did things to me ... and someone could look at me, and think what fun he'd had and what a little slut I must be ... my God, Lina, there wasn't one fellow who'd been at that party that I didn't stare at and cringe when he glanced back, not one! Others, too ... if a man smiled too knowingly, if a bloody shop assistant gave me a friendly nod ... I'd wonder, and feel sick and guilty all over again. And it was Clive? It really was? He came to that party,

232

said he'd seen me ... announced his intention of taking care of me? My God, I could kill him for that!'

'And he's never told you, never apologised for what he did? Oh, my God, could I be mistaken? Perhaps it wasn't him, perhaps he came afterwards ...' but Clare was shaking her head.

'No. Of course it was him, if I'd had the faintest idea that he was anywhere near Norwich ... no wonder he walked in and rescued me when he heard Mother shrieking, no wonder! It was the bloody least he could do in the circumstances ... and I was so touched, so grateful ...' Her voice faded for a moment, then returned, stronger than ever. 'He married me to make up for what he did ... as if anything could make up for that ... and then never had the courage to tell me he was Sal's father! Mother would have killed me if she'd known for sure ... she'd have sent me away to some sort of home for bad girls ... I thought he'd saved me from that because he really loved me, but it was just a bad conscience, because he'd done it to me! I wasn't a bad girl, truly I wasn't, Lina, but I've lived with being a bad girl for fifteen bloody years, thanks to Clive!'

Selina must have spoken; dimly, far off, Clare heard a voice talking on and on, but all she could see was Clive's face through a red mist. Clive's face telling her that she mustn't get a job, musn't see Selina, that she made him nervous when she drove the car so she had better let him drive, that he'd prefer her not to wear jeans when they went out together because skirts were more womanly, that since his time at home was so short he'd prefer that she didn't have friends round whilst he was with her. And over it all, the feeling which she had never quite managed to conquer that he had bought and paid for her, that he gave her money to look after his house, keep it nice for his return, and go to bed with him.

Many times she had felt like a prostitute, going to bed with a virtual stranger in return for money to feed and clothe herself and her illegitimate child. He could come home after a ten-month absence and take her to bed within ten minutes of his arrival; she was still trying to look him in the eye she felt so shy and he was so eager to get her on her back he scarcely listened when she spoke and certainly wasted few words on her.

Rage, hurt and a desire for revenge fought within her and Clive's face, in the red mist, swelled and shrank as she screamed soundless abuse for his cruel deceit. If he had only told her, how willingly she would have forgiven him! But the agonies of guilt she had suffered, the number of times she had swallowed her own feelings because she had believed he had been tricked into accepting another man's child, the ignorance which had caused her to search for a likeness in Sally's child-face to that man who had used her when she was too drunk to resist ... she was a fool, she should have known! Why should he have dropped the beautiful, golden Selina for quiet little Clare Flower, unless his wicked action in raping her had forced him into it? And never told! Never admitted, not when he held her in his arms and they were as close as two people can be, even then he had not been able to bring himself to tell her the truth.

Someone was shaking her. Someone slapped her face hard, a single blow like a pistol shot. She screamed, tried to slap back ... and came to herself. She was standing on the landing, a broken mug at her feet, hot chocolate splattering her skirt and legs. Selina was shaking her so hard that her head bounced and her upper arms hurt from Selina's grip.

Clare said: 'It's all right, Lina, it's all right. I'm me again, it's all right,' and Selina stopped shaking and dropped her hands to her sides. They stared at one another.

'Clare? Oh my love, what have I done?'

Selina's warm, purring voice was thin, higher than usual, her eyes desperate. Clare was shivering, clutching her arms with her hands, her flesh cold as death. She looked around the landing and was astonished to find it unchanged. Apart from the chocolate sinking into the carpet no one would have known that it had been the scene of such pain and heartbreak ... why was she so cold? Why did Selina look so frightened? What on earth had been said to make her hate Clive so, to put her into such a state that she longed to look over her shoulder but feared to do so? She felt as frightened as though a mad axeman lurked on the stairs behind her, waiting to strike her down.

Suddenly Selina seemed to give herself a shake and return to her normal, self-confident self. She took Clare's hand and led her into her bedroom. She turned back the white broderie anglaise quilt and the pink top sheet and sat Clare down. Then she swung Clare's legs into bed as though her friend was incapable of movement, pushed her gently back against the pillows and covered her right up to her chin with the quilt.

'Will you be all right alone for a moment?' she said gently. 'I'm going to get you a hot-water bottle and a hot drink. You're in shock, but you'll pull out of it once you're warm and settled. I'll get some aspirins . . . or I wonder whether a whisky might be better?'

Clare did not answer. She was shivering too hard, her teeth were clattering like an electric typewriter and she desperately wanted, of all the absurd things, to forbid Selina to leave the room, to grab her and hold and to simply stop shaking.

But she could say none of these things through the convulsive shudders so she simply lay there, the bed bounding to her shivers, and presently Selina returned. She carried two hot-water bottles which she shoved under the covers and a mug which steamed gently. She manoeuvred Clare into a sitting position, held the mug to her lips and tilted it. Hot sweet tea with what tasted like brandy in it invaded Clare's mouth. She swallowed because it was easier than spitting and then swallowed again – line of least resistance – and then took the mug and drank deeply, until it was empty. Then, without being told, she shrank down the bed again and cuddled the nearest hot-water bottle with desperate love. Selina sat down on the covers. She was almost smiling, Clare could tell, though the anxiety was still uppermost on her gentle, beautiful face.

'Better, poppet?'

Nod nod nod, went Clare's head.

'Getting warmer?'

Nod nod nod.

'That's grand. If you can just go to sleep you'll feel fine when you wake up in the morning. Shock's like that – horrid

235

and frightening for a bit and then gone like frost in sunshine. I'll stay here with you until you nod off.'

Clare, cuddling her hot-water bottle, didn't answer. Her lids felt heavy, beautifully heavy. Her body was warm and the quilt was tucked round her just as it should have been. Very soon now, very soon, she would simply disappear into the sea of sleep which beckoned. And Selina had said that by morning she would be herself once more, so there was nothing to worry about, nothing to be afraid of. Very soon now she would sink into lovely sleep – oh, she was tired – but until she did Selina would be there, safe and solid and reliable, on the edge of the bed, to protect her from mad axemen and all perils and dangers of this night. No one would get her, not with Selina there. Not Clive, not even that man who had got into bed with her and begot Sally . . . oh, but that was Clive, of course. Odd how she hadn't realised all these years. Odd how she had not even considered that it might be Clive, had never questioned him concerning his whereabouts that night. But of course she had known Clive was in Scotland and anyway it didn't really matter, none of it really mattered. She was a kid again and it was Clare and Selina against the world and when the chips were down, Selina would take care of her.

At last she slept but even as her senses reeled away from her she was conscious of the still figure sitting on the edge of the bed.

She slept so deeply for the next few hours that she woke in exactly the same position. She opened her eyes and it was still dark, though a tell-tale shape, lighter than the rest, told her where the window was. She looked around without moving anything other than her eyes and saw the clock . . . it was luminous and she could read the time quite easily, it was ten past five . . . and registered that there was no need to get up or even think about getting up for a couple of hours yet.

She closed her eyes again and discovered that she was wide awake so she moved to try to get into a cosier position and discovered the cooling hot-water bottles. Odd! It was summer, wasn't it? She kicked the coolest bottle spitefully out of bed and heard it thump onto the floor with triumph. That would teach it! On the other hand she must have put the bottles into her bed for some reason – had she been cold, earlier?

She moved and her cramped limbs creaked; she had indeed slept soundly! She moved a bit more, then rolled onto her back and for some reason this brought everything into focus. She remembered going to sleep with Selina sitting on the bed, the reason for Selina's presence and her own distress.

She sat up and reached for the cup by the bedside. It was heavy with liquid. She sipped and it was nice cold lemon squash, very welcome when you had a thirst. She drank it down, then her fingers encountered something else on the bedside table. Something oblong and crumbly and ... a shortbread biscuit. She ate it quickly, then took another drink, then lay down again. What about going back to sleep until the alarm went off, then? Her mind and body thought about it and dismissed the idea as futile. Better think herself into some sort of coherence before the day began. Heaven knew she had got enough food for thought, what with Selina's admittance that she had slept with Clive after Dan and she had split up and the other business.

Odd, really, that it was easier to accept her husband's unfaithfulness than his behaviour towards herself. If only he'd told me, she mourned now, wondering why Selina had not pulled the bedroom curtains. Outside, the walnut tree moved its branches and she heard the familiar creak one branch made in a wind when it rubbed against its neighbour. Why on earth hadn't Clive admitted that it had been he in bed with her that night? Why had he never reassured her that Sally was his daughter?

Five minutes serious thought, however, made her realise that Clive was not the only one to blame. He must have assumed, as it appeared everyone else had, that she knew who had fathered her baby, who had lain with her on the fateful night in that smart, soulless house.

But that would not do because if he thought she knew it was he, why had he never mentioned it, never apologised to her for what had been a pretty greedy, selfish sort of act? She had been frightened and in pain, enjoyment, so far as she was concerned, had not come into it.

But a little more thought brought understanding; if he had admitted it, she might well have sent him packing, hated him for it. She remembered weeping and a hand smoothing the tears from her cheeks, muttered words which might, she supposed, have constituted some sort of apology but which had seemed both at the time and later, to have put the responsibility for what had happened on her, for being so pretty, so helpless, so drunk. She believed now that he had probably married her, intended to tell her once the knot was tied, and then had simply lacked the courage. Or perhaps he had even thought there was little point in explanations which would be painful and difficult for them both when he had done the right thing by her and atoned for his behaviour.

That was the worst, most damaging thought of all; that he might have married her simply from guilt. But by six o'clock, with the sky brightening outside the window, she told herself that it was not guilt, he had never behaved like a guilty man but like a loving, dictatorial one. She decided she must tackle him about it however, come what may. She would ask him the very next time he came home, what on earth had possessed him to rape her and then say nothing. But if she did that he would know that she had intended to deceive him, had deliberately not told him that she believed herself to be pregnant by another man.

By six-thirty she had decided she must pretend to herself that she knew nothing; did not know Selina had been his mistress, did not know he had committed adultery with her friend, had no idea that it was he who had raped her and then left her alone in the bloodstained bed to make what excuses she could to her hostess.

By seven, when the alarm went off and she jumped out of bed, she had decided something else as well. What was sauce for the goose, she told herself, putting on a clean pink shirt and a full grey skirt, was sauce for the gander. She had been good, obedient and grateful to Clive, to say nothing of faithful and uncritical. She had believed herself to be labouring under such a weight of gratitude that nothing had been too much trouble if it pleased him. Well, all that was over. She was going to see a bit of life herself for a change. And she would start with Oliver. If he really did want her, and Selina had more or less said she thought he did, then he should jolly well have her – and this time it would be a conscious decision on her part to play an away game. I'll go all the way, she said vengefully to herself, downstairs in the kitchen making a cup of tea for Selina. I'll throw my cap over the windmill – the Dutch one, ho ho – and have fun whilst I still can. I'll kiss, cuddle and carry on with anyone who comes my way ... see how you like that, Clive Arnold!

CHAPTER
12

When Sally woke on Saturday morning she turned over in bed, tried to shrug the quilt up over her shoulders, and discovered at once there was something wrong. The quilt seemed to have disappeared and what was in its place was thinner, not so cosy, and somehow elusive.

She opened an eye and saw through the slit a strange, whitewashed wall not an inch from her nose. Someone had drawn a cartoon inexpertly upon its surface with a blue felt-tipped pen and someone else had colour-washed over it, but not well enough to entirely obliterate the blue lines. With some difficulty, for she had talked until the early hours, Sally wrenched open the second eyelid and saw that she was in Dee's bedroom. She rolled over to make sure and there was the other bed, with a lump in it which must be Dee, still snoring no doubt.

Sally sat up. The bed had a thin sheet and two equally thin blankets on it, and all three were rucked up and concertinaed against the wall. However, it was quite definitely morning and she and Dee had a lot to get through. Sally looked round for a missile, found the book she had been reading last thing, aimed and fired. The book struck Dee on the hip but did not wake her – at least she gave no sign of it – so Sally sighed, got out of bed, picked up the book and tugged at the top of Dee's hair, which was the only thing outside the covers.

'Dee! Get you up, gal, we've got a lot to do today!'

From deep below the covers a voice thickly requested Sally

to get stuffed and leave her alone. Sally tweaked again and Dee moaned, then emerged, red-faced, from her seclusion beneath the blankets.

'What do you want, Sal? That's early, Mum isn't bawling us yet, or I'd have heard.'

'It's past six,' Sally said righteously. 'Time we got up, you said we had to help feed and exercise the dogs and . . .'

'Past six? Lor, gal, it's Sat'day, innit? We don't get up till eight, Sat'days.' Dee burrowed back beneath the covers and disappeared.

Sally sighed, whacked Dee's rump half-heartedly, and returned to her own bed. She took the book with her and opened it, then fished a chocolate bar out from her overnight bag, kept handily close to the bed.

'Oh, all right, if you won't get up I suppose I can read for a bit. Want some choc?'

A rude mumble from the other bed told her what to do with her chocolate. Sally laughed, bit at the bar, and snuggled down again. She would read for a bit and if she got terribly bored, she would get up and go down and take a look at the dogs and the rabbits and things. If there was one thing she could not stand, it was lying in bed on a fine day when you could be better employed outside.

At seven, Sally was dressed and guiltily making herself a bacon sandwich in the kitchen because she was absolutely starving and the chocolate seemed to have made her hungrier, if anything. She was also thirsty – the chocolate's fault again – and made up some orange squash in a mug. Despite a certain amount of noise during these activities the house remained locked in slumber, not even Dee's parents stirring. I could be a thief, Sally thought rather crossly, I could have rifled the house and stolen the family jewels and no one would be any the wiser.. Not even the dogs had raised a yelp.

The bacon was cold in the fridge, the loaf standing out on the side. Clare would have winced at a loaf left to stale in the open air but Sally enjoyed the extra-crustiness. She got the cold bacon out of the fridge and knew at once that her mother would have had a word or two to say about the bacon, as well. It was not on a plate or anything like that and it must have been in the fridge for a while since it was dusted with other foodstuffs . . . a bit of lettuce, a few crumbs of cheese . . . and had that stiff and waxy look common to foods which are considering growing whiskery mould growth tomorrow.

Sally relished it, though. She cut two thick wedges of bread, put the bacon between them, and sank her teeth into it. It was lovely all right, but it lacked something. She glanced round and decided it needed mustard but the pantry seemed to lack this essential condiment so she went for the brown sauce instead and it proved to have a good strong tang to it, though it was some very runny make which Sally had not previously encountered.

Presently, with the bacon sandwich half-eaten, she decided she might just as well go and talk to the dogs. If they barked and woke someone all well and good – she would apologise prettily of course, and explain that she had tried to be quiet so that they could continue to sleep, and they would forgive her and be very jolly about it and come down and make a proper breakfast. Cereal on a Saturday for a start, then bacon and egg and fried bread and beans and perhaps a sausage and some mushrooms, then coffee and lots and lots of buttered toast with marmalade or Marmite to spread on it.

Sally wandered, sandwich in hand, out of the back door. It was a fresh, bright morning, with the sun actually shining for once and in the distance a mist hanging over what she guessed must be the river. A hazel copse in a hollow was wreathed in mist too and looked mysterious and exciting. Sally chomped her sandwich and considered the prospect. She could very easily reach both the hazel copse and the river – if it was a river – before anyone was stirring, but she had no particular desire to go exploring by herself. If she could take a dog with her, now . . . there was a handsome retriever grinning at her from one cage, she could take him.

However, when she went towards his door she saw that there were two dogs inside the wire and changed her mind about taking him anywhere. One dog was fine, two could be a problem. So she walked along the wire, examining the occupants hopefully, until she reached the last cage of all.

Inside there was a most enchanting little dog the like of which Sally had not seen before. It looked like a greyhound, but it was much smaller than greyhounds are as a rule, and it was an enchanting biscuit colour. It had big dark eyes, the thin, long nose of its race, and ears too large for its face which, when they pricked forward, reminded Sally of nothing so much as a cartoon kangaroo.

'Hello, Joey,' she greeted it, and the dog grinned at her and lashed its tail and jumped up at the wire.

Sally examined it, decided she could cope, and undid the door. The dog was wearing a thin collar with a silver name tag on it, and objected not at all to Sally's slipping the belt of her cotton dress through the collar and leading it down to the gate. In fact it leaped and bounced and licked her hands until she was quite in love with it and wondered whether Clare would have any objection to owning a second dog. Tish, bless her, was wonderful but she was also very large. This little Joey was so small he could curl up in the carrier on the front of her bicycle, or go into her school bag on the bus.

By this time of course, Sally had ascertained that it was a dog and not a bitch and was well down the lane. When she reached the last house she turned right into an enchanting little loke, with trees growing at the top of high banks and arching overhead. Wild flowers grew everywhere, the leaves, still the clear bright green of an early – and wet – summer, danced in the slight breeze, and sunshine took advantage of every gap in the foliage to come pouring down on her head and shoulders.

Sally, unlike many girls, was a good walker. She thought nothing of striding the country lanes for miles with Emma up on Pegasus and herself on foot and now it simply did not occur to her that anyone might worry because she was not in the house. It was full daylight, she was young and strong, and besides, she was accompanied by a dear little dog. So she went blithely on until the lane ended in a wood, and then she pushed her way in amongst the trees and emerged in a broad, upward sloping meadow.

Sally, wise in the ways of the country, glanced around her. Right up at the top of the meadow there were a couple of cattle grazing; they looked sturdy and indifferent and were definitely not bulls. And down at the bottom of the meadow was the river. Still with a tantalising scarf or two of mist blurring its gleaming surface it hurried between its banks, majestic and sown with long strands of weed, inviting, enticing, reminding Sally of *The Water Babies*, mermaids and paddling. Sally headed downhill, the dog tugging impatiently on the cotton belt, as anxious as she, apparently, to take a closer look at the river.

And when she reached it the river was as irresistible as Sally had thought it. There were some boulders sticking out of it which simply invited the bold to use them as stepping stones. It was deep in some places – you could see the current swirling wickedly – and shallow in others. There were tiny sandy beaches and yellow-flag irises raised their bright heads above the reed beds on the opposite bank. It was, without doubt, a really good river and Sally forgot her great age, her considerable sophistication and her status as a guest. She sat on the bank, flipped her sandals and socks onto the sand beside her, and jumped joyously into the water. The little Joey-dog, released, wandered along the margin contentedly sniffing at every passing strangeness and raising a leg against a sandstone boulder. Sally reached the first stepping stone and climbed aboard. She jumped to the second, and was above a deep pool. She crouched, staring intently into the depths. She wanted to see fishes ... or water babies ... and continued doggedly staring downwards until she began to make out movements which were not just currents or floating debris. She saw a spotted trout and wished she could reach down and try to tickle it, as in books. She saw a shoal of minnows, darting like quicksilver through the water, and a creature which she took to be an eel since she did not believe in water snakes. Then, because her crouching position was giving her cramp in her left calf, she stood up and made for the bank, calling to her little Joey-dog as she did so.

'Come on, Joey, let's go home for breakfast!'

If silence had greeted her ears it would have been bad enough, but now that her attention was off the river, what she heard was infinitely worse.

Baaing. A noise like thunder. More baaing. And then, even as Sally started to run towards the noise, the first bark.

The hedge was impenetrably thick for Sally, though clearly not for Joey, but fortunately Sally spotted a gate and was over it in a minute though on the far side horror stopped her short for a vital second. Joey was in amongst the sheep. Fat woolly bundles, baaing and fleeing, were on every side, panic-stricken by the calamity which had fallen upon them. And Joey, looking the embodiment of evil, was actually grabbing a fat ewe by the throat, undeterred by the fact that when she swung her head in wild panic he was lifted off his feet and actually dangled, for several seconds, in the air.

'Joey!' Sally shrieked. 'Come here this moment, you wicked dog!' But Joey was deaf to entreaties and threats alike. He was having the time of his life and nothing short of physical assault was going to stop him doing his best to decimate the flock.

For ten really dreadful minutes Sally chased, shouted and made wild swipes at Joey, and Joey dodged, ran like the greyhound he very nearly was and snapped at woolly heels, woolly hides and woolly heads. Sally was very soon in tears – and so, metaphorically speaking, were a good few sheep. Fortunately none were in lamb but they were by now in trouble. One ewe fell down, panting, distressed, and Sally nearly got Joey then because he grabbed the fallen one's ear and worried furiously at it until he saw, from the corner of his eye, Sally's approach and set off once more.

What Sally would have done had not help been at hand she had no idea, because she was worn out and breathless and Joey, it seemed, did not know the meaning of the word exhaustion. With hideous visions of a bill bigger than Pegasus's feed, shoes and supplement account plus all her pocket money for the next thousand years, Sally ran, croaked – her voice was going fast – and pleaded with Joey, all to no avail.

And then the miracle happened. A figure appeared on the far side of the pasture ... and Joey, with an eye warily on Sally, did not see it! He ran straight into the arms out-stretched to receive him and Sally, whose earlier tears had dried with the speed of her going and the need to keep shouting, burst into a whole fresh flood and rushed across the grass to her rescuer.

'Th-thank you,' she sobbed breathlessly. 'Oh, I can't tell you how awful it's been . . . are they your sheep? I had him on my belt . . . he broke away . . .' not for worlds would she have admitted her fault. '. . . He's not my dog, I had no idea he was a sheep worrier . . . Oh, I am grateful to you!'

The boy, for he was no more than eighteen or nineteen she supposed, grinned down at her over the top of Joey's bright-eyed and unrepentant head.

'They int my sheep,' he said positively. 'Good thing for you I aren't old MacDonald, though. He wun't be pleased to see them sheep abounding and apanting.'

'Are they much hurt, do you think?' Sally said fearfully. 'He's only little but he's a real swine.'

'He ha'nt done much harm,' the boy said consolingly. 'He skeered 'em all right, but sheep is duzzy fules, one minute they're all of a lather, the next they're wonderin' what the fuss wuz about. No blood, is there?'

Sally stared at the sheep, then at her scratched and muddied legs and then, broodingly, at Joey.

'No sheep blood, and only a bit of mine,' she admitted. She rubbed her wet eyes with her knuckles and then grinned at her rescuer. 'Sorry I made such a fuss, but I've been chasing him for hours, or it seems like hours. And he's not mine, he comes from . . .'

'Don't tell me; you're Sally,' the boy interrupted. 'Little gal stayin' wi' our Dee. Am I right?'

Sally's eyes had widened and now she nodded eagerly.

'That's right, I'm Sally Arnold and this is one of Dee's Mum's boarding dogs. I thought I'd take him for a walk . . . gosh, thanks again whoever you are.'

'I'm a chap what lives . . .' he broke off. Sally followed his glance which was fixed on her bare feet. '. . . Do you usually go walkin' without neither shoes nor socks?' he enquired, grinning. 'Strange habits you Norwich folk have!'

'I'm not from the city, we live out near Loddon . . . well, in that direction,' Sally said defensively. 'Look, thanks again, you saved my life ... well, the sheep's and Joey's,' she amended. 'But I think I'd better be going now or Mrs Spooner will think I've gone home for my breakfast.'

'I'll walk along of you, keep a-hold of the dawg,' the boy suggested. 'You run and git your shoes, there's a good gal.'

'Can we let him walk?' Sally said hopefully, as she and the boy sat on the river bank and she pushed her wet and muddy feet into her sandals. Her socks she had pushed into her pocket, not relishing pulling them on over damp feet. 'He'll start wriggling and fighting to get down soon and my belt isn't broken, it's just a bit raggedy.'

But the boy shook his head.

'That may not be broke, but that's seen better days,' he said judiciously, examining the chewed-looking strip of cotton. 'And you know what a dog's like when he gets a taste of mutton ... he'll pull free soon's he can and run straight back there.'

'Oh, lor, have I created a monster?' Sally said nervously. 'I should have beaten him up, but I was too tired!'

'I reckon he knew the taste already, else he'd have been happy enough wi' you and the river,' the boy said. 'Come on, we'd best step out. Did you know it was half-past eight?'

'No ... damn, Dee said they got up at eight, Saturdays,' Sally remembered with lively dismay. 'I expect they'll be ever so cross when I get back. And I was supposed to exercise the dogs for them, too.'

'You've exercised one of 'em,' the boy commented, grinning. 'This here Joey, he'll sleep for a week now.'

Sally laughed and fell into step beside him.

'Yes ... I'll have to tell Dee and her mum what happened, though, and I dare say they won't trust me with their dogs again.'

They were about to leave the meadow and re-enter the wood; Sally's companion however, stopped in his tracks to stare at her.

'Old Ma Spooner, not trust you with her dawgs? Why, gal, she's a careless mawther, that one. She'd trust you with 'em if you'd come back smothered in sheep blood with a dead hen adanglin' from your paw!'

Sally, on reflection, thought that this was quite probable and the two of them continued on their way in perfect accord.

When they reached the house despite the fact that it was nearly eight forty-five, the front curtains were still drawn and there was no obvious sign of stirring.

'I'd ask you in – you've been so kind – but it might look a bit rude if they're still in bed,' Sally said uneasily, swinging the gate back and forth. 'What do you think?'

'Here, take the mutt.' The boy deposited Joey in her arms quite gently, then turned on his heel. 'See you!'

Sally started to speak, then called, 'Thanks again!' and turned to go up the side of the house and in the back.

Out there she saw a sign of life at last. Mrs Spooner, as draggled as ever, was waddling down towards the runs, a bucket in one hand. She was singing loudly and tunelessly and did not, at first, see her guest. So Sally went quietly along the path between the runs, waited until her hostess was bending down and facing in the opposite direction, digging something out of her bucket and putting it into the trough from which, presumably, the dogs ate, then she slid Joey back into his natural home and turned towards Mrs Spooner.

'Hello, Dee's Mum! I'm sorry I wasn't around earlier, but I took one of your dogs for a walk and went further than I meant.'

'Thass all right, gal,' Mrs Spooner said. 'Din't know anyone was up yet, bar meself. Go you in and put the kettle on, and do. We'll have a cuppa while the rest of 'em get going, then I'll start a bit of breakfast.'

'Sure,' Sally said. She lingered for a moment though, looking curiously at the food which Mrs Spooner was tipping into the troughs, then at her hostess. The older woman's curlers seemed to be a permanent fixture, for she had been wearing them when Sally and Dee had got back from the city the previous evening and was wearing them still, and Sally wondered whether she ever wore anything on her feet but ragged slippers; the grey toe sticking out of the end of the right shoe was probably permanently coloured thus.

Mrs Spooner finished in the run she was serving and came out, waving the spoon under Sally's nose, her face amused.

'Fancy a bite? That's good, that is, a grand old sluther! That 'ud put some beef on your bones, young Sally!'

Sally laughed with her, but retreated into the house.

'I could eat it an' all,' she called back. 'But not before that cuppa, Mrs S!'

'Where did you go then, Sal?' Dee's face in the mirror was bright, interested. 'There int nowhere to go, round here!'

'Of course there is. I went to a river. I took an odd little dog with me.'

Sally hesitated, wondering whether to confess, but decided against it on the grounds that she might make trouble for someone, either the dog, herself or the boy who had rescued her. She wondered if she would see him again since he was obviously friendly enough with the family to know that Dee had a friend called Sally staying with her. But on the other hand, when you thought of the Carters and the way Em's family chattered, if all villages were like hers then probably there wasn't a person for miles who didn't know most of the Spooner business. And she'd travelled home on the work-bus ... she might easily never see that chap again.

'Well, you int a bad kid, then,' Dee said, smiling at her through the glass.

Sally was standing behind Dee watching as Dee applied her make-up. It was a fascinating business, far more complicated than she had supposed, with Dee cleaning an already clean visage, smearing it with stuff she called moisturiser, spreading a thin, pinkish film over it, powdering it, colouring different parts of it different shades and finally drawing thin dark eyebrows very neatly over her natural ones, which had been carefully and efficiently plucked away. The new eyebrows gave her a slightly surprised look but Sally was bound to admit that they also helped to give her face height and breadth – or at least she admitted it when Dee had explained what it meant – so supposed that it was all worthwhile. Not that she could imagine herself going to such lengths just to turn a nice little face into a no doubt sophisticated but rather unnatural creation.

'It's quite warm outside,' she said at last, when Dee turned away from the glass, apparently satisfied. 'Are you going to wear a dress or jeans? If you're wearing jeans I'll change.'

'Oh, I always wear jeans weekends,' Dee said. 'That's casual clothing, int it? Everyone wears jeans, weekends. Well, they do if they're in a skirt all week.'

Sally, who was in jeans from the moment she cast off her school uniform to the moment she had to put it on again, was happy enough to change and to wear her new shirt, a gaily checkered garment in blue and green, but she had only got faded old denims which had gone baggy at knee and bottom and felt very ordinary beside Dee in her pale-blue sloppy joe sweatshirt and a pair of jeans so tight that she might have been poured into them. However she was forced to admit, awful though it was, that had Dee paid as much attention to her body as she did to her face, she might have thought twice about the jeans. Dee's bottom was broad and slightly heavy but her legs were thin-thighed and her knees sturdy. She looked rather comic; Sally had to be very firm with herself and think sad thoughts or she might have showed something of what she felt on her face. Though she wondered whether Dee would have noticed − or cared. She was fashionably dressed and that was what mattered.

It had never occurred to Sally before to look at her own back view, but as she went out of the bedroom she glanced over her shoulder into Dee's mirror. A small, neat bottom and long legs met her eyes, topped by the naturally falling folds of the shirt.

I look nice, Sally thought, astonished, and went down to breakfast with an added spring in her step.

When Clare was up, dressed and almost ready to leave, she tiptoed upstairs with a cup of tea for Selina and found her friend sleeping heavily, curled up like a dormouse under the covers.

Clare hesitated, unwilling to rouse the other woman, but just as she was about to tiptoe out of the room again Selina stirred. A hand emerged from the bedclothes, waved about wildly for a moment, and then a voice said imperiously: 'Put the bloody light on ... no, don't, pull the curtains!'

'I might if you said please,' Clare remarked, going over to the window and swishing the curtains back nevertheless. 'Gosh Lina, you sleep like the dead. Here, drink this and return to the land of the living.'

Selina sat up. She looked even lovelier *en deshabille*, with her heavy hair loose and her face clean of even a trace of make-up. She held out a trembling hand for the cup and smiled at Clare, then gave a jaw-cracking yawn.

'God, I was tired! I can see you're fine this morning, but last night you scared the shit out of me.'

'Lina, what a ghastly expression! Yes, I'm sorry, I don't know what came over me as they say. Look, go back to sleep, I don't finish work until five so the day's your own.'

'I sat on your wretched bed until two in the morning, that's why I'm knackered,' Selina said, sipping her tea. 'Oh dear oh dear, will I never learn? However ... when do you leave?'

'In ten minutes. Why?'

'I'm coming with you, that's why. Oh, not all the way, just as far as Gran's. And don't think we'll talk about you because we won't, I wouldn't do that to Gran. And besides, I've not seen her new house yet or new flat or whatever. And from there, so she tells me, I can walk into the city.'

'You can. Gran does. But honestly, Lina, I dare not wait for you or not for very long, anyway. Mavis is marvellous, but Saturdays she's off and I make do with Saturday girls. One of 'em is almost as good as Mavis but even so ...'

'I shan't wash, then,' Selina said. She drank her tea, whimpering at the heat of it, then jumped out of bed and grabbed a handful of clothing apparently without prior selection from the top of her case. 'Can I use the bathroom?'

'Sure.' Clare looked at her watch. 'I'll go down and carry on as though you weren't coming and when I'm in the car I'll pip the horn and give you five minutes. If I drive fast I won't be late even with dropping you off at Gran's.'

Selina, disappearing into the bathroom, did not waste words on a reply but Clare had very little hope of being accompanied into the city and no intention whatsoever of waiting longer than she had promised. However, she did everything she had planned, kissed the top of Tish's head and

251

was only half-way to the door when a thundering on the stairs gave advance warning of an arrival and Selina cantered into the room.

'Well? Ready to roll? And I washed!'

'I always knew you could work miracles,' Clare said, as the two of them made their way out to the Mini. 'You look smashing, as well. What's your secret, Ms Bothwell?'

'Bothwell, indeed – I haven't been a Bothwell for a lifetime, or so it seems. But I feel a Bothwell again, isn't it odd, and no doubt Gran will transport me straight back to the seventies.' Selina settled herself neatly into the passenger seat, snapped her belt on and lowered her window a couple of inches. 'Right you are, drive on, pet. Do you approve of my ravishing new outfit by the way?'

The ravishing new outfit was a flying suit in a deep shade of rose pink with chunky glass beads in the neck and high-heeled white sandals on the feet. Despite her hurry Selina had brushed her hair up on top of her head and secured it there, in a fat and gleaming cushion, with two rose-pink combs. Clare felt small, ordinary and dull, but it did not matter; it never did matter with Selina because a few words with her and you knew she considered you fascinating, sophisticated and bursting with wit and humour. That was her gift and she used it to the full.

Traffic was heavier than usual, perhaps because it was a Saturday or possibly because Clare was a little late, but they talked as they queued, which made it easier to bear. After a little preliminary skirmishing, Selina put the question she must have been dying to ask ... she wanted to know whether Clare was going to accuse Clive.

'No. It would be stupid,' Clare said decidedly, glad of the hours she had spent vacillating earlier so that now she could give a considered answer to such questions. 'I certainly can't blame him for sleeping with you before we were married, nor can I really blame him for that one night ... you know. I still wish it hadn't happened, but I can't lay blame, especially when you consider that the one person who could and should have helped you then was me. I had the opportunity and I didn't do it because, frankly, I was afraid of what Clive

252

would say if he came home and found me up in London with you.'

'And what about the other business? Sally, I mean. Don't forget I'm only telling you what I believed to be true. Are you going to face him with that?'

Clare moaned, then laughed and turned her head to pull a face at Selina. Selina gave a squawk and Clare hastily returned her attention to the road, then answered without again looking away from it.

'Don't think I wouldn't love to do just that, because I would. When I think of the misery I've gone through ... but you can imagine, and anyway I spilt a good few of the beans last night from what I can remember. However, being practical, I can't say a thing about that either. He deceived me all right but by golly, I deceived him too! I thought I was foisting another man's child onto him but did I 'fess up? Did I make a clean breast of my wicked ways? Did I even mention that bloody party? No, I didn't. I still think the biggest fault of all was his, but if I tell him so I lay myself open to more criticism than I think I can take.'

'I'm glad; just don't let it fester inside and get bigger and bigger until one day it ruins your marriage,' Selina said seriously. 'God knows with two husbands behind me and consequently two ruined marriages I'm not one to give advice, but other people's problems and the solutions are always crystal clear to me even if my own life is rather clouded. The way I see it, you've a really good marriage and it would be a crime to spoil it after all this time.'

'A good marriage?' Clare tried to pull out to pass a bus and got hooted at by oncoming traffic. She muttered a curse and drew in once more. 'Lina, sometimes I don't feel married at all, that's the trouble. He's here for six weeks out of the fifty-two remember. That isn't marriage, it's legalised prostitution!'

'Aren't all marriages, when you come down to it?' Selina's warm, chuckley voice said gently. 'You said something like that last night, when I was trying to get through to you with such little success. You said he seemed like a stranger for the first week, but he still expected full marital rights from the

253

moment he stepped over the threshold. But sweetie, Clive won't see things like that; he's longed for you all year, to him you're the embodiment of a year's dreaming. He sees you exactly as he saw you twelve months earlier, his woman, in his home. That's not prostitution, legalised or otherwise, or no more than any marriage, anyway.'

'You can't possibly understand unless you've lived like it,' Clare said obstinately. 'No one could. All right, say I have an extended honeymoon with the guy once a year. Add the weeks together ... God knows I've done it often enough ... and the total is ninety weeks. Divide that by four and it comes to seven and a half months. That's the length of this marriage of mine you admire! Seven and a half months, strung out over fifteen years!'

'And each time, in a way, you feel you're sharing your bed with a stranger?' Selina touched Clare's shoulder lightly. 'You poor kid – and I've envied you, thought you had the best of both worlds! Independance without the worries.'

Clare laughed. 'Power without responsibility, eh? Oh no, just the opposite ... responsibility without power, that's what it's been like. Do everything, take all the decisions, heal the sick, tend the wounded, and then make yourself beautiful once yearly for the conquering hero when he comes home and stalks round your domain, admiring some things, criticising others, and taking your acceptance of everything ... every single little thing ... for granted.'

'You said in your letter, though, that Clive was thinking of coming home for good. Won't that be better? More natural?'

'For Christ's sweet sake, how am I supposed to know?' Clare shouted, exasperated. 'I've never had a proper marriage with a nine-to-five husband and a fifty-two week year! I'm scared stiff at the prospect and everyone expects me to cheer and throw a party! I'm more likely to throw up!'

'Yes, of course. How crass I am, and insensitive. Poor old girl, all these years I've envied you your lovely, stable relationship and never once have I thought how hard it must be to cope alone for months and months.'

'It isn't hard to cope alone!' Clare took her foot off the accelerator and swung the car violently into the kerb, then accelerated and banked like a jet fighter round into a quieter side street. 'It was, once, but it isn't any more. What will be hard is to have Clive back here all the time, interfering in everything I want to do, lugging me up to bed when I'd rather fiddle around in the garden, coming into the bathroom when I'm trying to shave my armpits in peace, taking over the car and telling me I'm a lousy driver ...'

'You are,' Selina said fervently as the pavements flashed erratically by. 'Do slow down, Clare, you'll bag a dog or a child in a minute.'

'Oh, am I rushing? Sorry.' Clare slowed to a more normal speed and giggled abruptly, putting her fingers across her mouth and then glancing at Selina over the top of them, every inch a schoolgirl again for one fleeting second. 'Actually I'm a darned good driver, but when I'm agitated I go a bit too fast, sometimes. Sorry. Where was I?'

'You were impressing upon me that it was no longer Clive's presence you longed for so much as his absence, I think,' Selina said carefully. 'How long have you felt like this?'

'I don't know. It came out into the open when he tried to make me give up the job, and it came out even more when he said he was going to come home. It isn't just me, even Sal's a bit wary of a change as radical as that.'

'I see. You're thinking of him not as a companion to help but as an additional burden who'll walk in, boss you both about and constantly carp and criticise. The trouble is obviously that you're used to being without him now and enjoy things as they are. It's change you're not keen on.'

'You're probably right. It isn't even as if he had a job to come back to though, Lina, because he hasn't. He said something about buying a smallholding or a little shop but we'd both hate that. Even a cafe of our own wouldn't be the same if we both ran it, because he'd boss me about all the time and take all the decisions and I've had fifteen years of making up my own mind, I can't become a yes-woman overnight.'

'But you were very much a yes-woman when we were kids,' Selina reminded her. 'I don't like to say this, sweetie, but you always waited for other people to take the lead or tell you what to do. Even now you don't strike me as the bossy type.'

'No, that's the odd part. I'm not bossy really, not even with Sal. I let her go very much her own way ... too much, perhaps. The only person I want to boss is me, but Clive won't even let me do that!'

'Look, the way I see it ... oh hell, have we arrived?'

Clare was drawing up beside the square of grass which was more outside Gran's flat than anyone else's and was considered as her 'garden', if you could honour a square of grass with such a grandiose title. Gran was not supposed to have any part in the cultivation of the ground outside her flat but naturally she ignored the fact and had already planted a good number of her favourite flowers under the window.

Today, when Clare looked sideways, she saw that someone had dug a round bed out in the middle of the grass and planted rose-bushes. There would, of course, be trouble but that was Gran's affair. If she wanted rose-bushes then the chances were she would keep them. If it were me, Clare thought wryly, those roses would never have got planted, but then Gran's got all the overt determination and courage which were left out of my nature. Or perhaps they had not been left out after all, they had just been kept under by years of first motherly and then husbandly despotism.

'Yes, that's Gran's flat, the one with a peony by the front door and the roses in the middle. How about coming into the caff for your lunch? We could have it together. Or if you're busy then, come in at about half-four and we'll have some tea and leave together at five. How does that sound?'

'Marvellous, love.' Selina unwedged herself from the front seat, patted Clare's shoulder and headed for the front door. She called, 'See you at lunch-time, then,' and added a wild 'Coo-eee!' for the front door had shot open, framing a beaming Gran.

Clare waved, then drove slowly off down the road. All her thinking in the early hours and all her talk with Selina had made her see much more clearly that whether Clive stayed in Saudi Arabia or came home for good, they would no longer be able to ignore their differences. They would have to discuss her job, Clive's desire to come home, their financial situation, with complete honesty and freedom from restraint. If they could do that, could learn to understand one another's feelings, then it was quite possible their marriage could withstand the shock of Clive's being at home all the time. If they could not ... well, it's only a matter of time before we split up, Clare thought, and was surprised by the stab of real hurt which went through her.

I don't want him to go, she realised, turning out onto the main road once more and heading for the city. I want things to stay the same, only Clive must understand that I need a life of my own other than keeping the house nice and mothering Sally.

'Gran! My goodness, you've not changed a bit ... prettier than ever!'

Selina's arms went round Gran in a gentle hug and Gran hugged her back, beaming all over her face.

'Ah, it's good to see you, love. Come in, come in ... what a turn up for the books, eh? I'll show you round first, then we'll have a nice cup of coffee, early though it is ... have you had breakfast? No? Good, then we'll indulge ourselves. I bought some lovely bacon last time Sal came to stay, smoked of course, and there's some of that left ... a few eggs which Clare brought over ... a new loaf of course. There's nothing like new bread. What else?'

She glanced round her perfunctorily; they were in the living-room and Selina recognised every article of furniture, every ornament, every picture on the walls. Clare had told her that Gran had simply cottaged the flat, now she knew what her friend had meant.

'What else? You've mentioned just about all my favourite food so we don't need anything else. Where's the kitchen? Don't think our Clare didn't feed me, it was my fault, I slept late and we had a scramble to get off.'

Gran led the way into the kitchen which was small, square and airy. The window overlooked a central courtyard but since the windowsill was positively heaving with pot plants in exuberant flower and since Gran, or someone on her behalf, had affixed a window box rampant with herbs to the windowsill outside, one scarcely noticed the view.

Selina glanced round. She recognised the fridge, the small freezer, the ancient wooden kitchen table with its scrubbed and pitted surface and the cupboards. New to her were the units, shinily clean in primrose plastic with chrome handles, and the sink, which was stainless-steel and modern, with crystal-topped taps and a fancy draining rack.

'I wanted posters on the walls,' Gran remarked, scrabbling in the bread bin. 'New ones, I mean. But I wasn't going to throw away my old ones and there wasn't room for both.' She stood up, the loaf clutched to her chest, and gestured at the walls. 'Make the place seem homelier I always think.'

The posters were the same, of course. Posters cadged or charmed out of various travel firms. Italy drowsed in the sun, a long beach announced that the Caribbean was everyone's dream holiday. A painting of ancient pink-stoned buildings and blue distance bade the viewer to come to Florence for history and weather both of the best. Selina patted the Caribbean as one might a dog or a small child.

'It doesn't half take me back, Gran. The times I've stood and stared at that picture and dreamed of going there one day. And now I've been and it's marvellous, and I wouldn't swop ten days there for ten minutes with you.'

'You always were a nice child, my favourite Bothwell,' Gran said placidly, slicing bread with a knife whose blade was worn down until it was as thin as a razor. 'How do you find Clare?'

'Oh, unchanged ... no, not unchanged, even better than before. Nicer, but more resolute ... oh, I don't know. Clare's been almost a part of me for so long that it's difficult to think of her as someone who has led her own life for the last fifteen years.'

'Hmm. Do you like your bacon cooked or frizzled?'

'How odd that you've known me all my life and we've never had breakfast together before! I like it cooked on the meat and frizzled on the fat, please.'

Gran heated a pan and dropped the bacon in it, then turned

her attention back to Selina once more. She looked severely at Selina's pink flying suit.

'Daft garment – what do you do when you want to wee in a hurry? Answer me that, Miss! And why are you waltzing all round the raspberry bush over Clare, instead of giving me a straight answer, eh? We both know Clare's changed and I know it's for the better and so should you. Her mother let go of her the moment she married Clive, I let go of her as soon as she wanted me to, and of course Clive's home so little that she's been her own mistress for years. What worries me is that she's at a loose end with Sally so grown-up, and she's ripe for mischief.'

'Well, what do you expect? Sal's fifteen, full of life, pretty as . . .'

'Not Sally, you foolish girl, Clare! Clare's ripe for mischief! Do you mean to say you've been with her since last night and haven't noticed? She walked in here after she'd got that job and I sensed a change.' Gran nodded to herself and cracked eggs into the pan. 'She's looking round for something to prove she's got a mind of her own and can use it any way she pleases. First the job – that was all right, a sensible thing to do – but what's next? What's next, I ask myself?'

Selina walked over to the cooker and kissed Gran's cheek. Gran patted her hand, but absently, then began to dish up onto two warmed plates.

'Lay the table, there's a good girl. I do worry about Clare you know Selina, old though she is. Life's been too easy for her in some ways and too hard in others. All those miscarriages . . . and never a word against Clive, though the doctor told her she probably wouldn't carry a child full-term with her man so far away.'

'I don't see why she should have blamed Clive . . .' Selina began, and was very firmly shown the error of her ways.

'Not blame Clive? Who got her pregnant, then? Five miscarriages that girl had before Clive let her go on the pill – five! Don't tell me she wanted another baby, I know she wanted one, but she wanted one more because Clive wanted a son than for her own sake. She had Sally and her home, she was happy enough with that.'

259

'I never thought of it like that.'

Gran and Selina settled down at the table and Selina eyed her plate with pleasant anticipation. Gran had always been a marvellous cook, who else could make bacon, eggs, fried bread and fried tomato look so temptingly delicious? 'Gran, don't worry about Clare. She's grown up a lot. She can take whatever the world throws at her, really she can. And Clive's talking about coming home, which should make things easier.'

Gran snorted and pushed half a fried egg into her mouth, then spoke through it, her voice a little muffled.

'He'd better come home and take better care of her, otherwise when he comes he'll find the bird has flown. Don't gape, dear – hadn't it occurred to you that Clare's a pretty woman with taking ways, and that she's been left alone too much? Someone's going to notice her one of these days and when it happens she'll go off. Because she's ripe for mischief, as I said.'

'Oh, is that what you meant!' Selina sipped her coffee and then began to tackle the bacon, which was delicious. 'Would you hate it if she did that, Gran?'

'What, behaved like a trollop?' Gran cocked her head, giving the matter her full consideration. 'Hate it? That's a bit strong. I'd probably think it served Clive right ... but it's not in Clare's nature to behave like that you see, and so it might hurt her. I won't have Clare hurt.'

'Well, I'll do my best to see she remains uninjured,' Selina said. 'Do you know, Gran, when I asked Clare to drop me off here she said she hoped we wouldn't spend all our time discussing her and I said of course we wouldn't, nothing was further from our minds. Yet here we are ...'

'You're right. Then I'm wrong to worry? She's not going to do anything foolish?'

Honesty forbade the instant placebo. Selina looked at Gran's green eyes, a bit faded but still bright, and at the slender, white-skinned hand which lay on the table. Gran was old ... but her heart was young, so she could understand many things which a younger woman, like Mrs Flower, would find a complete mystery. Nevertheless, she chose her words carefully.

'Nothing can stop you caring, Gran, and that means you are right, in a way, to worry. You were also right when you said she was ripe for mischief, because I think she is. But if she does ... kick over the traces, toss her cap over the windmill, act a bit wildly ... if she does do that, I don't think she'll regret it, or feel guilty. I think she'll enjoy it and then go back to being our own dear Clare.'

A lesser woman might have questioned, argued, continued to niggle at the point. Gran merely nodded and got up from the table.

'I understand. Would you like some toast now, dear? I don't approve of white bread, but wholemeal makes delicious toast and I've some home-made marmalade ...'

'But Sally, darling, you know what I said, I said you could have Dee back here, next. You can scarcely expect Mrs Spooner to want to have a visitor every weekend!'

It was Friday morning. A whole week had passed since Sally had set off so happily for her first weekend away from home and yet here she was, insisting that she wanted to go to Dee's again. It was not fair, Clare felt, that the child should simply batten on the Spooners, and ignore poor Em and push aside the suggestion that she go and take a look at Pegs with the explanation that she had ridden him every evening for a week and wanted a rest from it. Sally wanting a rest from riding was like Dracula declining a pint of blood!

'Oh, but Mu-um, Mrs Spooner wouldn't mind, she'd like it. I enjoy taking the dogs for exercise ... it helps Dee ... why can't I go?'

The two of them were sitting at the kitchen table eating breakfast with their usual absent-minded ferocity since once again they were a bit late. The previous weekend had gone without a hitch, Clare and Selina had lazed, laughed, gardened, told each other every detail of their lives since they had last met and taken turns to cook. Selina's cooking was slapdash and uninspired but she could take instruction, as she pointed out in her own favour, so Clare sat on the kitchen table and told her what to do, Selina did it, and they both enjoyed eating the result.

Sally had come back from her weekend away all smiles; yes

she had had a wonderful time, no she had not felt homesick, yes the Spooners had been very kind to her and she had, at the appropriate time, given Mrs Spooner the big tin of chocolate biscuits which Clare had provided and the azalea in a pot which she had bought with her own money.

Because it was exam time the week in between had been fairly uneventful with Sally not even chasing off to visit Em after school and with Clare hearing revision each evening. In the caff things had pursued an uneventful course; Dee talked a bit about the weekend but not much, Mavis went on, rather, about a mysterious ability which she, and she alone, had spotted in her youngest grandson, and occasionally she made remarks which caused Clare's heart to sink into her shoes about another long weekend in London so's she could explain to Lionel. What she wanted to explain and why it was necessary to have a long weekend she did not say and Clare was far too confused to ask. But the thought of being landed with Lizzie Treece again so soon filled Clare with dire foreboding.

'Mum, why can't I go?' Sally's tone would have been described as a whine by a parent less fond. 'Why do you want me to stay here, all alone, when you keep saying I don't mix with other people enough?'

'It isn't that. As for being alone, what about Em and Pegs? They've always been enough for you in the past. You must have heard words like reciprocal visit, though, Sal, and that's what I mean. In the time-honoured fashion kids visit turn and turn about, or they did when I was one. It's Dee's turn to come here.'

'Oh, but she'd be bored ... she's longing for me to go back there, we didn't do half the things we meant to do, there wasn't time!'

'Has she invited you?' As she spoke Clare glanced at her watch and gave a muted shriek, leaping to her feet as she did so. 'Heavens, the time! You are a little beast, Sal, making me forget the time ... No, you can't go to Dee's again, not unless her mother gets in touch with me and invites you. Dee hasn't said a word about it and though I'm sure she'd love to have you it may be very different for Mrs Spooner. They aren't very well off, you know.'

'So if she rings and asks you, you'd say yes?' Sally persisted as they shut Tish in and made for the garage. 'If she rings you at the caff you'd let me go?'

'Well, I suppose ... but just you come in at four this afternoon my girl and no messing. Oh damn, I've left the fruit cake on the side, we'll need it this afternoon and the tin too, to make another for Monday. Be a dear and fetch them both.'

Sally shot out of the car and made for the back door just as the telephone started to ring. Raising her eyes and both fists to heaven Clare made to follow her, but then she heard Sally's voice and instead of going right in she only went as far as the kitchen where she picked up the cake, its tin and the bag of mixed fruit which she had borrowed from the caff for its manufacture and returned to the car seconds ahead of Sally, who was smirking from ear to ear.

'Guess who that was?' Sally said as she bounced into the front seat. 'It was Mrs Myers – Ella's Mum, from Mattishall. They're having a tennis party on Saturday, they're short of a girl and she wondered if I'd like to go for the weekend.'

'What did you say?' Clare asked cautiously, well aware of what Sally usually said when invited to a social function, but on this occasion Sally leaned over and gave her mother a kiss on the cheek.

'Since you're so mean and won't let me go to the Spooners I said right, I'd be glad to go. They're taking me home straight after school tonight with Ella and I'll go to school with her on Monday morning and come to the caff afterwards as usual. Is that all right or are you going to spoil all my fun and stop me doing that as well?'

'No, darling, as if I would!' Clare said, scandalised that her daughter should believe such a thing of her. 'But what about clothes? And pyjamas and things? You can't possibly go for a weekend with what you're standing up in!'

'No, that's a bit difficult. But I thought if you could bring me some stuff down later I'd get Ella's Dad to pick it up at the caff on his way home.'

'I don't see how I possibly can...' Clare began, then turned the car in the road and headed home. 'Look, we'll be late for once. You rush up and pack a case and I'll bite my nails and wait for you.'

'Mum, you're a jewel,' Sally said, jumping out of the car as soon as it stopped. 'You're the best Mum in the world, I'm sorry I was so horrid earlier, I'm glad, now, that you said no to the Spooners. I'm sure I'll have much more fun with Ella and her friends.'

After her child's display of annoyance earlier this was balm to Clare's feelings and she helped Sally to pack and agreed to all the arrangements her daughter had made without demur. It was only much later, when she was in the caff and peeling a mound of potatoes, that it occurred to her to wonder whether she had been rather neatly manoeuvred. Tennis parties and weekends with friends during exam fortnight were not usual; had Ella planned it weeks ago and got her parents to agree and was she now having trouble with other parents? It sounded like it. And possibly, when Sally had first been asked she had said, 'It's exam fortnight, Mum'll never let me,' and then this roundabout route had been tried.

Oh, well. The exams were important, of course they were, since the results would determine which GCSEs Sally worked for, but if most of her class were involved in this tennis weekend – and it sounded like that from Sally's enthusiastic chatter – then Sal would have no more of a handicap than they. Anyway, it was all cut and dried now, there was really nothing she could do except pray for fine weather.

Clare attacked the next potato and thought that when Clive came home – if he did – then he could jolly well do the heavy father thing and forbid events of which he did not approve. That would leave Clare free to commiserate with Sally whilst being secretly grateful for Clive's intervention. I bet most mothers do it, Clare told herself defensively, as she began to convert the peeled potatoes into chips. Not that Clive would object to a tennis party; nothing could be more acceptable to them both than to see Sally begin to mix with a nice type of girl. There was nothing wrong with Dee of course, nor with

Emma, but one day Sally would want to meet young men, and it was not with the Spooners or the Carters that she would meet boys of her own type.

Not that I know what her type is, Clare told herself, but then Mavis called an order through and she hurried to the slicer to cut roast beef. Sally's social life, so suddenly burgeoning, vanished from her mind in the dinner-time rush.

'Why did summer have to come without a word of warning?' Clare moaned to the Saturday girls, all of them suffering in the heat of the kitchen as the sun beat down on the city. 'If someone had said . . . but naturally I had to wear a dress with long sleeves and a high neck, and naturally the whole of Norwich decides to have the hottest meal on the menu. Typical!'

'Never you mind Clare,' Jane said. 'It's good for trade and you never know it might stay, now it's come at last.'

Jane was the oldest and most sensible of the Saturday girls. She had worked in the caff for three years and knew it inside out, and at eighteen, with six 'O' levels and two 'A's behind her, she was just starting a shorthand and typing course at the tech., having decided that she did not want to teach nor to spend the next three years at University.

'I've stopped believing in summer, it doesn't exist, it's a figment of our imaginations,' Clare said crossly. 'I'm going to take my overall off in a moment, I'm melting away in here.'

'Why don't you? It's not so bad for us, we aren't in the kitchen all the time, the caff's much cooler,' Jane urged. 'Or you could nip up to the flat and borrow a thin dress from Mrs P – she wouldn't mind, we often did it last year.'

'It would be nice, but can you four cope?' Clare looked thoughtfully round her Saturday staff. Jane, tall, dark-haired, pretty but not fetching; Adrienne, blonde, bubbly, with a head like a sieve but heaps of admiring customers; Frances, neat, methodical, plodding. A good worker, if you didn't mind waiting whilst she thought about things. And Pearl, who intended to be a model when she was old enough because she had such a good figure and who seemed totally

266

unconscious of her extremely plain and spotty face. They were good girls, every one.

'We can cope for twenty minutes or so, whilst you change,' Jane said calmly. 'I'll serve up, Frances can help me, and the others will wait. Go off now, Clare, and you'll be back before we've had time to miss you.'

'Oh well, thanks, you're good girls,' Clare said, and hurried up into the flat. Mrs P kept a cupboard full of what she called 'spares', so there would be some choice, for a lifetime of catering had taught her that the waitress has not been born who does not suddenly soak herself to the skin in gravy or fruit juice just as she is about to serve a meal to the mayor and corporation. Accordingly, she kept her spares so that a drenched staff member need not stay in her sticky clothing for the rest of her shift.

Clare chose a thin, blue cotton dress with narrow shoulder straps and only wondered whether it was a petticoat when she was half-way down the stairs again. But the Saturday girls said it was pretty, that it was most definitely a dress, and that she had better get a move on since every table was full, and she forgot her clothing in the rush that followed.

The day cantered on – briskly, for they were busy. Days only dragged, in Clare's experience, when one had little or nothing to do. But even so, five-thirty took its time arriving and was welcome when it did eventually make it. The Saturday girls, paid out of the till, took their hard-earned wages, chittering like sparrows over the spending of every last penny before they made their various ways home, and Clare tidied round, locked up and saw to the cats. A friend of Mrs P's did the Sunday shift with Hodge and Pocket, so she had no fear that the cats might be neglected but she did feel it politic, in view of the sudden increase in temperature, to leave a little top window open in the kitchen so that her charges would not suffocate during the night.

When at last she locked up and crossed the road she was really tired out and longing for a cold wash and a good meal. She unlocked the Mini, sat down and was out of the seat like a flash ... the leather was scorching, even if it wasn't leather really but some plastic imitation. What was more, the windows had been up all day and the air in the car was unbreathable; it felt like red-hot dust as she drew it into her lungs.

It took ten minutes to get the car even slightly habitable and another ten to get clear of the city but once both these tasks had been accomplished Clare began to relax and enjoy the drive home. Cool air blew in from the open windows, her body was grateful to be sitting down after a day on its feet, and she was looking forward to a quiet evening with she and Sally having a salad and the junket she'd made that morning and then sitting in front of the telly and . . .

Damn, no Sally! The thought jarred because she had completely forgotten her daughter's social whirl. And Selina was back in her London flat, no doubt roasting, but there was small consolation in that. And Mrs Flower had been working in the store all day and was out this evening, possibly with that fellow she had mentioned once or twice lately. Gran would be in . . . but Gran's flat would be hot and there had been trouble, just as Clare had predicted, over the roses. So Gran would not want to sit in the garden – or rather she would want to, but if they did neighbours would keep coming over to discuss the present state of the pro-roses and anti-roses lobbies, and peace would be entirely missing.

Never mind, Clare told herself, there's nothing to touch a cool bath, lots of talcum, and then a quiet meal. After that you can take Tish out . . . look, you've been with people all day long, don't tell me you're actually lonely?

I'm actually lonely, Clare told herself, and snorted with scorn at such wimpish behaviour, but that didn't make it go away, it merely made her more aware of her own foolishness, these past few years, in never making a social life for herself, let alone for Sally.

By the time she reached home though, she was beginning to accept her lot with more equanimity. She would have a quiet evening and then tomorrow, she would give one or two people a ring, invite someone to lunch, ask them over for tea. She would not simply sit back and feel neglected because Sally had found something better to do over the weekend than spend time with her mother.

Back home, all went according to plan. Tish dashed out, then accompanied her up to the bathroom and sat by the bath, occasionally putting her fringed paws on the edge of it and peering doubtfully down at the scented water until Clare emerged. Downstairs, wrapped in nothing but a towel, she examined the pantry and decided that she was too tired to cook, it would have to be a tin of crab, suitably garnished, and a salad. Her hair was wet but it was lovely to feel it cool on her bare neck and shoulders so she did not attempt to dry it. Instead, she found a packet of biscuits and began to eat them, absently, whilst pottering round getting a salad together.

There was a subdued knock on the back door and immediately her heart lifted. Sally had come back! She flew across the room and even as she tugged the heavy door back realised that it was far likelier to be Gregory. Damn the cat, raising her hopes like that!

Clare tugged the door wide.

It was not Gregory. Neither was it Sally.

Oliver Norton stood on the doorstep.

'Ooh!' Clare said. She took a step back and clutched her towel protectively.

'Ooh!' Oliver said. He took a step forward and also clutched Clare's towel.

For two identical sounds, they conveyed quite different messages. Clare was surprised and taken aback. Oliver was surprised and delighted.

Clare's 'Ooh!' was the sort of noise you make when you find a slug in your lettuce. Oliver's 'Ooh!' was the sort of noise you make when you see something delicious and forbidden before you, and there's nothing to stop you helping yourself.

Clare said, 'What on earth . . .' and moved back another step.

Oliver said, 'Clare, you look . . . you look . . .' and took her firmly and extremely possessively in his arms, towel, wet hair, and all. With one foot, he nudged the door shut behind him. Then he started kissing.

The kissing went on for quite a long time. Tish put a stop

269

to it. She had been circling the couple, squeaking and growling in the back of her throat, sure that this was not right, unsure how to make it better. At last a solution occured to her.

She grabbed Clare's towel in her mouth, gripped firmly, and tugged. Oliver's arms were gentle now, Clare was relaxed. When Tish tugged, Clare rotated. And the towel came off.

'Ooh!' Clare squeaked.

'Ooh!' Oliver moaned.

Tish, with her mouth full of towel, stood and watched as Oliver picked Clare up, walked out of the kitchen, and kicked the door shut behind him. The dog's forehead wrinkled in a puzzled frown, but then she noticed the packet of biscuits, fallen from Clare's nerveless hand when Oliver had entered the room. Tish picked them up, glancing round nervously as she did so, the whites of her eyes showing. She carried them over to her mat and lay down. Then, very delicately, she proceeded to rip off the packing so that she might eat the biscuits. If she heard the twang of couch springs, heard moans, squeaks, soft protestations and then other, happier sounds, she made no sign. She simply gobbled her stolen booty.

As, in the living-room, Oliver gobbled his. He swarmed over Clare, cuddling, caressing, kissing, until she scarcely knew what day it was. And then he somehow managed to shed some clothing, without once letting go of her or stopping his delicious, hypnotic lovemaking, and Clare found herself indulging in the oldest pastime in the world, only this time she was partnered by a man who had never given her anything, not money, not a home, not a child ... not even a tip! This man, she sensed vaguely, was taking what he wanted and, dammit, giving what she wanted. And that seemed to make it all right. Acceptable. More, it was wonderful, relaxing, terribly sinful but somehow none the worse for that. The only snag was it didn't last long enough but Clare, used to Clive's ten-month starvation, accepted this as part of the game. And when they gasped their last gasp, climbed their last mountain, and were rewarded, she simply rolled over onto her side and hugged Oliver tight, as though they had known one another all their lives – or for seven and a half months.

Oliver had managed to get rid of his shirt and his chest was hard and bare and brown, with hairs growing in a line down towards his stomach. He still had wellies on, and his trousers had only descended to knee level, but even though he looked a bit comical, Clare was not tempted to laugh. She stroked his chest and he heaved a great, contented sigh and stroked her hair, then pulled himself into a sitting position and turned his head to smile down at her.

'Well!' he said softly. 'Well, well, well!'

'Wasn't that nice,' Clare said dreamily. She looked up at him, her eyes suddenly widening. 'It was, wasn't it?'

'It was fantastic,' Oliver said solemnly. 'You're a fantastic lady, Mrs Arnold. May I ask who you were expecting?'

'I thought you were my daughter, I forgot for a moment that she's gone away for the weekend.' Clare smiled and rubbed her head against his upper arm. 'What did you come for?'

'How am I to take that? I had planned to ask you if you had any hay to sell.'

'And then?'

'Oh, then I was going to try to worm my way into your good graces by asking you out for a meal. I thought if I played my cards right and I'd softened you up a bit with food and wine I might get to kiss you in the car on the way home.'

Clare chuckled.

'Well, you kissed me all right. We do seem to have skipped a good few preliminaries though, now you mention it.'

'You're certainly right there. Did you say your daughter was away for the whole weekend?'

'I don't think I did ... but she is.'

'Then why don't we transfer this party to a nice double bed somewhere? Or are you ravenously hungry? I'd go and get you a cup of tea and a biscuit in the best tradition of seduction, only I'm afraid that great sloppy dog of yours might try and remove my trousers since I'm not wearing a

271

towel. Is she trained to do that, incidentally? It's a beautiful trick, she must do it more often when I'm around.'

'No, of course she's not. I am rather hungry, in fact. I say, do you realise I'm lying here naked as the day I was born with the curtains drawn back?'

'Well yes, I did. That's why I suggested moving the party to a double bed since beds are usually kept upstairs. The elderly man who just peeked through the window looked the type who might spread gossip ... what on earth are you squeaking for? He's gone now!'

'Oh, Oliver, you didn't...' Clare struggled to sit up, Oliver held her down with ease. 'Was there really a man ... I'll die of shame ...'

'There was certainly a prowler; it was a big ginger cat with a malevolent face,' Oliver said serenely. 'What do you want me to do? Draw the curtains across or lie on top of you again so no one can see you're bare?'

Clare giggled but reached for his shirt where it lay on the round oriental rug.

'I'll just slip this on ... Ooh, doesn't it smell nicely of you, Oliver!' Respectable once more, she stood in front of the couch smiling down at him, then gave a huge yawn and stretched luxuriously. The shirt rose indiscreetly and Oliver smiled.

'What a nice view! Look, I don't want to panic you but there are them as don't think a girl in a shirt and nothing much else is terribly respectable. Do you want to go and get dressed, and then we'll go back to my original plan? It'll be much more interesting though – I'll look at you across the table and think of you losing your towel, and you'll look at me and remember how nice I look with nothing on, and then we'll both eat up like crazy so's we can come back here and try our tricks on that double bed I spoke of.'

'I think you're dreadful, but I would like a meal,' Clare confessed. 'Somewhere small and quiet, though.'

'Intimate, do you mean?' They both laughed. 'Tell you what, how about a dirty weekend? Does that set your tonsils tingling?'

'Huh? Hasn't this weekend been dirty enough already?'

'No, you don't get the point. Why don't we drive down to Yarmouth, book into a hotel as Mr and Mrs Smith, and live on love for a couple of days? Would you like that?'

'Oh, I would! But how about Tish? And Greg? I've got Monday off, but I don't suppose you have.'

'Certainly I have, or I shall have. We could take Tish with us, she could sleep in the car. You could leave Greg food out, I suppose, assuming he's the ginger cat I mentioned. Don't you have a neighbour who could feed and water 'em both just for once?'

'Oh sure, I can just see me asking. Can you take care of Tish and Greg for me whilst I go off to have a dirty weekend with this guy who drives a horse-waggon and comes into the caff sometimes? Honestly, Oliver.'

He smiled, a flash of white teeth in his brown face, then came across and tapped her on the bottom.

'Go and change. We'll discuss this at leisure, over dinner.'

Upstairs, Clare ran a bath and got into it, then lay back and watched the steam swirl above her head and let her mind float off into fantasy. She had not meant to be wicked, to commit adultery, yet when it came to the point it had been easy, delightful and rewarding. She felt she had made a friend, rather than gained a lover. Try though she might, and she had tried hard to resist when Oliver had first carried her through into the living-room, try though she might this had not felt wrong. It had felt like a release, a bubbling up of feeling which she had been repressing half her life.

She tried to feel guilty over letting Clive down; the feeling of guilt refused to materialise. All she felt was that she could no longer blame Clive for sleeping with her friend, if sleeping with Selina had given him even half the kick that sleeping with Oliver had given her.

Outside the bathroom door, Oliver cleared his throat then spoke in a soft but carrying voice.

'Clare? Can you leave the water for me? I'll have a bath as well, it'll give me strength for the ordeal to follow.'

'What ordeal?' Clare splashed out of the water, unlocked the door, and peered round it, her flesh steaming, water still puddling off her onto the floor. Oliver groaned and swallowed, then put out one finger and touched her nose with it.

'Dreadful, temptress! How I want to grab you ... but you're hungry and so am I. If you've finished with the bath I'll get in next.'

'Be my guest.'

Clare had always been rather shy about her body. She could not understand her ease with Oliver, the way she continued to dry herself on a towel, rubbing her feet one at a time with a leg cocked up on the bathroom stool whilst he sat in the water watching her with hungry attention. But she liked it. She enjoyed feeling his eyes on her ... and she was sure she could feel them, like being stroked with a feather. Why don't I feel like this with Clive, she wondered uneasily. Why do I feel a bit sinful and rather rude when Clive sees me bare, yet with this almost total stranger I feel comfortable, at ease? But it was no use, she could not understand it so dismissed it from her mind and merely continued to enjoy the moment.

Presently, both bathed and both decently dressed again, Oliver in slacks and a dark shirt with a hacking jacket over it, Clare in a white and gold silk two-piece, which she loved because it was cool and clinging and made her feel rich and cosseted, the two of them descended the stairs and went into the kitchen.

'We'll go down to Yarmouth, spend a night in a hotel there, and come back late Sunday evening,' Oliver announced, as Clare fed Tish and put food into a saucer for Gregory. 'You'll enjoy that without having to worry about the animals. But I suppose we'll have to take the dog with us.'

'I'll drop her off at the Carters,' Clare said, visited by inspiration. 'I'll tell Mrs Carter that I'm going off first thing tomorrow to visit ... to visit an aunt for the day, and ask if I can leave her. They won't mind, they're awfully good and rather fond of Tish.'

As soon as Tish had wolfed her dinner Clare put her on the lead and took her down to the Carters. True to her word, she came back without the dog.

'They were delighted, especially poor Em,' she said,

entering the kitchen and going over to the sink for a glass of water. 'It's awfully hot, Oliver, are you sure you want to drive all the way to Yarmouth?'

'Certain sure. Put your car in the garage and lock up, then we'll be off.'

As she obeyed, even as she stood Greg's saucers of food out on the old coal bunker, Clare found herself wondering anew how she could behave in such an irresponsible fashion. It was as if someone else inhabited her skin, someone with no conscience and no loyalties and no cares, either.

'Ready? Got your little bag? Come on then, let's go.'

Even climbing into the car beside Oliver, the bag slung onto the back seat, Clare felt no pang. If someone saw her . . . so what? She was perfectly entitled to take a lift from a friend. She might easily be going to stay with Gran as she had told Sally she would. She might be going to see an elderly aunt as she had told the Carters. But Clare thought it did not much matter; for a woman who has spent fifteen years under the mistaken impression that she had foisted another man's child on her husband, nothing she consequently did could be so very terrible.

The car was a bit like Oliver – streamlined, handsome and rather fast. Clare thought she would like to drive it and said so and Oliver agreed it was fun to drive other people's cars and promised to let her have a go once they were clear of the city traffic, or at once if she preferred to have her turn whilst in familiar surroundings. Clare drove the Mini because Clive's car, a lean, dark red sports model which he loved obsessively and kept swaddled in plastic sheeting and with its wheels on hay, was forbidden territory. She had never driven it and knew the one way to irritate Clive beyond endurance was to suggest that she might. So hearing a guy accept placidly the idea that she might like to drive his car was a novel experience.

'I'll drive it later, when I've watched you a bit,' she said, however. She'd probably make a fool of herself, get into the wrong gear and be unable to get out again, if she had a go too soon. Better watch how Oliver drove first, and then imitate.

'I've only ever driven the Mini, so I might find it a bit hard to handle,' she added.

Oliver nosed out of the drive, then accelerated down the road. He looked at her out of the corner of his eye.

'You'd handle it easily,' he asserted. 'I've watched you drive your Mini, remember. I think you've considerable flair.'

'That,' Clare said breathlessly after a short pause, 'is easily the nicest thing anyone's ever said to me. Gosh! Flair!'

The car was the sort with a fold-down roof so conversation had to be carried on at a fairly high level and anyway it was exciting, hurtling through the countryside with the wind turning your hair into a plume which it flung this way and that. For a bit they simply drove, and then Oliver turned to her and shouted above the wind that there was a nice pub in about half a mile, and how would she like to stop for a drink?

She agreed, of course. The pub was a converted mill cottage, with the sails of the windmill painted coyly in brown and cream and a children's play area at one side full of plastic giants with steps up their legs and slides from their shoulders and huge metal spiders crouching on concrete mounds. There were quite a few children about but despite the warmth and the sunshine Clare was amused to see not one of them even glancing at the play area. They danced around the bar, raced up to the tow-path beside the distant cut and came back at a gallop, scattering the cattle on the meadows and the hens which clucked at the back door of the pub, but they ignored the entertainment which had been erected to attract them, probably at no small expense.

'We'll go into the bar and take our drinks out to the back garden,' Oliver said, taking her hand.

He ducked to avoid the low beam across the doorway, then went over to the bar. He raised a brow at her and Clare said, 'Oh . . . orange juice, please,' and was momentarily anxious in case he queried it or made some silly remark about it being alcohol-free, but all he did was order a shandy for himself as well and then carry both drinks out of the back door of the pub.

The garden was nice with apple trees, grass underfoot and of course the ever-present hens, a couple of speckled geese and two little calves, which came cantering hobble-de-hoy fashion across the grass and then stopped short, like shy schoolchildren before a headmaster, nudging and staring but not quite daring to come closer.

They drank their drinks and talked quietly. Oliver wanted to know what Sally was doing and was amused by the tennis party.

'Do you want to give her a ring, make sure she's all right?' he asked, but Clare knew that Sally would resent such motherly interference and shook her head.

'She usually rings me, but we chatted last night and she said she wouldn't ring again because with so many people in the house it seemed a bit unfair to use the phone. I told her I might be at Gran's, too, so I doubt she'd ring anyway.'

'That's all right then.' He picked up her hand and played with the fingers, then smiled into her eyes. 'One of these days I'll take you home to my place, introduce you to my young people.'

A pang of genuine alarm and something very like jealousy shot through Clare. She kept her eyes lowered though and tried to speak naturally.

'Oh? Do you have children, then? I didn't even know you were married.'

'No children, nor a wife. Horses, dear Clare, horses! And a herd of pedigree Jerseys whose milk yield is so high I'm the despair of my neighbours. A few pigs, fowl of course, bullocks for fattening on the top pasture up by Richard's place.'

'I see,' Clare said. Her heart leapt up from her lower stomach and she sipped her orange juice with renewed thirst. 'Oliver . . . have you never married?'

'No, never. I've had girlfriends of course, but I've never taken the plunge. Why? Does it make a difference?'

'Yes, it would,' Clare said unhesitatingly. 'I wouldn't want to spoil anything between two people, it wouldn't be right. Well, I don't think I could enjoy it.'

'What about me? Am I spoiling things between two people?'

This embarrassed her. It made her feel, for the first time,

smirched, even a little guilty. She felt her cheeks warm as colour rushed to them.

'Well, n-no, you aren't. Clive's away so much … you think I'm dreadful, I'm sure, terribly loose-moralled … to tell you the truth I don't know how … why … it isn't like me at all, I've never been unfaithful to Clive before and … and …'

He stood up and held out his hands, pulling her to her feet. He put his arm round her waist and pulled her close, then he bent and kissed the side of her face, which was turned away from him now in embarrassment and shame.

'Goose! You aren't taking anything away from your bloke, you're giving to me, and that's generosity, whatever some might think. I'm not into marriage-breaking either, that's all I was trying to say.'

'Oh.' They reached the car and he helped her into the passenger seat, then went round and got behind the wheel. 'Then you don't think too badly of me?'

'I certainly do not. Look, love, if a man goes off and leaves his wife for a year, and comes home for six weeks and then goes again, what does that make him? Faithful? Even if he never touches another woman it doesn't make him faithful in my eyes, it means he prefers making money to being in his wife's company. Is that fair?'

'I don't know,' Clare confessed. 'I've never thought of it like that. But lately, I've felt it isn't *enough*. I'm not very good at explaining how I feel, but I wanted a life of my own, even friends of my own.'

Oliver leaned forward as if to switch on the engine but Clare put a hand over his fingers, shaking her head.

'No, don't, let me think it out loud, would you? It might help.'

He leaned back in his seat.

'Go on, you tell me.'

'Well, it's never been said aloud, or not very clearly, but I've always known that Clive liked to think of me in a sort of suspended animation until he came home. When I say it aloud it sounds absurd, but that was how he wanted it. For the majority of the year I could keep house, mother Sal, and wait for him. For six weeks I was alive, his wife or mistress . . . his woman anyway, living fully. And suddenly I couldn't stand it, not any more. I wasn't even sure whether I really loved him, or whether it was just habit, and his generosity in marrying me. I-I wasn't very marriageable when . . . well, I was . . .'

'Pregnant? For such a loving, giving woman, you do have some odd hang-ups. What was wrong with being pregnant when you married? It happens to hundreds.'

'Oh, I know, but I was only sixteen and I was scared stiff of having a baby on my own, so to speak. He came in like a knight on a white charger and said he wanted to marry me . . . I was so grateful! It was like going under for the third time and suddenly feeling a hand grabbing you under the chin. I adored him, and it was enough for ages and ages. And then suddenly it wasn't enough any more. Only even then I didn't mean to behave the way I did with you. I just sort of fell into it.'

'Dare I say how happy I am that you did?' Oliver leaned forward once more and this time Clare let him start the car, put it into gear and move off the car-park. Darkness was staining the sky and over in a field to the left a cow stared at them. It was an odd looking cow, white all over save for two black patches around its eyes. It looked like a naked highwayman who had managed to retain his mask.

Clare leaned back in her seat as they drove, and peace stole over her. Confession was good for the soul it appeared, for now that she had told Oliver how she felt all the brief embarrassment over her bad behaviour had fled once more as though it had never been. She watched the countryside flying past, saw a field full of leggy, shaggy shire horses, another with ponies grazing, a third full of geese, and enjoyed the novelty of being driven by someone who had no hold whatsoever over her, either emotional or financial. Soon she had even more to watch. The lights of Yarmouth appeared on the horizon, a thousand points of brilliance against the dark.

'I know a good hotel . . . still hungry?' Oliver murmured as they crossed the bridge and headed for the town centre. 'I'm sorry I haven't fed you before, we shouldn't have stopped at that pub.'

'I don't mind,' Clare said drowsily. They drove along the promenade and she smiled out at the crowds on the pavement, at the brightly lit Leisure Centre, at the rowdiness of the sellers of chips, sausages, burgers and candy floss. Even with their engine going and the wind so strong she could hear the bingo callers, the rattle and squeal of the icky machines, the laughter and shouts of young people enjoying themselves.

They parked right at the far end of the prom, in front of a small, grey stone Georgian building, unpretentious, welcoming. Oliver carried her bag and his own briefcase in and a girl in a navy-blue dress with a cardigan slung round her shoulders entered their names – Jack and Jennifer Norton – in the register and gave them a key and directions and smiled at Oliver with frankly admiring eyes.

'Is dinner still being served?' Oliver asked, and the girl said yes it was, and if Mr and Mrs Norton would like to go to their room she would have a menu sent up.

The room was luxurious, all in muted tones of brown, cream and gold with a lightweight quilt on the bed and matching curtains at the window. Feeling shy but pleased with herself, Clare put her nightie on the bed and admired it secretly as she did so. It was a wisp of white nylon, nothing more. She was sure Oliver would like her in it. The fact that he would probably like her even more out of it crossed her mind but that was scarcely the point.

A woman came up with the menu, and Clare and Oliver sat on the bed and studied it, their heads very close. They chose something easy because they were very hungry and wanted to eat at once, and Oliver rang their orders down and was told that they could start their meal in fifteen minutes.

'We'll go and have a quick one in the bar,' Oliver said, taking her hand and pulling her to her feet. 'I can have a proper drink now, since I shan't be driving again for a bit.'

'Or I could drive,' Clare reminded him.

And he smiled and said, 'So you could,' and they went down to the bar in very good charity with one another.

The bar was nice; cosy, all red upholstery and yellowy

lighting. Oliver had a whisky mac and Clare another orange juice. Then they went into the dining-room and sat at a window table and had fresh shrimps with hot toast which was delicious, followed by steak Diane and french fries with a side salad and some peas. After that Oliver had cheese and Clare had fresh fruit salad, and after that they had coffee with two chocolate mints each.

'Full?' Oliver said as they sat lazily finishing their coffee. 'Fancy a run in the car before bed? It's still quite early.'

'You've had two whiskys and more than half a bottle of wine,' Clare reminded him. 'We could walk, though.'

'No. You can drive,' Oliver said.

They went out to the car together and Clare got behind the wheel. She felt nervous, but to her surprise and pleasure the car was beautiful, easy to drive, instantly responsive, with a wheel that turned in her hand as though it could divine her thoughts rather than merely answering to her touch.

They drove up the prom even further, to the far end where the river divides Yarmouth from Gorleston, and then Clare parked and they got out and walked along in the dark, clutching each other, avoiding the ropes which kept the ships in their places. They saw big craft and small, little boats from across the water and great ships from Norway and France and Sweden. They saw a Russian trawler anchored in mid-stream so that the crew couldn't sneak ashore and several ships bound for the oil rigs out on the horizon.

'Why doesn't Clive try for a job on the oil rigs?' Oliver said once, as they gazed, hand in hand, out to sea. And Clare said it was a good idea, and she would suggest it to him if he really did decide to come home for good.

The wind was still strong and it was cold now, so that Oliver's arm around her was a comfort. They walked back to the car and she drove them home and parked in the small space they had left, then she and Oliver, still hand in hand, climbed the stairs and let themselves into their room.

Shyness still refused to come. They pulled the curtains and Clare went into the small bathroom which was a part of their suite and took her clothes off and ran the shower. She washed thoroughly, dried herself on a nice clean hotel towel, and realised she had not brought her nightie through, so she shouted to Oliver and he came in with it in one hand, making rude remarks about cobwebs until she reminded him that he had not seen fit to provide himself with so much as a night-shirt, then he pulled a face at her and took her place in the shower.

When they were both dry again he took her in his arms and kissed her, then led her over to the bed. He did not let her climb in, he lifted her like a baby in his arms and lay her down on the sheets, then he kissed her some more, and then he turned out the light. The nightie floated through the air like the cobweb he had called it and Clare saw, in the moonlight which flooded in through the window, that he was a beautiful animal when he was naked, strong and clean-limbed, and that his face was gentle even when passion made it seem harsh.

When they lay quiet at last she rolled onto her stomach so that she might put her face against his damp, cooling skin, and she was filled with a feeling so strong and pure that she knew she loved him. She wanted him, too, though not in a physical sense: physically she was sated, drowsily and completely satisfied.

'Sleep now, love,' he said, and turned on his side, turning her too, so that they lay like two spoons, one curled protectively around the other.

It was going to be easy to sleep, tonight. I wonder if loving him will hurt me and complicate matters dreadfully, Clare thought drowsily just as she drifted off into dreams. Or perhaps it will make everything clear-cut and easy, when morning comes. Is it better to make love out of lust, or out of this other, nobler emotion? But she could not answer herself, perhaps she did not even want to do so.

CHAPTER
14

All the way home in the car on the Monday afternoon, Clare kept up a continuous stream of chatter; chatter which Sally sometimes answered with more than usual vivacity and sometimes appeared not even to hear.

She's noticed I'm different, Clare thought with horrid foreboding. Is it written on my forehead in letters six inches high – 'Adulteress'? But she soon realised it could not possibly be that since no one other than Sally had treated her oddly ... and, of course, my forehead isn't six inches wide, she reminded herself with mad practicality.

'So what did you do after that, pet?' she heard her voice asking gaily, but she did not really listen to Sally's answer, which seemed to include a great many names she had never heard before and a good few breathy giggles. Suffice it to know that Sally had thoroughly enjoyed herself with Ella – possibly nearly as thoroughly as I enjoyed myself with Oliver, Clare thought with guilty, intense pleasure. Oh, that weekend! Oh, the bliss of their lovemaking, the comfort of being with someone who made no demands, or at least, she amended, no demands which she could not instantly and happily meet.

Her mind arrowed back to Sunday morning, waking in bed beside him, getting dressed together, eating breakfast with neither of them so much as glancing at the Sunday papers set out on the sideboard in the dining-room because all they wanted was their shared companionship.

Summer had vanished with the previous evening, but despite a cold, high wind, grey clouds scudding fast across the sky, and rain every half-hour or so, it had been an unforgettable day. Better, possibly, than the previous evening and even night, since they got to know one another and their sense of being friends as well as lovers – or Clare's sense of the happy state – increased with each passing hour.

In the morning they played the machines in the amusement arcades, strode briskly up the promenade from the Gorleston end to the Caistor end and bought each other sticks of rock, doughnuts freshly cooked in extremely old engine-oil judging by the flavour, and silly hats which they actually wore for half an hour. Clare's had 'Who loves Ya, Baby?' written round the crown and Oliver's bore the legend 'Make Love not War'.

'I intend to follow this advice,' Oliver said, taking the hat off and reading the words aloud. Clare laughed. They did a lot of laughing.

They ate on the hoof, as Oliver put it. Greasy beefburgers inside large white buns with lots of onion and even more tomato ketchup, most of which dribbled down their fingers and chins. Then peaches of great size and splendour – more dribbles, not so colourful but much stickier – then ginger-beer out of cans.

'If you want a beer I'll drive home,' Clare volunteered, but Oliver said that one glance from her beautiful eyes was more intoxicating than five double whiskies and that in any case he thought they had had quite sufficient role reversal for the next few hours. This remark, referring to a much earlier happening, made Clare blush and seeing her blush made Oliver hug her, and a lot of ginger-beer got spilt, adding to the hilarity which had marked the day so far.

After lunch they bathed, mostly to get rid of all traces of their alfresco meal but also because Oliver, it appeared, could not set eyes on a stretch of water without wanting to be in it. Yarmouth is a trifle too well-populated for nude bathing and neither of them had a costume, but Yarmouth is also broadminded to a fault; no one commented or probably even noticed the two people, one in briefs and the other in panties and a bra, who ran down the beach hand in hand, plunged together, and stayed in until Clare, at least, was going pale blue with cold.

'And now for junketings in the bathing hut, grabbings and clutchings and lovely lovely letchings,' Oliver panted, as they tore up the beach.

But it was too cold for anything of the sort. And too sandy. Bodies rubbed vigorously dry with towels which have been carelessly left lying, lose a thin layer of skin and people who have just been skinned don't hang about nude in the wind off the east coast for long, even if they do have the doubtful protection of a beach-hut.

'Tea with me is the high sort,' Oliver said, as, warm and dry once more, they drove off along the prom heading homeward. 'I know somewhere good.'

He did. They sat in an unprepossessing wooden hut down by a Broad and looked out with sympathy at the ducks trying to keep their balance on the water whilst a gale fought to knock them sideways, and they ate a very high tea indeed – sandwiches, sausage rolls, a salad with cold chicken, fruit cake, scones, and of course a huge pot of tea. After that they drove more or less straight home, because Clare told him she would cook him 'Pork chops à la Clare', with apple sauce made from her own apples and followed by ginger pudding in a golden syrup sauce.

The got home in a rainstorm, so Clare put up her umbrella and dashed down the road for Tish, who was gratifyingly pleased to see her and even jumped up and licked Oliver. Then, because it was such a vile night Oliver lit the fire in the living-room whilst Clare cooked, then they ate the meal sitting at the kitchen table and in Clare's case at least, not even tasting the food because she was suddenly excited by his presence in her home. Then they went up to bed.

At some unspecified hour, Clare was woken by someone slipping into bed beside her and put out a sleepy hand saying, 'Worrizit?' in the way one does when still more than half unconscious.

'It's all right, don't worry. Only I've swopped the cars

round; your Mini's outside the back door on the gravel and mine is in your garage.'

Even in a state of semi-consciousness she was aware of a warm glow pervading her being. He did not want to get her into hot water. Oh, she loved him! She said as much.

'Love you, Oliver.'

He put his arm round her and pulled her close, saying nothing for a moment, and when he did speak it was in a tone of surprise which almost amounted to awe.

'Me too.'

'Mum, you're in another world! I asked you if you'd had a nice weekend – wasn't the weather fabulous on Saturday? Did you go to Gran's? I thought of you a lot.'

It jerked Clare back to the present, ill-prepared for questioning. For an awful moment she could not remember what she had actually told the Carters . . . something about an aunt, was it? . . . and then, with real pleasure, she recalled what Oliver had said. She took a deep breath and prepared to lie convincingly.

'No I didn't go to Gran's, but I had a marvellous weekend, really good. After work on Saturday I came home and who should turn up on my doorstep but a very old friend indeed – have you heard me mention Harry Mortimer, the girl who lived down at Yarmouth? She was a boarder, she came to stay with me a couple of times when I was a bit younger than you, about thirteen I was I suppose. Well, she's married now and back in Yarmouth and when I told her you were away for the weekend she whisked me off home with her, just for the day you know, on Sunday. It was fun . . . her husband's a nice fellow too. I really enjoyed myself.'

Full marks, she thought as Sally said how pleased she was and asked not a single awkward question. Now if I just remember to stick to it Harry Mortimer can be most awfully useful! She could see Harry in her mind as she elaborated a little to Sally about how wonderful the Carters had been, how the storm had nearly turned her brolly inside out when she had called for the dog. Harry was tall and fair, with short hair in an Eton crop so that she looked quite masculine in certain lights. No, she had better be dark, perhaps. She had a beautiful house ... she had plenty of money, they owned a farm as well ... a bit snooty though, you had to be careful how you treated her.

'So we both had a nice weekend, then,' Sally said contentedly as Clare stopped the car with a flourish outside the back door. 'Dear Tish, I bet she's missed me!' As they walked together towards the house she added, 'Will you go again, Mum, if they ask you?'

'Oh, yes,' breathed Clare, forgetting for a moment to use the sensible, practical tone of one referring to an old schoolfriend. She caught herself up hastily. 'But it may not happen, they may not ask me again.'

'So you'd go to them again if you were asked.' Sally's tone was triumphant. 'But if I want to go twice running to stay with Dee...'

Clare unlocked the back door and Tish was upon them. For a moment it was all they could do to retain their equilibrium, then nature called and Tish dashed for the lawn and squatted. Wails from Clare brought her sheepishly, dot and carry one, back onto the gravel – urine kills grass stone dead in no time – and then they were in the kitchen and Sally was returning to her attack.

'So you can go twice and it isn't rude but I mustn't. Oh Mum, if I'm asked again, can I go? Please?'

Clare swallowed and tried to erase the giddying vision of constant weekends spent in Oliver's bed. Still, if Sally really did want to have another weekend with Deirdre, where was the harm in that? It would give her the freedom to ... to ...

'If you're asked again I don't see why not,' she said as calmly as she could. 'How hungry are you? There's cottage pie in the freezer or we can have chicken soup and then omelettes and salad.'

'Anything, I don't mind. Oh, by the way, is it all right if I run up to Em's for half an hour? I won't be long, honestly. Only I was away all the weekend and she did see to Pegs for me and if I'm going to be away again ...'

She did not wait for a reply but headed for the back door. Clare watched her go, then, with a glance at the chilly grey sky, went to the freezer and abstracted two individual cottage

287

pies in their foil containers. They were both home-made by
herself and full of goodness, but because they were frozen she
would grate cabbage and do it, French fashion, in a spoonful
of oil and no water, with a panful of green beans from the
garden.

She was half-way through the preparation of the meal when
she realised something odd. She was still extremely happy.
Her stolen weekend was over, she and Oliver had parted
without a word regarding their next meeting, yet she was
happy, looking forward without even an intimation of what
the morrow might bring.

Was this happiness dependent on seeing Oliver again? Yes,
of course it was, but she had such faith in him that she was
sure he would make other meetings possible somehow.
Grating cabbage over a bowl, easily her most disliked
household task due to wear and tear on the nails and
knuckles, Clare began to sing.

Clive drove, in his own private dust-cloud, along the road
leading to the city. His thoughts were all pleasant anticipation, because he was going to surprise someone. Someone of
whom he was fond.

He had seen quite a bit of Della Knighton since the fateful
evening when he had given her the gold bracelet. Quite a bit.
One way and another. She was charming, he told himself
defensively when his old-fashioned morals kicked him in the
stomach for the way he was behaving, quite charming, and
what was the harm, anyway? He was a long way from home,
Clare had a job and other interests, there was absolutely
nothing to do in the Kingdom save for ... well, for what he
was doing, or rather was about to do, so no one in their right
minds would blame him.

Nevertheless he was not entirely comfortable about his
behaviour. Even if Clare was having it off with every
farmhand who entered the caff – and he knew how unlikely
that was, none better! – it did not entitle him to have sex with
an engaged girl whenever the opportunity occurred. But
Della did so enjoy lovemaking! She groaned and grabbed, she
bit and clawed and whimpered and screamed ... she knew

the *Kama Sutra* by heart and obviously enjoyed doing things the hard way from time to time . . . which was instructive for Clive as well as being great fun.

He had never really realised, until now, that Clare did not enjoy lovemaking. She was a good girl, she tried, but having seen Della in action he was sure that Clare suffered him rather than shared his pleasure. She never simply lay, that would have been far too obvious, but he could not recall one single occasion on which she had taken the lead, tried anything different, or behaved with abandon. Well, he amended, remembering one or two occasions, not with wild abandon then.

He had last slept with Della – if you could call it that – four nights ago and already his body was demanding another session, though perhaps that was because last time, she had been easily and early satisfied and less athletically inclined than usual. But when she had been told he could not see her for over a week she had not been at all pleased.

'Lover, why not?' she had said, biting his shoulder quite sharply so that Clive had hard work not to shout. 'I thought you were always free on a Wednesday.'

'I am, usually. But I've been invited to a party which I simply can't afford to refuse and don't suggest I take you with me, much though I'd like to, because it's at Sheik Yussufa's place which means men only.'

'Sheik who? What's so important about him?'

'Sheik Yussufa, and you pronounce it shake, as in wobble.'

He grinned to himself, remembering Clare, years ago, instructing Sally with those very words, but Della was not amused. A frown marred her smooth young brow and she dug her long nails into the soft flesh of Clive's inner thigh. Clive winced. One of the penalties attached to sleeping with Della was her considerable use of violence; he had scars all over his body to prove it, though fortunately she preferred biting, clawing and pinching at what you might call the undercover areas of the human frame.

'That hurt, honey,' he protested more as a matter of form than in the hopes of an apology, but for once he wronged her. Della suddenly reared up in bed and straddled him. She hung

289

her head over him so that her short, shiny hair flopped forward, then bent down still further, until her breasts were squashed against him and her nose rested on the tip of his.

'Sorry, Cliviekins; Della's very sorry. So you won't come round to see me next Wednesday?'

'Darling, it isn't won't, it's can't, honestly.'

The last word came out muffled since she chose that moment to try to push her tongue into his mouth. He did not resist; resistance, as well as being useless was also dangerous as his scars testified. Della explored his mouth with her tongue for a somewhat suffocating moment, then sat up and blew her hair off her forehead.

'Oh well, if you can't, you can't,' she said briskly.

She slithered off him and began an intimate caress which he knew, with sinking heart, meant she wanted him to make love to her again. Saying plaintively that he simply couldn't was no answer; she would look at him slit-eyed, and tell him to leave it to her and sure enough, he would find that he could after all. Only it was so damn' tiring! Her fingers squeezed and coaxed but he could see from her abstract expression that her mind wasn't on her work for once.

'So you can't see me on Wednesday,' she repeated presently, using her nails softly for once whilst Clive stirred uneasily and longed for a cold beer. 'But there's always Friday. Can you come on Friday?'

'Oh ... ooh ... but you're working on Friday evening, you always work on Friday evening,' Clive protested faintly. 'Next Wednesday, now ...'

'I'll swop my duties round if you can't come on Wednesday,' Della said at once. 'Well, no, perhaps I can't do that, but I can get off on Friday if you promise you can make it then.'

'I can manage Friday,' Clive said wearily. He wondered if being constantly aroused like this was as bad for a fellow as he suspected.

'You can?' To his astonished delight Della's fingers abandoned their self-imposed task and she slithered right out of bed, sat on the edge of it for a moment, and then got up and walked towards the fridge. The bedroom door was ajar and

290

Clive, with mounting hope, saw her open the fridge, abstract two cans, and return, her busy fingers pulling the tag of the topmost can as she came. 'Then let's have a drink to celebrate Friday,' she said as she approached the bed. 'One for the road, I think, lover . . . you'll be off in about fifteen minutes, I suppose?'

'Indeed yes,' Clive said, taking his watch off the bedside table and slipping it round his wrist. Della, who so enjoyed inflicting pain on him, did not enjoy finding his watch strap entangled in her hair at all and insisted that he take it off before laying a finger on her. 'One quick beer and I must dash.'

He had dashed, happily conscious of having preserved, if not his virtue, at least the last of his strength. Usually he crawled down to the Land-Rover, knees shaking, mouth dry, and barely made it back to base.

Yet so strange is the human mind that when Sheik Yussufa changed the day of his party from Wednesday to the previous Tuesday, he felt delighted. He would not need to disappoint Della, he would go on the Wednesday evening as planned and they could spend five hours together.

First, of course, he telephoned the hospital, because if she was still working he had no desire for a long, dusty drive for nothing. Sister was sorry, Staff Nurse Knighton had been on an early shift today and was at home now, probably resting. If you want to ring her, she had continued helpfully, I can give you her number.

But Clive, ever the gentleman, had said he would not break into Staff's off-duty for the world and had replaced the receiver, chuckling. So she was free and probably sitting in her air-conditioned living-room reading a romance and eating something sticky and indigestible bought from the bazaar.

He reached the block of nurses' flats, parked the Land-Rover unobtrusively round the back, and strode masterfully up the stairs. At Della's door he paused whilst he searched for the key she had lent him, then inserted it in the lock, turned it and entered. He stood just inside the door for a moment, listening. Half-way across the tiny hall he stopped because he thought he heard voices coming from behind a closed door.

She might have a friend with her, or someone who knew them both quite well. That would never do, so Clive left the flat again and closed the door softly behind him, then rang the bell.

It was quite a long time before the door opened. Della stood there in the long, white silk robe with the dragon embroidered across the shoulders which he knew so well. She gasped when she saw him, then shrugged.

'Clive, honestly, you said you wouldn't come round on Wednesday, so naturally I thought ... Well, there's someone with me.'

'Oh? Can you get rid of her?'

'No, I couldn't possibly, when you invite ...'

Behind her, the door opened. It was the bedroom door. A man stood framed against the light. To Clive's relief he was fully dressed but he was carrying something in one hand. It looked like a large sheet.

'Della, do you have a beer?' The man said, his voice unmistakably English, his accent respectable, even slightly familiar. 'I'm gasping for a drink my dear girl – mind if I help myself?'

Della, who had been looking undecidedly from one to the other, seemed to make up her mind.

'Come in, Clive. Of course I've got beer, Teddy, we'll all have one. Clive, Teddy's an old friend – a patient, actually – who's just popped in to change out of Arabic dress into European. I lent him my room. Teddy, Clive's another old friend. He was supposed to be taking me out tonight but a party came up which he couldn't miss ... only as you can see, he managed it.' Her voice was acid on the last sentence. Clive, who had been feeling both self-conscious (married man caught visiting single girl) and annoyed (married man catching another man with girl), decided not to make a thing of it. After all, she was entitled to have friends, who was not?

'Hello, Ted. So you wear a *thobe* sometimes? I do myself, particularly when I'm amongst the Sauds, otherwise you stand out like a sore thumb, I find.'

Teddy agreed that this was so and the three of them went

through into the kitchen where Della rather sulkily dispensed beer and they sat and talked whilst it sank in the glasses.

It might have turned into quite a party but for two things. One was Della, who sat between the men growing sulkier as the evening progressed. The other was that Clive could not make up his mind whether she was waiting for him to go or Teddy, so naturally he decided to be the last to leave. In the bright little kitchen he saw that Teddy was a man well past his first youth, possibly in his mid to late fifties, and this reassured him. A man of that age was unlikely to give Della the sort of all-night service she required, he was probably simply an old friend as she had said.

He thought that firmly and innocently and continued to think it until, with the hands of the clock pointing at midnight, he decided to call it a day and go home. There was always next Wednesday after all and sitting cheek by jowl with an angry Della was not conducive to thoughts of making love. Indeed, when he contemplated what she would probably do to him if she got him alone he was happy to be the first to leave.

When he stood up to go, however, Teddy followed suit, confirming Clive's decision not to regard the older man as a rival. He continued to think this as they descended the stairs side by side and walked out to where their Land-Rovers were coyly tucked away amongst the dustbins at the back of the block.

'Well, Ted, it's been grand meeting you; I take it you're working with the Yanks since I've not seen you about before,' Clive said with masculine camaraderie, shaking his companion's large, tanned hand. 'You must come out to our base some time, sink a few jars. You're an East Anglian, like myself, I believe, from your accent.'

'That's right, I hail from Norfolk, and I'll come out to your base any time you're free to take me into the bar,' the older man said easily. 'I work all over the Gulf, liaison mainly between the big oil companies and the sheiks, but I'm heading home for good in a few months. I can afford to leave now, I reckon.'

'I'm thinking of doing the same,' Clive said. 'I've been out here sixteen or seventeen years, and my wife's coped alone for fifteen, I reckon that's long enough.'

Teddy chuckled.

'I've been here more than thirty years,' he observed. 'My wife does very well without me I imagine, since I've not set eyes on her for longer than that. Odd little thing; thought sex was a dirty word until she tried it and then thought it was a dirty deed as well. I was lucky to get away with my life I think sometimes.'

'That's strange.' Clive, frowning, leaned against the Land-Rover and looked across at his companion by the light of the great golden moon above. 'I've begun to wonder, lately, if my wife isn't a bit like that. Oh she doesn't think sex is dirty, exactly, she just . . .'

He stopped short. Ted, with an exclamation, was taking off his shirt. He was saying something about it being too hot to put the *thobe* on over the top of his clothing as he did so.

His chest and shoulders were criss-crossed with scratches, black against the paleness of his skin, and there was what looked like a bite at the base of his strong neck.

Ted glanced at him as he emerged from the shirt, looked down at his own chest and chuckled.

'You take your life in your hands when you go to bed with Della,' he said conversationally. 'Likes to play rough, doesn't she! Still, she's good value compared with some – they think a few kisses, a fumble and a quick bonk behind the Land-Rover are all a fellow's after. I need time and a bed at my age.'

'Er . . . yes, indeed. Yes, I think . . .' Clive turned to get into his own vehicle, then stopped and turned back. 'Look, you talk as if you've known Della for years, but she was telling me she'd only been here six months and . . .'

'Six months! Oh well, this time round, yes that'ud be about right. But she was here four years ago and don't I know it! She went home for a long leave, I think she thought she might marry and settle down, but she came back.' He shook his head, chuckling. 'Oh, everyone knows Della, she's a popular little lady.'

'How old is she, then?' Clive asked. 'She told me she was nearly twenty-two.'

294

'Add ten or a dozen years to that and you won't be far off,' Teddy said with cheerful disloyalty. 'How come you'd never met her before, though, if you've been in the Kingdom for fifteen years? I'd swear there wasn't a soul in the Gulf who didn't know Della . . . and I use the word "know" in all its senses.'

'I don't know . . . I only started taking an interest in the nurses when I thought I might go home for good. You see . . . no, it's too long a story.'

The older man sighed, glanced at his watch, and then caught Clive's arm.

'Come on, I know somewhere we can get a drink and watch a belly-dancer whilst you tell me your troubles. You don't want to go comparing your wife with Della, you know,' he added as Clive obediently fell into step beside him. 'Della's one hell of a girl I grant you, but it takes half a dozen men to keep up with her – she's a nympho of course, but even for a nympho she's hard to satisfy.'

'She is, isn't she?' Clive said fervently. 'I'm glad I met you Ted, I was beginning to wonder how on earth I'd manage if I really do go home for good, because I couldn't keep that up for a week, let alone for a year!'

'Yes, well, there's two extremes in women; Della's one end of the spectrum and my wife's the other. If I had to choose,' he added reflectively, 'I don't know that I wouldn't choose my wife at that; reckon a feller would live longer.'

He laughed. After a moment, Clive echoed it. They walked on through the city together.

'So you see, Cheepy my son, there's a lot more goin' on than any of 'em knows,' Mavis concluded, having reported the day's doings to her little friend. 'Clare's goin' around smiling at everyone but she don't even know what day it is half the time, and that feller . . . Coffee an' Book . . . comes in and sits in the corner and watches her and you can see he knows 'er for all they pretend to be nothing to one another . . . think they fool old Mavis, Cheepy-love? No, acourse they doesn't. I waits inside, 'e waits outside, and soon's I go orf for me bus, in 'e pops and God knows what goes on then!'

'God knows, Cheepy my son,' the bird said, in imitative sing-song. 'God knows, Cheepy my son, God knows Cheepy, Cheepy, pretty-boy, Mummy's pet!'

'You're a clever little bugger,' Mavis said from the depths of the cane-bottomed chair. She stretched out her shoeless feet and wiggled the toes at herself. She was going to fetch fish and chips for her tea and damn the money. Why not? She'd had one hell of a day at the caff, Dee was in a rotten temper, said her arm hurt, had twice been caught by Mavis crying in a corner. Clare was too cheerful by half, which was almost worse. And Sally seemed to have changed completely from the sweet, cheerful little girl who came noisily into the caff and begged cream cakes and milk from them into a stiff, almost sullen teenager who contradicted every word her mother said, spent hours staring into space and chewing her finger-nails, and bit anyone's head off who ventured to remonstrate.

Of course on the bright side there was the old lady: Gran, Clare called her. A nice old bird and quick as they come. No hanging back wondering for that one; straight out with whatever she was thinking and damn 'em all. My style, Mavis thought with satisfaction, and decided to have curry sauce with the chips and a bottle of red pop. Or perhaps a gin and tonic.

First they'd had Clare's Mum, and a right snooty one she was with her bust nearly touching her chin and her tight skirt and rigidly perfect hair. But she'd liked the caff, said it was good of its kind – Mavis sniffed in outraged recollection – and admitted Clare was better working than stuck at home being bored. Mavis, who had secretly dreaded someone persuading Clare to leave, had actually smiled at Mrs Flower ... daft name ... and would have winked had she not thought Mrs F might take exception to such an over-familiar gesture.

Gran, now, was quite a different kettle of fish. Shrewd, that was Gran. She'd come in, walking upright and quick when you considered she was the wrong side of seventy-five, and given the place the once-over with a glance like a knife. Mavis had been glad, she wouldn't deny it, that she'd just wiped down the tables and brushed the floor. Then Gran had sat quietly down at the corner table in the window – by a coincidence, the one favoured by Coffee and Book – and had simply watched, gimlet-eyed, as they all went about their business. When there were no customers she had chatted, too, and came behind the counter and used the coffee machine, obviously intrigued by it and giving little clucks of disapproval when she could not, at first, get it quite right.

She knew there was something up with Clare, Mavis had no doubt of that. And she was a bit anxious over Sally, too, though Clare herself seemed to take it as just teenage silliness and assured everyone who commented on it that it would pass. But Mavis wasn't so sure, and she didn't think Gran was so sure either. Nor, for that matter, young Deirdre. Dee was difficult, now, with Sally. Stiff, formal, as though they had had a row which she could neither forget nor forgive. But it couldn't be that because Sally was as friendly as anything towards Dee, more natural and easy with her friend than she could bring herself to be with anyone else.

Mavis had wanted to have a word with Gran, because she liked the old bird and wanted to reassure her, but it had just not been possible. There were too many people in and out, both customers and staff. So in the end she had been forced to make do with a muttered message.

'I'll keep me eye on 'em, let you know if things go wrong,' she had whispered as she passed Gran's table.

Gran's bright eyes had met hers and she had given a quick little nod of the head, but ... she was pretty old. Who knew what she might have thought she heard? Who knew whether she had made out a word of Mavis's message? Only if things did go wrong, and they had a way of doing just that when you started deceiving people in Mavis's experience, then she would rather have Gran's advice and help than try to soldier on without it.

The clock on the mantelpiece whirred, clicked and struck four. Which meant it was half-past six and the chip shop would be open. If she didn't get a move on a queue would be forming and all the biggest pieces of skate would be taken. Mavis struggled to her feet, forced her shoes on, and reached

297

for her handbag. It wasn't far to the shop, she scarcely needed a coat but she liked to carry a handbag even though it would have been easier to slip some change into her pocket. My generation needs a handbag for self-defence, she told herself as she opened the front door. A good, heavy bag full of the accumulation of a lifetime and swung at someone's face was more than a deterrent, it was a tooth-remover.

Outside, she discovered that the sun had come out since her dreary journey back from work and the wet pavement gleamed gold. Momentarily the worries about Clare, Sally and Deirdre vanished from Mavis's mind. At least it meant that her letter to Lionel would be full to bursting, for Lionel was a great student of human nature, which meant he was dead nosy, so far as Mavis could see. But for whatever reason, he enjoyed seeing the rich tapestry of life at the caff unrolled before him, which meant that though Mavis worried, at least she did not have to search around for something to put in her letters. There was an over-abundance of news, just lately.

Slapping along the pavement, for the chip shop did not merit high-heels so Mavis wore her scuffies, she told herself she would remind young Deirdre that they were supposed to be having a weekend down Yarmouth. Perhaps that would cheer the girl up. Not that she was depressed all the time, often she forgot her woes, whatever they were, and talked and laughed with the best. It was something to do with Sally ... if I could get Sally to one side and have a word with her I wonder if that could put things right Mavis asked herself, avoiding a puddle at the last moment with the recollection of the hole in the bottom of her right shoe. Sometimes she saw herself, poised above the action, as a sort of benevolent mother-figure who watched over Clare, Sally and Deirdre at work and Cheepy, Sondra and the boys at home. This benevolent mother-figure could solve all their problems if only they would let her.

Mavis reached the chip shop. It was nearly empty, the queue consisting of a small Indian boy picking his nose whilst reading a *Beano*, a mother with a baby in one arm and another clutching at her skirt, and a couple of truckies, one of whom was actually daring to smoke in the shop though there were at least three notices requesting customers to refrain from their unhealthy habit.

Behind the counter Mr Arrovali shouted, in an operatic Italian accent, for more spuds. His small, dark-haired assistants leaned over their glass-topped counter and tried to reason with the customer who was smoking. The mother and child repeated their order three times . . . the assistant did not know what she meant when she said did they do child's portions, he simply kept repeating fish, pie, chicken, pasty, as though it were the only English he knew. Then he swore at the man who was still smoking, and Mavis realised he had quite a good grasp of the language.

Mavis launched herself across the greasy floor and joined the end of the queue. There was a nice piece of skate already cooked, she could see it through the glass. Unless someone else in the queue was after it, it would just suit her for her supper. With so few people in front of her she shouldn't have to wait long.

She was about to take her turn at the counter when, for some reason, she thought of Clare again, as she had seen her that very afternoon. Clare had been serving a customer and Mavis, who had nipped out to the shops to get some more bread because they had unaccountably run out, had been looking straight into Clare's face as someone behind her had raised a hand and waved. And Clare's face, which had been smiling and pretty and happy anyway, had suddenly been transformed by a radiance which could have only one cause. Clare Arnold, Mavis thought crossly now, don't you dare go falling in love with a feller you scarcely know! That Coffee and Book, he's just a fly-by-night, just a horse-waggon driver who would be off as soon as he'd got what he wanted, and then where would Clare be?

'Yes, luv?'

'Coffee and . . .' Mavis stopped short and actually blushed; at least her neck went remarkably hot. 'I mean . . . skate and chips, please, and curry sauce.'

'Skate . . . we got any skate, Uncle Carlo?'

'Course you have,' Mavis snapped. She pointed, then her finger curled itself back into her palm. The skate had gone.

'Gotta cooka new pieca skate,' Uncle Carlo roared from the room behind the shop. He appeared in the doorway, a wing, well battered, dangling from his hand. 'Itsa gooda pieca skate,' he said encouragingly, waving the fish at Mavis.

Mavis sighed, then nodded.

'I'll 'ave that bit,' she said. 'How much?'

Gran was watering her roses. They were fine little bushes and they no more needed water than she needed to fly but they were in sore need of fertilizer and she dared not put good, old-fashioned horse-dung round their roots, not after the fuss the council had made over the roses' presence in their wretched community grass.

So she was using Liquinure, and the neighbours, no doubt, were using their binoculars to see what she was up to this time.

As she watered, Gran chatted. Roses needed a chat from time to time and it helped her to discuss her worries, even if the flowers did not answer back.

'Clare's happy,' she was telling the nearest bush, which promised to be very fine in a year or two though at the moment it was nothing more than a few small, apricot-coloured buds. 'Now why should I worry about her when I know she's happy, you ask. Well, the answer's simple. She's happy because the little idiot's gone and fallen head over heels for some unworthy young man. What do you think of that?'

The roses, not surprisingly, made no reply, but this did not deter Gran.

'You think she's a married woman and should be ashamed of herself,' she informed the roses. 'Ah, but you don't know the situation, that's why you think that. Clive ... he's her husband ... Clive's not been good to her, though you'll be told otherwise, of course. It's not good to leave a beautiful, lively girl like my Clare alone for fifteen years, only coming home for six weeks each summer to have it off with her, as they say these days. Now she's not over-sexed and she's a wonderful mother to Sally, but that six weeks wasn't enough, it wouldn't have been enough for any red-blooded woman.

Now I'm not saying the sex-side wasn't enough,' she warned the nearest rose-bush, wagging an admonitory finger at it, 'but the warmth, the love, that was what my girl missed. Oh, for years she thought Sally was enough but Sally's a big girl now, she's looking for love on her own account, I dare say. She's out of the house more than she's in it and my girl's lonely. She's wasting her life, you could say. Or she was. But not any more, no not any more. She's found someone who appreciates her, that's what I think, and good luck to her!'

Gran stared aggressively down at the roses, daring them to contradict. But the roses remained silent; it was Gran who was murmuring, 'Poor Clive, poor old boy, poor Clive,' as she made her way back to her flat. And she did not even realise she was speaking aloud.

Deirdre knew that something was up with Clare, otherwise she would have noticed and commented on Deirdre's own preoccupation. Does she know what Sally's up to? Deirdre asked herself half a dozen times a day, but she could not answer. Surely Clare could not be so dumb that she saw no change in Sally? But it was plain as a pikestaff that Clare had other things on her mind. Better things. Deirdre watched events at the caff as closely and obsessively as Mavis did, but she was too involved to have Mavis's clarity of vision and anyway she was handicapped by the fact that she knew no old person could possibly fall in love, and although Clare was great, the best boss you could ask for, though she was extremely pretty and full of life, she was also old. So having dismissed the possibility that Clare might have fallen in love, Dee's view of events was, so to speak, two-dimensional.

Sometimes she wondered about Coffee and Book, though. He came in so often now, particularly around four o'clock when she was thinking about going home. Dee still admired him, of course she did, but she would have had to be very conceited indeed to believe that the gleam in his eye was for her, and Dee was a down-to-earth sort of girl. Instead, she assumed that Coffee and Book must be interested in Sally. There was no doubt about it, Sally was blossoming. She had actually started to grow a pair of small, pert breasts, and although she never wore make-up, or not so's you could notice, Dee could have sworn that Sally's eyelashes were longer and glossier, her eyes brighter, her lips more soft and full.

Of course Dee was well aware that Sally had interests other than Coffee and Book. Who should know better than she, who had suffered most when Sally suddenly decided she was interested in boys after all? But that had died the death when she, Deirdre, had obstinately refused to have Sal to stay every weekend and Sal, to be fair to her, had been grand about it and had showed not the slightest sign of annoyance. Indeed, she had been very sweet to Deirdre ever since ... only, although of course it was nothing to do with Sally, not any more, Dee seemed to have lost Quack's regard which was precious to her, and she found she could not forgive Sally for that quite so easily.

Hence the coolness. To have invited Sally for the weekend when she was so sure that Quack was about to ask her out had been kind, she considered. To turn round and find that Quack, ostensibly visiting her, could scarcely take his eyes off Sally had been a poor return for her hospitality. And Sally, who only liked older men she had said, had definitely liked Quack enough to go off on the back of his motor bike twice, to share a bag of chips with him whilst he fished by the pond, and to be caught red-handed by Dee on the second evening of her stay cuddling with Quack in the bushes near the kennels ... though Quack had said he was mucking around, wrestling, and Sally had said she was sorry and wouldn't have let him fool about if she'd known Dee would mind.

It had spoiled the spontaneity of their friendship, though. Quack was cool, offhand, and Deirdre, bitterly hurt, turned the coolness and offhandedness on to Sally. Sometimes though, she wondered whether Sally wasn't a bit thick, because she never seemed to notice her friend's change of heart. Why, she had even asked Dee if she would like to stay one weekend, and had appeared downcast but not shattered by Dee's prompt refusal.

So if Coffee and Book were interested in Sally, and if Dee

302

could pass on this titbit of information to the surely still besotted Quack, would not her true love see the hopelessness of his passion – if he was still keen on Sally – and turn to her once more? It was all very upsetting and perhaps the most infuriating thing of all was that Hecky Smith, who was taller and stronger than Quack and who had been the terror of the upper juniors when she was in school, had actually asked her out ... and Dee had refused, because she could not contemplate going out with Hecky whilst there was the faintest chance of getting Quack.

These thoughts were whizzing about in Deirdre's mind as she walked two of her charges along the familiar lanes. She went to the pond, but Quack was not there; an enquiry elicited the information that he'd gone off, on his bike, and wouldn't be home till late.

'The boy Quack's courtin',' the girl who informed on him said laconically, her mean little eyes fixed on Deirdre's face. 'Got a woman, Quack has, out Dereham way.'

'Then who's going for chips?' Deirdre asked briskly; she did not intend Vi'let Cummins to have a laugh on her, that she did not! Vi'let looked at her with some respect and offered to go down herself, on her push-bike. Deirdre offered to walk alongside so's they could chat, like, and the two girls set off.

All the way to the chip shop and all the way back they talked. But Deirdre did not once mention Quack and Vi'let volunteered no information. Only when they were in the queue did she say idly, 'How's your friend Sally? Int seen her lately. Nice kid, is she?'

'Very nice, but as you say, only a kid,' Deirdre said kindly. 'Mad on horses, she is. Know all about 'em too, young though she is.'

'Ah. Strange how you'll get a gal mad on horses, can't think of nothin' else. I knew a gal like that once.'

Deirdre ate her chips, giving her dogs a couple, and then walked away from the pond alone. But not for long. Hecky caught her up. He had a motor bike at home, as she well knew, but it was always ailing and Hecky was no mechanic. After a few yards, silently, he took one of the dog's leads from her hand. Deirdre did not have the heart to snub him and snatch it back. If Quack really had a woman . . .

'Comin' out, come Sat'day?' Hecky asked presently.

Deirdre sighed.

'I might.'

CHAPTER
15

As though love could even affect the weather, the sun suddenly decided to shine not only on Clare and Oliver, but on the rest of Norfolk as well.

Sally went off most weekends, either to play tennis, or to stay with a friend or simply out on Pegs for a whole day at a time, taking a packed lunch, a flask of iced lemonade, and a bag of apples for her dauntless steed. Whilst she was gone, however, Clare was no longer lonely. Oliver had only to hear her voice on the telephone to drop whatever he was doing and come running. They were careful at first and took precautions against being seen, but soon it no longer seemed possible that their idyll would end and they drove away from the house quite merrily on a Saturday night, after dark to be sure, and drove back equally merrily on the Sunday.

The first time that Oliver came into the caff and waited for her to tell her that he loved her was a Red Letter Day. Clare had been rushed off her feet for hours and was tired and cross, Mavis was full of a letter she had received from her youngest grandson extolling the virtues of his mother's new boyfriend, and Deirdre's arm was out of its sling so Dee was talking non-stop about going down to Yarmouth come the weekend to have a swim in the briny, as she insisted on calling it. Sally was off to stay with Ella again; Clare sometimes wondered if Ella had a brother and if so whether he was keen on her daughter, but Sally just scoffed at any idea of boys being interesting.

Amidst all this toing and froing, Clare cooked on, in the heat of the kitchen, wondering aloud every few minutes why she had insisted on keeping her job when Clive had suggested she give it up. No one took any notice of her, which did not help, and she was really getting very short-tempered and wondering whether it would be worthwhile blowing her top and making everyone feel aggrieved, when she saw a familiar figure enter the caff and lounge over to the corner table.

Immediately her temper improved and the sun, which had been shining all day, came out above Clare as well as over the rest of the city.

She hurried through into the caff, smiling, and went to Oliver's table.

'What would you like?'

They both loved this phrase, but today Oliver's smile was perfunctory.

'A moment of your time. Can you get out? I have to see you.'

It sounded serious, even a little worrying, but of course Clare knew it was nothing of the sort because Oliver's eyes were smiling at her and his mouth, though it looked serious, had a quirk in one corner, as though he was smiling inside.

'Well, I could. Ten minutes time? Outside the Press Office?'

'Right, only I'll have a quick coffee first. You follow me ten minutes after I leave. Got it?'

'Got it.'

The whole exchange had been so quick, their voices so low that Mavis, clattering dishes in the kitchen, must have missed it and Deirdre, taking an order at another table, did not so much as glance across.

'One coffee please, Mave,' Clare said as she returned to the kitchen, and Mavis left the sink and went to the coffee machine, because Clare was making a pavlova, to be served presently with fresh strawberries, and no one expected her to wait on when she was cooking.

Clare watched through the doorway though and ten minutes to the second after Oliver finished his coffee and left she clapped a hand to her forehead and put down her whisk.

'Gosh, I'll forget my own head next! Dee, my love, can you finish off the pavlova whilst I run up to the newspaper office? It was this week that Mrs P said to start the summer holiday advert, wasn't it?'

'That's right.' Mavis, who had come through to catch up on the washing up, turned away from the sink. 'We always get it in the week the schools break up, then the mums bring the little perishers in 'ere because of the 'oliday specials.'

'Right.' Clare shed her apron, tidied her hair with her hands and set off across the kitchen. 'Shan't be a tick; you can manage without me for ten minutes or so, can't you?'

'Sure can,' Deirdre said happily. She was gradually growing more cheerful as her social life picked up again. Once or twice lately she had mentioned someone called Hecky, though without too much enthusiasm. Mavis merely grunted. Rhetorical questions annoyed her.

Out in the air Clare relished the sunshine and the balmy breeze as she made her way at a brisk trot up the road until she reached the steps. She glanced up them. There was Oliver, leaning on the parapet which surrounded the terrace, looking down at her with a gentle but wicked smile. Returning the smile, Clare fled nimbly up the steps and went and leaned on the parapet beside him.

'Well? What's eating you?'

'You are. I wanted to tell you.'

'Go on then, spill the beans.'

'What a culinary conversation,' Oliver said with a sigh. 'Well, I woke up in the night and turned over, and you weren't there.'

'True. It's mid-week and Sally's home. I'm never there mid-week,' Clare said regretfully. 'I've yet to visit your palatial pig-farm or whatever you call it, remember.'

'Yes, I do, but shut up or you won't hear what I've got to say. So I turned over and put my arm round you . . . only you weren't there. And I woke up and wanted you . . . wanted you badly, Clare. Not because I wanted a woman but because I wanted you. I'm not that sort of a bloke, not really. I like women, admire them even, but I've never felt my happiness depended on one particular member of your sex.'

'That's a lovely thing to hear, but fancy telling me when we're perched above the city, the cynosure of all eyes, so I can't even give you a little kiss!'

'I know. What are we going to do, Clare?'

Clare turned her head and looked up at him. His Red Indian's impassivity was no match for her loving eyes. He was, in his own way, trying to tell her that he loved her; wasn't that enough? What else did they have to do save to enjoy their mutual feelings?

She voiced the thought aloud, but Oliver shook his head.

'It's not enough, not with Clive coming home.'

'Well, not until Christmas, that's months away and he won't be home for longer than a week, or two at the outside. Don't meet trouble half-way, Oliver, it'll be all right, you see.'

'Right, but I've explained how I feel. I don't want a casual affair, not any more. I want you. Any chance of meeting tonight?'

There had been no chance. Sally had been at home, Clare was entertaining Gran to tea in the city and then all three of them were going to the cinema, and Oliver was driving his stallion up to Northumberland next day and needed an early night.

But Oliver's declaration of his feelings had made Clare realise that their affair could not go jogging along indefinitely. At first this thought made her miserable, for she did not want to have to choose between the two men. No matter how difficult Clive might be, no matter how wonderful Oliver was, she knew she owed Clive a lot. He had been her sole means of support for fifteen years, he was Sally's father, and he loved her very much. The home they shared had been paid for with his money and he was as fond of it as she. Furthermore, she acknowledged for the first time what she had always secretly known. Clive was a lonely man and Oliver was a loner. Oliver could exist perfectly happily alone; she was pretty sure that Clive could not. And fifteen years of belonging to a man leave their mark. Right now her feelings towards Clive were pretty ambiguous, but underneath, at bedrock, she loved him in a quiet, undramatic, unromantic sort of way which would be difficult to cast aside. The splendid passion she shared with Oliver, the delight they took in each other, the ease and familiarity they were growing to enjoy was just as hard to lose, however.

Finally of course, she sat herself on the fence.

'I don't want to hurt Clive, and I can't bear to lose you,' Clare told Oliver the following weekend as they lay, shame-lessly naked, in the double bed in the spare room. She had drawn the line at sleeping with Oliver in Clive's bed, though she still thought she was being a bit silly. After all, it didn't matter where she slept with him, she was being unfaithful to Clive whether she committed adultery on a clothes line or in a double divan. But Oliver did not care so long as she was happy, and he liked the spare bed and it was he who mattered right now.

'But what if he really does come back for good?' Oliver groaned. 'I can't bear to think of you in someone else's arms. I'd go mad, imagining, wanting you.'

'I know, I'm the same. But I can't do anything about it, not yet. Just enjoy what we've got, love, and we'll worry about the rest when we have to.'

He did not approve, she knew that just by the quality of his silence. Once, he would have been perfectly happy to take whatever he could get and then move on, he had told her so, with painful frankness. Now it was different; she had made herself, in some way he could not understand, special. Important. Now he wanted her all to himself, he wanted to find her there when he needed her. He wanted to acknow-ledge their love.

But when he had gone back to his farm and she was alone, Clare was aware of another want which Oliver had not put into words.

He wanted to own her. He wanted to be able to say 'mine, all mine,' the way Clive had done for the past fifteen years. And deeply though she loved him, she was not sure she wanted anyone to be able to say that.

'I can't think why I said I'd work in the caff during my lovely summer hols,' Sally grumbled. 'July's almost over, Dee, and

I've hardly ridden Pegs at all. Still, at least I've got money of my own for a change.'

The two girls were taking their lunch break not in the caff since the sun was shining brightly, but in the Castle gardens. Or to be more accurate, half-way up the Castle mound, where the grass grew long and sweet and you could feel the sun on your face and hear the traffic noise muted by distance and kid yourself you were in the real country.

'When did your Mum deny you money?' Deirdre said lazily, biting into a Cornish pasty. 'She let you have whatever you ask for, gal Sally!'

'Well yes, but it's not the same because I have to ask. This way, with my own money, I can do what I like.'

Deirdre was lying on her back, not a sensible way to eat. A bit of pasty went down the wrong way and she sat up the better to cough, then turned and looked down at Sally through watering eyes.

'If that's true, then that int fair,' she observed. 'I've been earnin' best part of a year and I still have to tell Mum what I'm up to.'

'Then you haven't trained her properly, or you don't know her well enough to shift the conversation when it gets dangerous,' Sally said lazily. 'Or perhaps it's because your Mum isn't up to anything, so she's got more time to wonder about you.'

'Up to anything? Lor, gal, Clare int up to anything! She just works hard, that's all.'

'No, of course she isn't up to anything, not in that sense,' Sally agreed. 'But she's having a lot more fun lately, and people phone up and ask her out, so what with the caff and all she doesn't have as much spare thinking time as she once did.'

'I don't know as my Mum can think.' Deirdre finished her pasty and reached for an apple; Clare believed in the young eating fresh fruit whenever they could be persuaded to do so. 'She's got an evil mind, my Mum; perhaps that's the difference. There int nothing she don't believe I'd do, given my head.'

'Sign of a misspent youth,' Sally said, quoting her grandmother. 'Was she a bad girl, your Mum? Mine was. There was a huge row before Mum and Dad married and when I was down the Carters a while back Mrs C said something about my parents' wedding anniversary which made me wonder. So I poked around at Gran's and got the pictures out, and I wouldn't be at all surprised if they didn't have to get married – Mum and Dad. I think I'm a love-child.'

'A love-child? Oh, a bastard, you mean. Well, what's wrong with that? I am.' Deirdre dropped her bombshell without blinking and Sally, who had only just evolved her own theory about her parents, stared at her open-mouthed.

'You are? How d'you know?'

'Oh, Mum's told me, many a time. Has a laugh over it, she do. How she insisted on being married in white though she stuck out like the prow of a ship, and how nervous Dad was. He wanted to get wed she says, but not so soon. Still, it put them at the top of the housing list, and that was important in them days. Still is, I dare say. Not that I'd let Hecky carry on like that, not till I'm a lot surer than I am now.'

'How far do you go, then?' Sally asked, having digested this information. 'Not ... all the way?'

'Not yet. Course, he's always on at me to,' Deirdre said hastily, lest it be thought that her desirability was less than absolute. 'But that's different for a feller.'

'What about the pill? If you've got the nerve you can go to your G.P. and get a supply, so they say. But I wouldn't have the nerve.'

'Nor the need, I trust,' Deirdre said with mock severity. 'If you get the pill that means you're going to do it, see. It means you've made up your mind you fancy him hard enough. Anyway, what about AIDS?'

'Oh, that. Does your Mum nag about AIDS? All the girls at school say their parents go on and on ... at least you have to say that much for mine, she scarcely ever mentions it. I don't see there's much risk so long as you don't take drugs or go with men who've gone with prostitutes. Is that right?'

Deirdre shrugged, biting into her apple with haste now, since a glance at her watch had shown her that they were due back at the caff in about five minutes.

'Dunno. Mum don't say much but I watch telly so I know

they're all worried stiff, even the Government. If I decide to let Hecky do it, I'm going to tell him he's to get a packet of them things, and use 'em, too.'

'What, those rubbery things?' Sally pulled a face. 'I wouldn't want one of them poking around in me, I bet they hurt.'

'Hurt? How can they hurt, for God's sake? It's the chap what hurts, or so they tell me, and that's only the first time. After that it's all lovely and you wish you'd been doing it for years. Hecky says.'

'Hmm.' Sally looked sideways at Deirdre, who was poised, arm raised, to hurl her apple core. 'I heard . . . one of the girls at school said . . . that if they wear a condom . . . is that the right word? Yes, if they wear one of them it's like being done by a great lump of rubber hose. Really stiff and dry and horrid.'

'I don't believe that,' Deirdre said stoutly, but with an undertone of worry in her voice. 'If that's true, how come so many people use 'em till they want kids? All the village boys use 'em . . . the ones that don't have a regular girl, that is. The ones with a regular girl think she's on the pill.'

'Well, when I get a regular fellow I'm going on the pill, or I'll just chance it,' Sally said firmly. 'I'm not into rubber hoses.' She stood up, dusting pastry off her short grey skirt. 'Come on, we'd better get back to work or Mum'll nag.'

When Clive failed to visit Della two Wednesdays in a row, she rang him at the base. She sounded very young and hurt and sweet, but Clive told her unkindly that he was not into time-sharing and rang off. Afterwards he was rather proud of himself because tiring though Della was, it had not been easy to deny himself access – occasional access – to her charms.

Teddy had been sure that Della would accept him on an occasional basis, too.

'She's a good enough girl when she's not biting lumps out of you,' he had said as they drank chilled beer and watched a belly-dancer obsessively rotating her tassels. 'She won't take it amiss if you cut your visits down, provided she can fill the gap you leave . . . and I don't meant that as literally as it sounds. Or do I? Yes, of course I do. Nymphos, my boy, can't afford to be choosy because they go through men like kids go through chocolate; they're always searching for new ones.'

Clive and Ted had got on very well indeed once Clive had got used to the idea that they were sharing a nurse. What Clive found stuck in his craw was the other men, the fact that probably a couple of hours before he dived into Della's bed, some sticky Arab taxi driver or swarthy American driller would have dived out of it. Worse, almost, was the deceit. She had told him she was just a girl whereas she was older than his Clare, and she had let him think he was the only man she had ever had as well as the best lover. He wanted to believe the bit about the best lover, naturally, but although Clive flattered himself that he had done his utmost, he had all the Englishman's distrust of his own sexuality and feared that a randy Arab, with a dozen wives at home to practise on, probably outclassed him in bed without any effort.

Odd though it seemed, however, his liaison with Della had done some good. He now had a friend. He and Ted found they had a lot in common. Ted had once known Norfolk well, he even knew the village, though most of the shop-keepers and barmaids he remembered were either no more or had moved on. It seemed that Ted would be going home for good soon as well, and the pair of them sat in the bar at base with a warm beer each and wove for each other's admiration beautiful pictures of life in England as it had been and life in England as it would be, when they returned to the fold.

Not that Ted had a fold, exactly, to which he could return. He had a wife who must have divorced him in his absence twenty or more years ago and a child he had never set eyes on. He talked about his daughter sometimes ... her name was Annabel ... but such talk was of necessity largely wistful conjecture. Clive thought that Ted would have liked to get to know his daughter but his own behaviour had clearly made that impossible. One could not walk out on a woman on one's honeymoon, send her money for three years without, most of the time, so much as a one-liner with the cheque, and then ease oneself unobtrusively out of her life without building up a certain amount of bitterness. Ted knew his wife must have put him right out of her mind by now, probably she had told the child he was dead. To go back, to resurrect himself, was both selfish and unfair.

'You can come and stay with me and we'll go out to a pub and reminisce about Della and her extraordinary abilities,' Clive said, grinning. Ted grinned too. Free of her thrall – for Ted had likewise forsaken Della's arms – the two of them got a good deal of malicious amusement out of remembering aloud the hoop through which Della had made them jump, and eyeing her 'replacement dicks', as Ted crudely nicknamed Della's new suitors, whilst wondering to each other how they managed such-and-such a position.

Although you could say truthfully enough that Ted did not have much helpful experience in the way of being married, it was equally true that he gave Clive a great deal of sensible advice.

'Don't worry she'll expect too much of you just because she's only had six-week honeymoons,' he advised the younger man. 'I'm told women find perpetually lying on their backs even more tiring than a man would find being perpetually on top of them.' 'Don't think you won't get work,' he advised in the same vein. 'Remember you're an engineer and you know all there is to know about oil; the North Sea is as crowded with oil rigs as Piccadilly is with people. They could use your experience, and even if that fails there are hundreds of small firms who want a bloke who can drive, do the books and use high-tech computers.'

Clive showed Ted a photograph of Clare and Sally. Ted looked at it for a long time and then said shortly, 'You're a lucky chap', and handed it back without another word. He did not even say how sweet Sal looked or how beautiful Clare was, but Clive understood. Old Ted knew what he had missed but was too big-hearted to let his suffering show.

Plans for Clive's return to the UK were going ahead slowly but surely. He had given in his notice and was training a replacement, a callow lad from South Wales whose sing-song voice and timidity with foreigners would ensure he neither went far, nor far wrong. Clive still did not know exactly when he himself would go, though. Wait and see how Davie got on, wait and see how the drilling went, wait and see, wait and see. He bought Clare a gold necklace so heavy that the first time she wore it she would probably end up face down in her cornflakes, but Clive wanted to show her that she deserved the best. He got Sally a necklace too, but it was lighter, daintier, with a matching bracelet.

Clive liked buying presents so he got Gran an ivory camel to stand on her mantelpiece and his mother-in-law and mother brooches. Richard and Rachel would receive watches and he got earrings for Sally's friend Emma and the same for Deirdre, because she seemed a nice girl. Even Mavis warranted a gift, because she had been good to his wife. A gold leopard brooch was expensive, but with her husband out East she needed spoiling a bit.

Clive was beginning to look forward to his eventual return home. Every time he went round the souk now he purchased bits and pieces which he knew he would never find in Britain, things which would remind him of his time in the Kingdom, because the souk had its fascination and it would be annoying if, when it was too late, he remembered that piece of silk which would have made Clare a lovely evening dress, or a rug which would have set off the parquet floor in the living-room. He even bought Pegs a marvellously complicated bridle, for shows.

In Clive's quarters the pile of presents began to take over; they spilled over the bed and onto the floor, they were hung all round the walls, they crowded out his shorts and shirts in the small, cramped cupboard. Simon, coming in one day to fetch him over to the mess, blinked and remarked that Clive would be forced to leave simply in order to rehouse his presents somewhere more spacious. Clive smiled politely and bought a vast striped travelling rug for the spare room. He decided to send his presents home by sea, though. One had to be practical!

Mavis's long awaited break had arrived at last but she was not going to Yarmouth with Dee because her young friend had got this boy and thought of nothing else. Me and Hecky are going to the flicks, me and Hecky are going to a pop concert, me and Hecky, me and Hecky ... it was like a gramophone record stuck in a groove.

Still, Mavis didn't mind because as soon as she wrote to Sondra, rather disgruntled, saying her little holiday was off, Sondra wrote back urgently telling her to keep that particular week and asking her up to Earls Court to meet Russell at long last.

'I don't know as a week up there with all them Pakis and bimbos is my idea of an 'oliday, exactly,' Mavis had grumbled to Clare, but secretly she had been delighted by Sondra's prompt response. A whole week with her grandsons, a whole week of being given tea in bed first thing, a whole week, furthermore, of being so near Lionel that she could visit him daily. Except they wouldn't let her, of course. But she could go in two Saturdays running and that was bloody marvellous after once in six weeks.

She had so much to tell Lionel, too. Not about the caff and that, because she got all that out of her system in her twice weekly letters. Crammed with news, her letters was, simply crammed! Lionel knew all about Clare and her feller – or he knew as much as Mavis did, even if that was largely conjecture – and he heard every detail of Mavis's words with the milkman, her tiff with Lizzie Treece, the evil day when Pocket did a dirty on the second stair from the top and Mavis hadn't discovered it until she trod in it and slid the whole flight in one fast, blaspheming swoop.

He knew that Mrs Parnell had written to Clare and told her she would be back in mid-September and would probably then split the week with Clare. This would mean more time off for Clare and they were all pleased, since Clare did not really need the extra money she got at the moment but could do with the time. He even knew about Gran's battle with the council over her rose trees, and quite a bit about Mrs Flower's efforts to fix herself up with a meal-ticket who wouldn't expect no bed-sharing. Not that Mrs Flower had been quite so blunt when she told Mavis, in a moment of weakness, why she was hinting so desperately to Clare that Grosvenor Parkinson was really rather a nice man and might well become something more than a friend, 'if ... but only if, mind you ...'

'Are you going to marry him, Mother?' Clare had said at last, clearly amused by the thought, and Mrs Flower had said crossly that Clare was a silly girl and that marriage had never appealed to her and nothing was further from her mind.

After that Mavis had made a point of visiting Mrs Flower in-store, so to speak, and had managed to get most of the story out of her whilst the two of them sifted through a pile of bras for the one Mavis said she wanted.

So Lionel knew all about Mavis's life in Norwich. What he didn't know about was Desmond's potential, because Mavis had very soon realised it was too important to tell in a letter. Besides, suppose she was wrong? Suppose it was just grandmotherly fondness and had no foundation in fact? The disappointment to Lionel would be cruel and she was just not prepared to risk it.

Her week's holiday would not just be relaxing, therefore, it would be her best opportunity for testing out her Desmond-theory. Would he really be able, at his young age, to prove her right? Mavis thought so. But she had said nothing to Sondra because you never knew with girls. Sondra adored both her boys but Rupert was rather a favourite, what with being older and more help and that. And Mavis had never been absolutely certain that Sondra wanted her boys to excel in Lionel's career. After all, no one wanted to see their son spending time inside, and despite Lionel's excellence, this was not his first prison sentence.

But right now, Mavis was about to climb aboard the London-bound bus, and already the caff and her friends were spiralling off into the mist whilst London and Sondra got nearer and nearer. She got a window seat, then glanced around to see who would sit by her. She had been lucky last time in that tea-shop lady. Who would partner her this time?

A woman with a headscarf wrapped round her head and her face turned away came up the bus. She was alone, you could see that. She was looking timidly into passengers' faces, then moving on, but when she got to Mavis she sat down, still rather on the edge of the seat, then turned so that the other woman could see her at last.

'Anybuddy settin' here, lady?' she asked.

Mavis's heart failed her. A spade! Well, probably a Paki, but not English, anyway. Firmly, she nodded her head.

'Me friend'll be along in a tick,' she lied. 'Sorry.'

The woman sighed and stood up. She was wrapped in a long, transparent scarf-thing which covered her hair, neck and shoulders and then fell in graceful folds to her feet. Beneath the scarf she wore a shimmery dress in shades of red and blue, all embroidered with silver thread. She had a round red mark in the middle of her forehead, gold rings in her ears and her narrow nails were varnished silver.

'Right,' she murmured, moving further down the coach.

Mavis sat back, feeling at once righteous and rather mean. She did not want to spend a five-hour journey to London sitting beside a black woman who wouldn't be able to talk to her! Where was the fun in that? The journey should be part of the holiday, she and the tea-shop lady had agreed on that. You didn't go on holiday with a black woman all done up in carnival colours with paint on her face and no hair showing. Besides, they smelt funny, and Mavis had always been particular about smells.

Presently, the woman came back down the bus. Mavis pretended to look out of the window but she had put her handbag squarely on the seat beside her. She glanced up though, once the woman was passed, and wondered why she had not settled herself in any of the other seats. Most of them already had two people in to be sure, but one or two contained only a single passenger.

Someone else climbed onto the bus; it lurched as the person made his way down the aisle. He was a big, shambling man with wildly untidy greying hair and a squint. Mavis knew at once, of course, that he would sit next to her; it was in her stars, because she'd turned the black woman away with a lie. Hastily, she jumped to her feet and turned round to peer behind her. The big man and the black woman were face to face, the woman trying to squeeze herself into nothing so the man could get past, the man pawing and leering and obviously drunk. Mavis raised her voice.

'Here, Missus ... I don't reckon my friend'll show up now, you better sit yourself down 'ere.'

The black woman scuttled back down the aisle, thanked Mavis with a shy glance, and sat down. The man lurched past. He smelt horrible, Mavis noted; a waft of unwashed male, stale alcohol and socks nearly stifled her for a moment. She pulled a face and rolled her eyes and the black woman jerked her chin and gave Mavis a tiny, conspiratorial smile.

Mavis smiled back, but tightly. Incoherently, she felt that she and a black woman should not laugh together at a drunken white man. Why not? It was not loyal and she was a great believer in loyalty. On the other hand though, Clare had been talking a lot lately about women standing up for themselves a bit more, insisting on their right to be people as well as wives. Did that mean that, of the two, Mavis owed more loyalty to a fellow-woman than a fellow-white? Mavis turned slightly towards her fellow-passenger and sniffed as unobtrusively as possible. The woman smelt slightly spicy, slightly sweet, and very clean. Mavis could just make out the faintest whiff of Imperial Leather. She turned her face to the front again, then glanced quickly at the other's profile. She had lovely clear skin even though it was brown, and her lips, which were a sort of purply shade, held a gentle line. Ahead of them, the drunk stumbled over someone's feet and fell into a seat. The man beside him got up and moved into the aisle. The drunk promptly fell across both seats, striking the window quite a whack with his head. He then either fell asleep or was knocked unconscious, since he remained in the same position for the rest of the journey.

Once when they stopped and Seliaka and Mavis got out to have a drink and to stretch their legs, Seliaka went over and looked at the drunk, then came back and reported merrily that he was snoring and bubbling, so at least he was not dead. She and Mavis laughed over this as they drank their tea. Seliaka helped her husband to run a restaurant called Gateway to the East, so she and Mavis had quite a lot in common, actually. It was scarcely Mavis's fault if Seliaka managed to get the impression that Mavis, too, owned a restaurant. They exchanged recipes and suggestions most of the way to London, and Seliaka, who was going to spend a week with her mother-in-law and her husband's three unmarried sisters, said that she would keep a seat for Mavis next week, if she reached the coach first.

'You must come into our restaurant and have a meal, whilst you are in Town,' Seliaka said in her musical, precise voice. She spoke much better English than Mavis did, except when she was nervous.

'We might, at that,' Mavis said. But she did not mean it. It was all very well talking to people on coaches, but introducing your daughter and grandsons to them was quite another matter. Sondra would be shocked at finding her mother thick as thieves with a black woman!

When they reached Victoria though, it was rather nice that they were both bound for Earls Court, so they could travel the rest of the way together. Seliaka was going to go on the underground, but Mavis dissuaded her. Come by bus, she urged, and then we won't have to cart our cases down all them stairs. Seliaka agreed, then suggested they share a taxi, but though Mavis would not have grudged the expense, she pointed out that her grandsons would be meeting the bus, so it would not do to arrive by any other means.

She did wonder, rather uneasily, whether Rupert or Desmond would say something about Seliaka's colour or choice of clothing, but the question did not arise since Seliaka stayed on the bus for two stops more than Mavis did and so was carried on whilst Mavis was still fussing with her case and kissing the reluctant brow of Rupert (too old for kissing) and the eager cheek of Desmond (too dirty).

'Is Russell at home with Mum?' Mavis asked as they made their way through the streets, but the boys said no, not right now, he was in Paris, but he'd be back this time before she had to leave.

'Do you still like him?' Mavis asked teasingly, and was rewarded by a chorus of approval. He was great, apparently.

Back at the small, familiar house, Mavis was surprised to find that Sondra appeared to be in the middle of packing.

'Not going away somewhere are you, love?' she asked as soon as Sondra had stopped hugging her. 'Place looks a right mess!'

'We're moving,' Sondra said proudly. 'Oh, not far, just about half a mile away. We're moving in with Russell.'

'Oh, Sondra, is that wise? Your dear little house – what if it doesn't work out?'

'It's got to,' Sondra said quietly. 'We're getting hitched. Well,' she amended, seeing her mother's open-mouthed astonishment, 'we will if we stay together twelve months. And in the meantime, we're keeping this house on, we'll pay the rent and all. My friend Susie's moving in, keeping it warm for me in case.'

Mavis sniffed. She had met Susie, who owned a small boutique in the West End. Sondra worked there from time to time modelling Susie's clothes for her and the two girls had always been close. But Susie was a red-head and Mavis had a theory that red-heads were naturally sly and not to be trusted.

'Huh! Well, keep your eye on the gas meter, that's all I'll say. And don't go leaving none of them lovely modelling clothes here, or she'll make good use of 'em, you mark my words.'

Sondra laughed and turned away from the work surface where she was making a tray of tea and sandwiches. She crossed the small room and kissed her mother's well-rouged cheek. Mavis sniffed again, enormously pleased.

'Soppy thing,' she declared. 'Just you let me get at that tea, don't fuss round me with kisses!'

'Later today you and me'll go round to Russell's place; he said I was to take you there,' Sondra said to her mother next morning as the two of them sat companionably on opposite sides of the kitchen table, sipping the inevitable tea and eating buttered toast. The boys had been and gone long since; a group of youngsters had carted them off in their midst to the nearest playground where they would spend the morning and most of the afternoon, with a break in the middle for a quick dinner. 'But first, what do you want to do? Shopping? A trip up West? You can't see Father until afternoon, can you?'

321

'Nah, but I'll be first on the doorstep, you can bet your life. Let's do a bit of shopping, eh? Up that big market I seen yesterday.'

Mavis had her spending money in the top of her knickers, she'd sewn a pocket there specially, but it would only be the work of a moment to go upstairs, abstract a few notes, and return to Sondra's side. Accordingly she went to her room, rearranged herself, and then went downstairs again. Sondra was on the telephone, her big blue eyes shining, her mouth curved in a smile.

'Yes, of course,' she was saying. 'Oh yes, love. I'm never too busy, you know that! Well, any time, like I said. Yes. Yes. And me. Take care ... don't waste time watching other pretty ladies, because I'm always...' she saw a movement out of the corner of her eye and broke off abruptly. 'Hello, Mum, you did come in quietly!' She turned her attention back to the receiver cuddled close to her mouth. 'Darling, of course! Take care. Mm hmm. See you soon. Bye.'

'That was Russell,' she said unnecessarily, as she replaced the receiver. 'Sent his regards and he'll be home Thursday or Friday at the latest. I told him he'd got to make it by Saturday, because you go back then, and he said what did I take him for, he wouldn't miss you for the world. Now then, ready to go?'

'That I am. Love, there's something I've been meaning to ask you.'

'Anything, Mum,' Sondra said, picking up her cream jacket – she was wearing cream slacks, an apricot shirt, and totteringly high-heeled cream sandals – and heading for the door. 'We'll do our best to see you and Father happy, Russell and me. And the boys, of course.'

'It's about the boys, actually. Desmond, really. I wonder if you've ever thought how like Father Desmond is.'

Sondra, half-way out of the front door, paused, her china-blue eyes widening.

'Like Father – Desmond? Oh no, Mum, he's a dear little boy but he's got no style, no panache, not Des. You mean Rupert, do you?'

'No, love, I mean Des. It isn't looks,' Mavis said,

remembering her grandson's mouse-nibbled hair and the big, gappy grin. 'Nor it ain't figure. It's something inside. I think it's charm.'

'Charm? Desmond? He's a nice little boy, ever so helpful, but I don't see him as charming, exactly.' Sondra, obviously thinking of his physical appearance, giggled, then clapped a hand over her mouth. 'Sorry, Mum, I shouldn't laugh, but Desmond's an odd little chap.'

'I dare say,' Mavis said somewhat shortly. 'Then you won't mind if Des and me takes off one afternoon for a sorta experiment?'

'No, course not. Just let me know when you want to go off and I'll see he's got a clean shirt.'

In some ways, Mavis found herself thinking as she and her daughter made their way towards the market, Sondra was almost too typical a mother; all she could think about, when her parent suggested an outing with her younger son, was a clean shirt. Though in a way, Mavis admitted to herself, a clean shirt would be a help, especially if allied to clean finger-nails and a decent haircut. Then she scolded herself for her unbelief. Desmond did not rely on looks for his particular brand of charm. All her youngest grandson needed to make people like and trust him was himself. Or at least so she hoped to prove.

Three days later, on a mild and sunny morning, Mavis and Desmond set off for a day in the West End. Mavis had sandwiches in her bag and money for a drink but if all went according to plan she intended to treat Desmond to the best lunch money could buy. Desmond, completely unconscious of any undercurrents, was all set to enjoy a day out with his favourite person. He was in the happy position of almost always being with his favourite person since his nature dictated pleasure in the company of anyone who did not actively dislike him. And since he loved Mavis and knew himself loved by her he bounced alongside her, a grubby hand in hers, words pouring out of him like water from a can.

'Where'll we go, Nan? Can we go to the Tower of London? I've never been there. Or the Zoo ... only we went to the Zoo last time. Or there's vat place where the Chamber of Horrors is ... except you'd scream, Nan, because there's blood, so we won't go there. Roop went to a place where there was a dinosaur ... imagine that, Nan, a real dinosaur, bigger'n a room, Roop said, bigg'n a bus ... bigger'n a house, probably. You can go right up to it, it ain't kept in a cage nor nuffin', and you can touch it on the nose if a keeper lifts you up. But perhaps that ain't much for ladies, dinosaurs, so perhaps it'ud better be the Tower. You'll like the jools, Nan, ladies always like the jools.'

They went to the Tower and saw the jewels and the tower where the first Queen Elizabeth was imprisoned when she was only a princess. Then they paced out the length of Sir Walter Raleigh's walk when he was a prisoner there and then they looked down on Traitor's Gate and listened to the story of that same princess sitting down on the steps and refusing to go any further because, she had said, she was no traitor.

Desmond enjoyed it all, particularly the Beefeaters and the ravens. The Beefeaters chatted to him and the ravens consented to eat one of his sandwiches, tearing at it disdainfully with their wicked grey beaks and watching him cornerwise as they did so.

And all the time, in the depths of Mavis's handbag, half a dozen little old glass bottles nestled, waiting for their moment.

Mavis had intended to experiment first and then eat, but her nerves were not as good as she thought them and every time she opened her mouth to suggest that Desmond might do something for her, she shut it again. But at last she could delay no longer. Desmond wanted to go for a boat-trip along the Thames, their sandwiches were long finished and the day was clouding over. Her grandson, despite the best efforts of his mother and herself, no longer looked the Little Lord Fauntleroy who had got on the bus with her what felt like half a lifetime ago. His hair stood on end, his paws were grubby, and his shirt and blazer had marks of sandwich on the latter and marks of red fizzy pop on the former. He looked like any other small boy out for a day with an indulgent grandmother.

No one could possibly accuse her of using Desmond's appearance to aid her experiment.

'We'll go on the river presently, Des,' she said, fishing about in her handbag. 'The trouble is, we'll need a good hot meal before we leave and I don't know that I can run to both. But I've had an idea. Do you see these little glass bottles? They're all ever so old ... they're probably nearly as old as the Tower of London, imagine that! Now what I want you to do ...'

'Look, dear one, take a deep breath, count to ten, and then start again. I can't make head or tail of it! I got as far as you and young Desmond at the Tower of London and then you started on glass bottles and Americans and how he did it easy ... For heaven's sake start again!'

Mavis and Lionel were sitting on opposite sides of their table and Mavis was reliving, for her husband, the previous Tuesday's outing with Desmond and the splendid, the unbelievably splendid, end to the day.

'I keep trying to tell you, only it was so exciting ... like seeing you, Li, as a young feller starting out, only it was Des. Now I'd got these glass bottles in me bag, see ...'

In simple terms, Mavis had decided that she would ask Desmond to do the impossible, and that was to sell air ... to sell someone nothing, in other words. She had bought the bottles cheaply from one of those rag and bone, broken gramophone, cracked flower vase sort of shops which abound in certain areas of all big cities. The man in the shop told her they were old, they certainly looked old. But she did not think them valuable or anything like that, otherwise the man in the shop would scarcely have sold them to her, as he did, for five pence apiece.

Having got the bottles she left them dirty because that made them look more old and interesting and then she enlisted Desmond's help.

'Americans like to think they can take a bit of old England back 'ome with 'em, when they go,' she said earnestly, as they sat, side by side, on a bench overlooking the mighty Thames. 'Some buy antiques, but antiques is expensive and not all of 'em can afford much. Some buy old pictures and books and tell themselves they've got a bit of old England. But I reckon you and I, Des, can really give 'em some old England . . . or we can sell 'em some, rather.'

'I see. They want it and we've got it,' Desmond said, bright eyes fixed on her face. 'They'll give us money and we'll get a slap-up dinner before we goes down the river. Sounds awright.'

Mavis wished he had chosen almost any phrase other than 'going down the river,' it had an ominous, almost prophetic ring, but she nodded eagerly despite this.

'You've got it, Des. And do you know what we've got in these bottles?'

Desmond scrutinised the bottles all together, then one by one. Then he looked up at his grandmother and his face was split by an enormous grin.

'Air!' he announced. 'Just air!'

'That's it. But all the time we was goin' round the Tower of London them bottles was unstoppered, open. So the air . . .'

'The air in them bottles is as old as the Tower of London,' Desmond cut in triumphantly. 'I bet they'll fall over themselves to buy that air, Nan!'

He was right, they did. Mavis kept well away, explaining to Desmond that it would not do if she was nearby, someone might smell a rat, but Desmond, who loved people, was perfectly willing to take himself and the bottles off to where the crowd was thickest whilst his Nan had a nice hot cup of tea at the cafe by the walls.

'And he did it,' she ended her tale triumphantly, while Lionel stared. 'He sold every one of them bottles, charged a fiver apiece, and came back to me with twenty-eight quid in 'is 'and . . . someone couldn't quite make the full amount, so he sold it to 'em cheap, as goodwill, 'e said.'

'That's amazing,' Lionel said slowly. 'Just to Americans, I suppose? Did they know how much money they were parting with?'

'Not just to the Yanks,' Mavis informed him triumphantly. 'The last bottle of all he sold to one of the Beefeaters, I swear

326

to God it's true, I thought it was all up when he went over to 'em, but the feller paid up like a right'un.'

'I'd never have thought it of Desmond,' Lionel admitted. 'But ... don't you wonder what he told them, my darling? Did he really tell them he was selling them thirteenth-century air? Or did he ask for money to take his old Gran out to dinner?'

'Knowing Des, he told 'em what he knew they most wanted to hear,' Mavis said with considerable perspicacity. 'That's 'is way, after all. But he certainly told some of 'em he was selling air ... I heard him start his spiel before I walked off.'

Lionel was silent for a long moment, staring down at his hands. For one awful moment Mavis thought wildly that she had done the wrong thing, Lionel did not want Desmond to take over his career, he wanted Rupert or no one. Perhaps he did not even consider that selling air to the citizens of the United States of America was a true con – she had tried so hard to please him but perhaps she had got hold of the wrong end of the stick and upset him, instead.

Then, as she watched, his shoulders began to shake; not much, just a tiny bit. And she saw his mouth curl, a deep crease appear across one cheek, and his shoulders shook more.

'Is ... it is all right, Li?' Mavis asked anxiously. But Lionel, though he nodded, could not answer; he was laughing far too hard. When at last he sobered up, he leaned across the table and put a hand over hers.

'You're a wonderful woman, Mave my love,' he said tenderly. 'And that boy of ours is wonderful too – if he can do that at the age of six God knows what he'll do when he's ten! Give him a big hug from me and tell him Grandad's proud of him.'

CHAPTER
16

August was always hell in the caff, thanks to a combination of Mrs P's tried and true advertising campaign, the proximity of the car-park and the fact that school parties visiting the Castle very often left their coaches right opposite and thus got a good view of the caff both on leaving and returning to their transport. Clare had the Saturday girls in for various shifts all through the week as well as on Saturdays, she came in early in the morning and left late each evening, she made Sally come in at least three days out of the six, but even so she was always looking round for another pair of hands.

When the tummy bug struck half-way through the month she was even harder pressed. Girl after girl, or so it seemed, rang in to say she was incapacitated, prone on her bed except for brief periods when she was galloping to use the loo with one end or another. Even Mavis, the iron-stomached, succumbed and for two awful, nerve-racking days Lizzie Treece reigned in her stead and Clare quite longed for the bug to grip her round the larynx and bowel.

Yet she and Sally and Deirdre as well remained unaffected, they stood firm whilst all around them were losing theirs. Clare had begun to feel they might survive after all when she woke one fateful Friday morning with an uneasy feeling in the pit of her stomach which grew more and more uneasy as the hour neared eight.

It was a good thing, really, that she did not make it out of the drive, or even into the Mini. She was actually standing in the stable, one hand on the door, when an earthquake occurred in her stomach. She belted desperately for the back door, fumbled for the key, and cast up her morning cup of tea and a horridly altered round of toast, almost on her own feet. The next lot, providentially, made it into the sink, and she managed to do the stairs by a dint of holding her breath, closing her eyes and running like Seb Coe so that the bathroom was gained in time for the third lot.

Naturally, Sally was staying away. Of course! Nothing in life was ever simple, Clare thought bitterly, staggering, weak and empty, across the landing and collapsing onto her bed. For half an hour she felt too ill to do anything, but at the end of that time she picked up the phone and dialled.

Mavis answered the phone after the sort of pause which represented, Clare knew, shouting instructions to Deirdre, probably threatening the customers, dodging the cats and hurrying up a flight of stairs and across Mrs P's living-room carpet. We ought to have a phone downstairs, she was thinking as Mavis breathed a greeting of sorts into the receiver.

'Hello Mavis, it's me,' Clare said. Her voice sounded husky and rough and she had barely started on her career as a sick person. I'll be voiceless as well as hollow after a whole twenty-four hours of this, she told herself helplessly, but there's nothing I can do, you've just got to get through it, everyone's said the same.

'Oh, Clare. You've got it, then!'

'I have indeed.' Indescribable feelings began to churn inside Clare. 'It'll be a couple of d ... Mave, I must ...' She just managed to clatter the receiver back onto its rest before the next wave hit her.

By eleven o'clock she was convinced that whatever everyone else had suffered from, she had food poisoning. By lunch-time (ugh!) she knew it was dysentery as well. At two o'clock, faint and giddy, she picked up her bedside phone and, with a quivering digit, dialled Oliver's number.

He sounded irritatingly healthy, even slightly impatient, when he answered, but Clare was too eager to tell him of her fate to quibble about tone.

'Oliver, I've got it!'

'Got what?'

'Oh darling, the bug!'

'Really? On the phone? I didn't know you thought people were listening in.'

Clare took a deep breath, waited a moment, and then spoke as to a child.

'I've got the illness that all the girls have been off work with; I've been dreadfully sick and when I'm not being sick I'm doing the other. I feel so weak!'

'Poor love!' His voice, she was glad to hear, was vibrant with sympathy and affection. 'Is there anything I can do? Have you rung the doctor?'

'You can't ring the doctor when half the world has had the same thing,' Clare said querulously. 'Oh, darling, I feel so dreadful, and I look awful as well. My hair's gone all limp and greasy and I feel blotchy and beastly.'

'Poor love. If you're sure you don't need the doctor, get Sally to go down to the chemist for you when she gets home, he'll probably give you something to settle you down.'

'Sally's not here, and she won't be here until aftr the weekend,' Clare said miserably. 'All I've had all day is water, I don't think I've got the strength to go down the stairs.'

'I wish I could do something; that's the curse of being so far away,' Oliver said worriedly. 'Look take care, do you hear me? If you're no better tomorrow, give me a ring . . . no, I'll ring you about nine, see how you are.'

'Couldn't you come round now?' Clare asked piteously. 'I need you, really I do. I'm so weak!'

'Darling, I've got a stallion covering a mare, she's only a little thing, I can't just walk out on them, and I've got to do the milking today, my chap's off to see an agricultural show in Suffolk somewhere. But what could I do, anyway? Everyone says the doctors are advising nothing but water for twenty-four hours, and you've got water upstairs. Other than that it would just be a drive for nothing.'

'You could hold my hand and tell me I'll be better in the morning,' Clare argued. But Oliver, though he laughed and called her his poor love again, was clearly adamant.

'I wish I could, darling, but I can't. Keep your pecker up and get well soon and perhaps I'll see you tomorrow.'

They rang off and Clare, miserably disappointed, started to cry and reaching blindly for her glass of water with her eyes full of tears, managed to spill it all over the bed.

Foiled of a visitor, foiled, she felt, of even adequate sympathy, she turned on her side, buried her head in her wet pillow, and slept.

She woke an hour later to more feelings of nausea, more stomach churning. She lost yet more of her stomach contents, took another draught of water, and got back into bed again. She looked hopefully at the clock but it must have stopped since its hands pointed to a quarter past four. She watched it narrowly and saw that it was still working. Checking with her wrist-watch, she had to admit that the clock was right; she had only slept for a couple of hours.

The day continued on its boring, agonising course. By ten o'clock, when she was absolutely dead tired and longed for sleep, her ribs and back ached so much that she was sure she would lay awake all night. She drank more water, tottered over to the window and opened it so that the cool night air might blow in and take away some of the smell of sickness and despair, washed her face and hands at the basin in the corner – that was nice – and returned to her hot and nasty bed.

She had just decided that she would never sleep again and was trying to gather sufficient energy to go downstairs and make sure that Tish was all right – she had gone down at six and fed the dog and cat, awful though she had felt – when she fell asleep with the abruptness of a man stepping over a cliff. What was more she stayed asleep, she did not even dream, and when she woke it was because some unfeeling swine was telephoning her and the bell, kicking up a fearful cacophony, was only inches from her semi-conscious ear.

'Wha ...? Clare mumbled, getting hold of the receiver upside down and speaking into the earpiece. 'Whozzat? Wharrer ...'

'Hello, sweetheart; feeling better?'

Never had Oliver's voice sounded less welcome, never had Clare so longed for the strength to throw the instrument across the room so that it would never break into her dreams again. Awake, all the discomforts of the previous day rushed back. Her mouth tasted indescribable, her ribs announced that someone had been trying to fillet her, the light burned into her eye-sockets and her brain was definitely made of green cheese . . . or was that the moon?

'What?'

'Are you better, darling? You were ill yesterday, remember?'

'I'm ill today,' Clare snarled into the receiver. 'You woke me up! Go 'way!' She slammed the receiver back onto its rest and tried to curl down and recapture slumber, but sleep had gone and would not be wooed back. Presently she sat up. It took time, she could almost hear her joints creaking, but she made it at last and put out a hand for her drink of water.

The glass was empty. Cursing weakly did almost no good so she climbed painfully out of bed, crossed the room, still semi-bent like a witch in a fairy-tale, and arrived in the bathroom. She ran the cold tap, filled her glass, and staggered back to bed. Between the sheets once more, and bed had never felt better, she took three sips of water and relished every mouthful, took two more sips – and realised she needed the loo.

It was tough going but she made it, and balancing on the seat with her glass of water still in one hand, she sipped and swished and thought hopefully that by taking water in at one end and voiding it at the other, she might well cut out the middleman so to speak and be able to stay in bed for a while without having to pay visits.

Vain hope! Her bed seemed crumpled and full of crumbs, she had not pulled her curtains the previous night and the light hurt her eyes. And downstairs she could hear the pattering feet, the outraged moans and occasional barks which meant that Tish needed to go out and was growing desperate.

I'll ring bloody Oliver and make him come over, Clare told herself vengefully, picking up the phone. What on earth is the matter with him? If he'd been ill I'd have rushed over yesterday, I wouldn't leave it a whole day!

She confidently expected that her call would bring him running, but this proved not to be the case. He was very nice on the phone, said he'd come as soon as he could and just as she was relaxing, deciding she had been too hard on him, he added that unfortunately this might mean tomorrow, but that she was to take good care of herself and start eating light meals quite soon now. Clare put the phone down half-way through this good advice and when the phone rang again, seconds later, ignored it until it stopped.

However, she was beginning to worry about Tish, so she got herself downstairs somehow, let the dog out into the yard, fed Gregory, and was about to take herself upstairs to bed once again when the room began to spin and turn in a very odd fashion. Before she had had time to wonder just what was happening Clare found herself eyeing the kitchen tiles from close range and what was worse, they were behaving just as oddly as the room had done. She saw them through smoke, then through water, and then for a moment they disappeared altogether and Clare knew no more.

She came round to find herself still on the kitchen floor with Tish's long, anxious face staring at her from an inch or two away. She spoke, which reassured the dog and then, inch by inch, she got herself onto all fours. Ignominiously, she crawled slowly across the kitchen, through the door, across the hall and began, still on all fours, to ascend the stairs.

Half-way up she felt Tish's cold nose against the backs of her knees, but a stern order sent the dog scuttling down again and Clare continued with her humiliating progress.

It took time, but she got back to bed without fainting again, though twice she was forced to stop whilst her surroundings steadied. In bed, she lay back against the pillows, panting and breathless, and stayed quite still until she felt capable of movement once more. Then, very slowly, she picked up the receiver. She held it for a moment, then, still slowly, she dialled a number.

*   *   *

'My dear girl, you didn't seriously think I'd hesitate for one moment?' Gran's imperious eyebrows rose in astonishment. 'Of course I didn't, as soon as I put the telephone down I rang for a taxi and made him drive here, hell for leather. "The girl's very ill, so get your finger out," I said. This is no time for creeping along at thirty miles an hour just because you happen to be in a speed limit – give her all she's got, I told him, and I'll deal with the police if they try to stop us!'

She would have done, too, Clare knew. She could imagine a traffic cop's astonishment at finding himself trying to book Gran. The lecture she would give him on how he could be better employed, the words she would use, the rich phrases, made it almost a pity that the taxi driver had escaped unscathed. But Gran was here now, so Clare could relax.

'A wash first,' Gran was saying, walking around the bed with a blue bowl in one hand and a clean towel in another. 'Then I shall heat up some of the chicken soup I saw in the fridge. We'll see how you are after that.'

She was as good as her word. Clare was washed in warm water with scented soap, which Gran had brought with her in the taxi. Then she was powdered with talcum and helped into a clean nightie. Then she sat in a chair by the bed, with a tray on her lap, and drank chicken soup very slowly and sedately whilst Gran changed her sheets.

'Where's Sally?' Gran had asked at one point and upon being told she was staying with a schoolfriend asked why the child had not been sent for as soon as Clare realised she was going to be ill.

'I didn't think of it, she's only a kid,' Clare said, shamefaced.

She would have thought of Sally at once, only she had wanted Oliver so much more. She still couldn't understand why he hadn't come to her, but people reacted differently to illness, she knew. Presumably Oliver was one of those healthy types who cannot abide illness, even in others, so he had kept well away even though it was she, Clare, who was ailing.

'Well, next time you ring me right away, don't leave it a whole day,' Gran instructed, grim-faced. 'I've nursed you through worse than this, Clare my love, and you know how bossy I am, I've always thought I would have made a good nurse. Come to that, I'd have made a good prime minister, but that isn't given to everyone.'

Clare followed the logic of this, though not without difficulty, and gave Gran a tired but grateful smile. How lovely it was to be domineered over and told what to do and how nice to feel safe at last. She had been extremely frightened to realise she was so weak that she could not even stand upright without fainting, but now that Gran was here she knew she would be all right.

After the chicken soup Gran brought her a hot cup of very weak tea and when she had drunk that without ill effects Gran marched into the room with a handful of Sally's jeans which needed patching and announced that they would listen to some radio together. She fetched the radio out of Sally's room, turned it on low, and sat down on the bedside chair.

'Just close your eyes and listen to the music,' she advised her granddaughter, 'And before you know it you'll be asleep. You could do with the rest, even if you did sleep all night. You're still weak from the illness. And when you wake up I shall make you some more chicken soup, only this time you can take a slice of dry toast with it.'

Clare had always done as Gran told her because Gran never asked anyone to do anything which was bad for them. She slept immediately, yet even in her dreams she could hear the gentle melodies which the radio was playing, and knew that she was safe with Gran.

Mavis hated the caff when Clare was away, and with so many customers it was even worse than usual but she soldiered on, knowing that Clare would be back as soon as she could. Sally was away too of course and to do Mavis credit it never crossed her mind that Sally was not at home or she would have rung Gran herself.

But since she assumed Sally would be looking after Clare, Mavis did nothing other than run the caff. She did think about sending for Lizzie Treece but decided against it since Lizzie, in her experience, would prove more trouble than she

335

was worth. The Saturday girls, moreover, were good little souls and quite willing to work like slaves to see the place right in Clare's absence.

It was hard on Mavis, but despite having had the dreaded bug a week before, Mavis was on a high. Her holiday with Sondra had been such a marvellous success, her delight in Desmond's accomplishment so great, that not even three days off with the bug could damp her feeling of elation.

It was a pity she had been unable to meet Russell, but that was going to be remedied any day now. Sondra had rung her at work when she got back and had said that Russell was home from Paris, full of apologies for having been delayed, and she was going to bring him down to Norwich to see her mother any day now, because she had refused point-blank to move into his house until Mavis had given them the go-ahead.

Mind, Mavis told herself now, frantically frying eggs and bacon whilst Deirdre, behind her, made cakes and scones faster than lightning, if his home's anything to go by he'll do all right by my girl. Russell's house was only a mile from Sondra's, as she had said, but it was a lot more than a mile above it, figuratively speaking of course. It had a wall round it, a high wall, and a real garden, not just a bit of grass and a few flowers. A country garden almost, with apple trees in the back and a hedge of fuchsia along one side which made Mavis think, sentimentally, of Devonshire lanes and clotted cream teas.

It was a big house too, though not the sort of place Mavis was used to. There was a big hall, lofty she supposed you would call it, with a black marble floor and the walls painted white, the better to show the huge photographs which Russell had hung all over it. They were mostly studio portraits of famous people, but not stiff, posed pictures. In Russell's photographs women swung on swings, men dug the garden, children had fist fights or pulled faces at each other, or stared hopefully in at shop windows, their souls in their eyes. The surprise was often when you recognised the face yet saw in it what most cameras had missed – the reality behind the famous mask worn by men and women whose business was being seen.

The photographs were kind of stunning, Mavis supposed, but the rooms themselves took your breath away too. Huge rooms, with high, old-fashioned ceilings, with polished wood block floors and full-length windows, they had casual, expensive furniture scattered about them which managed to look both good and extremely comfortable at the same time. In the main living-room, for instance, there were three splendid sofas with jewel-bright velvet cushions scattered across them, and white goat-hair rugs on the floor. One wall was lined with books, another had a series of beautiful water-colour landscapes scattered across it, a third was all window and a fourth had a larger then lifesize photograph of Sondra hung on it. The photo-Sondra had no clothes on, but she had a little kitten perched on her knee right where it mattered, so Mavis supposed, a trifle doubtfully, that it was all right.

'How will the boys get on here?' Mavis asked at length, when she had done the full tour – three reception rooms, kitchens in the plural, a garden-room – which was apparently the modern word to describe a conservatory – and six bedrooms to say nothing of three bathrooms and four toilets, including one downstairs which had, amazingly, a shower complete with curtain, towel rail and cork floor in one half.

'The boys adore it ... the space, the brightness ... and of course there's the garden,' Sondra said. 'Why, Mum? Don't you like it?'

They both laughed. Mavis adored it, it was the kind of house she would have loved had she been able to imagine it.

'You're daft, Sondra, as if anyone wouldn't like it! But it ain't that, I'm sure the boys will love it, it's ... how'll they get on? They aren't saints, no boys are, and they're bound to make messes and muddles, scratch furniture, mark wallpaper, that kind of thing. What'll he say if they carry on as normal?'

'He isn't like some blokes, he really likes kids, he understands 'em, too,' Sondra said earnestly. 'The bedroom with the pear-tree right outside the window, that'll be the boys' room. We're going to have it done out for them, so's they can play there, make all the mess they like. But they aren't savages, I've told 'em there's to be no breaking things, no spoiling things, and they've both said they'll be good.'

'Well then, I reckon you've landed on your feet,' Mavis said slowly. 'If he's good to my gal and my little lads, I won't have no quarrel with Russell.'

So now, frying bacon and eggs and working her hardest, Mavis planned the rest of her day. Customers slowed down at about three o'clock as a rule, though by four they could be crammed with people wanting tea, but come three o'clock she could usually nip out for any shopping that Clare needed. Today, there being no Clare, she would have to make her own shopping list but even so she would get some chops, a bag of potatoes and some frozen veg for herself when she did the marketing. She had been doing it every day so far this week, so that when Sondra and her Russell came she would be able to produce a decent meal, give them the idea that she always ate well, took care of herself.

If Clare had been here Mavis would probably have picked up the odd piece of meat, a few spuds and a tin of peas or some broccoli from the caff and taken it home without so much as a twinge of conscience, but because she was in charge she could not do that. She would make sure that no one else did it, either, whilst she was managing here.

Another reason why she could not take anything home was because with only Deirdre to bake they were stretched to their limit for home-made food. Deirdre was a good little cook and she made the cakes a treat, but she needed help with meat pies and the fancier savoury dishes. Still, if I buy chops later, Mavis thought, and put them in the fridge at home they'll do for tomorrow night if they don't come today.

Because of Clare's absence, Mavis rang a Saturday girl who was not supposed to work on a Tuesday and bribed her to come in with promises of an extra couple of hours' work. Half-way through the morning they had to send a girl flying out to buy in some sliced roast beef, which made Mavis purse her lips at herself, and before the caff shut at six she knew that unless Clare was better, which really was impossible if her illness was to follow the course everyone else's had run, they would be in deep trouble the following day. Clare would have taken homework, so to speak. She would have loaded her Mini with ingredients and would have spent all evening cooking. But Deirdre could not possibly do that what with bussing and all.

Finally, annoyed with herself, Mavis went up to the flat and dialled Clare's number.

Gran answered; Mavis had only heard her voice a couple of times on the telephone but she knew who it was at once. Poor Clare must have had it bad if Sally couldn't cope, she thought.

'Mrs Forsyth? That you? Ooh, we're in dead trouble, really we are. Not a bite to eat in the place, though I've bought in more beef and the egg and cheese man comes tomorrer, thank God, but not so much as one scone let alone a bitta cake! I felt I'd gotta ring Clare!'

'Well, she won't be back tomorrow,' Gran said, sending Mavis's heart down into her scuffies with a rush. 'However, I am a steady sort of a cook and no doubt Clare won't mind me using her cooker. Let me see now, how can I get ingredients at this time of night?'

'Aint there anyone who could come in and fetch 'em, before I goes off?' Mavis asked anxiously. 'I'm alone here now, but I've shut and locked up. Only I can't see me managing a pile of flour and that on the bus, let alone by the time I reached you it 'ud likely be midnight.'

'I dont think we need go to such lengths,' Gran said thoughtfully. 'After all, though the house is remote, there are such things as taxis and neighbours. Look, dear, what sort of cake do you need most? You give me a list and I'll find the ingredients somehow.'

'Well, you're a wonderful woman, Mrs F,' Mavis said, the weight on her heart lifting. The telephone was by the window and she was glancing incuriously out as she spoke. A car, big and shiny, had drawn up outside the caff. I'm not opening for anyone, Mavis told herself grimly, specially not for someone in a great old limo, who could afford somewhere real good like the Castle 'otel. She leaned forward. A woman was getting out, crossing the pavement.

No doubt Mavis's shriek startled Gran, waiting for a list of cakes and cooking, but she was far too sensible to panic.

'Did you drop the phone?' she said as Mavis gibbered into

the mouthpiece that all their troubles were solved, that she'd been a-looking through the window ... 'Let me work something out, Mavis. I might even give Clare's brother-in-law a ring if you think ...'

'It's awright,' Mavis got out. 'Someone's arrived ... we'll bring everythink you'll need to the 'ouse in no time. See yah!'

She clattered the receiver down and flew for the stairs.

She reached the door of the caff just in time; Sondra was turning away, going back to the big shiny car and shaking her head, talking to someone Mavis could not see in the dark interior. But she turned as Mavis unbolted and ran back across the pavement, her face breaking into a big smile.

'Mum! Oh, great, we thought you'd left, I was getting quite worried. Russell's driven me down, Susie's got the boys, so we thought we'd stay the night, take you out for a meal, and leave sometime tomorrow. That okay?'

'Oh love, it couldn'ta come at a better time,' Mavis said. 'You don't know the trouble I've 'ad ... I was just wondering how on earth I was going to get a load of flour and that over to Clare's place and I looked through the winder and there you were. Can you take it for me? I know the way, more or less.'

'Of course we can,' Sondra said soothingly, 'and still be back in time for a meal. Look, you go and get the stuff into a couple of boxes and I'll go and explain to Russell.'

Mavis hurried back into the caff, her heart beating fast with excitement. Fancy that marvellous car belonging to her daughter's feller, and him going to run an errand for her and all! She had packed a big box with all the ingredients Gran would need to make chocolate cake, scones and some fruit pies and now tried to lift it, but it weighed a good bit so when she saw Russell standing against the light she smiled in his general direction and waited for him to carry it out to the car for her.

He was a tall, strong man. He came over and lifted the big box whilst Mavis was struggling to get the smaller one comfortably settled in her arms and Sondra held the door open for both of them.

He said to Mavis in a deep, rather posh voice, 'Here, leave

that, I'll come back for it,' but she assured him she could manage and followed them out.

Half-way across to the car she noticed that due to some peculiarity of the light her future son-in-law was very difficult to see once he had slipped into the driver's seat. But she climbed into the back without making any comment and waited whilst Sondra sat down and then turned to her. Russell turned too.

'Mum, this is Russell. Russell, this is my Mum. You've both heard a lot about each other, so it's nice that you're meeting at last.'

Russell's hand shot out. Mavis took it. Against her thin, ageing skin his fingers looked black. What a deep tan he had! He was smiling at her, his teeth flashing white against his dark skin, his eyeballs whiter.

Mavis tried to speak but no words came out. She did smile and mutter something, but she had no idea what. Shock had rendered her dumb.

For Russell, the rich photographer, the limousine owner, her daughter's lover, was as black as it was possible for a human being to be.

'She's a lovely old lady, that Mrs Forsyth ... Russell was really impressed, wasn't you, love?'

'Most certainly. I asked if I could take her photograph and she said she was far too busy, and then she thought of something and asked if I came from a newspaper; if so, she said I could take a picture of her tending her roses. She gave me a real wicked look when she said that.'

'She's a very good cook,' Mavis said in a faint, far-away voice.

How she had lived through the last half-hour was more than she could understand! When he had walked into Clare's kitchen, bold as brass and black as your hat, she had nearly passed out from embarrassment. Not that Gran seemed to notice anything, she thanked him, offered him a drink, accepted the fact that he did not drink and drive so changed it to a coffee, made Sondra laugh over her crisp description of Clare suddenly deciding she wanted to get dressed, so Gran

341

had hidden her clothes ... If only he hadn't been black, Mavis thought with anguish, what a pleasant visit it would have been!

Clare had not set eyes on him, which was cold comfort when you remembered that Gran and Sally had both done so. Gran's explanation of Sally's sudden arrival in their midst – that she had sent for her – had puzzled Mavis until Sally had told her she had been staying with some family out Mattishall way and had only just got home. Then into Mavis's awful introspection over black, had come the realisation that poor Clare had been forced to go through the worst part of her ordeal alone, and she had apologised to Gran and explained that naturally she thought Sal had been at home, otherwise she would have visited Clare herself or at least rung for a doctor.

'When I was bad Mrs Williams from next door dropped by on the hour every hour,' she said impressively. But then Russell said good neighbours were a very real blessing when one was alone and brought his unrepentant blackness to everyone's attention again and Mavis fell silent.

Every now and then she glanced at Sondra and wondered how her daughter could behave the way she had. With a black man! Probably in bed! Putting her beautiful white hand in his black one, going around with him in public, letting him take a picture of her with nothing on but a kitten! If Mavis hadn't been real fond of Sondra she would have thought, 'She's no daughter of mine', but even Sondra temporarily going off her head did not merit that sort of reaction.

Now, sitting silent and shaken in the back of the car, Mavis tried to reason out why Sondra hadn't warned her – nor the boys for that matter. They could have told me, Mavis brooded bitterly. It wouldn't have been such a shock to me system if they'd told me. You couldn't even pretend that he wasn't terribly black or say he was dark brown because he was black all over – so far as she could tell. His hair was frizzy and you couldn't get much blacker than that.

Sally had been good, mind. Only a kid but not the slightest surprise did she show on walking into her kitchen and finding a black man sitting in the chair by the Aga, drinking coffee. Indeed, her surprise was reserved for Mavis; she had rushed at Gran, kissed her, said hello generally and had then turned to Mavis, her eyes rounding.

'Mave! What on earth are you doing here? Don't say something awful's happened at the caff?'

Mavis had reassured her, still in the thin, polite little voice which was all she seemed able to produce, and the talk had moved to other spheres. Indeed, Gran had seemed positively sorry to see them go, she had come to the car with them, thanking them over and over, and had waved them off like old friends, promising to get a taxi to take Sally into the city the following day complete with a couple of boxes of baking.

So now Russell, Sondra and Mavis were driving back into the city as if nothing had happened, and Sondra and Russell were arguing over where they should take Mavis for dinner and Mavis was trying to find a polite way of saying, 'You're not walking into a public dining-room with me, young black man! If you want dinner out you can either go alone or go to one of them big, noisy places, a MacDonalds or a Wimpy, where they don't care if you're yeller with pink spots so long as you pay!'

'Which would you like best, Mum?' Sondra said at last, turning her clear eyes onto her mother sitting scrunched up and silent in a corner of the big back seat. 'You're very quiet all of a sudden!' There was amusement in her voice, Mavis could not imagine why.

'Isn't it a bit late?' she said hopefully. 'Why not let me make you a meal at my place? Or we could get a . . .'

She stopped short. She had been about to suggest getting a Chinese! What would he have thought? Or said? Fancy suggesting that a black man might eat Chinese food!

'No, Mum, you aren't getting out of it,' Sondra said. She was laughing, the cheeky bitch.

'I don't know what you mean,' Mavis said heavily. 'I'm tired, that's all. I've had a long day.'

'So've we, and we want a meal out,' Sondra insisted. 'Shall we let Russell choose?'

'Yes, that seems better,' Mavis said, perking up the tiniest bit. All he'd know would be MacDonalds and such. At least

343

in a place like that you didn't have waiters hovering and other people, posh people, staring at you.

'Right. What do you like to eat best, Mrs Cannaway?'

'That's daft, Russ; you should call her Mum,' Sondra said. Mavis tried not to shudder, but it forced her to at least semi-accept the situation.

'You call me Mavis, Russell,' she said. 'After all, you aren't a child.' More like a gorilla, she thought cruelly. Oh why had Sondra ever met him? Why was he rich, when deserving English men were poor? Why had she not brought Sondra up to respect herself and others? Why was Lionel in clink, when he might otherwise have saved Sondra from herself?

'Here we are, then ... best little fish and chip shop in the east,' Russell said, scattering gravel. Mavis dared not look; it sounded posh gravel to her.

It was. A country house hotel, with a flight of steps up to the door and a feller in uniform at the top. The dining room was the size of Mavis's entire house and filled with flowers, white napiery and solid silver cutlery. It was also crowded with people. Mavis half-shut her eyes, raised her chin and stepped forward, in the wake of Russell, Sondra, and a feller with a black tailcoat, a white bow tie, and not a lot in the way of hair.

She was half-way across that rich, deep carpet before she realised she was still wearing her scuffies.

After their visitors had gone, Gran and Sally sat on opposite sides of the kitchen table and had some soup. Then Gran pushed back her chair and fixed her great-granddaughter with a clear, commanding gaze. Sally met it for a few seconds, then looked down at her hands, the bright colour rising up her neck and flooding her face.

'Sally, my dear child, just what are you up to?'

'I don't know what you mean ... I'm not up to anything, Gran.'

'You aren't? Well, did Mrs Myers tell you I'd rung?'

There was a breathless silence. Sally continued to subject her hands to close scrutiny, Gran's eyes remained on her great-granddaughter's face, cool, speculative.

'Did she, Sally?'

At last Sally looked up; now her expression was rueful, her glance twinkling.

'Oh Gran, you know she didn't, because I wasn't there – I suppose she told you that, did she? That's why I ring Mum every day when I'm away, so she won't ever need to ring anyone up and ask about me.'

'Where were you?'

The twinkling look vanished; Sally looked hunted.

'With friends. It's all okay Gran, honest. It's just ... just ...'

'Just what, love? What is so important that you're prepared to deceive your mother and me?'

'It's just that I must be free,' Sally said earnestly. 'You don't know how awful it is to have to tell someone else everything, and then to have to do as they say when you know they're just being silly and old-fashioned. I'm earning money now, at the caff, I'm fifteen years old, old enough to get married ... well, nearly old enough. Not that I want to get married, I'm going to have lots and lots of fun first, and see foreign lands and live in London and ... So you see, I let Mum think I was at the Myers' because I didn't want to have to tell her everything.'

'And she never suspected? Never asked awkward questions?'

'Oh no, not Mum,' Sally said at once, airily destroying her own avowed claim to need more freedom, 'She isn't like that at all, she's so busy, you know, and so happy. She's got these friends, the Mortimers who live in Yarmouth. Quite often she goes over there for a whole day, which she couldn't do if I was left alone at home, could she? So my being asked out so much has been good for her as well as for me.'

'Yes, but who asks you, Sally? And where do you go?'

The mulish look threatened to descend again, then Sally sighed and the look fled.

'Oh, Gran ... I go and stay with a girl from school mostly. She's an awful bore and plain as a pikestaff, all she thinks about is her pony, but she's flattered to have someone like me wanting to stay in her house and she thinks it's awfully romantic if I go off with a boy for half an hour ... it's all right, really it is.'

'I dare say,' Gran said shortly. She was remembering how poor little Clare had behaved fifteen years ago, how she had hated to feel any hand on the bridle, whether it was Anne's clumsy tug or Gran's more sensitive touch. Oh, the misery her headstrongness had caused! Anne weeping and nagging, poor little Clare so ill and unhappy ... only Clare had been lucky, the boy had owned up, done the decent thing by her, and they had married to give Clare's baby a father and so that Clive could have a wife to come home to.

'So you won't tell Mum, will you, Gran? It would hurt her ever so much.'

'I ought to tell her, I know I ought. But darling, if you promise on your honour never to deceive Mum and me again, then I'll think about keeping it to ourselves. Only the staying away must stop I'm afraid. You'll have to grow up a bit and get our trust back before you can go off for two or three days at a time again.'

'But Gran, Mum won't be a bit pleased, she'll think I'm ever so fickle, and I can't just stay at home, I'd go mad! You'd better tell her, or I will. I'm sure she'll understand and let me go over to Prue's place again.'

'Then you tell her and see what she says,' Gran advised. 'Promise you will, darling? On your honour?'

'Yes, of course. And Gran, I'm sorry I was bad.'

The two hugged, then Gran began to prepare her oven and her cooking things whilst Sally ran up to tell Clare the visitors had left and ask what she would like to eat.

It was not until she was in bed in the spare room that night, with the satisfying knowledge of full cake tins in the kitchen below, that something occurred to Gran. This girl Prue that Sally had described was only keen on her pony ... would that Sally still was, Gran yearned just before she fell asleep.

CHAPTER
17

Perhaps because she had got so dehydrated Clare took a full week to recover from her illness, and all the time Gran stayed with her and she did not speak to Oliver at all. Once Gran was ensconsed, indeed, she did not even think very much about Oliver but simply enjoyed being fed, ordered about and made to rest by either Gran or Sally, because Sally was a help too having been forced, Clare imagined, to return to the fold.

But on the Saturday morning Gran came in and sat on the bed whilst Clare ate cereal, toast and bacon with a good appetite and then drank orange juice – she had gone off coffee – and announced that she would be leaving when she had made Clare's lunch.

'Something light, I think, probably a nice piece of cod in a parsley sauce,' she said judiciously, giving Clare time to get used to the thought of being alone again, with only Sally for company. 'You're very much better now, dear, and you'll be back at work on Monday no doubt, so this way you'll have a full day on Sunday to get used to being independent.'

'I feel guilty at having kept you her so long already,' Clare said remorsefully, sipping her juice. 'I really could have managed without you, only I didn't want to – I love having you near me.'

'Well, I like being here,' Gran said honestly. 'But I like my flat too and the people round about. I don't believe in the old battening on the young if they can help it ... it's different

347

when they're ill and lonely of course, but I'm neither, thank God. Now, is there anything you want me to do for you before I go?'

'You've done it all you wonderful old Gran you,' Clare said, patting Gran's hand. 'I've been spoiled to death and I've thoroughly enjoyed it but you're quite right, I've got to start standing on my own two feet again and I won't do that with you in residence – you won't let me.'

'True. Two women in one kitchen won't go,' Gran said, as she had said many times, over the years. 'I've ordered a taxi for two o'clock.'

It was odd after she'd gone. Sally mooched round for a bit, then said would it be all right if she went and fetched Emma, so the two of them could go up and see to Pegs. Clare said she could because she did not want to cramp Sally's style, but she was worried about her daughter. True to a promise she had apparently made to Gran, Sally had admitted she had only stayed with the Myers once, and that on all the other occasions she had been staying with a girl called Prue Gundry, of whom Clare had never heard, out in the country somewhere. It worried Clare that Sally had thought it worthwhile to lie – she had no more enthusiasm for a Gundry than she had for a Myers and vice versa – but she was still not sufficiently recovered to make an issue of it.

And of course as soon as Sally had disappeared, taking Tish, and the house was quiet, Clare wanted to ring Oliver. Indeed, her hand stretched out of its own volition, so used was she to the pathways of deceit; when the house was empty or the caff full, that was when it was safe to ring.

But now she hesitated, her hand poised above the instrument. She had spoken to him last four days ago and to the best of her knowledge he had not attempted to get in touch with her since. He had neither rung nor visited, or she did not think he had. She had no means of knowing, of course, whether he had popped into the caff, to be told that Clare was ill but that her Gran was looking after her. If so it was natural that he had neither rung nor called, though she found herself wishing that he had. After all a friend calling to ask after her would have occasioned no suspicion in Gran's mind, but then he might have feared Sally's presence and her daughter would definitely have thought it odd if Coffee and Book turned up at home.

With recovering strength she had wanted him more, though still not with much urgency – she had only wanted to see him or even speak to him, the thought of making love to him had occurred to neither her weary mind nor exhausted body. But each day she was also a little more conscious that he had let her down when she needed him and resentment, even if it did not precisely fester, was definitely present when she considered the situation.

Clare's hand returned to her lap; perhaps she would not ring him just yet. She was lying on the couch feeling a bit weepy but oddly peaceful and she could see, through the open window, that the fowl had got out of their run at the bottom of Mr Atkins's garden and one of them, a handsome cock bird, was picking off the heads of a bed of dahlias which were just breaking into bloom. I wonder if I ought to go and shout at that bird before he does more damage, Clare was thinking when the telephone rang. She jumped six inches, then grabbed the receiver and held it to her ear.

'Norwich three-five-seven-five ... Hello?'

'Clare, it's so good to hear your voice! I've been terribly worried, love. Are you all right? Is Sally looking after you as well as your Gran? I wanted to come round so badly but it was too much of a risk, it would have caused talk.'

'Oh, hello, Oliver,' Clare said a little stiffly. 'I'm much better, thanks. Gran went home a couple of hours ago and Sally's out with a friend, but I'm well able to take care of myself now. Fortunately.'

'I should have come,' Oliver said miserably. 'But I wouldn't have been any good, I never am good with illness. I always leave it to the experts ... not that I've had any experience of being ill, because I never am and when the men are ill their wives look after them, I suppose.'

'Yes. Well, I don't happen to have a wife but as I said, I managed. Did you ring for any particular reason, Oliver, or was it just to make sure I'd not died this past week?'

'You're annoyed,' Oliver said acutely. 'Oh damn, sweetie,

what can I say? I've been into the caff each day and always made a point of getting some sort of information out of them about you, but when I spoke to your Gran she was very precise and severe ... did she say I'd rung?'

'Oliver, you didn't!' But Clare felt the first stirrings of pleasure that he had been concerned. 'That was daft, and awfully dangerous.'

'No it wasn't, I said I was different people each time. Once I was a man who was interested in selling your daughter a horse, the next time I was a wrong number, just to check that she was still with you, you see. The time after that I was a wholesaler who wanted to know whether you'd be needing more frozen peas when I was next delivering in Norwich, the time after that ...'

'Do stop,' Clare said, clutching her aching side and mopping weak tears of laughter from her cheeks. 'How could you be so crazy, you've got a most distinctive voice, I bet Gran wasn't fooled for one moment. Oh, dear, but it's good to hear you again ... wish I could see you.'

'You can, in a moment! I'll drive over straight away, I'll be knocking on your door before you've put the phone down, just tell me it's all right to come and you'll hear the roar of an engine ...'

'No, no, you can't come, not really,' Clare said quickly. 'Sally's not away, she's only gone down to the field with Em to have a ride on Pegs and make sure he's all right. If you come over she's bound to come back, it's the law of averages.'

'Can't you send her off to visit friends?' Oliver said plaintively. 'I've got to see you, Clare!'

'You've managed very well without seeing me for a week,' Clare reminded him. 'You'll just have to put up with it, I'm afraid. There isn't a chance today, and as for tomorrow ... Well, I suppose I could go out for a little drive in the Mini, just to make sure I'm okay behind the wheel, and then we could meet for half an hour. But only if I feel well enough.'

'Ring me tomorrow,' Oliver said, suddenly practical. 'Couldn't you give Sally a packed lunch and send her off on the pony for the day? Or you could get an urgent message from a friend and rush off. We could have a meal out and then find a quiet spot somewhere . . .'

'I'm not too keen on eating right now, and as for finding quiet spots, that would be far too athletic for one recovering from my complaint,' Clare said, but she was laughing. 'Ring me tomorrow, and . . .Oh lor, I'll have to go.'

'Come on, darling, don't rush off, remember it's been a whole week since I saw you last and . . .'

'Cheerio, darling, we'll talk tomorrow. Hens are invading my flower beds,' Clare said truthfully. She replaced the receiver and went over to the window. The lower half of the sash was closed, the top open, so she quickly reversed them and clambered out. Mr Atkins's cockerel had been joined by half a dozen of his wives, all of whom were trampling flat-footedly across Clare's most precious and tender plants. A shout, a quick, arm-whirling foray, and the birds scattered though the cockerel did cast a mean, calculating look at Clare's legs, stoutly defended by denim jeans. If I'd been wearing a dress that swine would have got me, she told herself, climbing back in through the window having routed the enemy. I'll have to get Mr A to keep his hens under control or I won't have any dahlias worth looking at in that bed.

'So if you don't stand by me, I'm a goner,' Sally said tearfully to Emma as the two of them groomed Pegasus in his stall at Mr Blower's stables. 'Gran knows much too much and she made me tell Mum a bit and I just can't simply let my whole life be ruined by two old women!'

'But if they know, what makes you think they're going to let you come out for a day with me, far less overnight?' Emma asked practically. 'Your mum's no fool, Sal, and nor's your Gran.'

'Oh, I know . . . but Mum doesn't want me hanging around the house whining, which is what I do when I'm kept in,' Sally said shrewdly. 'You've no idea how nasty I can be when I'm thwarted. You see, I'll go home in half an hour and spend the whole evening moaning about being shut indoors and people not trusting me and by tomorrow when I suggest us going off with Pegs for the day she'll jump at the chance.'

'Oh, all right then, if you're sure. I know you'd do the same for me if I ever needed it.' Emma stood back and examined the pony's legs. 'If I brush much more he won't have any hair left on his hocks,' she observed. 'Shall we call it a day and go home, now?'

'Might as well. And I'll tell her we'll go to that show in the paper and probably get home late, so I'll stay with you. She can pick me up first thing in the morning if they need me at the caff, but the chances are she'll let me lie in and then we can go off somewhere for the day,' Sally said. 'Em, you're the best friend in the world, I don't know what I'd do without you.'

'You'd find someone else, like you did over the past few weeks,' Emma said, not sharply but practically. It was the first time, by word or deed, that she had reproached Sally for her faithlessness and Sally knew it was richly deserved.

'I'm sorry, Em, I know I've been awful, but you don't know what it's like, it's as if you've got to go, as if your life depended on it and you don't really think about who you hurt or upset when you've got that urge driving you.'

'Is that what they call a sex urge?' Emma asked. But Sally could not tell her.

'I shouldn't think so,' she said thoughtfully, after a moment. 'It's more like a sort of itch that you have to scratch. Wait till you get it, though. It's worse than missing a train, I can tell you, it just rules your life.'

'Then I hope I never do get it,' Emma said placidly, as the two of them made their way out of the stable. 'That sounds foul.'

'It's only foul when they try to stop you,' Sally said. 'Otherwise, old Em, it's sheer heaven. Take my word for it.'

'Really Mavis, I don't know what's the matter with you,' Clare said sharply, coming into the kitchen to find Mavis, mop in hand, pushing it absently across a perfectly clean floor. 'You've had the bug or I'd think you were going down with it. What ever is up?'

'I can't understand my Sondra going with That Man,' Mavis said heavily, putting the mop back in its bucket and staring mournfully at Clare. 'What have I done to deserve it, eh? She was well brought up, went to a decent school . . .'

'What was wrong with Russell?' Clare said, rolling pastry. 'Gran said he was lovely and even Sal thought he was fanciable. What was wrong with him for God's sake?'

'They didn't say nothing about his . . . about him?' Mavis's face was a study, except that Clare knew of no reason for this sudden preoccupation with Sondra's fellow. 'Not Gran nor Sally? Nothing about his . . . his . . .'

'His what? No, they just said he was charming, had a lovely voice, was obviously in love with Sondra. Come on, tell your Auntie Clare.'

'He's black,' Mavis hissed at her. Clare, who was just cutting out the pastry and fitting it into a dish for apple pie, did not catch what she had said.

'What? Do speak up, Mave.'

'He's black . . . he's a nig-nog.'

'He's what? Oh, black! Well, what's wrong with that? Over half the world's population is black so I believe. Is he nice? that's what matters.'

'I didn't notice, pertickler,' Mavis said bitterly. 'I couldn't think of nothing but 'is blackness. When they asked me about coffee at that posh place . . . and me in me scuffies, I coulda died . . . I went and said "black," because that was what I was thinking about, and I got me coffee without so much as a drop of milk in it.'

She sounded so aggrieved that Clare bit back her involuntary giggle. Instead she said seriously, 'Mavis, you mustn't be prejudiced just because someone's skin isn't the same colour as yours. You must accept him for his merits . . . What does Lionel think?'

'Sondra says her father likes him, but then Lionel's soft with Sondra. Not that she'd lie, mind . . . but I daresay Li doesn't know he's black either. Sondra didn't see fit to mention it to her own mother, which was a facer I can tell you.'

'Well, neither Gran nor Sally saw fit to mention it to me,'

Clare said with unimpaired cheerfulness. 'Anyway, Sondra may change her mind and move out of Russell's lovely house. So why are you in such a state?'

'They're married,' Mavis disclosed. 'Married! Well, that's to say they will be, come next Saturday. Sondra begged me to go ... begged me ... but I said I was working and couldn't get away. How could I go and see her marry that man, knowing the heartache what's in store for her?'

'There's absolutely no reason why they shouldn't be very happy indeed and remain married for the rest of their lives,' Clare said. 'You're old-fashioned Mave, really you are. People don't look down on mixed marriages the way they used to, you'll find Sondra's generation will just accept that her husband, who is rich, successful and charming, also happens to be black.'

'Huh! Well, you oughter hear Mrs Williams going on about the way they take all our jobs and breed like rabbits,' Mavis told her. 'I'll never live it down, never! The neighbours will whisper behind their curtains, they won't come right out with it and tell me what they think, but I'll know, I'll know.'

'And it won't matter to them that he's got a huge house and a marvellous car and is a famous photographer and can speak seven languages?' Clare asked shrewdly, tipping sliced apple into her pie case. 'They'll be so busy despising him because he's black that they won't listen when you tell them Sondra's going to the Greek islands for her honeymoon and wears a real leopardskin fur coat, and that the boys go to the most exclusive school in London?'

There was a long pause; Mavis was gazing at the apple slices as if she had never seen such things before. When she spoke it was slowly, even reverently.

'Well, d'you know, I believe you're right? I believe that'll make up for any amount of blackness! Even Mrs Williams 'ud have to take heed of that!' Her unfocussed gaze left the apples and focussed sharply on Clare's face. 'D'you think I oughter go to that wedding?'

'I'm sure you should,' Clare said solemnly. 'You'd make Sondra's day, Mavis, really you would.'

'I'll go,' Mavis decided. 'What's more I'll tell Mrs Williams meself that there's good in all. You did say they was honeymooning on the Greek islands?'

'Well yes, but . . .'

'Good.' Mavis picked up a tea-towel and went over to the sink to dry up for Deirdre who was diligently washing away. 'Yes, it's about time I told that Mrs Williams a thing or two.'

Later in the day, when Deirdre and Clare were having their lunch together, because with the place so busy you had to take turns, Deirdre asked Clare how she had known about Sondra going to the Greek islands.

'I didn't, I was just supposing, but I dare not admit it now,' Clare told her. 'What's more, I doubt if Sondra will ever have a real leopardskin coat, what with conservation and everything. Still, I dare say Mrs Williams will get the message.'

'Mavis did,' Deirdre observed. 'Is Sally in tomorrow?'

'Yes, she is. By the way, she made some remark about wanting to go away with you to Yarmouth if I'd cough up the cash. Has she said anything to you?'

'Not a word, but it 'ud be great,' Deirdre said promptly. She hesitated, then lowered her voice. 'I dare say you didn't notice, but a few weeks back Sally and I had a sort of row.'

'No, I didn't notice I'm afraid, but then I hardly saw you together once the holidays started. I'm sorry, Dee.'

'That's awright. I got a bee in my bonnet, tell the truth. I had this feller – Quack – and when Sally come to stay he liked her, see? And when she left he seemed to ha' gone right off of me. So I blamed Sal in a way, though I knew that weren't her fault at all, really.'

'And you've got Quack back now, have you?'

'No, but I've got Hecky and I like him more.' Deirdre smiled. 'So if Sal 'ud like to come on holiday with me, I'd be that glad.'

'I've got Christmas presents to buy – might as well get 'em here – and then still some more things to bring home for good, so I've got a great deal of shopping,' Clive said as he and Ted sat in Clive's room whilst Clive made out his shopping list. 'I think I'll get my mother a brooch. Mrs Flower – that's Clare's mother – likes what she'd call something good, so I dare say a gold brooch would be acceptable to her too.'

'Mrs Flower? It's a common enough name, I dare say.'

'I am spending an arm and a leg on Clare,' Clive said unheeding, 'but she's worth every penny. My God, when I think about the narrow escape I had with Della I turn cold all over and can't wait to get home! Now let me see, what else do I want?'

'A cold beer, I hope,' Ted said. He glanced around the bare little room. 'Is that your Clare?'

The photograph on the wall had been taken at least ten years ago but Clive was fond of it and never considered replacing it with something a bit more up to date. Besides, Clare had changed very little. He said that it was and Ted walked over and scrutinised it, though he had seen better and more recent likenesses.

'Nice to have a picture looking down on you,' Ted said. 'Come along, old man, let's get our skates on, I want some grub before we visit the souk.'

They chewed the fat over their return to Britain for most of the evening. Ted accepted an invitation to visit Clive once they got home, only he said that he'd wait for a few months.

'You'll want some time to yourselves to sort out the honeymoon feeling first,' he said. 'Though when I remember my honeymoon . . . I'd have been glad of a friend popping in! Did I ever tell you about my wedding night?'

'I gathered it wasn't a success, but you didn't go into detail, no.'

'Well, it was pretty bad because she fought me off and sobbed and didn't like the physical side of it at all. She undressed in the dark and then complained because I put my finger in her eye when I was trying to uncurl her in bed.' He shook his head chidingly when Clive laughed. 'It's all very well for you, I was only twenty and dam' nearly as scared as she was, to tell you the truth. But what put the kybosh on it was breakfast next morning. The silly girl had prunes, because she said cornflakes were too noisy and she didn't like

356

porridge. And then, of course, she was far too inhibited to spit out the stones, so she swallowed 'em! Yes, she swallowed every one of the stones and then wouldn't let me lay a finger on her for the rest of the week; said she was getting appendicitis or some such, hated me for laughing when I saw what she'd done ... Put me off marriage for good and all to tell you the truth.'

'I suppose you got married after a whirlwind courtship, and hadn't realised what a prude she was?' Clive asked, taking a drink of his beer. 'I can't imagine why you married her so quickly, to be honest. Why didn't you try it out first? Give her the odd fumble and see how she reacted?'

'In those days?' Ted guffawed. 'My dear chap, in those days you could scarcely kiss a girl let alone touch her breast without signing a betrothal certificate first! And then of course after a honeymoon like that I was right off sex for years. For twelve months afterwards I couldn't have got it up even if I'd been handed Marilyn Monroe to do with as I willed. Besides, I was a decent country boy, I believed in the devil and all his works, knew a man didn't get any but a bad, dirty girl to sleep with him before her wedding night. So I simply kept away from women until I was twenty-five and discovered that I was capable of giving and receiving pleasure. Then, of course, I got the taste for it and knew I'd have to keep well away from my wedded wife. Because I knew that one glance from those icy eyes and I'd never fornicate again.'

Clive, laughing, agreed that such an experience would certainly scar a man.

'Sure, just like Della does only worse,' Ted agreed. 'How are you going to explain those scars to your wife, by the way?'

Clive, blanching, said that he'd calculated the scratches would be invisible by Christmas and asked Ted whether he would not consider marriage now, if he met the right woman. Ted scratched his head.

'Now? I'm not sure. Some days I feel eighty but in fact I'm only fifty-four with a good few years ahead of me, if I'm lucky and keep fit. There are two things against it, actually.

The first is that I simply don't know any women at home and precious few out here if you don't count Della. The second is that so far as I know my wife never actually divorced me, which could make marriage difficult, not to say illegal and bigamous.'

'And you wouldn't consider going back to her, starting it all up again?' Clive expected a quick and cross denial but to his surprise Ted stared down at his beer for long moment before shaking his head almost reluctantly.

'No, I guess I wouldn't. How could I, when you think about it? No matter how badly I was treated I got the girl pregnant and didn't stand by her, save financially, and I only paid up for the first few years. She didn't want a baby at all, wrote that she'd had a terrible time, and all I did was increase the size of my monthly cheque for a little while. No, I couldn't possibly go back.' He sighed and drank, then wiped the back of his hand across his mouth. 'Ah, but she was a pretty thing, a very pretty thing. Lovely figure, gorgeous hair, legs like a chorus girl's and a natural dress sense which could make the cheapest little cotton rag look like Bond Street. All wasted, of course, because she had no sex drive and absolutely no sense of humour. You need both to make a marriage work. Still, you never know; I've thought about going to Australia, seeing if I can make a home for myself over there.'

'We've both got a hard time ahead of us if you ask me,' Clive said, draining his beer mug. 'Clare and I aren't used to being with each other all the time, she's become a very independent girl over the years and try though I do, I can't say I find it easy to accept. I don't really like to see her driving; in an odd sort of way it shocks me when she gets behind the wheel and puts the car in gear.'

'Because women aren't allowed to drive over here,' Ted said, nodding. 'Ever suggested Clare covers her face when you go out?'

'No, of course not! But I didn't like it when she started to work, it's such an unfeminine thing to do, especially if you don't need the money. And there are other things ... she wears jeans; I think women look much prettier in skirts. And she can ride a horse astride, which always seems more a man's pastime than a woman's, although I admit she looks very pretty and feminine in jodphurs, on horseback. She's a quiet girl, which is why I married her I suppose, but she's become terribly practical – she can hang wallpaper, paint a ceiling . . . oh well, I dare say she'll stop doing things like that quite happily when I'm there to do the work for her.'

'Unless she's better at it,' Ted said softly.

Clive nodded. 'Exactly. She's been doing things like that for fifteen years, I'm not at all sure she won't run rings round me. Oh hell, when I think about it in practical terms I'm quite dreading some things about going home.'

'Face up to it and you'll find you've worried over nothing,' Ted advised. 'Wish I was married; wish I had a nice little wife to go home to.'

'You are and you have, only you're as scared of yours as I am of mine,' Clive said, and then wished he had worded it differently. But Ted only laughed and shook his head.

'You love her and she loves you; that'll see you through the difficult times,' he prophesied. 'Let's drink to it!'

'In less than two weeks I'll be back in school. Boring, boring!' Sally chanted as she and Deirdre cleaned down in the caff. Mavis had left early and Clare was cooking in the kitchen so they had the place to themselves.

'School in't that bad really,' Deirdre protested, safe in the knowledge that she had done with it for ever. 'I quite liked it, looking back. Any road, you're coming down to Yarmouth wi' me, first.'

'Yes, that's true.' Sally grabbed Deirdre's arm, nearly causing her to drop the mop. 'Look who's coming in!'

Deirdre looked up, then continued to mop.

'It's only Coffee and Book; he come in a lot lately. I've got accustomed to him, he don't seem special no more.'

But Oliver was still special to someone; Clare heard the nickname and hurried through into the caff ostensibly to put out a tray of scones to cool, really to have a word with her lover.

Not that he had been her lover since her illness, because he

359

had not. Despite Sally's various wiles she had not managed to get Clare to let her go out overnight again and that meant that though Oliver and Clare could and did meet during the day, their chances of getting it together were restricted to say the least and Clare found herself not sorry. She still loved Oliver, or thought she did, but his behaviour when she had been ill rankled; he could jolly well wait to resume full relations until she felt he had been punished for his neglect.

But now she went towards him, smiling the special smile she kept just for him and receiving, in return, one of Oliver's most intense looks.

'What can I get you?'

'Coffee and toast, please.'

'I'll do it,' Sally called, but Clare told her she would do nothing until the tables were cleaned down and the floor fit to eat from. So Sally returned to her task and Clare made toast, turned the tap and filled a cup with coffee, dashed milk into it and carried it back to Oliver, sitting patiently at his corner table.

'Any chance of seeing you tonight?'

He spoke so low that no one else could possibly have heard, but even so Clare was nervous; Sally was a sharp little blighter, you had to be terribly careful what you said in front of her.

'I doubt it.' Clare raised her voice. 'Sally, what are you and Dee doing this evening? If you're coming home with me then I want to pop down the road for some meat.'

'We're going to the flicks and catching the last bus,' Sally said at once. 'We'll have our tea here if it's all right with you, Mum.'

She had grown polite again, Clare thought, with the approach of school and the need to be nicer to her mother so that she might go on holiday with Deirdre to Great Yarmouth. Little did she know that her mother had planned to use that holiday to recommence relations of a naughty but nice nature with Oliver, now crunching toast at the corner table.

'Yes, that'll be fine.'

Oliver gave a small nod, and Clare knew she would find a big waggon on her tail as she left the city, though he would not come straight back with her. He would go home, clean up, get out his car and come back to her in that. But she always enjoyed the bit of the journey when they drove in convoy, both thinking of the other, remembering the first time he had tracked her home.

'What time can we go, then?' Sally asked, when they were all in the kitchen once more and all the customers, even Oliver, had left. 'Do we have to pay for our tea?'

'No, I'll treat you both,' Clare said grandly, making Deirdre giggle. 'I can recommend the meat and potato pie and the chips since we've got plenty of both left, and Dee made a fresh fruit salad which several customers commented on, earlier.'

The girls ate rapidly, helped Clare to lock up and then left. She watched them make their way down Cattle Market Hill, giggling and nudging each other, and then turned back into the caff. She would make the cats tidy for the night, then give Gran a ring to make sure she was all right, then set off for home.

Ten minutes later she was putting on her coat and thinking that the best laid plans ... Gran's phone was either out of order or she was in bed or possibly even out, only she enjoyed Clare's calls and usually waited for them so that the receiver was snatched up at the first ring.

It was a couple of weeks since Clare had had the bug, but she was still a little anxious in case Gran should catch it from someone. Gran pooh-poohed this idea, pointing out with perfect truth that she had nursed Clare without ill effects, but Clare still worried. She could not forget that awful moment when she had fainted on the kitchen floor, and knew that an old lady like Gran whose bones were brittle could do herself a lot of harm from a fall.

On the car-park, she waved frantically to Oliver in his waggon until he came over, brows rising, looking so deliciously dark and masculine that her stomach gave a little lurch. She explained that she would not be going straight home, however, since she must call on Gran first, and he said in that case he would arrive at her house at eight precisely, and would expect a warm welcome.

On the way to Gran's she planned the evening to come. She would have to look lively if Oliver was not arriving until eight and she meant to feed him first ... she did not examine that important little word, first, in case she did not like what she saw ... because Sally's last bus got in at ten twenty and she always met it since by then it was very dark to walk alone along the summer lanes. Still, she thought she could manage it. Steak was quick, a salad could be made in no time, and she had picked some beautiful greengages off the old tree in the orchard; they were lovely eaten raw or combined with other fruit in a compote of some sort.

Drawing up outside Gran's flat she considered potatoes in their jackets; they took hours really, but if she par-boiled a couple of medium sized ones, surely they would be ready to eat by say eight-fifteen? It was not as if they ever ate at once, they would have a drink, a few kisses ... her stomach was still lurching over the thought of the kisses when she noticed that Gran's rose-bushes were missing.

Odd, Clare thought, leaving the car parked by the kerb and crossing the now bare grass. The round garden-bed was still there, but there was no sign of the roses. She reached the door and tapped; no reply. Odder and odder – worrying, too. She knocked louder. Nothing.

Now thoroughly frightened, Clare nearly beat the door down, only to have the window of the next-door flat fly open. An elderly, rather moth-eaten head poked out.

'You after Mrs Forsyth? She int there, m'dear. She's in 'ospital.'

Clare's heart stopped, then started up at twice the speed. She walked nearer to the head. 'In hospital? Why? What happened? Where are the roses.'

'It was them roses caused it. The feller from the council come, had orders to dig 'em up, he said. Your Gran ... she was your Gran, I remember her telling me you was her granddaughter ... your Gran told 'em to lay off. Ooh, awful language she used,' the elderly one went on in a sprightly and awed voice. 'Awful! Believe it or not there was a struggle ... ought to be ashamed of themselves, young fellers like that, trying to drag the bushes away from an old lady.'

'Which hospital?'

'I don't know, m'dear. I think t'was a heart attack, or maybe a stroke. Anyroad, she fell down, still with the roses in her arms ... they'd dug 'em up then, and she was going to put 'em in again after they'd left, like she did last time ...'

'Last time? Do you mean she'd had this business once already?'

'Oh yes, dear, didn't she tell you? Three times they come and dug 'em up, and three times your Gran carted 'em indoors, kept the roots moist, and planted 'em again next day. Bad for the bushes maybe, she said, but better than being flung on a council tip.'

'And today was the fourth?' Clare groaned. 'Oh why on earth didn't she tell us? We'd have done something ... why shouldn't she have roses if she wants them, anyway? People need flowers — some people do.'

'You're right. Still, seeing them roses in and out of the ground was interesting, too. Wondered who'd win, we did. Some of 'em betted, but not me; I knew she'd win, in the end. She's not one to quit, your Gran.'

'I'll have to ring round the hospitals,' Clare was beginning, then remembered something else. 'Did they get in touch with anyone, do you know? A relative?'

'Someone give 'em a name ... Flower, was it? They'll have rung there.'

Thanking the head, Clare dived back into the Mini and drove as fast as she could in the direction of the nearest telephone box. She reached it and dialled her mother's number. There was no reply. Then Mother's at the hospital, Clare reasoned. She'll ring me, of course, but I can't go home, it'll take too long, waste too much time. There's nothing for it, I'll have to ring round the casualty departments ... no I won't, what a fool I am, she'll be in the Norfolk and Norwich, where else would they take her?

It was not very far to the hospital, though she had to cross the city more or less. Afterwards, she did not remember much about the journey save that it was fast and that an indignant motorist who hooted at her as she spun past the nose of his Ford got treated to a hoot back which went on twice as long as his original blast, the victory sign in reverse, and a word which Clare had not known she knew.

She parked the car anyhow on double yellow lines and ran into the hospital. In the huge reception area she collared a clerical person and explained that an elderly lady had been taken ill at her home ... she gabbled the address of the flats ... earlier in the day and was almost certainly now on one of the wards. Could someone please tell her which one it was, since she was the next of kin?

They were good, they were even patient, but they could not find Gran. Someone suggested another hospital. Clare had got it into her head that Gran was here, so she decided to become fierce. She demanded to see a senior official and when someone was fetched, told him that if he could not produce her grandmother then she thought the least he could do was to ring the other hospitals in the area to which Gran might have been taken, and ascertain just where Mrs Forsyth was.

Clare afterwards felt that she might have continued to search all night and try to knock some sense into various official but wooden heads, except for the good offices of a pale young doctor who looked as though he had seldom eaten a square meal and had forgotten the meaning of the word sleep. He was passing through reception when Clare's voice, raised in yet another cry of '... An elderly lady with red hair and most beautiful green eyes ... even if she was too ill to give her name, someone must remember her ...', must have caught his attention. He came over to the desk and cleared his throat.

'Excuse me ... they did bring a woman into casualty, thought she'd had a minor heart attack, but she was discharged about two hours ago.'

'Oh, thank you,' Clare said, restraining herself with difficulty from falling on his neck. Gran was not dead, she could not even have had a heart attack! 'Was she sent home, do you think?'

'No, not home. She went to a relative's.'

364

'Thanks,' Clare shouted over her shoulder. 'She'll be at my mother's place. Thanks again.'

There was a police officer standing beside the Mini. Fortunately he was young. Clare gave him her most blinding smile and grabbed his arm.

'Oh, Officer . . . my grandmother's had a heart attack, I've got to get across Norwich . . . could you tell me the easiest way to St Edwins Avenue?'

Any doubts the officer might have felt about the parking of a Mini, crosswise, on double yellow lines disappeared at this challenge. He rapidly but extremely efficiently sketched out a route on the back of an envelope which Clare found in her handbag and stopped the traffic in order that she might get into the flow. Clare waved a gay goodbye and proceeded to put her foot down to such good effect that she was outside her mother's house in St Edwins Avenue a good five minutes before it should have been possible. There, she parked the car a little more conservatively and ran up the short path. She hammered on the door, noticing with some surprise that the light was on in the bedroom but not in the rest of the house. Had her mother put Gran to bed, having decided that the old lady needed rest? But if so, why no other lights?

In answer to her knocking the window above her head was thrown open and Mrs Flower's neatly coiffured head emerged. She looked downwards and did not immediately recognise her only child.

'I'm very sorry . . .' she began in the formal tones of one about to utter a large lie. Then she recognised her daughter. 'What on earth are you doing her, Clare?' she said, her voice outraged.

'I came to see if you'd got Gran here,' Clare said. 'But you haven't, have you? Oh, hell!'

'No, I haven't, and I don't see why you think I should have,' Mrs Flower said peevishly, preparing to shut her window. 'I was trying to have an early night . . . what's Mother up to this time?'

Clare, however, did not intend to bandy words with anyone, because she knew very well where Gran was; ought to have guessed as soon as the doctor had said a relative, in fact. Gran would be at her home . . . and a quick glance at her watch made her groan aloud and turn without a word of farewell to her mother to leap into the Mini. Gran would be at home all right, and since it was eight-fifteen, so would Oliver!

CHAPTER
18

To say that Clare hurried home would have been to understate the case. She flew. The wiggling road through the villages straightened out beneath her wheels, cyclists leapt for ditches, other motorists blinked and she was gone. She gripped the wheel, pushed her foot hard down on the accelerator pedal, and tried not to think.

It was impossible to keep the mind a blank, however, when so many appalling events might have occurred; if even the mildest of them had happened she needed to rehearse, in her head, everything that she would say, how she would explain away her absence and Oliver's presence.

Who had got there first? Gran, obviously. But both Oliver and Gran knew where she kept the spare key, so if the doctor had got the hour of Gran's discharge wrong, and if Oliver had arrived early ... Clare groaned and took a corner so close that she later found a bunch of grass wedged beneath the passenger door handle ... if he arrived early and saw fit for some weird reason to get undressed and lie in their bed, how on earth would she explain that away?

Even the thought that it would be Oliver who had to do most of the explaining did not ease her foot on the pedal. She told herself at least a hundred times that Oliver was not that sort of bloke, he was in his way as conventional as Clive. Well, perhaps not quite as conventional as Clive, but very nearly. He was very unlikely to answer the door to Gran wrapped in a sheet, or to shock her by leaping out from behind the curtains and shouting 'Surprise!' so she had better simply get home at once and find out what had occurred.

As she turned into her own particular lane, it happened to her that Oliver might be late. Something might have happened his end, too, which would have prevented him from arriving on time. She glanced at her watch. Heavens, it was only eight-thirty. You never could tell, it just might . . .

She swung into the drive and there was Oliver's car, parked in her garage out of sight from the road but plain as a pikestaff from where she was. Clare drove the Mini round the corner, near the old hen run, and parked. Her heart had been hammering like fury but now that she knew the worst – Oliver and Gran were both in the house – it actually slowed down. She climbed out of the car, locked up, and went in through the kitchen door. Tish gave a strangled yelp but she was not in the kitchen; someone had relegated her to the living-room. Gran and Oliver sat in opposite chairs at the kitchen table, prosaically eating what looked like scrambled eggs on toast. Cups of tea steamed at their elbows.

'Clare . . . forgive the intrusion,' Gran said, turning to beam at her. 'Your friend was cooking you a meal when I arrived, but he insisted on my lying down in your sitting-room for a while and instead of getting on he came and chatted to me, which held things up. And then when you didn't come back I guessed you were probably combing the city for me, but I was hungry and so was Oliver, so he very kindly scrambled us both some eggs.'

'So I see,' Clare said. She crossed the room and put her arms round Gran's shoulders. 'Gran, I've been so worried! Are you really all right? What happened at the hospital? They shouldn't have let you out, they should have telephoned.'

'I told them you weren't on the phone, because I knew you'd be out and I didn't want to worry you,' Gran said placidly. 'It was a good thing Oliver had arrived or the ambulance driver wouldn't have left me, he said so. But as soon as he saw I was going to be well looked after he was perfectly amenable.'

'What happened in the garden, then?' Clare asked, beginning to have a most unworthy suspicion. 'Did they get the roses?'

'Indeed they did not! The brute of a man was actually trying to pull the bushes out of my arms ... what could I do? I pretended to have a fit, or a faint, or something like that. I crumpled up slowly, of course, rolling my eyes and moaning, otherwise I might have hurt myself. They rushed off for the ambulance, but I clung onto the roses, I wouldn't let go – or not until Billy Keeble from down the road came over, when I gracefully relinquished them into his care. I came round, of course, as soon as I saw the ambulance, I didn't want taxpayers' money wasted on me, but they made me get in and they did all sorts of tests before they'd let me go.'

'Gran, that was awful,' Clare exclaimed. 'You might have ... well, you might have ...'

'It worked,' Gran said, looking smug. 'The neighbours are getting up a petition, I heard them talking about it whilst I was unconscious. They say if the council interferes again they're going to cut a bed out in front of every single flat and plant roses and see how the council likes that!'

Clare shook her head helplessly. It was never any use nagging Gran once she'd made up her mind. Now, she glanced diffidently across at Oliver.

'Hello ... sorry I wasn't here to make you dinner, but you seem to have done awfully well without me.'

'Yes, indeed.' Oliver's slight smile was at its most saturnine. 'We've been very civilised, we had a sherry before our meal,' he waved a hand at the scrambled eggs. 'And of course a pot of tea with it. Can I get you something?'

'Nonsense, Oliver, the girl's quite capable of making herself a sandwich and pouring a cup of tea,' Gran said briskly. 'Eat your eggs before they go cold.' She turned to Clare. 'I recognised him as soon as he opened his mouth, of course,' she added. 'I said ... oh, you rang me up several times when my granddaughter was ill. Let me see, I said, weren't you some sort of a cheese salesman? When you weren't trying to sell Sally a pony, of course. And then you were a wrong number ... so courteous! And after that a hay merchant ... oh yes, I recognised him at once!'

'Poor Oliver,' Clare murmured, pouring herself a cup of tea. 'I don't think I'll bother with a sandwich, I'll just grab some bread and butter.'

'You've got to get up very early in the morning to catch me out,' Gran boasted, eating her eggs. 'I wondered whether I'd ever meet the mystery man on the telephone and now I have!'

'Yes.' Clare pulled up a chair and sat down. 'I'll have you know I drove them mad at the hospital, trying to find you. They wouldn't let me scour the wards personally, and they tried ringing up the other hospitals in the group and asking for you there, name and description, in case you had been too ill to give your name because I know hiccups do occur between the ambulance staff and ward staff, but of course nothing worked.'

'Well, it wouldn't, since I'd left,' Gran observed. 'Finished your eggs, Oliver? How about some of that delicious apple pie I saw in the pantry, second shelf down on the left? No? Well, I'll have some Clare dear, if you'll be so good as to get it out for me.'

'Right.' Clare got up, fetched the apple pie through, and cut Gran a slice. She raised her brows at Oliver but he shook his head; he was still looking amused which was a good thing, since Clare was beginning to feel more and more murderous. What on earth had she done to deserve this? Apart from the obvious, of course.

'Since I've finished I'd better be making tracks, I think,' Oliver said, having cunningly, Clare now saw, waited until Gran was heavily engaged with apple pie and cream. 'Goodbye, Mrs Forsyth, it's been a rare experience meeting you. Clare, can you come and see me out? I put the car in your garage to get it out of the way.'

'All right,' Clare said. Gran made signs as if she would struggle to her feet but for once Clare was not having any of it. 'Just you sit there, Gran,' she said firmly, 'I want a word with Oliver before he goes and I don't want you listening.'

'That was a bit unkind,' Oliver said as they left the house, closing the door firmly behind them. 'She wouldn't have followed us, would she?'

'How many old ladies do you know who would fake a

370

heart attack in order to embarrass council officials and keep a few rose-bushes?' Clare said tartly. 'Actually, she's marvellous and she might well not have come out, but you can never tell with Gran. Can you tell me what happened, please, and just what she thinks is going on?'

'She knows just what's going on I'm sure, though she may not guess the full extent of it. As she told you I was here, peeling potatoes actually, when I heard something come into the drive. I opened the back door without a thought ... imagine how I felt when I saw the ambulance! I thought, Oh God, she was hurrying, she's smashed herself up ... and I rushed across the gravel just as your Gran descended, looking very Queen Mother I might add, bowing right and left to the ambulance men − well, she gave that impression − and obviously, I thought, making for the wrong house.

'I was about to say so when she said in tones of ringing clarity, "Ah, my granddaughter is clearly still at work as I warned you she might be, but her man will take good care of me." Which of course put me more or less in the picture right away.'

'And then?' Clare prompted, fascinated despite herself by the picture of Gran taking the discovery of a strange man in her granddaughter's house completely in her stride. 'How did you feel when you realised she'd sussed us − I take it she has, having recognised your voice on the phone?'

'Oh yes. But I'd have told her anyway, I think.'

Clare stared at him.

'You'd have told her? Why, for God's sake?'

'Because it would have made you do something, instead of just letting life go on. Even now ...' He glanced quickly back towards the house, then pulled her into his arms. He hugged her strongly, steadily, then put her away from him so that he could look down into her face. '... don't you see that we're going to have to come clean? Your Gran knows I'm your lover, and she isn't horrified, so why ...'

'You told her we were ... Oliver, how dare you!'

'I didn't say we were lovers, sorry, I didn't mean to give you a false impression. I told her I loved you and because she asked, I said I thought you loved me too. But Clare, surely you want to be with me all the time and not just have to sneak a few hours together? I want it ... it's the only time in my life that I've felt like this and I want everyone to know!'

'Look, we'll talk later,' Clare said, making a snap decision. 'I'll ring you tomorrow. Only don't take things for granted ... I'm a married woman, even if you're fancy free.'

'If you were married for twelve months a year, this situation would never have arisen,' Oliver said quietly. 'What are you going to do, then? Stop seeing me when your husband comes home? Simply push me through the door, slam it and pretend I never existed? Because if so, we'd better stop seeing each other right here and now. We'll say goodbye and I'll find somewhere else to read my book and drink my coffee.'

'It isn't as simple as that,' Clare said with anguish. 'I'm not sure of anything any more. I loved Clive ... no, that's wrong. I still love him, but you're easy and he isn't. Only that doesn't mean it's right to love you and to leave him, does it?'

'What do you mean, I'm easy?' Oliver said, grinning. 'I thought women were easy, not men!'

'No, I don't mean that. I mean you're easy to talk to, easy to laugh with, easy to understand, even. Clive isn't. He's like a tightly sealed safe, you've got to know the combination to get inside and even then everything's in code. Oh, it's a lousy explanation, but it's the best I can manage, right now. Do go!'

Oliver was no longer smiling. He got into the car and revved the engine, then backed out without glancing at her – he had never had any difficulty in reversing out of the garage, that had been a ploy to get her to himself for a few minutes. When he reached her, he wound down his window.

'Well, love? If this is the moment of truth. Shall I go for good, or are you prepared to talk about permanence?'

'Oh ... oh ... We'll talk about it,' Clare said agitatedly. 'I do love you, Oliver, but I've got an awful lot of responsibilities which you don't even consider!'

'I'm one of them,' Oliver said grimly. 'Love is a responsibility, Clare. I'll ring tomorrow.'

He backed round in a neat, smooth curve, then he was off, a hand raised but no smile. Clare stood and watched his rear lights until they disappeared, then walked slowly back to the kitchen. And Gran.

'Why didn't I want you to know? For heaven's sake, Gran, decent, respectable married women don't have ... have men friends. I didn't want to hurt you, nor Sally, nor my mother, even. Far less Clive.'

'And is that how you still feel? That you don't want to hurt Clive?'

Clare nodded. The two of them were sitting in the kitchen – why do all the big events in my life happen in kitchens and never in living-rooms, Clare thought peevishly – on opposite sides of the Aga, sipping fresh tea whilst Tish golloped her supper and Greg sat like a stone statue as near Clare's legs as he could get.

'Well, dearest, you're going to hurt Clive if this affair continues and Oliver if it stops. I know you too well to think you'd simply go to ground with this man, you'll either put an end to it or leave your husband. Which is it to be?'

'You don't know me as well as you think,' Clare said gloomily, 'because frankly I'd go to ground like a shot if Oliver would let me. After all, Clive talks about coming home but really I bet it'll just be six weeks here and then he'll be off again. I can't take it, Gran, not any more. I'm lonely, I've been lonely for fifteen years, and that's long enough. If Clive goes then I'll boomerang straight back to Oliver and you might as well know it.'

'Sally's away a lot,' Gran nodded. 'She's growing up, of course. How would it be if I left my dear little flat and moved in with you?'

'It wouldn't stop me being lonely,' Clare admitted, not even having to think about it. 'I adore you, Gran, and always shall, but I need ... I need ...'

'You need a mate,' Gran said, not mincing matters. 'Someone to make love to you, to scold you, to laugh with you even. Someone to support you when Sally's difficult, someone to take Tish to the vet when she's poorly and you're busy. You need a man. If Clive comes home for good, isn't he just what you need?'

'I don't know. Do you know, Gran, I've only been on ... on close terms with Oliver for a couple of months, but I know him a great deal better than I do Clive! If I tell you something, will you promise not to pass it on to anyone else, ever?'

'Certainly. I never grass on my friends,' Gran said with dignity. 'Go on, shoot!'

'I never did know for sure who Sally's father was. I thought it couldn't possibly be Clive, but I married him when he asked because I thought he was so wonderful. I never told him I was pregnant either. Then he went off to the Kingdom and Sally was born and somehow he never mentioned she'd come a couple of months before she should have, and I never did either.

'And then, recently, I found out what I should have guessed just from looking at her, that she is Clive's daughter. Gran, can you imagine what that did to me? Clive knew all along, he was at that party ... Gran, he seduced me and never said a word about it! Believe me, a man like that isn't easy to love. I've carried guilt and gratitude around with me like a ton weight for fifteen years and when I discovered that it had been Clive all along I felt ... well, at first I felt very angry, but then I felt relieved! Light, unburdened, as though at last I could make up my own mind, do what I wanted to do, because I wasn't married to a selfless saint after all, I was married to a seducer of sixteen-year-olds who hadn't had the gumption to come clean!'

'And now you despise him? My dear Clare, you both behaved abominably! If I'd known you believed you were foisting another man's child on Clive I would have given you a good spanking, besides a telling-off. What else?'

'What else? Isn't that enough?'

'Well no, it isn't dear. I imagine that Selina told you when she stayed for the weekend – am I right? Yes, I thought so. And if you think I wasn't well aware that Selina and Clive had an affair before he proposed to you, you must think me dreadfully stupid. Didn't you know about that either?'

'No, I didn't. I was pretty self-engrossed about that time. But Selina let slip that she and Clive had spent the night together after her first husband left her, and what with that and the other business, I just felt I wanted . . . oh dear, this is awful . . . I wanted to get back at him. I more or less fell into the affair with Oliver, but underneath I was determined to show Clive that two could play at the game he'd played . . . or perhaps I should say four – Clive with Selina, me with anyone else who was willing.'

Gran leaned foward and twittered to Greg, who promptly got up and leapt lightly onto her lap. Clare saw the long, white fingers trembling as they caressed the cat's thick fur and knew that Gran was playing for time whilst she pulled herself together. It must have come as a horrible shock to find her granddaughter was not only blithely committing adultery but had done so for that most unworthy of reasons, revenge.

However, it appeared that she had underestimated Gran.

'Well dear, if you think I'm shocked you're quite wrong, because in your shoes most women would have done the same. I certainly would have. What would shock me very much would be to know that you intended to continue being unfaithful to two men – Oliver and Clive.'

'Oh, Gran, I do love you!' Clare knelt on the rug and grabbed Gran's hand, carrying it to her cheek. 'You've been the only constant thing in my life, I wish I'd told you about Sally before, but it didn't seem fair to her or to Clive. I thought Clive wanted to believe he was her father, you see.' She sat back on her haunches, smiling up at her grandmother. 'But how can I possibly be unfaithful to two men, when I'm only married to Clive? I don't see that at all.'

'Love calls for faithfulness just as much as marriage,' Gran said severely. 'Really, Clare, you should know that without having to be told! Poor Oliver loves you very much, or so he claims. Would you take another lover before his eyes?'

'No, of course not! But I'm married to Clive, I can't simply refuse to go to bed with him because of Oliver. It would be absurd!'

'Then, since you love Oliver, surely it must seem cruel to let him imagine you with Clive.'

375

'He shouldn't imagine,' Clare said. Even to herself her voice sounded sullen. 'It's none of his business ... we're married!'

'But my love, you didn't behave married,' Gran said triumphantly. 'That's the whole point, you're like Marie Antionette, you want to have your cake and eat it, and you can't, it's not allowed! It's a choice, Clare. Either or. It's up to you.'

'I want them both,' Clare wailed miserably. 'Clive's Sal's father, so I want him to be just that, but Oliver ... oh, Gran, how can I give Oliver up?'

'Either or,' Gran said with finality. 'Dear me, look at the time! Are you going to take Tish down to meet Sally's bus? If so, dear, I'll stay up to make us all hot drinks and I'll see if I can find some biscuits, but then I'll make my way to the spare room if you don't mind. It's been a full day.'

Next morning Clare awoke with a jump to find that it was broad daylight and that her alarm had failed to go off. She was just about to indulge in some panicky leaps and bounds when she remembered that it was Sunday and lay back again.

But not for long. Last night's conversation with Gran niggled and niggled at her. 'Either or.' 'You can't have both.' 'Take your choice.' Why not? she asked herself rebelliously, knowing the answer. Why shouldn't I have Clive for six weeks and Oliver the rest of the year? Men did it all the time, as she knew very well. Selina's first husband had been carrying on with at least two other girls whilst he was married to her friend. Sally was always talking about girls at school who visited their father one weekend in four, and came home with tales of small step-sisters and abandoned lovemaking between their ageing father and a teenage ex-secretary.

But you were either that type or you weren't, and Clare knew very well that she was not. She could not possibly live a double life, even if she had done so quite successfully now for nearly two months. Once Clive came home for good – if he did – she would have to stop seeing Oliver, or she would have to leave Clive.

She was considering the possibility of staying with Clive

376

until Sally was say twenty, when she heard someone slapping along the hallway, making for the bathroom. That would be Sally, presumably, getting up early so she could take Pegs out for a canter round. I'll go and remind her that Gran's here, because otherwise she'll be out of the house before Gran's even up, Clare decided, and hopped out of bed.

She went straight to the bathroom, but it was empty. Sally was in the loo. The door was pushed half shut but from the sounds coming from within, the poor child was not using the toilet for its usual purpose.

'Sal, my love ... you poor kid, you've gone and got the bug!'

Sally heaved, panted, and then sat back on her heels. She looked round at her mother. Ghastly pale, with running eyes, she was no advertisement for outdoor living. Clare, clucking, put an arm round Sally's waist and helped her to her feet and into the bathroom next door where she ran her a glass of water and sat her down on the cork-topped bathroom stool.

'Drink that slowly, just a couple of sips,' she advised. 'Well, love, you won't be riding Pegs today, that's for sure. It's bed for you until it clears up.'

Sally looked up. Colour was returning to her cheeks and her eyes looked brighter, less lost.

'Oh it won't make much difference, Mum, I don't think it's your bug at all. I was sick yesterday morning just like this and it cleared up in no time and I felt fine, after. And I was sick the other evening, too, at the stables. It can't be much or I'd feel ill, and all I feel is sick for a few minutes, then I am, and then I'm okay again.'

Clare stared at her daughter. Sally stared back. Wide, innocent eyes set in her little-girl face. A simple little shift nightie ... Clare looked down at her daughter's small breasts. They were not so small, at that. The nipples were swollen, pushing against the cotton ... now what did that make her think of? Suddenly it came to her.

'Sally! You're pregnant!'

She kept her voice down, remembering Gran in the spare room. She pushed the door shut behind them, then locked it. She pulled Sally to her feet and held the nightie flat against her stomach but there was no sign of even the slightest bulge. Only her instinct and the way Sally's breasts had developed backed the sudden judgement. Sally was shaking her head vehemently, looking suddenly smaller, younger and more afraid than she had for years.

'Mum! How can you say that? Do you know what you're saying? As if I could possibly be pregnant!'

Her voice rose a little on the last few words. Clare shushed her with a finger on her lips.

'Hush, love, Gran's staying the night don't forget. Sally love, this happened to me once, and I know.'

'Mum, you're wrong, you don't know. I couldn't possibly be pregnant. I'm not old enough to have a baby ... I don't want one, I don't understand about them.' She shook her head as though ridding herself of a bad memory. 'Please don't say that, Mum. I'm not pregnant.'

'Are you telling me you've never done anything with anyone which could get you pregnant? You've never been with a boy?'

More head-shaking. But Sally's lips were shaking too. Her voice had a plaintive note.

'No, I've not done anything. I'm all right, really I am.'

But Clare had gone through it herself and knew that giving way now would help no one in the long run – not if her hunch was correct.

'Right, if you tell me one more time I'll take your word and stop bothering you. But ...' she held up her hand as Sally began to speak, '...but if you tell me one more time then I'm going downstairs and I'm going to speak to Mrs Myers, see if you ever went to a tennis party there, and then to Mrs Gundry and ask how often you've spent a weekend with her over the past few weeks. Is that all right? Because Sal, my love, I have to know.'

Sally stared down at her hands for a long time. Her face was flushed now, her mouth sulky. But at last she looked up and met her mother's anxious eyes.

'I still don't think I'm pregnant,' she muttered. 'But ... don't ring them. I wasn't there.'

'Who was the boy, love? Was it a boy or was it a man?

378

Don't worry, it's probably no more his fault than yours, I never told you anything, never warned you ... you seemed such a child still to me. Please, Sal, trust me. Was it a lad of your own age?'

'Yes,' Sally whispered. 'Oh, Mum, I'm scared!'

Clare's heart went out to her daughter, but all was not yet lost.

'The boy ... is he likely to make a fuss? Does he know?'

'No, of course not, I didn't know, Mum, I promise you I didn't know. But now you've said, it would account for other things. What will I do?'

'The boy's name, love.'

'Well ... you wouldn't want us to get married, would you? Because he wouldn't want to do that – nor me.'

'Nothing's further from my mind, darling. Who was it?'

'Oh, Mum, it was Quack ... Eric Dolman he's called really.'

'Quack? But that's Dee's boyfriend.'

Sally sniffed and wiped the back of her hand indiscriminately across nose and mouth, then eyes. Clare blinked back a sudden rush of tears. She was such a child!

'No he wasn't, not really. But I don't want to marry him, Mum, if you don't mind. I don't even want to see him again. If I'd known he was going to give me a baby I'd never have ... I thought it was all right if you took the pill, Quack said it was.'

'But you aren't on the pill,' Clare said, forgetting to keep her voice down in her astonishment. 'How could a child like you get a supply of the pill?'

'Well ... you won't tell anyone, Mum?'

'No, of course not.'

'We nicked 'em, Emma and me. Just for a giggle, really. You see Mrs Carter was on the pill for a bit last year, just for a couple of months. She'd been having painful periods, Em said. So the doctor gave her a supply only she's ever so old-fashioned, Em's mum, and she wouldn't take 'em, kept 'em upstairs in her bedside drawer. Em thought it would be a giggle to take one or two and see if we felt any different. They're hormones they reckon at school – we thought they might make our busts grow. Only I took mine when ... when I was seeing Quack, which is why I thought I couldn't possibly have a baby.'

'It doesn't work like that though, darling,' Clare assured her daughter. 'A doctor would have advised you, or the clinic. Look, do you want to go through with it, have the baby?'

'No! I hate it,' Sally said energetically. She looked hopefully up at her mother. 'Could I take another pill and make it go away?'

'It isn't as simple as that, I'm afraid, but I'll have a chat to ... to someone I know, see if we can make some arrangements,' Clare said, her mind flying wildly to Selina who lived in the sinful city of London and could surely fix a little thing like an abortion. 'Go and get dressed, pet, and go off with Em and Pegs for the day but don't tell Em anything, understand me? Wait until I've seen what I can sort out.'

As soon as Clare saw Sally off she had breakfast with Gran and then took Tish for a walk, stopping off at the nearest call box to phone Oliver.

'What is it?' Oliver said at once. 'Can I help? Shall I come over?'

'I can't say much on the phone,' Clare told him, 'But I'm in trouble; Gran's still with us but after lunch I'm going to get her to rest for an hour on the bed. I'll walk down as far as the little wood – you know – and we'll meet there and talk.'

If Gran noticed Clare's preoccupation that day she said nothing. She never commented when Clare walked up and down, bit her nails and answered at random. She must have assumed that Clare was still struggling over whether to renounce Clive or Oliver but actually such a thought never crossed Clare's mind. All she thought about, all that long morning, was her daughter. When Gran said that she'd stay to lunch but then, if Clare would be so good as to run her home, she would have her rest in her own flat, Clare agreed. She would have agreed to anything which got her the solitude to phone Selina so that they could tackle Sally's problem properly, without Gran suspecting.

At last, however, lunch was over and Clare took Gran home, settled her in, told the neighbours that she was back in residence and returned to the house. She had gone down to the telephone box again and informed Oliver of the change of plan, so now she sat in the kitchen with her eyes on the drive, waiting.

The car drew up outside and Oliver came in, took one look at Clare's drawn and worried face, and took her in his arms.

'Darling, what's the matter?' he asked tenderly. 'What can I do for you?'

Clare outlined Sally's predicament in two words. Oliver stared.

'Pregnant? That child? Impossible! If you'd said . . .'

He stopped, the words unsaid. It was Clare's turn to stare.

'Go on! If I'd said it was me who was pregnant you were going to say. What next? Would you have been pleased?'

'I'm not sure,' Oliver said. 'Yes, I think I would have been pleased after the initial shock. I think I'd like a child.'

'Would you? Well, I wouldn't, not with Sal fifteen and about to start living her own life. Oliver, what shall we do?'

They were still standing in the kitchen. Oliver took her hand and turned her towards the hall.

'When's Sal coming back? Do we have time . . .?'

Clare snatched her hand away.

'My God, how can you even suggest it? I'm in dreadful trouble and in a good deal of distress and all you want to do is go to bed!'

'My dear love you aren't in any trouble, and not all the distress in the world can help Sally now! She'll have to grin and bear it, and don't think I'm cruel or cynical, because I don't mean to be. It's her life and her body, you'll just have to stand by and support her as best you can. But you don't let it ruin your life and you don't offer to mother it instead of her. Be sensible.'

'I'm being sensible. I'm going to suggest . . .' A movement outside the kitchen window caught Clare's eye and she frowned. 'Oh, hell, Mr Atkins's fowl are in my garden again, I can see the cockerel lording it over his hens and leading them right across my wallflower seedlings for next year. Perhaps I'd better ...'

'They won't do any harm,' Oliver was beginning. He tried to take her hand again and it was clear to Clare that he was still thinking mostly of bed. She jerked her fingers out of his reach and was about to speak very frankly when more movement in the garden caught her attention. She ran over to the window.

Outside, bedlam reigned. The cockerel was attacking a small red animal, the hens were leaping and shrieking ... and the small red animal, apparently not acknowledging the size and ferocity of the rooster nor the number and noise of his wives, was attacking everything within reach with complete lack of discrimination. It was Greg, and he clearly did not understand the essential difference between a sparrow and a Rhode Island Red.

'Greg's killing the hens!' Clare shrieked, diving for the back door. Oliver followed her out, she heard his feet scrunch on the gravel, but Clare was already deep in feathers and the fray. The cockerel had its cruel beak buried in the side of Greg's head, it had him by the ear but it was plainly as bent on mayhem as Gregory himself. Meanwhile Gregory, almost lifted off his feet by the cockerel's grip, continued to hiss and threaten for all the world as though he were in complete control of the situation.

Clare tried to grab the nearest bit of Gregory, which happened to be his tail, and was beaten to it by a hen which, emboldened by the behaviour of her lord and master decided to lend a hand, or rather a beak. Gregory lashed out viciously with unsheathed claws and now the feathers which flew were blood-stained.

The noise was astonishing and Clare was unaware she was adding her own shrieks and exclamations to those of the poultry and Greg until she suddenly stopped, having collared quite a bit of Greg. She pulled. The cockerel pulled too. Gregory squalled and wriggled and Clare trod on something soft which out-squawked them both.

Someone was laughing. Hands seized the cockerel and applied some form of persuasion, for the bird's beak opened

382

and the claw buried in Greg's back suddenly went slack enough for Clare to tear him free, though she left quite a lot of ginger fur behind. Oliver had the cockerel, he held him triumphantly high ... then dropped him. Scarlet furrows ran down his bare arm beneath his shirt-sleeve and his slacks were streaked with chicken dung. In Clare's arms, Greg was growling like a thunderstorm and struggling like a mad thing, but she clung on. He was digging his claws in at the same time, it was like being injected with red-hot needles, tears of laughter and pain ran down her cheeks but she would not — dared not — let her small but ferocious captive go. She got into the house somehow, slammed the back door and sagged, boneless and exhausted, into the nearest chair. In the yard outside she could hear Oliver herding the poultry out of the garden, back in the general direction of old Atkins's hen run. The shouts and cackling grew muted by distance and, on her knee, Gregory retracted his claws, gave a couple of smug, faint purrs, then began to wash.

Presently Oliver opened the door and came in, ruefully grinning.

'Can I get cleaned up?' he asked without preamble. 'That bloody rooster's ruined my shirt as well as most of my skin.' He displayed his arms, criss-crossed with claw marks. 'Come to that, I could do with a luxurious bath and someone to scrub my back.'

He looked hopefully at Clare and it was then, she thought afterwards, that she finally grew up. You could not blame Oliver because he was still on the other side of the fence she had just cleared, but it was plain that he had completely forgotten Sally and her problem in the excitement — and pain — of rescuing Gregory. Or perhaps they had rescued the cockerel, she was still not completely sure.

'Yes, love, you go up and have a bath,' she said comfortingly, 'I can't come and scrub your back though, because first I've got a telephone call to make and then I'll have to wash and change myself. But don't hurry, I shan't need the bathroom, I didn't get nearly as injured as you. I'll make us a meal, shall I? Then we can eat together when you're recovered.'

Her tone had been motherly – thus would she have spoken to Sally – but Oliver only heard the affection and his eyes gleamed.

'Right. I'll borrow a robe ... will that be all right? ... and chuck my things downstairs. Perhaps you'd give them a quick rinse, just over the worst bits, and then I'll put them on later, after ...' he hesitated, but her calmness remained, her affectionate smile was still in place. '... Well, after we've eaten and so on.'

Oliver went up the stairs and she heard water running. She was already on the telephone, though waiting for the operator to reply, when a pair of slacks and ripped shirt landed, with a thud, in the hall.

'All right, I'll deal with them,' she shouted, and heard Oliver's answering hail closely followed by the closing of the bathroom door.

He was a long time in the bath, which was a blessing. It enabled her to get his clothes clean, if not dry, to prepare a meal from the freezer, and to get her long-distance telephone call in peace when the operator rang her back.

'Hello? Clive? Darling, it's me ... can you come home right away? There's been a bit of trouble. No, we're all fine, no one's ill or anything like that. It's just that Sally's ...'

They were cut off. Not by the exchange, simply by static of such ferocity that there was nothing she could do but put her receiver down, ring the foreign exchange operator, and ask her to reconnect if at all possible.

It was not possible. All through the meal with Oliver she waited, half hoping the call would come, but it did not. Finally, at nearly twelve o'clock that night, when Oliver was long gone and Sally had been in bed for an hour, the operator rang back with the information that there had been a breakdown of colossal proportions in Saud; they would ring her as soon as it was possible to put a call through.

Clare went to bed edgy, to put it mildly. She had sent Oliver away without what he had so plainly come for and had been friendly and understanding over his unhappiness, yet almost untouched by it. Whatever her future was to be, she intended to work it out without emotional blackmail from anyone and right now Oliver's emotional blackmail was just a nuisance.

What was worrying her now was whether she had done the right thing for Sally. She had intended to ring Selina about an abortion and instead had followed a suddenly strong, almost psychic instinct, which had told her, in no uncertain terms, to get Clive. The trouble was she had not managed to tell him why she wanted him to come home and he would obviously wait until the lines had been reconnected before making any moves. In the meantime, would it not be wisest to get in touch with Selina? And yet every nerve in her body was against it, every strong feeling in her said she must wait for Clive.

Sally had come home from her day out with Emma and Pegs a different person from the stunned, miserable child who had slunk out of the house hours earlier.

'I knew you'd think of something to save me, Mum,' she had said as she drank her night-time drink and fussed Tish's long ears. 'You always look after me. I'm very sorry I've been so silly, I won't ever do it again.'

'I hope you will, one day, when you're married to some nice young man,' Clare had said, laughing and hugging her. 'Oh Sally, I'm glad you're back.'

'Well, you said go out for the whole day and have supper at Em's if she asked . . .' Sally began, but Clare only laughed again and kissed her on the nose.

'I didn't mean today, I mean from weeks ago,' she said, and Sally thought she was talking nonsense and laughed too and Clare found she could not – did not even want to – explain how totally her daughter had appeared to leave her whilst her mind and body were involved with Quack.

At two in the morning, without having closed her eyes, Clare went down to the kitchen and made herself a pot of tea. She sat at the kitchen table drinking it, whilst at her feet Tish, a frown on her beautiful, silly face, tried to sleep despite light, company and the warm smell of the tea. Clare was having a belated attack of conscience because she had not even rushed Sally to a doctor for a pregnancy test but had simply leapt to conclusions, mostly because she herself had suffered from nausea and sickness almost from the moment of conception, not only when she was expecting Sally but from the start of her five miscarriages as well.

The trouble was she did not want to see Sally tread the path she had taken happy though she had been, by and large. Sally was not only more than a year younger than she had been, she was mentally far less mature. Long ago, Clare had been going around with Selina, who was nearly two years older. Now, Sally mixed mostly with Emma, who was five months younger than she, or the girls in her own class at school or, lately, Deirdre. Clare had been cooking, cleaning and marketing either for her mother or for Gran for at least twelve months, but Sally was indifferent to domestic chores and frankly preferred eating to cooking. I was searching for a mate even if I didn't know it, Clare told herself. Sally was just searching for a bit of excitement. It isn't fair that she should lose her youth . . . she has so much more to lose than I did.

Clare went back to bed on the thought. It was true, she and Clive had done their damnedest to see that Sally had a proper country childhood. Sally was just beginning to blossom into a teenager, she would be wanting to wear pretty clothes instead of jeans and jumpers, she would go to parties and give them, exchange secrets, go out with a variety of boys and possibly find the one who was most right for her. If she had this baby it would change everything, and for the worse. But the decision was not just hers and Sally's, this time Clive must be able to show how he cared, how much he mattered to them.

On the thought, whilst still steeling herself for sleeplessness, Clare suddenly toppled into slumber.

CHAPTER 19

'The wedding was wonderful, I wish you coulda been there!'
Mavis's face shone beneath hair dyed amber and faultlessly set
specially for the occasion. She looked very different from the
caff Mavis in her checked overall and scuffies. She and Clare
were sitting in Mavis's kitchen, since Clare had brought
Cheepy home to his mum as soon as the caff closed, on
Mavis's return from the big city.

'It must have been lovely,' Clare said. 'When will the
photographs be back?'

'I don't know, one of 'is friends took 'em. Oh Clare, me
only sorrow was Lionel couldn't be there but 'e was there in
the spirit, I tell you straight.'

'Mavis, don't, it makes him sound dead,' Clare protested.
But Mavis explained you're as good as, once them gates clang
shut on you, and then went on to add that Lionel was very
cock-a-hoop having been told that, with remission, he would
only serve a further three months.

'Out for Christmas,' she exulted. 'Think of that, Clare!'

Clare, still on pins over the telephone call which had not
yet come through and longing to get home, sat on in the
kitchen. She had taken Sally home after work, picked Cheepy
up and come straight back to Mavis's place and now felt it
would be unkind as well as ungracious to rush off before
Mavis had told her about the wedding. Besides, the more
Mavis told her today the less she would have to tell her

tomorrow and if she did not get lots of cooking done the next day the caff would grind to a halt.

She had taken Sally round to Emma's before she left though, just in case the call did come through. She had no desire to put Sally on the spot by being in the house when Clive phoned back – if he did – and watching Sal settle down with Em and two of the Carter boys to play Monopoly eased her mind a lot.

'Yes, 'twas a dream wedding,' Mavis mused. She put the kettle on and got a cake out.

Clare pretended not to recognise it and decided she really would have to leave the caff last, in future. Then she remembered how hard Mavis worked and how willing she was to stay late and changed her mind back again. 'Let them eat cake,' she decided; Mavis deserved some perks.

'What did Sondra wear? White, I suppose. Was it a long dress?'

'It was cream-coloured, all lace like and real low-cut. Ballerina length she said it was, not real long. She wore spike 'eels and the biggest bouquet you can imagine.'

Mavis tried not to recall a ribald suggestion, overheard at the reception, that her daughter might presently appear on the stairs with nothing but the bouquet between her and her guests, and might then complete their enjoyment by throwing the flowers to honoured persons. Mavis had favoured the would-be comedian with her most basilisk stare, knowing full well that her Sondra wouldn't never do nothing so common.

'It sounds beautiful,' Clare said encouragingly. 'Were Rupert and Desmond pageboys?'

'Nah! Rupert wouldn't, said it was sissy, and Des doesn't 'ave the looks.' It no longer worried Mavis, however, that Desmond was not a handsome child; she and Lionel knew his true worth. 'They was there, acourse, sat one each side of me and Des lent me 'is 'anky to cry into, when Sondra said 'er vows.'

'So Sondra and Russell have gone off for their honeymoon, leaving the boys with friends, I suppose. Where did they go, incidentally?'

Mavis shook her head indulgently.

'As if you didn't know! To them Greek islands, just like you said. The boys are with Suzie, the one what keeps the boutique, but some time soon when Sondra an' Russell come home, they're all coming 'ere. Lovely, that'll be. Sondra says they'll go on the Broads if the weather's fine or up to the Castle if it's wet.'

'They'll have a great time,' Clare said, finishing her piece of cake. 'Well, Mavis, we'll be jolly glad to see you back tomorrow. I had the Saturday girls in, but though they try hard it's not the same.'

'Well, I've 'ad the experience,' Mavis said, rising to her feet as Clare got up. 'You've got to get back, I suppose. Thanks very much, my love, for taking care of my boy.' She bent over the cage, peering lovingly at the small occupant. 'Was you good, Cheepy my son? Was you a good boy for your Auntie Clare?'

'He was very good,' Clare said as they made their way up the dark little hall and out of the front door. 'The only thing is, Mave, he did say something which might embarrass you; he said ...'

But Mavis, who obviously felt she knew quite well what Cheepy said, overrode any explanation.

'Where he gets these expressions from I'll never know, unless it's off the telly,' she said, accompanying Clare to where her Mini stood at the kerb. 'My word, your car needs a clean, dearie! Real dirty, it is. Never mind, perhaps you'll find time to put it through the car wash, now I'm back.'

Clare, driving off, laughed to herself. Trust Mavis to turn what might have been an embarrassing explanation of how Cheepy came to say the things he did into a sideways swipe at her dirty car! But now that she was on the move once more she began to relax. She would telephone Saud again as soon as she got home and see if she could get hold of Clive before Sally came back from Emma's place.

'Pamela Forbes is in the caff with her father,' Sally remarked, coming hastily into the kitchen. 'He's not bad looking when you consider his hideous child. Steak and kidney and mash twice please Mum, and a child's sausage and chips.'

'Where's Alan Whatsizname?' Clare asked jokingly, reaching for three warmed plates. 'Don't say he's not with them!'

'Huh, they probably broke up months ago,' Sally said. 'He's too good for her, much too good.'

It was Tuesday and though the telephones in the Gulf were working once more Clare had not yet managed to reach Clive and to her annoyance he had apparently not thought it worthwhile to ring her back. Or perhaps she was wronging him, perhaps he had tried and been unable to get through.

Deirdre came through with her order pad in one hand and smiled brightly at Clare. She had been disappointed when told that Sally could not go on holiday with her to Yarmouth but not heartbroken; it transpired that Hecky had a sister with a boyfriend who was also off work that week ... a foursome had been arranged and Dee was anticipating enormous fun.

'Clare, could you take through my two gammons? I've got a big order here, all bits and bobs, I'd better deal with it myself.'

Clare got the gammons out from under the grill, piled chips on the plate, added a garnish and headed for the caff. It was for table three and she recognised Pamela Forbes at once. The man opposite her was dark with hair silvering at the temples. Clare looked, blinked, and then realised where she had seen him before; he was Tom Forbes, the young man who had carried her up to bed on the night of his sister's wild party. He was very like Pamela; no wonder she had thought the girl looked familiar!

'Hello, Tom,' Clare said, setting one plate before him and the other before his daughter. 'It's a good few years since we met – do you remember me?'

He stared, then grinned. Once, Clare thought, I'd have looked at him sideways, wondering whether he was a bit like Sally in certain lights. Now I can see a nice looking man who was once a handsome youth. I can smile at him knowing he isn't smirking over the fact that he seduced me sixteen years ago. I can even smile with a hint of mischief because he won't misinterpret it, won't think it's a come-on from a naughty girl who let a virtual stranger make love to her and then palmed the resultant child off on another fellow.

'Clare! That's right, isn't it? Clare Flower. Do you know I don't think we've met since my sister's party ... what was it, twenty years ago?'

'It was sixteen years, actually, and I've not seen Tracy since either,' Clare said. 'Of course I didn't know her terribly well, she was a year older than me, I only got asked because of the Bothwells ... remember Selina? She was a great friend of mine.'

'That's right. You wouldn't have seen either of us much after that of course because the party was Tracy's farewell to her friends ... Dad had got a job in Ipswich, we'd sold the house and were off in a week or so. Actually, Tracy married a Suffolk lad and lives there still, it's only my part of the family who moved back to Norfolk. We came back ten years ago so Pammy is very nearly a native, like her dad. She's at your old school ... by the way, what's your married name?'

Clare was glad he assumed she had married; she did not like to think she looked like a spinster, but you could never tell.

'Arnold. Clare Arnold.'

Tom Forbes clapped a hand to his brow.

'Of course ... I remember a fellow coming to find you long after the party was breaking up. He said his name was Arnold ... tall bloke, curly hair, about my age. So you married him, then.'

'Clive Arnold,' Clare said. 'I don't remember Clive being at the party.'

'No, you wouldn't.' He grinned at her, then at his daughter. 'I'm sorry, I've not introduced you. Clare, this is my daughter Pamela. Pammy, this is Clare, a part of my past, one of your Auntie Tracy's pals.' He turned back to Clare. 'You won't mind if I tell Pammy you were a bit the worse for wear? Well, you were only a kid, I carried you up to the spare room and Tracy tucked you in and we left you to sleep it off. So anyway your fellow turned up and we sent him up but he couldn't wake you. He came down after about half an hour and said you were still sound off and he'd better leave you to wake naturally. Poor kid, I bet you had a headache next morning!'

Not only a headache, Clare thought grimly whilst smiling and saying that she had felt like death. They talked for a bit, bringing Pamela into the conversation, Clare mentioning Sally and her own job here in the owner's absence. Then she left them to eat their meal and hurried back to the kitchen, where only her presence averted several culinary disasters. Sally was inexpertly mashing a huge bowl of potatoes with a very small fork and Deirdre had cut wedges of meat pie which would have bankrupted the caff for a week had Clare not halved each piece.

As she worked and the girls scurried back and forth, Clare reflected that school would be starting very soon now. She hoped Clive would get in touch before then because she felt, uneasily, that a decision should not be long delayed and if Sally wanted an abortion she would need a cast-iron reason for being off school since this was her 'O' level year. Far better all round if they could get everything done before term began.

Oliver had not been into the caff since the weekend; Clare found herself hoping he would not do so for ages, not until she had sorted things out. But of course there was always the telephone; he would not ring her in case Sally answered, but she could always ring him.

She did not, however, feel any urge to do so. She was too busy waiting for the call to go through, or for Clive to contact her.

'Mum, do you think you could drop me off at Em's? Now I'm working at the caff so much I hardly see her and next weekend there's a show quite near, we could get there without having to hire a horse-box. We're going to take turns to put Pegs over the jumps and if we do go to the show we really need to practice.'

'Well, love ... what about Tish? And your supper?'

'Em and I can get some chips, but I'm not hungry really. I know it's a bit unfair on you but if I go straight to Em's then

392

we can ride before it gets dark, and I'll be home in time to take Tish round the block. What time is it now, Mum?'

'Let me see ... only ten-past six, that's not too late.'

'There you are, then! I'll be home by eight. Can I, Mum?'

Some old road, same old questions; the only thing that is different is me, Clare thought, and was surprised at her immediate acceptance of the fact. Even Sally was the same really, wanting to spend all her spare time with Em and the pony. She might be pregnant but that was just a physical accident. Underneath she was just Sally, a little girl who had played at being a woman for a few hours and got herself into deeper water than she was prepared for so had hastily reverted to being a child again.

I'm different though, Clare told herself, driving skilfully along the twisty road. No one will ever ride roughshod over me again, not even in the name of love. I'm not worrying, any more, over how my actions will affect other people. Why should I? Other people don't! Not Clive, not Oliver, not my mother, not even Gran. Gran had never given Clare's anxiety a thought when she decided to fake a heart attack, she just wanted to have her own way over the roses. Oliver hadn't shared her crippling anxiety over Sally, he had just wanted to get her into bed. Even Clive had not bothered to ring her back to see why their conversation, if you could call it that, had terminated so abruptly. Probably he had thought it was just Clare, fussing again.

'Here we are, then.' Clare drew into the verge outside the Carter house. 'Give Em my love and give Pegs a kiss on the nose, and if you're back promptly at eight I'll make you something nice and light for your supper.'

'I'll be back.' Sally dived out of the car and up the Carters' long front path, between the dripping rows of vegetables. Naturally, it was raining. 'See you, Mum!'

'Back by eight, then,' Clare called through her open window, then wound it up and set the car in motion once more. Another lonely home-coming, with Tish rushing out into the rain to wee and bringing mud into the kitchen. Greg would come stalking in, cross over the weather, annoyed that the house was cold, the Aga dead, the rain beating down on the window panes. She would get the place warmed through, put the kettle on, listen for the telephone and try not to worry about Sally, or Oliver, or anything but what was on telly, later.

She stopped on the gravel with her usual scattering of the tiny stones, jumped out and ran for the shelter of the house. To her surprise the back door was slightly ajar ... caution should have stopped her, made her either return to the Mini or at least approach with less noise and rush, but caution was blurred and belittled by the driving rain. She entered at the double, pushed the welcoming Tish aside and saw a man standing by the Aga, turning to face her.

Rain was in her eyes and her hair fell lankly across them, but even so she was cross. How dared Oliver come here, make use of her spare key, walk into her home the way he no doubt expected to walk into her life, without so much as a by your leave! Clare's face began to burn, her eyes to sparkle ...

'Just what do you ... Clive!'

The last word was shrieked rather than spoken and even as she said it she dived across the room and Clive caught her in his arms.

He had set out at once, as soon as the line had gone dead. Well, not at once perhaps, since first he had made desperate efforts to get the call reconnected and then he had rushed to the airport to make a reservation on the first possible flight. He had been lucky though, someone had cancelled at the last moment and he had simply got on the plane, sending a message to his boss by a passing employee informing him that Clive Arnold had gone home to deal with a crisis and would be in touch as soon as possible.

'No suitcase? No pyjamas?' Clare said wonderingly, with her arms still round him as tight as they could go. It was so totally unlike Clive, whose conventional soul winced at the idea of shedding his pyjamas even in the torrid summer heat of the Kingdom.

'Not even a toothbrush,' Clive corroborated. He smiled, and the little white wrinkles round his eyes disappeared, making him look younger and happier. 'Are you surprised when you think what I must have thought?'

'Well ... what did you think?'

Clive rocked her gently, from side to side, looking down into her face. 'I think Sally's having a baby. Am I right?'

'Yes, I think so. But darling, how did you guess? I'd barely said her name before we were cut off.'

'I heard you say Sally, that's about all, but the moment I thought about it I was sure that's what it would be. Look, you never phoned me to come home when you had your miscarriages, you were so determined to cope that you soldiered through them alone. If it had been you ill or in trouble I was all too bitterly aware you wouldn't need me. But if it was Sally ... that was different. Even then I knew you could cope with illness, because she had all the usual childish ailments and you never phoned. But the other time you needed me – the only other time – was because of a baby, you see.'

'When I was having Sally, you mean. Not that I ever got in touch with you, then.'

'No, love, but you needed me then and weren't ashamed to show it. I loved having you need me, you've no idea! Every time you got a bit more independent, when you learned to drive, when you found out how to paint and wallpaper, when you coped with burst pipes and worse, I felt you'd moved another step away from me.'

'I did,' Clare said. 'I thought that was what you wanted – an independent wife who could manage everything beautifully whilst you were away. Come and sit on the couch, I've got a lot to tell you.'

Comfortably curled up, her head against his shoulder, Clare started. She tried, for the first time in their lives together, to explain how it felt to be married to a man who was only home for six weeks a year. She admitted the twin bogeys of sexual yearnings when he was away and the feeling of being obliged to sleep with him when he was home. She put into words the fact that she felt like a prostitute when he first slept with her because he seemed like a stranger, and that in any case the dignity of choice was always denied her because he was home for such a short time and also because she was so dependent on him financially. She told him how difficult it was to adjust to being told what to do instead of making up her own mind, and then of the worse difficulty of adjusting back again, when the six weeks were over and she had no one to consult or share with.

'I'm a hermaphrodite, neither one thing nor t'other,' she explained, scowling down at her hands. 'I'm married, but I don't have a husband to come to parent-teacher evenings or social events. I'm married but I can't produce the evidence, so to speak. I've probably got more in common with a widow or a divorcee than with other wives. In a big city maybe it wouldn't matter because I'd make friends with other women in the same position but in a village that doesn't apply. You're either married or not, you can't be half and half.'

Clive nodded and said he had never dreamed ... but listened again as Clare continued, determined this time to say it all, to be as honest as was kind and necessary.

'When we married, I had no idea Sally was your daughter. I'd been taken up to bed, drunk, by someone and left to sleep it off. I woke to find a fellow – Clive, how could I have guessed it was you? – in bed with me. Hurting me. Then I slept again, and in the morning it just seemed like a bad dream.

'Then Mother guessed I was pregnant and you came along, rescued me from her and asked me to marry you. I was just sixteen, scared silly, desperate for help and understanding. I should have told you I was pregnant but if I had, would you have admitted you were the father? I was wrong not to confess, I admit it, but you didn't simply do wrong, Clive, you did a wicked thing. You never told me, never let me have the satisfaction of knowing who Sally's father was. Every man I looked at might have been the one. Whoever it was knew who I was, might have been laughing up his sleeve at me whilst he served me with fish and chips or talked to me about Sally's progress in reading. If I'd told you, and Sally had been fathered by someone else, how would you have felt? Perhaps I was young and silly but I believed you'd be happier thinking Sally was yours than in hearing an unpalatable truth.

I thought you wouldn't understand, that you'd believe I was immoral, a real little scrubber who slept with a fellow she'd never met before, so I kept quiet. Why did you keep keep quiet, Clive?'

'Because I knew I'd done an awful thing,' Clive muttered. 'You were sixteen, I was twenty-five ... and you were drunk, in no state to defend yourself! But I swear to you, love, that I only got into bed with you because you were shivering with cold, weepy, maudlin ... I meant to warm you up with cuddles and then take you home. Only you were very sweet ... you clung to me ... does it make it any better if I tell you I'd wanted you for months, only Selina was always there, always in the way?'

'Oh, Clive! But why didn't you tell me later?'

'That I'd raped you when you were too drunk to resist? You'd have hated me ... I couldn't have borne that. And afterwards, when you didn't say anything, I told myself that you were such a kid you probably didn't realise Sally was conceived that night, I thought you probably thought we'd started her respectably, after the wedding, and she was premature.'

'Premature? At eight and a half pounds!'

'Yes, well ... I didn't know what tiddly things babies are as a rule, she looked quite small to me ... and then she was so like me, people were always remarking on it. How could you possibly have doubted that she was mine?'

'Clive, I knew you were in Scotland, or I thought you were,' Clare said forcibly. 'Besides ... Richard was at the party. In my worst moments I thought it must have been him.'

'Richard?' The disgust in Clive's voice was enough to make Clare's lips twitch. 'You thought that toad could have fathered Sal? My God!'

There was a short silence. Clare broke it.

'Then you didn't know I was pregnant when you asked me to marry you, which means you might have asked me anyway ... in time.'

'Good Lord, yes! Don't ask me why I fell so heavily for you because I don't know the answer, but I did. I only started going out with Selina so that I could get to know you. I'd have asked you out and courted you in the normal way but for finding you crying and your mother attacking you that evening. Selina said you were unhappy and so on, but I didn't know how bad it was until then. And that, of course, gave me the courage to ask you to marry me.'

'Did you know I was pregnant? Come on, tell me the truth, it's about time!'

'I knew your mother thought you were,' Clive admitted. He squeezed Clare's shoulders and then kissed the top of her head. 'When I think of what I made you go through . . . if I'd known . . . thought . . . used my imagination . . . I'd have spared you so much.'

'It would have been better,' Clare said with careful understatement. 'When I found out it was you that night I flipped, I went a bit mad, but I've come to terms with it more or less, and I want our marriage to go on. Only there's got to be more give and take Clive, honestly. You'll have to come home and share everything, the bad bits as well as the good. Do you want to try it?'

'Yes, I do. Clare . . . how did you find out? Was it Selina?'

'Tom Forbes told me,' Clare said, with only partial untruthfulness. 'I met him for the first time since that party and he told me how he let a chap called Clive Arnold go upstairs to try to wake me up and take me home. He said you came down again after about half an hour and said it might be better to let me wake naturally. In a nutshell. Selina knew, then?'

'No . . . but I often thought she suspected. That was why I asked you not to go up to her flat for a holiday in London,' Clive said. The partiality of his truthfulness comforted Clare for her own shortfall in the line of total honesty.

There was another pause. A comfortable sort of pause, Clare reflected. Sitting in the circle of his arm she realised that all her worries over Sally had eased, you could say they were literally halved. This was the one person who could truly share her feelings, the right and proper person, Sally's father. She was sure, now, that if she had known it was Clive right from the start the difficulties of living with a part-time husband would have been minor irritants rather than major catastrophes and the Oliver episode would never have happened. Crippling gratitude and guilt are no substitute for love and shared responsibility. Because she felt guilty over having, as she thought, deceived Clive, she had not turned to him for love and understanding, she had turned to Oliver.

'I'm glad you came back,' Clare said presently. 'You were right – I need you.'

'We need each other,' Clive said. He turned her very gently in his arm and kissed her mouth; it was a loving kiss, far more restrained and far less ... less suggestive ... than his early home-coming kisses usually were. Clare kissed him back without her usual fluttering nervousness, without the contracting stomach muscles, the fear of being thought too eager, the agonising uncertainty which had characterised their embraces in the past. If it works this time, Clare thought with a sudden bubble of amusement, it will be partly thanks to Oliver!

Clive held her in his arms and she was more precious than she had ever been, yet the nervous, ravening urge to make love immediately, the fear that he would be in some way unsatisfactory after his long love-fast, were missing. He wanted her all right, but he had no intention of rushing anything.

If it works this time, he thought with an inward grin, it will be partly thanks to Della!

'She's come round and she's going to be fine!' Clare crossed the small waiting room – very discreet with a thick-pile carpet and flowers on the central table whilst the magazines were all glossies – and hugged Clive, smiling into his anxious face. 'She wants to come back with us tonight, but I explained they want to keep her in just for a day or so. The nurse says you can take a peep at her if you want to, but not to go right into her room. She's still sleepy and a bit fragile, but she's our own darling baby, you'll see.'

The nursing home was quiet and discreet, set opposite a sober London square. From Sally's room you looked out over grass already touched with autumn and flower-beds with dahlias hanging their heavy heads as the days shortened. Clive turned away from the view he had been staring unseeingly at and followed his wife along a short corridor, up a flight of stairs and over to a white-painted door with a glass panel in it. When the nurse saw them she smiled and beckoned so they went in, on tiptoe, Clive a little in the rear. Sally smiled sleepily up at them, pale-faced and heavy-eyed but only from the anaesthetic. Clare's heart faltered at what they had done to Sally, then strengthened as Clive gripped her fingers reassuringly. They had offered Sally the choice and the child had not hesitated. Clare was glad; she saw no reason why Sally should suffer what amounted to a life-long punishment for a sin which was more ignorance than wickedness.

'Hello, Dad!' Sally sounded almost perky. 'I say, I feel as if I've been knocked on the head ... I'm terribly thirsty, can I have a drink?'

'I'll call the nurse, she said you could have a sip of something,' Clare said. She went outside and found a nurse who came back with her, allowed Sally to wash her mouth out with pale pink fizzy liquid and then settled her down again.

'I think Doctor wants a word with you before you go,' she said to Clare in a discreet undertone. She turned to Sally. 'Will you be all right now, dear? Mum and Dad will come and see you again tomorrow, but now I think you should have a little sleep.'

'I am quite tired,' Sally murmured. She turned her head wearily on the pillow and Clare thought she slept even before they were out of the room. Clive lingered for a moment but the nurse waited so that the three of them walked up the long corridor together.

'Doctor's in here,' the nurse said at last, stopping outside yet another white-painted door. She knocked, then opened it. 'Mr and Mrs Arnold, Doctor.'

'Come in. Please sit down.'

The doctor, who was tall and thin and no older than Clive, smiled nicely at them. Private medicine gives one absolution, Clare thought guiltily, taking the proferred chair. She noticed

400

that the doctor had an impeccable pair of charcoal-grey trousers under his white coat but saw, as he came to shake hands, that his shoes were dusty. He waited until they were both seated and then returned to his own chair behind the desk.

'Now, Mr and Mrs Arnold, your daughter's going to be fine. In fact, we aren't absolutely certain that she was pregnant; if so it must have been the very early stages. I take it she'd had tests and so on?'

Clare tried to suppress a huge wave of guilt which threatened to swamp her and carry her down to the depths; dear God, had all this been for nothing? Had she suspected it? Was this a Freudian method of teaching Sally the evils of haphazard sexual intercourse? But Clive reached out and took her hand. His fingers were warm and firm and his voice was steady as he answered.

'We didn't have any tests done, Doctor, since my daughter seemed to be following the same pattern my wife followed in all her pregnancies; um ... constant nausea, swollen breasts and stomach ... that type of thing.'

Uneasy as she was, Clare still gave an astonished mental gasp at Clive's casual use of words such as swollen breasts and stomach; feminine functions tended to make his eyes slither uneasily and brought a strangulation to his throat.

'Ah, I see. In that case she was probably in the early stages, difficult to diagnose. Yes, I remember you said no more than a month ... anyway, the main thing is that she's pregnant no longer. She's very young, even for fifteen she's young and you wanted to be sure, no doubt.'

'That's right,' Clive said, still easily. 'She begins her GCSE year in a few days and we wanted her to start on even terms with the rest of her class. Will she be able to go back to school next week?'

'Good lord, yes. Fit as a fiddle. Umm ... we usually ask girls in her position if they'd like birth control advice, but Sally's only just fifteen ... I thought I ought to have a word with you first perhaps.'

'It won't do any harm,' Clare said. Her voice sounded pale, which just about described how she felt. 'She was talking about AIDS the other evening though, with a good deal of horror. Do you suggest condoms these days rather than the pill?'

'We advise, we don't do much else and of course these days as you say we tend to suggest a barrier method rather than simply the pill. Well, someone will have a word with her. So if you'd like to come here tomorrow after breakfast, you can pick her up. Keep her quiet for a day or so, then let her slip back into her school life as if nothing had happened. I assume you've not talked about it back home . . .' he glanced down at his notes, '. . . in Norfolk?'

'No,' Clare admitted. 'I don't think anyone would guess, you see the boy wasn't a regular boyfriend as such, he was chance-met you could say, so friends and relatives still assume she's only interested in ponies.'

The doctor laughed and looked ten years younger. Then he got to his feet and held out his hand.

'Right; perhaps this will make her return to ponies as an interest. Tell her if she boasts about it to her friends she'll be sorry one day and perhaps she'll listen to you. And if you'll take my advice you won't try to keep her in or show you're watching her. In the end that sort of reaction from parents makes the child fight harder to get away and it breeds resentment, which sensitive treatment and a good deal of understanding can avoid. But I probably don't need to say this to either of you, you obviously love your daughter very much and are young enough to understand her. At least, so far as anyone past nineteen can understand a teenager,' he added, smiling at them as he shook hands.

Clare thought back to the summer, when she and Sally had both behaved like wilful women. She thought of Sally's sudden freedom to get away with people her mother had never met . . . had it not been for her own preoccupation with Oliver she would have realised something was wrong with her daughter and would have taken steps which might easily have nipped Sally's affair in the bud. She could never blame Sally for what had been so much her own fault; she had ignored the importance of being a caring parent in the pleasure of having a lover, Sally had suffered for it and now she was suffering too, because it was something she could not possibly share with Clive. Her own part in Sally's downfall could not be mentioned because she knew it would place far too great a burden on their marriage, however good confession might be for the soul.

'After breakfast; we'll be here by nine,' Clive said, as he shook the doctor's hand. 'And we'll treat her with kid gloves.'

The doctor smiled, then shook hands with Clare.

'No, Mr Arnold, not with kid gloves, she might resent that as well. Just try to forget it happened; treat her normally.'

'We'll do that,' Clare said. She tucked her hand into the crook of Clive's elbow and they left together, on Clare's part at least with a lighter step.

'Ought we to ring Selina?' Clare said as they walked back to their hotel. 'Just for a few words?'

Selina was staying at the house, looking after Tish and Gregory and having a restful few days, or so she said. Clare had lent her the Mini and told her to keep an eye on the caff and help out if they needed it but Mavis had been confident she, Deirdre and the dreaded Lizzie Treece would manage very well.

'There'll be no trouble from Lizzie, not with me in charge,' she had said darkly. 'I know 'er you see, Clare.'

But now, with their arms still linked and mutual relief giving Clare the impression of walking on air, Clive shook his head.

'Better not. After all we rang her last night to say we'd arrived safely. I don't want anyone to suspect anything, not even Selina.'

'Perhaps you're right, though I wouldn't say a word, but Selina's got sixth sense sometimes,' Clare agreed, having thought the matter over. 'Anyway, with the babe coming out of durance vile tomorrow, I suppose we'll be home in time for lunch.'

Clive, however, shook his head.

'Nope. She'll look pretty silly after a three-day stay in London if she's got nothing to talk about. We'll take her round a bit for the next couple of days ... after all, you did tell Selina we'd be away Monday to Saturday so she won't be expecting us back.'

'Yes, and Sally will love to see the Tower and perhaps go to a theatre ... you don't think it will seem ... well ... it'll give her the wrong impression? ...'

'Like a reward for going through it? Well, what's wrong with that? Clare, darling, we're her parents, we've got to take some responsibility for the fix she was in, wouldn't you agree? I'm not blaming you, God knows it was me who was never on hand, but if I'd been around more it might not have happened.'

'And me. You've never said it was the job, but ...'

'It wasn't! Look, the quack gave us good advice back there; we're going to forget it as fast as we can and make sure Sal doesn't suffer for it and in doing so we'll make sure we don't suffer either. Good enough?'

'Good enough.'

'That was quite the nicest meal I've ever eaten,' Clare said much later that night as the two of them climbed the stairs at the Carlton Grange Hotel. It was a medium-sized place since Clive had been very conscious of the fact that he had come in with two female companions and for this one night his party had shrunk to just himself and Clare. He had a story all ready about a chance-met school friend but by the time their meal had been consumed the foyer was deserted so they were able to make their way upstairs unchallenged, and by the following night Sally would be with them once more.

'Yes, it wasn't bad,' Clive agreed, fitting his key in the door and handing Clare Sally's. 'Go and rumple her bed, there's a love, then if anyone asks we'll say she went out early to meet someone.'

Clare, rumpling obediently, thought it was all a bit cloak and dagger, a bit unnecessary, but it made Clive happy and that was enough. Her sudden growing up had included an ability to appreciate the reason for some of Clive's hitherto annoying habits. Over-cautiousness was often kinder all round than an easy-going attitude might be and his leaping aboard an aircraft without so much as a pair of pyjamas or a toothbrush had impressed Clare mightily. That's love, she told herself dreamily now, disarranging the bedding and casting garments from the wardrobe in appropriately teenage fashion onto floor, chair and dressing-table. Love isn't grand passion and candlelit dinners and kisses that set you on fire, or at least that isn't all it is. It's the mundane, little things ... the arrival in the nick of time, the hand held when one is making a difficult telephone call to one's best friend and telling her what amounted to lies for the first time in one's life. Love is going right through the London Telephone Directory for the right nursing home for one's child, ringing up colleagues and asking veiled questions, behaving out of character because it no longer mattered if people sneered or giggled. What mattered was saving a dearly loved daughter from the consequences of her own folly.

Although the candlelit dinner had just been very enjoyable of course, she reminded herself, staring out of Sally's bedroom window at the brightly lit street beyond. And the kisses were pretty dam' good as well. The passion bit was all right too – less frantic, more leisurely, as though Clive had learned some lessons about love as well. Perhaps it was because he was not going back to the Kingdom, save to collect his things and work a last month out of loyalty to his firm, but she preferred to think that it was because they were so much in accord. Her needs were now understood and therefore important to Clive.

She finished rumpling, gave the room a last look, and then returned to her own room, careful to lock the door behind her. Tomorrow Sally would really be here and they could start living properly again.

'None of this would have happened,' Clare said later, as she lay in bed with her mouth very close to Clive's. 'If you and I had decided I should have an abortion nearly sixteen years ago.'

'An abortion? My God, I was a fool, but not that foolish. I loved you desperately, I wanted you to have our baby, and so far as I can recall you seemed quite keen on me!'

'I was wild about you; still am,' Clare admitted. 'Shall we turn the light off?'

'No. Want to look at you in the nuddy.'

'Well, you can't, I've got my nightie on,' Clare reminded him.

'That's soon remedied!'

Clare squeaked and her nightie sailed through the air and draped itself provocatively across the mirror on the dressing-table.

'If that's how you behave in London hotels . . . we must visit the place more often!'

'Was that nice?' Clive asked sleepily some time later.

Clare yawned, stretched, and replied that it had been very nice indeed and how was it for him. Even the light, she realised, had not impaired her performance and Clive, who was shy, had seemed to revel in illuminated sport, if such it could be called.

'I'd better get my pyjamas on,' Clive said presently.

He leaned over and rumpled her hair, then got reluctantly out of bed. He was still a very conventional man in some ways, Clare knew. Whilst she could sleep without a nightie and never think twice, Clive would be uncomfortable in the nude. It was a warm night, so Clare remained where she was, lying indolently against the pillows, watching her husband re-robe.

'What are those scars on your shoulders and the top of your chest?' she said idly, as Clive climbed back into bed. 'You look as if you've been in a fight with a cockerel.' Horror filled her as she realised she was talking to the wrong man – it had been Oliver who had borne those particular scars – but Clive appeared to notice nothing unusual.

'What, those? Oh . . . they're just little scratches,' he said offhandedly. 'It wasn't a cockerel, they don't run to them in Saudi, but those little monkeys they hand you in a bazaar to be photoed with can get spiteful.'

'I can imagine.' Clare pulled his jacket to one side and examined the damage some monkey had inflicted on her man.

'Never mind, they're fading already; by Christmas you'll not be able to see them at all.'

'That's what I thought,' Clive agreed.

The two of them settled down, Clare curled up with her back against Clive's front, Clive curled round her. Like two spoons.

Very soon they slept.

CHAPTER
20

'Bring her round then ... gently, gently!'

Oliver grabbed the rein from his lad and immediately the mare, who had been wild-eyed and terrified, prepared to spook at the least thing, calmed. Oliver talked to her quietly for a moment and then said, without glancing round, 'Get the stable door open, Nick.'

Behind him he heard the stable door creaking open but he made no move to change his position. He continued to gentle the chesnut until he could sense her change of attitude; she was no longer fretting over her recent experience but beginning to turn her mind to the hay in her net and the good feed which would presently be brought to her stall. Only then, still with hands and voice reassuring, did he wheel round to face the doorway and Nick standing by it.

'You'll do, you'll do, my lovely.' The words, crooned out in an almost hypnotic tone, accompanied his slow and steady walk stablewards.

With no more trouble the beautiful seventeen-hand mare was taken to her stall where she began immediately to tug hay from the net, her ears pricked to catch his voice to be sure but almost idly, as an afterthought. What mattered now was the sweet hay and the familiar dimness of this place. She was forgetting the swaying of the horse-box, the terror when it had tilted as it entered the yard, throwing her to her knees. Thank God the straw was thick and she isn't scarred, Oliver said fervently to himself, signalling Nick to leave the door open for him. It had been his own carelessness which had nearly signed the chestnut's death warrant, for once she was down she could easily have broken a leg in her attempts to rise, could easily have killed herself and Nick too in her panic-stricken efforts to escape from the box by kicking the door down or the side out.

'Shall I get her a hot mash?'

Nick knew perfectly well it was no fault of his, but he still sounded apologetic. Oliver turned and grinned at him. Better set him straight, lads as good as Nick should not have their self-confidence destroyed, they were, in their way, as sensitive as a thoroughbred mare.

'Sorry about that, old man, criminally careless of me. I clean forgot I'd told Sid to get the old flagstones up on that side of the yard whilst I was up North. Like a fool I was daydreaming as I came round the corner and drove straight onto mud where I'd expected flags ... lucky it was no worse.'

He had not been day-dreaming, of course; far from it. He had been going over and over, for the thousandth time, his last encounter with Clare. Where had he gone wrong, for God's sake? He had been concerned over Sally in his way but she was not his child, he had naturally been far more concerned over the possible effect her pregnancy might have on Clare. What was more, Clare had seemed to think it contemptible that he had wanted to go to bed with her ... When you remembered that they had been lovers for two months and had, because of her illness, been apart for a fortnight, surely it was natural that he should want to make love to her the first time they met?

What really rankled, of course, was the fact that Clare had made no secret of her feelings; when it came to the crunch it was that wimp Clive she wanted and not Oliver. It was the first time Oliver had been literally cast aside by a woman in favour of her husband and he was not enjoying it one bit. What was worse, it was also the first time in his long and amorous career that he had actually urged a woman to leave her home and her husband in order that their affair could continue.

He loved her, dammit! Standing in the dimness of the

stable, watching the mare lipping at her hay and occasionally rolling an eye to make sure he was still near, he tried to tell himself that Clare was only a woman just like all the others. Fun to be with, fun to kiss and cuddle, great in bed and out of it . . . but dispensible. More, replaceable. The trouble was, he did not believe his own propaganda. Clare was not just another woman, not replaceable. He could not imagine ever feeling quite the same over another woman, getting the same kick out of her company, sharing the same sense of humour, knowing the giddying pleasure of holding her, possessing her.

He forced his mind to think of the others: Gloria, whose long hair had touched the base of her spine when she brushed it out at night. Susan, a teenage nymphet whose appetite had, after a couple of weeks, reduced Oliver to thinking himself little better than one of his own stud stallions. Bet, a luscious divorcee, blonde and sweet and cuddly, whose understandable eagerness to get Oliver into bed had only been outweighed by her inexplicable eagerness to marry him. Going further back there was Helen, twice married, a steeplechase jockey the present incumbent. He had met her at a race meeting; the thought of her bottom in jodphurs still had the power to make his muscles clench in an extremely stimulating fashion. They had had a lot in common, she had been magnificent in bed if a trifle demanding, but he had never for one moment felt anything other than a nice, healthy lust for her.

Clare. She was not as pretty as Gloria, not as eager as Susan, not as well-endowed as Bet, not as randy as Helen. She was dark-haired – he had always had a weakness for blondes and red-heads – she was of medium height and built when by and large Oliver liked his women either tall and willowy or curvaceous and cuddly. Now that he came to consider it, what on earth had he seen in her? He did not know, could not put it into words. All he did know, he mused, leaving the stable and walking towards the house, was that he yearned for her, thought about her twenty times a day . . . no, twenty times an hour.

He missed her. It was a new and unpleasant experience to

410

eel a constant ache in the back of the mind, dulling the
enses, clouding the sunshine, taking the taste from food and
he kick from alcohol. It's impossible, Oliver had told himself
vhen he had first noticed this fact. Clare gone is Clare gone,
t's my mind trying to tell my stomach a load of nonsense and
ny stomach's gone and passed the news on to my taste-buds
nd all I need is willpower and commonsense and I'll enjoy
ny food and my beer as much as ever.

It did not work. His taste-buds continued to insist that the
lavour was mysteriously missing from food and his stomach
nade it worse by confirming that it was not really hungry.
Oliver had to be very firm indeed with himself, forcing down
asteless meal after tasteless meal. Do you want to lose weight
over a woman? he asked himself severely. Women are the
ones who pine and sicken, men move on. Only this man, this
virile, fascinating brute, had somehow got himself wrong-
ooted into the role reversal he had teased Clare about.
Because Clare was looking grand, there was no possibility of
us thinking otherwise. He had spied on her, followed her,
urked behind walls and crouched between cars and watched
er as she went about her business. She had never looked like
e felt, which was lonely, aching and depressed. She moved
round the caff swiftly, she laughed, she ran out to her little
ar when the place closed, eyes bright, hair shining, the soft
kin of her tanning to a golden brown as the weather
mproved and the days shortened in an Indian Summer of rare
beauty.

Not even in his most self-indulgent moments could Oliver
ee Clare as either deprived or pining. No. All too clearly she
vas happy and successful. He assumed that this Clive fellow
had solved the problem of Sally's pregnancy – if she had been
pregnant – and was now filling the gap that Oliver's own
absence must have left in Clare's life so satisfactorily that the
voman never gave him a thought.

So what to do? It seemed obvious. Clare was happy
because she had Clive, so it stood to reason that Oliver, too,
could be happy if he could replace Clare. The only snag was
hat for some absurd reason he had no urge whatsoever to
pick up the chase where it had apparently ended . . . with first

the capture of Clare and then her defection back to Clive. I[
the ordinary course of things he should have been lookin[
round now for the next because that was his way. Love 'er[
and leave 'em. But to start again, knowing that the quarry[
when he finally pulled it down, would not satisfy him in th[
way Clare had, was no spur. He looked at every woman h[
met and found he was comparing them – to their detriment [
with her.

It was like some dread disease for which there was n[
cure. Finally, as he re-entered the house, he decided h[
simply must do something about it. He would not lur[
outside the caff tomorrow, he would go boldly in an[
demand a few words with her. He dared not ring her in cas[
the wimp answered the phone. Even in his unhappiness h[
would not have done anything which might hurt Clare.

What will I say when I see her? he asked himself, stridin[
across the kitchen and through the back hall to his study, nc[
even noticing his housekeeper's open mouth and half-spoke[
words of greeting until he was too far away for a belate[
apology for absent-mindedness. Shall I tell her I'm ill wit[
wanting her? Scarcely; he would sound as wimpish as th[
wimp. Perhaps if he could persuade her to come out with hir[
a couple of times a week and he could see the love in her eye[
turned to mere friendship, that would complete the cure. A[
sort of innoculation, he mused. If she knew how he wa[
suffering surely that would not be too much to ask? H[
would not let himself admit that his belief in his own abilit[
to charm a woman into his arms was still alive, thoug[
distinctly groggy. When she sees me, hears my voice ..[
when I get my arms round her ...

He reached the study and poured himself a stiff whisky. H[
drank it. It tasted like a urine sample and the second one gav[
him heartburn. Damn all women, Oliver thought furiously[
pouring another and then leaving it, untouched, on his desl[
Damn them all ... except the one who's going to get me ou[
of this!

'Well, hello, stranger!'

Mavis's greeting was a bit sarcastic but Oliver did not care. He grinned at her.

'Hello, Mavis. Could I have coffee and toast for two, please?'

She would come out; she was bound to come out. She could not leave him sitting here, munching his way through two rounds of tasteless toast and sipping two mugs of tasteless coffee. She had a heart . . . she was a generous, loving woman, that was the trouble.

The place was not full, but it was not empty, either. Mavis brought him tea and toast, then went off to serve other people. Deirdre popped out, blushed in his direction, then popped back again. There was another woman moving about in the kitchen, but it was not Clare. He knew, abruptly, that she was not here. Could he ask? He could.

'Dee . . . where's Clare?' He had to grab her overall as she went past but she was a polite girl; even with a loaded tray in her hands she stopped for a moment.

'She's off today.'

He stayed at his table until the toast and coffee were gone, then left the money and a tip and abandoned the place. If he went to her home he might be seen by the wimp . . . but there were other people who could tell him where she might be today, or if she was working tomorrow. He would try the Bretts half a mile up the road past her place.

'Lookin' for Mrs Arnold, are you?' Mrs Brett was a friendly soul who made it her business to know as much as possible about her neighbours, even if they did happen to live half a mile down the road. 'Well, my dear, you're in luck . . . I reckon she's seeing her feller off . . . back to that Arab place he go to most o' the year. Yes, I see her on Thorpe Station this morning, with Mr Arnold and a pile of luggage that 'igh.' Mrs Brett stood on tiptoe to indicate the size of the pile. 'Howsomever, she'll be back now . . . well, I know she's back, 'cos as I come down from getting myself a mess of plums from the Carters just back the road there, I see her drive up in that little Mini of hers. That was when I put two and two together, like. When he's home they drive the big

413

car, see? Mini gets put into the garage. But when he go back out come the Mini.'

'She's back?' Oliver's heart rose from its new position in his boots to its customary nook. He felt wonderful ... the wimp had gone and Clare was actually at home, no more than half a mile down the road! But it would not do to seem too eager; he nodded casually. 'That's good, I've some pony-nuts on board the waggon, she wanted some, I can drop them off with her.'

'Well, you could always leave 'em here ... but there, since she's home ...'

Mrs Brett waved him off and Oliver waved back, then swung the big waggon round in her yard and headed for Clare's place. He sang loudly as he drove and fancied steak pie and chips followed by sherry trifle only slightly less than he fancied Clare herself.

Selina had had a most enjoyable day. She had picked Gran up and together they had driven round to various friends, being lunched here and tea-ed there. Gossip had been dug out – fifteen year old gossip – and aired, new husbands and children discussed, dreams dreamed and visions wistfully remembered. Now, back in Clare's kitchen, trying to persuade Clare's Aga to light so that she could make herself a meal, Selina wondered, not for the first time, how she would have enjoyed being married to Clive for fifteen years.

I don't think I'd have been faithful to him, like Clare has, was her first thought. Not with his absences so long and the house here so lonely. Of course, she supposed vaguely, having Sally must have made a difference, and perhaps the sex side of it had not been so important to her friend as it would have been to her. But ... I'd have been driven to find myself a lover, Selina told herself ruefully, turning away from the Aga and deciding to have a nice salad until such time as the brute turned itself on in the course of nature. I could not have borne being abandoned here for months at a time without so much as a grope to keep me happy. As for the job ... well, I'd have been desperate for a job all right and nothing, no

Clive's most earnest pleas, would have stopped me from getting myself one.

Selina went to the fridge and got out the makings of a salad, though when she remembered what she and Gran had been through in the cause of other people's hospitality it was odd that she could even consider eating the stuff. She ran lettuce under the tap half-heartedly, picking off tiny slugs, then put it into a bowl and began to slice cucumber over it.

Naturally, her mind returned to Clare, whose house this was, whose daft great dog had eaten an enormous meal and flung itself down in front of the still unmoving Aga, and whose food she was about to devour. Clare was astonishing, but then Selina supposed she always had been, really. Trying to please Gran, who was loving but extremely eccentric, trying to satisfy her mother, who had never wanted a child, and then getting involved with Clive, bringing up a daughter who she believed to have been chance-begot ... the mind boggled. And doing it all alone, what was more, save for six or eight weeks each year. Possibly those six weeks had been one long, torrid session, but even so! I'd have taken a lover, Selina decided crossly for the second time in ten minutes. Bad it might be, but I wouldn't have had the character to manage alone.

Someone knocked on the back door. Tish raised a sleepy head and thumped her tail on the floor. Good, Selina thought, someone who knows Tish probably knows Agas. I'll get whoever it is to switch the bloody thing on for me and then I can have something hot.

She opened the back door. She and Clare's visitor stared, almost nose to nose, into each other's startled eyes. Oliver, in his eagerness, had been inside the room and all but on top of Selina before he realised she was not Clare. And Selina, thinking about lovers, recognising him without at first realising where she had seen him before, let recognition and dawning interest show in her face before putting on a more neutral expression.

'Oh!'
'Oh!'

Oliver stepped back and shut the door behind him. Selina

was, for once, speechless but Tish rushed forward, beaming. Oliver patted her head but you could see he was unaware of the dog's affectionate prancing.

'Clare?'

'She's in London, I'm ...'

'In London? But I thought ... Mrs Brett told me ...'

Selina was a tall girl but Oliver could give her a good four inches. Now she tipped her head back to look into the dark face above her own and saw such an expression of unguarded misery, such unhappiness, that she very nearly put her arms round him. This being liable to misinterpretation however, she just took his hand in both hers.

'It's all right, it'll be all right. I'm sorry, you thought she was here, but she and Clive and Sally are away for a few days and I'm taking care of the house and the animals. Look, sit down.'

He moved like a sleep-walker and sat down on the arm of one of the chairs. Selina sat opposite. He had very long eyelashes, she saw, and very dark-blue eyes, the same colour as the shirt he was wearing, but he was not seeing her; disappointment and distress were breaking over him, like waves. What on earth had Clare done to this luscious man to make him so much her slave that he did not even see Selina's own considerable beauty, nor appear aware of her warm interest in himself? The thing to do was to distract him, she decided.

'Look, I'm awfully sorry you've had a wasted journey,' she said, giving him her most beguiling smile. 'But actually, you could be most awfully helpful if you would. I can't get the Aga to light and I'm dying of hunger ... could you possibly show me how to start it up?'

For a moment he just stared at her, then he made an obvious effort and pulled himself together. She even saw a spark of interest in those dark eyes.

'Of course.' He got to his feet and went over to the clock mechanism. Deftly, he twiddled the knobs, pressed things and waited whilst it clicked, muttered, then burst into life. He turned to her, smiling. 'Better? It'll take a few minutes to warm up but you should get your meal shortly.'

'You're a life-saver,' Selina said fervently. 'Um ... I wonder if you'd like to share my meal, make up for wasting your time? Clare's left me enough food for an army, if ...'

'That's awfully good of you.' He stood there, incredibly tall and dark and desirable, apparently considering her offer, but then he smiled and held out a lean, tanned hand. 'Thanks, I'd love to share your meal. I'm Oliver, and you'll be Selina.'

'Yes, that's right. Clare left me a curry ... do you like curry? Or there's a meat pie in the freezer which wouldn't take long to thaw out, we could have a drink whilst everything's cooking ...'

'I'll fix the drinks.' Neither commented on the sudden ease and friendship which came to them as Oliver went unerringly to the drinks cupboard, found glasses, poured, came back for ice and finally handed Selina a glass. 'Is that all right for you? Not too dry?'

'It's delicious,' Selina said, sipping. 'I've put the curry on the hot-plate, it won't be long, and the water's boiling for the rice.'

'How domestic.'

Selina shot him a quick look but he was not being sarcastic, he was simply commenting. He dived into the pantry and came out again with a packet of peanuts and some other dried stuff which Selina did not immediately recognise. He smiled at her, then opened the packets and poured them into two small brass bowls which Clare always used for nuts and raisins.

'Here we are, then, cocktail snacks. Do you prefer peanuts or Bombay Mix?'

'You aren't hopelessly fickle just because it doesn't look as though you'll die of unrequited love after all,' Selina said three hours later. She and Oliver were sitting on opposite ends of the couch with the curtains drawn and the lamp glowing gold whilst the fire flickered lower in the grate. They had talked with rare honesty, Oliver from the depths of his disappointment and despair and Selina from her deeply hidden and seldom acknowledged loneliness. 'What you

didn't take into account was the time you met Clare and the
stage your development had reached.'

'Huh? You make me sound like a slow-witted child.'
Selina laughed.

'Was it patronising? I didn't mean to be. But what I'm
trying to say is you didn't fall in love so heavily with Clare
just because she was Clare. It was because you'd reached a
stage when you really wanted and needed one woman, all of
your own. To love and to cherish, forsaking all other, so long
as ye both shall live.'

'Marriage, do you mean?' Oliver's voice sank to a shocked
whisper, but Selina only laughed and shook her head.

'Not necessarily; what I meant was ... that biblical thing
... a time to reap and a time to sow ... a time to laugh and a
time to weep ... men and women come to a time when they
need stable relationships and a sort of settling down. I think,
consciously or unconsciously, you'd decided you wanted
stability. It was sheer bad luck that your feelings didn't
coincide with Clare's – her urge to settle down came earlier,
you see.'

Oliver snorted. It was the nearest he had come to a laugh
and Selina was encouraged by it.

'Came earlier? You mean fifteen years ago, when she met
the wi ... met Clive, I mean.'

'Yes, I suppose that is what I mean. I don't want to hurt
you any more than you've already been hurt, Oliver, but I
think she needed to know someone could love her for herself
not because she was pregnant, or unhappy at home, just
because she was Clare. And having found herself perfectly
lovable, she simply turned back to Clive, to where she felt she
belonged.'

'And you think she'll never glance my way again?'

Selina was sitting at an angle, so that they could watch each
other's faces as they talked. Now she turned her head to
glance down at Tish, sprawled on the hearthrug at their feet.
She liked Oliver and what was more, she trusted Clare's
judgement better, even, than her own. Clare had taken Oliver
as her lover and that must mean he was worth taking. He had
been honest with Clare and would be equally honest with any

418

other woman. Selina knew she wanted him and knew, sadly, that as yet he did not want her. Later, perhaps ... but she did not want to gain his interest through deceit. She had let her long hair fall forward, screening her face from his gaze but now she pushed it behind her ear and turned towards him.

'Oliver, I don't know, not for sure. She's always been a very loyal girl, you see, but that could mean either you or Clive. Except that she seems to have gone off with Clive right now.'

There was a silence whilst Selina told herself that he would now re-double his efforts to interest Clare, then Oliver sighed deeply and leaned over to tickle Tish's ear. As Selina had done, he spoke with his face half hidden.

'I know for sure. In my way, I know her as well as you know her in yours. If she sees me again she'll smile and chat and say – and mean, dammit – how nice it is to meet old friends. I'll bet it was the friendship she valued, not the other.'

'I think you're probably right,' Selina said gently. 'But that applied to you as well, didn't it? You didn't just value the lovemaking, did you, or you'd just have found someone else for that. You valued Clare.'

'I did. And now I've got to get myself sorted out and continue living life.' Oliver stretched, yawned, and got to his feet. Selina, startled, stood up as well and Tish moaned and followed suit. 'Thanks for letting me talk, Selina, you're a kind girl. When I've unscrambled myself a bit perhaps I'll get in touch. Thanks for the meal.'

They went, automatically, to the back door and Selina opened it and watched as Oliver crossed the now rain-swept yard and climbed back into his big waggon. Behind her the Aga muttered to itself and Tish shook violently and then padded over and squeezed into the doorway beside Selina, staring out, ears pricked, eyes rounded by the dark.

Perched up high, Oliver looked suddenly small. His hand, raised in farewell, looked light and brittle against the dark. Selina stood watching as the big waggon turned ponderously onto the road, stood watching until the headlights' beams disappeared, still stood until, far off, she saw the tiny twin pinpricks of the rear lights disappear too. Then she went back into the house and closed the door, intending to go miserably up to bed and think wistfully of what might have been. But Tish would have none of it. She barged against Selina's legs, whimpering and gazing, dancing on tiptoes, reminding Selina with every liquid glance, every quiver, that she always went for a walk before bed.

'You bloody nuisance,' Selina said five minutes later as the two of them, booted and spurred in her own case and collared and led in Tish's, made their way down the puddled road. 'The last thing I'll ever do is have a dog!' She stumbled into a puddle and swore as it splashed down inside Clare's Wellington boots. 'Unscramble himself and get in touch ... ha! I'll never see him again and it's probably a damned good job, all he'd want to do would be talk about Clare!'

'Lovely to see you ... 'ere, give your old Mum a kiss!'

Mavis grabbed Sondra and kissed her soundly, then tried to pat Russell's hand but he was having none of it, not now that she was his legal mother-in law. He gave a whoop and picked her up, right out there on the pavement by his car with the neighbours eagerly watching no doubt, and kissed her smack on the mouth.

'Hey Mum, put my husband down,' Sondra said, laughing, whilst the boys cheered and jumped around and Mavis struggled weakly and told Russell he was a devil, really he was. She reminded him that a feller carried his bride over the threshold, not his mother-in-law, but Russell told her that he had carried Sondra over the threshold a month ago, and now it was her turn. He continued up the garden path, through the front door and into the hall, then turned right into the parlour and lowered her gently onto the couch. Mavis felt the velvet cushions sag and hoped she had not marked them – she never used the parlour – but then she was so busy laughing and scolding Russell that it scarcely seemed to matter.

'There you are, Mum, safely onto the couch,' Russell said, blowing out his cheeks and winking at her. He turned to the boys. 'Now lads, when you're a big chap like me you'll be able to carry Nana around and mind you always let her down gently ... see?'

The boys adored him still, after a whole month of living in the same house, and he certainly seemed fond of them. Now, however, with a big high tea set out in the kitchen and the prospect of a trip the next day, the boys wanted Nana up off that couch and through behind the teapot as soon as could be. It was Friday evening and their boat trip was booked for the Saturday so it behoved Mavis to enjoy their company now. She had no intention of sharing a life on the ocean wave with her son-in-law, fond though she was of him. She feared his ebulliance, in a boat, might well cause a mishap of some sort. So she and Sondra planned to stay at home, do a bit of shopping up the city, and cook their menfolk a big tea for later on.

But right now the big tea was just waiting for her to start things off, so Mavis took herself into the kitchen with the family following, and put the kettle on the stove. It was already hot so soon boiled and Mavis mashed the tea, sat everyone down and began to pass the red salmon, the baked potatoes in their jackets and the salad complete with radishes and spring onions which had been ready for the past four hours.

Everyone was talking away nineteen-to-the-dozen when Cheepy started. At first Mavis ignored him, but then she saw Sondra glance sideways, saw a frozen look cross her daughter's face, and listened herself.

Cheepy was in fine voice. What exactly was he saying?

'Oh Cheepy my son, he's black, black as your 'at,' the little bird said in tones of utmost woe. 'What'll we do, Cheepy? He's black ... black as your 'at!'

Mavis could feel a huge scarlet blush beginning at her toes and working its way up to the top of her head. The boys fell silent as the bird chanted on and Mavis wanted terribly to get up and put a cloth over Cheepy – or, indeed, to wring his sneaking little neck – but she was glued to her chair, immobilised by the sheer horror of the moment.

Russell saved the situation.

'Well my God, that's an intelligent bird,' he said mildly. 'Who'd have thought he'd notice!'

Sondra looked across at her husband, started to speak, and then put a hand across her mouth. Behind it, Mavis could see she was laughing. Russell started laughing too, the big infectious laugh which people found so hard to resist, and then the boys started giggling. Without quite knowing how it started, Mavis found herself laughing as well. The whole family were in stitches. They hooted, they howled, tears ran down their cheeks, the boys rolled off their chairs and continued to laugh lying on the floor. And presently Cheepy started laughing too, his horrid little squeaky titter bringing fresh paroxysms of mirth in its wake.

Finally, to restore sanity he said, Russell got up and ceremoniously placed the cloth over Cheepy's cage, giving it a playful shake as he did so.

'Now who's black?' he said, grinning from ear to ear. 'Now who's black, Cheepy my son?'

CHAPTER
21

Clare, Mavis and Dee stood behind the counter, staring out through the caff's glass frontage at the car-park. Out there a wild October wind had snatched the leaves from the plane trees and was playing a kitten-game with them, tossing them into the air, casting them on the ground, swirling them round in a pile and then whisking them to every corner of the compass once more. The three women watched, mesmerised by the dance.

The Mini, in its usual place, had a pile of leaves on its snub-nosed bonnet but even as Clare tutted silently to herself and wagged her head at it – you look a fool, dear Min – the leaves were whirled away to join their fellows and Dee stirred and spoke, breaking the spell.

'I reckon that's worse to have a quiet day like this, even though you can rest your legs. The hours seem to last twice as long when there's no people in and out, no customers.'

'That's true, but it'll be nice later, when we need a spell o' quiet.' Mavis sighed, then bent to check her reflection in the gleam of the coffee machine. She patted her hair, still determinedly bronze though the wedding was long past. She owed it to herself to keep a good appearance, she told Clare, to say nothing of Lionel, who liked to see her smart. Besides, she was as good as a shareholder now, a person of conse-quence, and she wanted to look like one.

For Mrs P had come back as she had promised, but only to put the caff on the market so she could afford to buy somewhere nearer her daughter. And Clare and Clive, after much heart-searching, were buying two-thirds of it for what Clive thought was an exorbitant price, though Clare had assured him he was wrong. The other third was being bought by Mavis and Lionel.

Clare cast her mind back to when Mavis had first suggested a partnership. She had been agonising aloud over her inability to put up the full sum without borrowing from the bank when Mavis slid across the kitchen towards her.

'We've gotta bitta money, me and Lionel,' she had said, her voice hoarse with rare embarrassment. 'We'd like to 'ave a share, like. Lionel reckons you could make a gold-mine outa this place.'

'Oh, but Mave, your savings!' Clare had said, horrified to think of the responsibility such an investment would put on her shoulders. But Mavis, in a rare moment of complete honesty, had shaken her head and leaned confidingly close.

'There's more where that come from, Clare, and I tell you I'd sooner see it go into something steady, something Lionel couldn't muck abaht with, than see it put into a place of our own where Li might be tempted to go a bit too far, be a bit too clever.'

So of course she had said she'd talk it over with Clive and had done so, even to the point of telling him where Lionel would be spending the last few weeks before Christmas. She had held her breath, waiting for the 'I'm-not-going-into-business-with-a-crook' routine, but she had waited in vain. Once Clive had taken it in – and stopped laughing – he had said thoughtfully that everyone conned someone some of the time and perhaps it was a good thing if two of the world's more conventional people should profit by Lionel's wicked ways. Clare, who still remembered sometimes how she had once been far from conventional, agreed weakly that he was right and told Mavis that they would be happy with her and Lionel as partners in the caff.

They were happy, too. Mavis had always been hard working and energetic and being a partner did not stop her from continuing as before. This very evening they were going to stay behind when the caff closed to start stripping the paint

424

so that they could redecorate and Mavis would throw herself into the work with even more enthusiasm because she and Lionel were shareholders.

'Well, we'd better tidy round a bit, I suppose,' Mavis said now, having satisfied herself that her appearance left nothing to be desired. 'Next week's half-term, we shan't 'ave no time to stand around then, we'll be too busy for our own good, if you ask me.' She lived in fear, she had told Clare, that Mrs P would examine the accounts since Clare had come and would see how good trade was and put the price up accordingly. 'Still, it's all but signed and sealed now, eh, Clare?'

'It is all signed and sealed, we're just waiting for the transfer date,' Clare said reassuringly. 'I wonder if we ought to get the Saturday girls in for half-term week? Or isn't it that busy?'

Mavis sighed and cast her eyes at the ceiling.

'We'll be rushed off our feet, gal. Mrs P always had the girls in.'

'Then we'll do the same, shall we?'

Clare watched the play of emotions on Mavis's face with considerable interest. First came the weariness of one annoyed by rhetorical quesions, then realisation dawned that it was not rhetorical, but was one shareholder consulting another, then the urge to disagree just for the hell of it was quashed by the recollection of who held most shares. Dear Mavis!

'Hmm, yes, reckon we should, Clare.'

The door opened abruptly and two untidy mums, toddlers at heel, were blown in. Mavis gave Dee an unnecessary shove in the back and began ostentatiously to tidy the cake display. Dee cast a black glance at Mavis, grinned at Clare and then went across the room to take the order, pad at the ready. Clare, for her part, retreated to the kitchen where a good deal of cooking awaited her attention.

She was putting a chocolate cake in one oven and checking the pavlovas in the slow one next door when someone came into the kitchen. A voice said: 'Hello, sweetie! As it's so quiet I thought I'd start stripping the paintwork right now.'

Clare shut the oven door and straightened, pushing a wing

of flopping hair out of her eyes. She smiled at Clive, looking rather absurd, she thought, in a pair of brand-new blue overalls which he had bought specially for decorating in.

'Well, you've brought all your gear, I see. Have you asked Mavis if she agrees to you starting now?'

Clare knew Mavis would not mind, but she believed in plenty of consultation between partners, whether married or merely in business together. It was not talking enough that nearly wrecked our marriage, she told herself, whenever she was tempted to go ahead with something off her own bat. We don't want the caff to suffer like that, it has such enormous potential if we handle it right. As soon as they could they intended to convert Mrs P's flat into a dining room, and open in the evenings as well as all day, which should boost takings and bring in a different type of customer.

'Yes, I mentioned it on the way through. She said what about closing a bit early, as it's so quiet, then we can all wade in. She's right, if we do that we'll be able to start painting tomorrow. How do you feel?'

Clive, who had once taken all decisions as a matter of course, was now sensitive to her need to consult and be consulted; Clare smiled at him.

'I agree. We'll shut as soon as the women outside leave, then, and start cleaning down. We'll have tea here too, I'll put something out, then we'll not waste any time.'

By the time Clare had got her cakes out of the oven and their tea ready, Sally had arrived and the door was locked. Dee offered to stay late for love, but Clare insisted that she be paid, and it was a happy little group who began the messy but enjoyable job of stripping paint, cleaning down the walls and getting the furniture well out of the way of the workers. Indeed, by seven o'clock almost everything was done except the street door and its frame.

'I'll run Dee to her bus stop,' Clive offered presently, knowing that Deirdre would want to catch the 7.15. 'And at the same time I'll take you home, Mavis. Clare and Sal can clear up for us whilst we're gone and then we'll go home ourselves, and tackle the painting tomorrow.'

Deirdre demurred as a matter of course but Mavis was

426

happy to accept a lift now, as of right, and led the rush to the car. Sally and Clare, left alone, promptly seized the blow-torch, which Clive had been using, and the scraper and advanced purposefully on the door.

'I say, this is fun,' Sally said gleefully, aiming the torch at the door-frame. 'Trust a man to keep the best part to himself, I'm going to get the whole of this frame done by the time Dad gets back, see if I don't.'

Clare scraped for a bit behind the torch, then thought of the morrow and put her scraper carefully down on the nearest table.

'Sally, you keep burning for a bit, I'll come and scrape again presently, but since we're still here, I'm going to make up some scone mix for baking tomorrow. It won't take more than ten minutes to weigh up and mix it all into dough. All right?'

'Fine,' Sally said absently. 'I'll let you have a go with the torch when you get back.'

Clare went into the kitchen and began weighing into the big bowl. She was barely starting to knead the dough, however, when there was a shriek from the caff.

'Oh, hell! Water, water!'

That wretched door does leak round the bottom, Clare told herself, hurrying through to the caff with an old tea-towel to mop up floods. I suppose it's getting the wood damp so Sally can't burn off properly.

One glance through the doorway, however, disillusioned her. Sally, blow-torch still blazing, was struggling with the door, which was now wide open. The wind, crashing jovially into the caff and bringing a good number of dead leaves with it, had also somehow managed to set light to the door-frame, which was burning with increasing fierceness even as Sally dabbed ineffectually at it with a dirty paint-cloth which suddenly began to smoulder, then burst into flames. Sally dropped it and shrieked, 'Mum! Water!'

'Shut the door!' Clare shouted, hurrying over with her tea-towel. She tried to get hold of the door to shut it but the wind defeated her and the smoke, blowing into her eyes, forced her to abandon that course. She beat at the flames with her tea-towel, setting that alight as well, and was just trying to beat it out and dampen the flames nearest her at the same time when a figure burst in, grabbed the tea-towel from her hands and began crushing the nearest bit of briskly burning door-frame to the detriment of his own skin and clothing.

Even through the smoke and the howling wind, Clare recognised Oliver. Her heart, which had been hammering out a fast tempo anyway, speeded up and she had to force herself to remember the fire and to turn from him to go back to the kitchen, where she filled the big jug with cold water and hurried back to the caff, grabbing some tea-towels as she passed the rack. Outside, she dunked the tea-towels in the jug and handed one to Oliver, one to Sally and kept one herself. Feverishly, the three of them slapped their tea towels onto the flames.

Oliver only stopped his attack on the flames when they were clearly staggering and giving up and then he did what Clare had tried to do earlier. He grabbed the door and forced it partly shut. Then he put his full weight against it and the wind dropped as the door and frame at least partially met. For a few moments longer the three of them continued to douse the wood, which was now merely smouldering sullenly, then Sally stood back and the others followed suit.

'I say Mum, I'm awfully sorry, it was all my fault, but the door blew open when I fell against it and I forgot I was holding the blow-torch on one spot, I was trying to close the door . . . I say, it's Coffee and Book!'

'So it is,' Clare said rather drily. She turned to Oliver. 'I can't imagine how you happened to turn up, but I'm most grateful to you; we'd never have beaten it without your help, I wasn't strong enough to shut the door again and the wind . . . well, it was simply bound to spread.'

'You're a hero!' Sally said. Her face was filthy, pale and tear-streaked but the eyes which fixed themselves on Oliver's face were blatantly admiring. 'You must be most awfully strong!'

'I'm heavier than you two,' Oliver admitted. 'Hadn't you better go and clean up, young lady? You're black as the ace of spades.'

Sally giggled.

'You're not much better,' she said cheerfully. 'Okay, okay, I'm going to have first wash, you two can clean up afterwards. Shall I put the kettle on, Mum?'

'Please, love.'

Sally disappeared into the kitchen and they heard the taps begin to run. They turned towards each other. Oliver smiled down at Clare, a long smear of dirt decorating one lean cheek, his eyes full of mischief and something more, a sort of absent-minded tenderness.

'Hello, you,' he said softly. 'It's been a long time.'

'Oh, Oliver . . .' Clare began, but got no further. The door opened, causing them both to look round. Clive stood there, framed in burnt wood. He glanced from one to the other. He looked annoyed and somehow suspicious.

'What on earth's going on her?' he demanded. 'I've only been gone half an hour and I get back to find . . .' he glanced at the sea of water and smuts on the floor, at the filthy handmarks on the nearest tables, at the burnt and dirty tea-towels flung down at random.

'It was a fire,' Clare said wearily and rather obviously. 'I'm not sure how it started, but . . .'

'Dad!' Sally bounced back into the room, her face half obscured by grey soap suds but her eyes gleaming with excitement and her cheeks pink with it. 'It was all my fault, honest it was, though it wasn't my fault that the bloody door blew open. I was using your blow-torch you see, and when the door blew open I tried to shut it without turning off the flame.'

'I see.' Clive turned to Oliver who promptly shot out a grimy hand.

'Oliver Norton,' he said. 'I saw the flames from the car-park and came across. It could have been nasty – the wind, you know. An old building like this could easily go up in flames when there's a high wind.'

'I see. Thanks very much,' Clive said. Clare fancied she heard reserve in his voice, even a touch of suspicion. He turned to Clare again. 'Are you all right, love? No burns? And you, Sal?'

'I'm dirty, but that's all,' Clare said and Sally shouted from the kitchen that she was fine and had quite enjoyed the adventure so long as it turned out all right.

'And you, Mr ... er ... Norton?'

'Nothing that a good wash won't cure,' Oliver said. 'When Sally's finished at the sink I'll clean up a bit.' He turned towards the kitchen, adding over his shoulder, 'I'm a customer, or I used to be, I haven't come in for several months. I wonder if I might use your phone as soon as I'm a bit cleaner? I'm meeting a friend at the station, I'd like to let the staff there know I'll be late, then they can get her to wait for me.'

Her? Clare assured Oliver that after all he had done they would gladly lend him their telephone and offered to show him where it was as he turned from the sink. She preceded him up the stairs, then stood at the top of the landing whilst he passed her, having first flung open the lounge door and indicated the instrument. As he drew level with her he gripped her wrist, his fingers fierce, urgent.

'I burned for you,' he muttered. 'Twice, now. But it's all right, I've got ...'

'Clare? Come and have a wash, love,' Clive's voice urged from the foot of the stairs. Clare turned at once and made her way down the flight again. Had he heard? But if he had, what possible significance could he read into those words? She wondered if she looked as guilty as she felt, but there was no need, really. It had been months, she had not even seen Oliver since Clive's return.

She walked into the kitchen and went over to the sink. She ran the taps into the bowl, more cold than hot because she had sore palms, and jumped when someone put an arm round her shoulders and kissed the side of her neck, but it was only Clive.

'Poor darling, it just goes to show that I can't leave you alone for two minutes without you getting into trouble.' He was joking, yet Clare still sensed unease behind the mundane words.

'Well, all's well that ends well, and we'll soon put it right in the morning,' Clare said, leaning against him for a moment.

'It's not too bad really, it didn't go much deeper than the paint, thanks to . . . Oliver.'

'Yes, we'll fix it tomorrow.' Clive's arm slid from her shoulder to her waist and squeezed. 'Do you know, when I looked across from the car-park and saw the two of you standing in the doorway I wondered what the hell had been going on.'

Clare's heart gave a frightened leap but she said as calmly as she could: 'I'm not surprised, a fire doesn't happen every day, thank God.'

'No-o, but I didn't mean that. It was the way you were looking up at him and the way he was looking down at you. For a moment I thought . . . but as he said, he's only a customer.'

There was the faintest of faint queries on the last sentence but Sally pouring tea into four mugs, answered before Clare could open her mouth.

'Yes, he's only a customer, but he was a regular, once. Several times a week he'd come in and have a coffee and a round of toast. Then he'd read his book and off he'd go. We didn't make much money out of him, did we, Mum, but he left us a tip most times.'

'He had a piece of cake, once,' Clare said. 'And he was fairly regular too, as he said, but not for ages. I think people's lives change, because a customer who comes in every day for six weeks suddenly stops coming and you very rarely find out why. At first, you wonder if it's something you said or did but then you come to accept that it's just life.'

'I suppose it's natural. He's a good looking chap, though. When I came across the road from the car-park . . .'

'Thanks very much, I've alerted the British Rail staff, there'll be a chalked-up notice in the foyer telling my friend I'm late.'

Oliver lounged into the kitchen but waved away Sally's proferred mug.

'It's kind of you, dear, but I'd better be making tracks. Hope the fire didn't do too much damage.'

He was across the kitchen as he spoke and Sally hurried after him, tea slopping from the mug.

'Oh, do wait ... just have your tea!'

'It's all right, I can grab a cup at the station if the train's late,' Oliver said easily, over his shoulder. 'Mustn't keep Selina waiting!'

He was gone on the words, into the windy night, pulling the caff door shut behind him only it would not latch so Sally had to run across the room and grapple with it, and Clive had to lend a shoulder, and Clare was left to stand in the kitchen, by the sink, and try to still the stupid trembling and the ache which seeing him had resurrected.

She was glad he had left, grateful to him, even, because it would be so easy to give herself away. Just the stillness of her body might be interpreted rightly by Clive, made suddenly sensitive by the mere sight of them together. A word out of place and the careful wall she had built around that brief, heady love-affair could come tumbling down, injuring them all, wrecking their marriage. Once, she had ached for him despite having Clive in his rightful place, but that was all past, all gone, and must remain forgotten.

Clive and Sally returned to the kitchen, chatting easily. Clare picked up her mug of tea and sipped; it was very hot and the burns on her hands ... she had lied to Clive ... throbbed and stung where they touched the china.

'Didn't he say Selina?' Sally questioned, her clear young voice untroubled. 'How odd! Wouldn't it be funny, Mum, if it was our Selina?'

'It would be a coincidence, certainly,' Clive said, when Clare mumbled that she supposed there must be more than one Selina. 'Good bloke, that. Wonder what he does for a living?'

'He's a horse-dealer of some sort,' Sally said at once. 'He was meeting a train though, Selina always comes down by train, so it might be her. Wouldn't it be odd, Mum?'

'Jolly odd,' Clare said, sipping tea. 'How much longer will we be here, Clive, because if it's ages then I'll get us some cheese and pickle or something. I know we ate earlier, but I'm hungry again now.'

But Clive said that they would leave right away; there was no point in staying any longer, nothing they could do until

432

morning, so the three of them cleared down the kitchen, turned off the lights and did their best to close and lock the door, though it was not easy with the door warped and the frame charred. The Mini would spend the night on the car-park, they decided, since Clare's hands did not feel much like driving, and in any case Clive would have to be in early to deal with the burn damage.

'I still bet it's our Selina he's meeting,' Sally said, as she climbed into the back of the car. 'Why don't we go down to Thorpe Station and take a look?'

'Too tired, sweetheart, and besides I wouldn't want to spy on the chap. No, we'll go straight home, and straight to bed, because we'll have to be in before Mavis, tomorrow.'

'I know,' Clare said wearily. 'You're right, we need sleep. We'll be fit to tackle anything when morning comes.'

It was hard to sleep though, with her mind so active and the pain from her burnt palms. And curiosity is a lively beast and will not let the sufferer simply roll over and forget unanswered questions in sleep. Until the small hours Clare asked herself the same unanswerable questions but mostly she asked herself what Oliver had been doing on the car-park, if he was supposed to be meeting a train at Thorpe Station?

Finally she decided that he must have come there hoping to see her, to exorcise any faint, remaining tug their relationship had retained over him. He was going to see a girl, a girl called Selina, though there was of course not the remotest possibility that it could be their Selina, despite Sally's remarks. Perhaps he felt he wanted to start afresh, without any lingering desire for herself to spoil the new relationship.

Then, of course, Clive, who seldom talked in his sleep, began to mutter and mumble. At first, it was just vague, disconnected sentences which appeared to mean nothing, but then he spoke out loud, and clearly enough to be unmistakable.

'It's better to marry than to burn,' he said firmly. Then he turned over, flung an arm round Clare, and began to breathe deeply.

Clare cuddled his arm and thought how true it was, even if Clive hadn't meant a word of it. She enjoyed being married, being settled, having Clive with her all the time, or most of it, and looking back, the affair with Oliver had never been peaceful. She had burned for him, as he had burned for her, and there is precious little comfort in such feelings. But it was past, as past for Oliver as for herself, she was sure. Oliver was far more like her than he realised; she needed permanence and so did he. Looking back over their brief encounter earlier in the evening it occurred to her that he had changed. He was still good-looking, still darkly fascinating but he no longer looked dangerous. The sharp chiselled edges of him were blurred into a more comfortable image. Someone, somewhere, is taming Oliver down into the right material for marriage, Clare told herself. Wouldn't it be wonderful if it really was Selina, because she's such a marvellous person. But it can't be, of course. I'm not sure that I want it to be, that I could bear it to be ... but wouldn't it be poetic justice if it was? I took Clive away from her, so it would be only fair if she took Oliver away from me. Except that Oliver isn't mine, not any more. He could have been, but he wasn't what I wanted.

Clive's arm was a warm weight on the dip of her waist, the hand curled across her stomach touched her with lethargic possessiveness. She took his hand in hers and carried it to her mouth, then kissed the unconscious knuckles, squeezing his fingers convulsively. This is what I want, Clare thought, and the tears which squeezed from beneath her closed lids were tears for lost romance, not for a lost lover.

For a few months in the summer I was chasing rainbows and telling myself it was real life, Clare told herself. But now I've got real life and it's rainbow coloured.

She fell asleep then, her cheeks still wet. But she smiled as she slept.

ALSO AVAILABLE IN ARROW

First Love, Last Love

Katie Flynn
Writing as Judith Saxton

A powerful story of two sisters, and the love that changed their lives.

It wasn't a privileged childhood, but it was a happy one. Sybil and Lizzie Cream, brought up in a fisherman's cottage on the edge of the cold North Sea were content to leave privilege where it belonged: with their friends the Wintertons. Christina Winterton was the same age as Sybil and the two girls were inseparable, but it was Lizzie whom Ralph Winterton, three years older, found irresistible.

Then war came to East Anglia, and so did Manchester-born Fenn Kitzmann now of the American Army Air Force. At their first meeting he is attracted by Sybil's subtle charm, but before he sees her again her own personal tragedy has struck, and he finds her changed almost out of recognition...

arrow books

ALSO AVAILABLE IN ARROW

Someone Special

Katie Flynn
Writing as Judith Saxton

On 21st April 1926, three baby girls are born.

In North Wales, Hester Coburn, a farm labourer's wife, gives birth to Nell, whilst in Norwich, in an exclusive nursing home, Anna is born to rich and pampered Constance Radwell. And in London, Elizabeth, Duchess of York, has her first child, Princess Elizabeth Alexandra Mary.

The future looks straightforward for all three girls, yet before Nell is eight, she and Hester are forced to leave home, finding work with a travelling fair. Anna's happy security is threatened by her father's infidelities and her mother's jealousy, and the Princess's life is irrevocably altered by her uncle's abdication.

Set in the hills of Wales and the rolling Norfolk countryside, the story follows Nell and Anna through their wartime adolescence into young womanhood as they struggle to overcome their problems, whilst watching 'their' Princess move towards her great destiny. Only when they finally meet do the two girls understand that each of them is 'someone special'.

arrow books

You are my Sunshine

Katie Flynn
Writing as Judith Saxton

Kay Duffield's fiancé is about to leave the country, and her own duty with the WAAF is imminent when she becomes a bride. The precious few days she spends with her new husband are quickly forgotten once she starts work as a balloon operator, trained for the heavy work in order to release more men to fight.

There she makes friends with shy Emily Bevan, who has left her parents' hill farm in Wales for the first time; down-to-earth Biddy Bachelor, fresh from the horrors of the Liverpool bombing, and spirited Jo Stewart, the rebel among them, whose disregard for authority looks set to land them all in trouble.

arrow books

ALSO AVAILABLE IN ARROW

A Mistletoe Kiss

Katie Flynn

It was only a mistletoe kiss, Miss Preece told herself, stepping out into the icy December evening and locking the library doors behind her. A mistletoe kiss means nothing, everyone knows that; but this did not quench the warm glow inside her.

Hetty Gilbert is a canal child with no permanent address, so when she needs to join the library, she cannot do so. Miss Preece dislikes children, but Hetty's longing for books touches a chord and she stretches the rules to allow the girl to read on the premises.

Soon, Hetty's chief desire is to become a librarian like her friend. But with war on the horizon, their lives will never be the same. In 1939 Hetty joins in the war effort, for her knowledge of canal boats is desperately needed, whilst Miss Preece can only sit and listen to the dangers her young friend faces, knowing she herself can do nothing to help.

But her chance will come, and with it the meaning behind that fragile mistletoe kiss . . .

arrow books

ALSO AVAILABLE IN ARROW

Heading Home

Katie Flynn

Claudia Muldoon and her younger sister, Jenny, live with their parents and their gran in her house in Blodwen Street. Both parents have good jobs and the family assume they are settled for life, but then Grandpa Muldoon has a seizure and begs his son to return to Ireland and the family croft.

The Muldoons leave and Gran has to take in lodgers to make ends meet, for the Depression is beginning to bite. In Ireland, however, the Muldoons flourish and the girls love the freedom of their new life, though as they grow up, disadvantages become clear. Claudia has to find work, so both sisters return to Liverpool and to their old pal Danny, who still adores the beautiful Claudia and welcomes them back with delight.

But both girls' lives take an unexpected turn when Danny's friend, the flamboyant and successful Rob Dingle, returns from America . . .

arrow books

A Mother's Hope

Katie Flynn

Along a blacked-out wartime street a girl is scurrying, a basket on one arm. As the sirens begin and the bombs crash down, she is filled with panic and, with a heavy heart, abandons her burden in a sheltered doorway, meaning to return later. Even as she disappears in the resulting chaos, the bundle in the basket begins to wail.

Years later, two young unfortunates meet on a miserable November day. Martin has been desperately trying to hitch a lift along the lonely windswept road and when he sees a weeping girl in front of him, he hurries to catch her up.

Rose and Martin become unlikely companions until they go their separate ways, not expecting to meet again. However, fate decrees otherwise . . .

arrow books

ALSO AVAILABLE IN ARROW

The Lost Days of Summer

Katie Flynn

Nell Whitaker is fifteen when war breaks out and, despite her protests, her mother sends her to live with her Auntie Kath on a remote farm in Anglesey. Life on the farm is hard, and Nell is lonely after living in the busy heart of Liverpool all her life. Only her friendship with young farmhand Bryn makes life bearable. But when he leaves to join the merchant navy, Nell is alone again, with only the promise of his return to keep her spirits up.

But Bryn's ship is sunk, and Bryn is reported drowned, leaving Nell heartbroken. Determined to bury her grief in hard work, Nell finds herself growing closer to Auntie Kath, whose harsh attitude hides a kind heart. Despite their new closeness, however, she dare not question her aunt about the mysterious photograph of a young soldier she discovers in the attic.

As time passes, the women learn to help each other through the rigours of war. And when Nell meets Bryn's friend Hywel, she begins to believe that she, too, may find love . . .

arrow books

ALSO AVAILABLE IN ARROW

Forgotten Dreams

Katie Flynn

Lottie Lacey and her mother, Louella, share a house in Victoria Court with Mr Magic and his son Baz. Lottie is a child star, dancing and singing at the Gaiety Theatre to an enraptured audience, whilst Louella acts as Max Magic's assistant. But Lottie was in hospital for weeks after a road accident and has lost her memory. Louella tries to help but the white mist remains. Until Lottie meets a boy with golden-brown eyes who calls her 'Sassy' and accuses her of running away.

It is after this meeting that the dreams start, dreams of another life, almost another world, and Lottie, sharing them with Baz, begins to believe he knows more than he chooses to tell. But then Merle joins the act and Lottie feels Baz and Merle, both older than she, are in league against her.

Then the dreams begin to grow clearer and Lottie realises she must find out the secrets of her past, no matter what the cost.

arrow books